Praise for *This is Rage*:

"*This is Rage* is that rare book – a fascinating, fast-paced, really smart thriller. Part action/adventure story set in the wilds of Silicon Valley, and part insider's exposition of some of the major inner workings of our contemporary economy and of the secrets of today's High Tech 'Masters of the Universe' – Ken Goldstein succeeds in making this a debut that will make your heart race – even as it gives you plenty to think about."
– Naomi Wolf, author of *Give Me Liberty*

"I worked with Ken Goldstein at Disney: and since I knew he could write, I encouraged him to do just that, to write a novel. As impressed as I always was with him as an executive, I'm equally impressed with what he accomplished with a pen (or maybe a computer)."
– Michael Eisner

"Ken Goldstein knows the ins and outs of Silicon Valley – the customs of the land and where the bodies are buried. I would read anything he wrote, nonfiction or fiction, set on that fascinating terrain."
– Will Schwalbe, author of *The End of Your Life Book Club*

"Given Ken Goldstein's pedigree as a major Internet CEO whose vision has significantly shaped today's digital world, it's no surprise that his first novel takes us on a thrilling front-of-the-coaster rocket ride through the Valley of Silicon. While *This is Rage* is surely required reading for all high tech and deal-savvy action/thriller fans, it is an absolute crystal ball for radio broadcasters who are still scratching their heads as to the future of their industry."
– Mitch Dolan, Former President, ABC Radio Station Group

"Ken Goldstein has written a modern-day blockbuster! Smart, insightful, and engaging, the story takes us on a thrill ride through the circus-like madness of corporate American, the media, and government. It reveals with stunning clarity the inept and all-too-sinister characters that inhabit these worlds. You cannot help but think that Goldstein has had a front row seat and used his real life experiences to masterfully weave a fictional narrative that enlightens as much as it entertains. A must read."
– Gene Del Vecchio, author of *Creating Blockbusters!* and Adjunct Professor, USC Marshall School of Business

This Is Rage

A Novel of Silicon Valley and Other Madness

This Is Rage

A Novel of Silicon Valley and Other Madness

by

Ken Goldstein

THE
STORY PLANT

This Is Rage

A Novel of Silicon Valley and Other Madness

by

Ken Goldstein

The Story Plant
Studio Digital CT, LLC
PO Box 4331
Stamford, CT 06907

Print ISBN-13: 978-1-61188-071-7
E-book ISBN-13: 978-1-61188-072-4

Visit our website at www.TheStoryPlant.com
Visit the author's website at www.ThisIsRage.com
Join the online dialogue #ThisIsRage
Visit the author's blog at www.corporateintelligenceradio.com
Follow the author on Twitter @CorporateIntel

First Story Plant Paperback Printing: October 2013

Printed in the United States of America

0 9 8 7 6 5 4 3 2 1

For Shelley
Who tried to teach me Patience
Then never left me in the Wilderness

In My Life, I Love You More

Acknowledgements and Apologia _(not in that order)_

I didn't write much during the twenty years prior to this novel. It was a necessary choice based on a bunch of other choices I had made. I have no regrets about the other choices, but I do have issues with myself for betraying the writing—out of necessity—which had been a part of me since I learned that there was such a thing as writing. When you sign up for leadership and other people trust you with their talent, their needs come first, and the one thing human innovation has yet to invent is time. During my executive years, many business colleagues commented that there was something unusually polished about my memos, performance reviews, and PowerPoint decks. They often asked me if I ever thought of doing something else with my writing. I said the thought has crossed my mind, but it didn't seem sensible.

In hindsight, not writing was not sensible, and getting started again was no small trick. It started with my blog, www.CorporateIntelligenceRadio.com, which let me put words in front of readers, all of whom I thank dearly for letting me subversively take your temperature. Then I had to take my own, to get a reality check on whether this book was worth the next few years of my life. For not talking me out of it, but instead offering me tremendous encouragement to be brave when I most needed launch tinder, I must thank Will Schwalbe and Deborah Dugan.

My early readers were astonishing in their support, candor, and feedback. Michael Eisner remains the most wonderful mentor I could imagine, his creativity keeps me believing in magic. Naomi Wolf never missed an opportunity to show me, teach me, and evangelize my words. Gene Del Vecchio was especially gracious, reading and commenting on every draft, always a perfect sounding board. Mitch Dolan named my blog, refused to let me stop writing, and let me share his love of radio where we still have plans ahead. Lisa Queen was an early believer in the book and helped me grok the publishing world. Lisa Hickey at _The_

Good Men Project helped introduce the text to the online reading world.

Dan Sherlock, Robert Gonsalves, Sabrina Roblin, Mark Laudenslager, Kate Zentall, Tom Marcus, Jessica Ivy, Clint Ivy, Johanna Wise, Andrew Wise, Bryan Yates, Stewart Halpern — my brothers and sisters, thank you for trusting me with your time, and for letting me trust you at moments delicate, frightening, and critical. You gave me my first reviews, public and private, and for that you will always be in my heart.

Nora Tamada did a wonderful job copyediting the manuscript and offered some insightful notes late in the process, bringing much welcomed comfort to a rookie who slept a bit better with her delightful evangelism. Mick Spillane was an eagle eye proofreading the final pages. Allison Cronk has been a joy to work with in marketing, and is forever energized with new ideas for outreach. Marian Brown, a literary publicist of the first order, got on board with trumpeting enthusiasm, and continues to open doors of widespread promotion, be they physical or virtual.

My dad taught me a lot of important stuff. He taught me where we came from, and never to forget that. He taught me you can't work too hard, be too honest, or laugh often enough. He taught me to stare down injustice and unmask arrogance. He taught me it was okay to be me, which wasn't always easy, but always was right.

A very long time ago, a Norwegian woman who taught high school French and German came to see a revue I had written. She said it made her laugh, and that was kind of cool, but she thought I could do more with my words. I said I wasn't even sure I could do that, but I promised I would try. She said she would teach me to read Plato and Kierkegaard if I would loan her my Beatles and George Carlin records. She got beat badly on that trade. That was Dr. Berit Mexia.

I had a hard time shoehorning *This Is Rage* into a category for the traditional publishing industry. If I don't think you know what you are saying, I can be a very poor listener. Finding an editor I could trust with this book was no small challenge. Then came Lou Aronica, whom I met on Twitter, and the way I thought about words changed in real time, forever. I am doubly blessed to be published under Lou's visionary imprint, The Story Plant, and to have my work shepherded through both the creative and business process by an industry professional of his sensitivity and stature. Folks, he is that good.

On a page prior to this I have already dedicated this work to my wife Shelley, but to not thank her again for believing in me would be remiss. On our first date, about a quarter century ago, she asked me what I did for a living. I stole a line from the afore-mentioned Carlin: Make up goofy stuff and tell it to people like you. None of this would be without her. None of it at all. Yep, she is that good.

If you're actually reading this and still with me, I thank you. If you stay to the finale and post a review or reflection, I thank you again. If you do something about it, we all thank you. There is so much that needs to be done to make this place right, the notion of innovation for betterment can only be applied if we embrace it together—and remember to laugh at ourselves now and again, because we Earn Each Moment.

Mahalo.
Los Angeles, California
Summer 2013

FORM 10-K (Amended)
Summary of Contents

PROSPECTUS (Prologue)

1.0 THE VISION THING

1.1 In Tres Partes Divisa Est
1.2 It's Terrestrial
1.3 Never Bet Against the Bozos
1.4 Let's Get Small
1.5 No Such Thing as CEO School
1.6 Live from the Boulevard of Broken Dreams
1.7 The House Checks and Raises
1.8 If There Were Rules Who Would Listen?
1.9 Show Me Your Bulls

2.0 IN THE COMPANY OF KINGS AND GOATS

2.1 Format Disk
2.2 Functional Spec
2.3 Source Code
2.4 Test Compile
2.5 Debug Mode
2.6 Run Time
2.7 Event Loop
2.8 Upgrade Path
2.9 Blue Screen

3.0 THEATRICALITY

3.1 Oxygen is Underrated
3.2 All PR is Evil
3.3 Fundamentals are for Mortals
3.4 Exit, Stage Left
3.5 Buy Low, Raise Cash, Sell a Story

<u>Prospectus</u>

Imagine you were to embark on the Next Big Thing in global digital business.

Imagine that your mission statement would be To Save Advertisers from Themselves.

Imagine that your vision statement would be To Take on the Entrenched.

Imagine that you said these two things publicly and often.

And the market share that followed was without precedent or challenge.

That would be some company.

1.0
THE VISION THING

"When Adam Smith described the concept of markets in *The Wealth of Nations* in 1776, he theorized that if every buyer knew every seller's price, and every seller knew what every buyer was willing to pay, everyone in the 'market' would be able to make fully informed decisions and society's resources would be distributed efficiently. To date we haven't achieved Smith's ideal because would-be buyers and would-be sellers seldom have complete information about one another."
– William H. Gates III, *The Road Ahead* (1995)

"On Wall Street he and a few others — how many? three hundred, four hundred, five hundred? had become precisely that . . . Masters of the Universe."
– Tom Wolfe, Bonfire of the Vanities (1987)

1.1
In Tres Partes Divisa Est

Silicon Valley parties are notoriously dour. Some might call them misfit assemblies accompanied by hot and cold hors d'ouvres, mixers where thin manners connect the awkward with the hopeful. If you watched *The Social Network* in your dorm room, migrated your way to Palo Alto and thought your clever code would land you a Victoria's Secret model, you were playing for the wrong prize. Forget bikinis, forget bikini waxes; no clinging starlets in lingerie on this peninsula. Truly good wine, that you would find in abundance, and tension-filled stuffiness in every brief exchange. Quiet new money, a quantum inability to fully distinguish between the wackiest of ideas and the next Built-to-Last initial public offering, and elevator pitches that replaced pleasantries, these are the fabric of high tech social outings. Conversation is a conduit for data extraction, all else is a caustic slide to the next body behind the one currently boring you with an algorithm declared certain for patent award. If that was your idea of a party, you would have come to the right place.

Today's Sunday afternoon affair was no different. Truth is, manicured lawns were so far removed from geek reality, you had to wonder why you were even there. You were there because someone told you to be there. You were not coding and you were not having fun. What was the point? Fund or get funded.

The decade since Google's IPO was a time when doors could be opened with impossibly few words, depending on those in the discussion. Like any viable economic ecosystem, Silicon Valley had sized its hierarchy, although here the moving parts were more paradigm than absolute. At the top of any pyramid are always names of substance and continuity, and while every now and again a Buffett-like brand might escape to the public headlines, these were intentionally few. Fame was important in the Valley, but not public fame, that could cost you big money. The Valley was the home of the non-disclosure agreement, the NDA, a much honored but fully irrelevant ritual where The Parties agreed to plot in obscurity. Relationships were built on narrow fame, on reputation and track record, most evaluated by the size and financing arrangements of your private plane.

Three castes of characters ruled the Valley, which like Hollywood, had become far more a state of mind than a GPS specific location. While your name could move up or down within your own vertical, your caste was largely set by the way you tallied your hours. At the top of the world were Investors—venture capitalists, private equity managers, angels, anything that was not public money or widely available for the asking. The media would have you believe the world had changed and ideas were the currency of the information age, but the media were not even part of the calculus, they were exchange-traded aftermarket concessions who got just about everything wrong because no one ever asked them to sign an NDA. Nothing had changed. Current money was the fuel of all future value. Investors were Boss, Master, the Absolute Vote. Anyone who questioned that, well, good luck getting your Series-A.

Directly below Investors were Bankers. This was mostly unfair, but Bankers had little problem with it. In terms of starting salaries, they won. A top twenty MBA grad who was brave enough not to go into management consulting and smart enough not to get on the treadmill of corporate climbing could hit the ground running as an analyst and build a following quickly to ascend to managing director—never really adding specific value to any equation but always taking buckets of cash off the table in an IPO, private sale, equity raise, or debt placement. Ask any civilian what a Banker actually did and they would mention something about the desks behind the ATMs in the office at the strip mall, they had no clue. Bankers liked this, it was their secret society, they even invented language to describe new forms of deal constructs around which analogies were not even possible. Money for Nothing, but the hours were excruciating, the document generation an insult to the environment, and the career longevity dire. The old joke prevailed, "What do you call a forty-year-old Banker?" A failure.

At point three in the triangle were Operators, sometimes called entrepreneurs, founders, CEOs, presidents, general managers. They started companies, or took over from people who started companies, then built and ran things. They almost always came up through some functional discipline, perhaps two-thirds as engineering geeks and a third as sales and marketing wonks, then they became generalists, leaders, visionaries, creatures of passion. They were Operators for only one reason: they could not imagine themselves doing any other thing. Nor were they likely employable, who could manage such an unmovable beast? When you made things for a living, that was a life choice. The hours were equally abusive as those of Investors and Bankers, but the lows lower and the highs almost nonexistent. Way more products failed than succeeded, and on the few occasions an Operator found a win, the reward from Investors and Bankers was a request for a comparable forecast—what else do you have and when will you have it? Operators seldom had the academic credentials to become Bankers, but never forgot their own starting salaries were sweat equity while the Bankers flying first class too easily forgot to return their phone calls—until the Operator danced with an Investor, then the phone calls were endless. Operators stalked Investors like adolescent boys tracking high maintenance co-eds at a gymnasium dance, always ready to recite the elevator pitch, terrified of the response, clumsy to a level of vaudeville entr'acte that soon became annoyance. Sand Hill Road was the dance hall, Operators knew the addresses and the names, but until the first big win, that was mostly good for bar chat. After the initial hit, the mating ritual reversed—Operators became gold and Investors prowled.

Investors, Bankers, Operators. All three needed each other, no value creation without the triad. Each of the castes retained profound contempt for the others. None could figure out why anyone would do what the others had chosen as a career. Investors wondered why any Operator would work that hard, wagering it all on a single line item bet, allowing their failures to be publicly displayed and their successes shakedown exploited. If you were smart enough to be an Operator, you could be an Investor, so why didn't you? Many former Operators eventually did become Investors, only to discover that with few exceptions they had been hoodwinked, they could have bypassed the whole of Operating and gone straight to Investing. Oh well. Investors barely acknowledged that Bankers existed, they were support services, worthy of being interviewed even after they had done a dozen deals for you, unworthy of any praise. Bankers loathed Investors because, as sales people, they ceded all power to the client, and how can you possibly admire the power that can sever your fee with a phone call? Bankers laughed at Operators; who would ever want to weather mandates from Investors and be exposed to the wild odds set by Bankers? Operators had little understanding of what Bankers really did other than introduce them at conferences and give them thick documents that validated, with equal lack of predictability, why their companies were worth more or less than they thought they were. Investors and Bankers collected Tombstones, those acrylic shelf pieces with their company logos that marked liquidity events, and Operators noted their Tombstone collections were much smaller than those of the other castes. Investors and Bankers bet with their time and dollars. Operators bet with their souls.

Where did worlds collide? At parties, forced backyard affairs the nature of this one in the elite flats of Atherton, which just seemed like so much fun, you could hardly wait for the last passed tray of vegan canapés to go soggy and the valet to bring back your Maserati. There were others in attendance, lawyers mostly, but they were not in the club. Occasionally, a professor would sneak in, but almost always he was an aspiring minority Investor, limited partner, or board member to be. With real estate exuding fate like no other, Stanford had produced more than its share of invitees, and it would be hard to call this an accident. Today it was tenured Professor George Yamanaka holding court.

"Who could have guessed at the dawn of the twenty-first century, that the seminal technology upon which five thousand years of modern science had resulted in was the click?" intoned Yamanaka to a small assembly of would-be Operators. "Of all mankind's Faustian discoveries, efficient advertising has entranced the capital markets."

Yamanaka was reminiscing about the geyser IPO less than five years ago of EnvisionInk Systems, a company that had thwarted the search engines. Any chance to lecture, rehearsed or extempore, and the real Yamanaka would joyfully recite on cue. Prior to paid search advertising, companies bought their media blind. After paid search they bought it even more blind, but at least they could measure return on investment, so the peddlers of keywords told them. EnvisionInk had launched with a contrarian paradigm, showing much abused corporate customers how to beat the hype and save money through proprietary study patterns that suppressed overpriced clicks before bidders lost their bait. It was math, not magic, a practiced educator like Yamanaka knew any formula could be unspooled—but how to make every ad dollar work harder by applying history and context to reach and frequency, that was disruptive and defensible. These patented processes were theirs alone, the celebrated antidote allowing clients to save vast fortunes avoiding unprofitable keyword buys one at a time. Advertisers had been rescued, and EnvisionInk catapulted to preeminence through a combination of insight, execution, good timing in the face of skepticism, and a touch of luck. The company not only led the industry, it led the equity markets. So rare were companies this closely watched, the riches they generated made reason a punch line. Most academics could mine trends. Yamanaka had dug out something entirely more prized.

"You see that fellow over there?" continued Yamanaka. "That is Daniel Steyer. He was the lead Investor on Envision-Ink. He bet big on some students of mine when no one else

would. Later he was gracious enough to bring me on as a director. He is the fellow who saw it coming, that good clicks needn't
have to pay for bad clicks, and how dodging the wrong bits of
text could be transformed into white water cash streams."

"What do you suspect he's worth?" posed a would-be apos-
tle, donned in the Operator's uniform of vogue, the grey hoodie
sweatshirt.

The Professor found the question flat, a difficult bridge.
"How would one know?" he replied. "He has what he needs, ten
figures I suppose. I'm not sure his wife knows and they still like
each other. More important, he understands liquidity, without
which wealth is just a scorecard."

The young fellow who had asked the question seemed unaware he was out of line. Asking someone's net worth was chit
chat for the other end of California. In Brentwood or Pacific
Palisades you might schmooze around the topic of income. Glib
exchange always trumped tact south of Santa Barbara. In the
Valley, you either knew the answer or were polite enough not to
ask. Learning such etiquette took time and acquired polish. The
friend standing next to him seemed to understand and nudged
him accordingly.

"If we had an idea to pitch Mr. Steyer, would this be an
appropriate forum?" asked his buddy. Yamanaka sensed that
the words did not come naturally to this kid, in many ways just
another wide-eyed aspirant like so many around campus, but
too strained in the ask. He and his partner may have come with
a mission, but they had not had much practice. They were not
alone. Just as the North American continent tilted up and to the
right each spring for film students to roll west down Interstate
10 to Hollywood, the techies all slid down Interstate 80 along
the melting spring snow line, crossed the demon route failed by
the Donner Party and planted themselves in the Bay Area. That
is, unless they were from the Bay Area, in which case they were
likely to be even worse dressed.

"Daniel Steyer will listen to almost anything," said the Professor. "That's a meaningful component of what makes him
good. Your question should be, how many seconds of his time

can you command? He has seen more business plans than exist in all the world's finest business schools. You see, memory is key, and his is photographic."

The two hopefuls were not sure what to make of this, as Yamanaka so often scripted it. They wanted more, but Yamanaka found them light. With a polite gesture of his index finger, he ended the mini-lecture and made his way toward Steyer.

$ $

Daniel Steyer admired talent more than the people who possessed it, his ability to recall both unmistakably tagged to writing down losses or capitalizing the unimaginable. To say that he had a photographic memory was equal parts understatement and hyperbole. Certainly he could not remember everyone's name on the lawn, but he could remember in detail the first memory map for the XT he had financed in the early days, when so few could see what was coming. Steyer knew that manipulating memory was the key to getting a computer to do what it was not supposed to do, just as remembering what the talent wanted was the key to getting them to do what they were not supposed to do, or at least what they never intended to do. Computer memory had fundamental protocols. Violate those for your own shortcuts and you would be looking at a crash. People, too.

Steyer slid up to the bar, did not even have to ask, they handed him some medium-aged Cabernet he pretended to appreciate. All those private vineyards purchased for chatter, all those favors to secure the latest cult label, none of it made sense, so much money entombed. He was a fine-looking front man with a Jack Kennedy side part and just enough grey to let you know he had heard too many clichés for one lifetime. Noble trim at an uncompromised six feet, he had been at this well over thirty-five years now and cherished the recollection of what it was like to start with nothing, mostly because he helped new entrants do it every day. What he did not remember was the name of the fast-approaching pitch person suddenly targeting him, only that he was a peripheral Banker to whom he had said "no" more than a dozen times.

"Daniel Steyer, we among you." Steyer thought he might

vomit spontaneously, just to avoid the sales speak the B-team drone was not even trying to mask.

"You'll have to forgive me," choked Steyer. "I can't quite remember your . . ." The grape would get him through this, or so he prayed.

"Charles McFrank, Dardley Scott Silverman, we're a boutique investment bank. Focus on quick post-mezzanine sales, private to private, some public market currencies now and again . . ."

"I know your firm, you've pitched to me before," said Steyer. "I really don't have anything for you."

"Maybe I have something for you," said McFrank. "EnvisionInk is a flawless shop, no doubt, but I'm working with a new caching solution you might want to look at."

"I don't look at caching solutions," replied Steyer. "We have a management team that does that."

"And they are here, are they not?" asked McFrank. "An introduction would be much appreciated. You lead the trail by blazing it."

An introduction, thought Steyer, that was not much to ask. So why was he annoyed? It was his party, introductions were why he invited the crowd. So what if he no longer needed middlemen. He was admired for his willingness to broker a kind handshake. He was the introduction, the one that mattered, the one they would remember when valuations were set. Like Yamanaka said, Steyer put his firm's money where others were blind and had delivered for his partners a lottery ticket like few others, an uncharted win that would make the history books, top-tier compounding that most risk managers saw only in prayers. His photographic memory, that was his power jab. He had read the business plan of Calvin Choy and Stephen J. Finkelman with a scope of knowledge that conjured prescience. Steyer had seen in Choy and Finkelman the kind of company builders that made Yamanaka's campus assessment pay out. They were more than students—not glamour hounds, not reckless pivotors, but notably gifted software engineers whose disciplined studies unveiled chance where others saw obstacles. Choy and Finkelman were that solid, pure talent, gold in Fort Knox West stacked by the craft that Steyer wished to be revered as strategy, but really came down to balls.

"You want to meet the boys?" asked Steyer, turning away from the bar, acknowledging the irritant McFrank if for no other reason than duty. "Let me see if I can find them."

"There's a rumor on the street EnvisionInk may get bought by Atom Heart Entertainment," blurted McFrank. "It would be a heck of a way to for them to diversify. Institutional funds know convergence isn't going away in our lifetime. With fatter margins, they're prime to heavy up at choice premiums. Showbiz is now tech biz, the smartest people just have to stay in charge."

Steyer said nothing. McFrank's game was sloppy. Steyer had not risen to the throne by babbling innuendo. Steyer placed information, legally, selectively. Still there was something about McFrank that kept him from bolting. McFrank seemed starved, a guy who needed a big win real soon and would serve up value to reserve a favor.

"We've approached Atom Heart, pitched them hard with an honest story, but they're chiseled in with the Wall Street mausoleums," continued McFrank. "It would really make our name to advise you in a sale, ensure the fairness opinion supports the take out price—pushing comfort appropriately, more than worth the fee."

Steyer tried to admire his persistence, without the dogged there would be no Valley, but his patience was legendarily thin. "There's no deal to advise, we're barely out of the gate. I said I would introduce you to our guys. Should I change my mind?"

"No, I appreciate that," said McFrank. "Thank you, I'll be here."

"I know that," said Steyer.

"And I'll owe you," bid McFrank. "I never forget someone who helps me."

Steyer knew that too, but he was not sure about following through on the introduction. He knew he had to get away or the conversation with McFrank was going to turn toward insult, either that or an unintended violation of securities law. Steyer liked to sell as well, particularly the art of closing, but like most career money guys, he had little tolerance for being oversold. It was not that his ego was out of check, simply that he believed his time was of such immense value, he measured conversations in sentence fragments the way programmers counted lines of code.

Steyer looked around for Choy and Finkelman, but the landscape was a blur of breathable textiles. Not less than two hundred, not more than three hundred, all blue blazers except for the occasional hoodie accompanied by sneakers. Since this was a party of homage and prospecting, the crowd was over-weighted with Investors and Bankers. That did not give Steyer great pleasure, at this stage in his lifecycle he did not need to meet any more Investors or Bankers. His younger, better educated partners at the near mythic SugarSpring Ventures had suggested on more than one occasion they keep the invitation list narrow so their image reflected increased scarcity, but that had never been Steyer's style. His annual backyard gathering had become part of the tight-ticket-must-attend-if-asked circuit, but throughout the years the original purpose of talent attraction had never been lost on Steyer. Part old school, always the pragmatist, he knew without an open door talent could not get to him. A little friction to filter the poseurs, he could do that with an offstage glance, but they had to come through the gate. Talent was the lifeblood that mattered, a dream and a plan. The younger partners surely had a point, invention was rare, and while Steyer knew when to stop listening, lately he had begun thinking his tricks might be getting tired. Maybe it was time for him to get out, but not today.

Yamanaka intercepted him. "Tell me again why you do this every year," goaded the Professor.

"I was just thinking the same thing," replied Steyer. "You hearing anything about Atom Heart?"

Yamanaka looked surprised. "Not at all, not outside our circle. Is it leaking?"

"Yeah, I don't know how wide. Some Banker from Dardley Scott just asked me if we were represented."

"Not good," replied Yamanaka. "Especially since the seller doesn't yet agree we're a seller."

Steyer nodded. "We have to keep a lid on this or we're going to have a fiasco. Choy and Finkelman still aren't on board. If it gets out that we're considering something and we're not ready to act, we'll have to stay organic for at least a few quarters to keep the stock out of play."

"Also not good," offered The Professor. "Internal product development has been lifeless. Our stock price reflects that. No innovation, no improving multiples."

"I have enough trouble selling this internally, I don't need the SEC camping out in our cafeteria," defended Steyer. "Meanwhile, cash flow keeps getting stronger, our standalone position is enviable."

"But predictable," returned Yamanaka. "The ticker doesn't reflect our top line, because it all comes from a single source, no more triple digit growth rate."

"I love it when you teach me my side of the business," said Steyer. "Got any new students for me to meet, someone with a big idea we can leverage?"

"Not mine, but there are a few here I don't recognize," offered Yamanaka. "I was just chatting with two newbies across the yard. They weren't at all familiar with the terrain. You might want to wander over and see what they have."

"Great, my kind of crashers, the only reason for me to be here. Let's hope they can levitate a brick."

Steyer made his way back to the staging of Yamanaka's soap box and eyed the two lost hoodies in the crowd. As expected he did not recognize them, but that was not unusual. Deal memory placed all the Bankers and Investors into mind storage, but new blood had to be encoded. No chance these two were Investors or Bankers. They were Operators without invitations — Operator wannabes more likely. That was either a payday five years in the future or an exit whistle instantly. It would not take more than a minute to find out.

"Gentlemen, have we funded one of your companies?" opened Steyer.

There was silence. Boys among deity.

"Has someone else here backed one of your projects, someone I might know?"

Still silence. This was their opening, but it was not going in the right direction.

"Do you fellows have a new product to share, a business model of some sort?"

Steyer's gift of the one-minute hearing was ticking down to time out, but just at the moment he was hedging to turn away, he felt his legs buckle. It was as though something had hit him, he wasn't sure what, but there was acute pain behind his left knee. A blood clot? Snake bite? The possibilities raced through his mind as his weight overcame his balance. Next thing he knew his head hit the grass, he was on his stomach, face down. The only variant that had not registered in his brain was the incident actually occurring.

"What we have for you is not an ordinary proposition," said uninvited Hoodie One.

"We'll need for you to come with us," added uninvited Hoodie Two.

Steyer had hit the ground without much noise or prelude, so most of the party continued. As a small group nearby looked over to see if the fallen giant was okay, Steyer realized that uninvited Hoodie One had eased behind him during their brief, stalled conversation and walloped him behind his knee with something incredibly hard. That's when he saw what he had been hit with, the handle of a handgun.

"Guys, get out of here, this isn't going to happen."

Hoodie One awkwardly drew down on Steyer. "Let's go, Mr. V.C."

"You broke something in my leg," said Steyer. "I don't think I can get up. I know I can't walk. You need to leave."

Steyer tried to ignore the pain, to pretend a thick sweat

was not already building above his eyebrows. He could still see clearly, but he was not sure for how long. The crowd around him, his personal and professional guests all around the lawn, all at once they knew this was not just a bad party, it was a party interrupted. Steyer needed it to be contained. He could neither be the nucleus of rumors nor open the barn for wolves.

"I said let's go," continued Hoodie One. "I can carry you or drag you, your call."

Steyer was not budging, not only for pain, but for principle. "Guys, there's armed security all around the property, in about four minutes you're going to be in handcuffs."

"In four minutes we'll be in another zip code," said Hoodie One as he rammed the gun barrel in Steyer's mouth and yanked him to his feet. Steyer felt a dull, numbing pain in his upper jaw. He reached up to his mouth, trying to push it aside to let enough air into his throat to breathe. At least one of his front teeth was missing. He didn't know about the other one, the gun barrel lodged between his tongue and molars. He looked around him, at the yard of sycophants his fortune had attracted, at their near frozen state of fear.

Hoodie Two draped Steyer's arm over his shoulder and started to push-pull him through the crowd, his partner shadowing the death march with the gun still in Steyer's mouth. "Let us through or he loses all his teeth," shouted Hoodie One. Steyer again pushed past the pain. He heard concerned mutters in the crowd, but could not believe they were doing what they were told, standing back, no bravery to be had. Of course things like this did not happen in Atherton, but were these people on lithium? Here they were, sealed within an armed commando attack on a reserve canteen, and not one of them had a clue how to respond. Maybe it was more than that.

Postponing the despair of abandonment, Steyer saw his wife Riley, making her way across the compound, pushing through the chaos. As Yamanaka had hinted, Steyer was somewhat unique among his peers in that he had remained devoted to Riley all their many years, which paralleled his rise to distinction.

Most of his partners had suffered the expected mid-life crises and made spectacles of themselves with trophy accompaniment, but not Steyer. An award-winning author with a deft sense of the sardonic, Riley had been there on day zero, and she would be there on day last. Steyer wondered what she was thinking, the hope that this was not going to be day last, how with their security bill did two geek thugs get on their property with a gun, or why was no one helping her husband? Had she figured out what he knew, that everyone here had come to drink his wine and pitch their hearts out? She always wanted to have more faith in people than he could, but she never forgot that protecting him from his own opportunism meant calling out the heartless even when it meant leaving money on the table.

"Dan, they aren't going to get you off the property," she cried. "Security has the fence sealed and we called nine-one-one. This is already over, they just don't know it."

"Lady, if we don't get off the property, you're going to find yourself stupid lonely in this fairy princess estate," belted Hoodie One, stuffing the gun deeper in Steyer's mouth. "We're going, that's it."

"He has to be with us," said Hoodie Two, bracing himself under Steyer's frame.

Hoodie One and Two continued forcing their way toward the gate, the crowd stepping back, parting without prompting. Shock had replaced maneuvering, too many blue blazers, not enough street sense. Steyer tried to talk but could not, the gun was wholly jammed down his throat. It was all he could do to stay conscious while his feet bumped along the pathway. His knee was swelling, his jaw throbbed, his full weight now loading down the torso of Hoodie Two while Hoodie One managed to keep the gun in his mouth. Steyer looked at Riley and did not know if this would be her final memory of him, seeing him hauled away with mud stains by a pair of no-name criminals.

"Don't worry, Lady, you'll hear from someone, not us," offered Hoodie Two. "This can all end fine, we just gotta get out of here."

"You got the valet timed?" said Hoodie One.

"Car should be there waiting," said Hoodie Two.

"You valet parked?" cried Riley. "You crashed our party and you think you're walking out with my husband? You're really not that smart."

"We made the guest list," said Hoodie One. "We thank your husband for his open door policy."

They were almost to the gate now. At the rim fence stood the rent-a-uniforms, but everyone knew they were unarmed. Question was, how fast could nine-one-one respond, and how good were these guys at tying down their exit? They sure did not seem like pros. Police sirens wailed in the distance. Perhaps the Steyers' tax dollars had been better spent on municipal services than the cash retainer for security detail. It would be close.

As Steyer's knees pushed toward the gate, through his haze he saw his prodigies Choy and Finkelman arriving. They were young, and they owed him, he thought. Maybe they would do something. Imagine their surprise, arriving at Steyer's Tudor mansion, late to a fault, only to find uniforms on the street, sirens in the background, and their board chairman being dragged through his own yard with a gun barrel down his throat.

Steyer kept focus as the hoodies pulled him across to the street, where the three of them were equally startled by the sound of the lawn sprinklers. It was McFrank. He had found the throttle and turned the key setting of the irrigation system. No question, this was his in, heroics for a chance at serious commission. In seconds at the street curb, water was everywhere. At the same time, up the street were a pair of dispatched police sedans, blue lights spinning, a third of a mile away at most. Across the gate, Hoodie One and Two noted their retrieved SUV, ordinary as ten thousand others, parked and ready to go with a stored second set of plates primed to be deployed on exit.

McFrank dove at Hoodie One, the one with the gun down Steyer's throat. As all three men slipped in the water, the gun hit the ground. Hoodie Two quickly retrieved the loose gun, put it in Hoodie One's grip, then opened the tail door of his SUV. He knew they only had seconds remaining to finish the job, with very few options.

As McFrank struggled with Hoodie One, he found his attack stance far more valiant than his fighting ability. He was a Banker who picked up a lot of dinner tabs, and although he had wrestled high school junior varsity, that was several decades and forty pounds ago. Hoodie One had him by at least twenty years, and each blow to the head was weakening him. Steyer tried to pull away, but his head was even lighter, his focus unclear. Not allowing himself to pass out, Steyer saw Choy and Finkelman diving into the fray. They had figured it out, the numbers clearly on their side. Steyer thought this just might end reasonably, as his wife observed, the pair in control were not bastions of intellect. That argument might or might not hold, depending on their level of desperation, the look of confusion he saw in their eyes he had committed to memory. Unfortunately, he did not even hear the gunshot that ripped apart half of Finkelman's left lower leg. Finkelman was fast losing blood. Steyer lost consciousness.

$ $

It was all George Yamanaka could do to hold back Riley Steyer from lunging at the intruders, weaponless, but determined nonetheless to get to her husband, thirty feet of life risk beyond their driveway. Yamanaka would not let her go, he knew better, that this at least he owed Steyer. The mess around them was more than he could analyze, he simply knew there was value in winding down what he could, protect the wife. Less pain, just prevent more pain.

Hoodie One held up the gun. The blast had silenced the crowd again. Yamanaka saw that Steyer was out cold, too heavy to move. He knew that Hoodie One and his partner were out of time, they had to make a move, any move.

"In the car," shouted Hoodie One at Choy and Finkelman.

Hoodie Two started the car, then taking guidance from his partner, jumped to the curb, grabbed Choy by the midsection and managed to hurl him into the rear cargo section of the SUV. Hoodie One approached Finkelman, on his back, half under the hood.

"You want no legs?" yelled Hoodie One. "In the car!" Finkelman tried to drag himself on his one good knee away from the SUV, toward the gate. Hoodie One looked at him, then back at Choy. "In the SUV or your friend loses a leg, too. That's one warning more than you got."

Finkelman could not pull himself to his feet, but stopped crawling. He did not want his partner, his friend, to be where he was. "You gotta help me get there," said Finkelman. "I can't walk."

Hoodie One approached, paused, cold-cocked him with the pistol handle. Finkelman was out, same as Steyer, but he was closer to the SUV, and many pounds lighter. Hoodie Two was back at the wheel of the SUV, ready to drop it into gear. The police were now pulling to a stop, both cars, four officers. Yamanaka saw McFrank trying to wave them off, signaling them to pause, but they were still coming, hesitant momentarily in assessing the suburban calamity. Too much edge, it was all about to explode.

"Grab him," yelled Hoodie One at McFrank. You wanna be Superman, save his life. Help me put him in the SUV."

McFrank looked back at Yamanaka, his body still blocking Steyer's wife from coming at them. Yamanaka tilted his head guardedly to let McFrank know it was the right thing to do. It was clear McFrank had no choice, his options were to help load-out Finkelman or watch him take a second bullet and be memorialized in the street. McFrank nodded and lifted Finkelman's upper body. Hoodie One handed the gun back to his partner through the car window and heaved the lower half into the SUV's back seat.

As Hoodie One closed the car door and made his way for the passenger seat, Choy leaned over from the cargo hold, saw his unconscious friend, leg half blasted, and knew he was all in. In one swift move, he threw himself over the seat edge, hurling his body at Hoodie Two's gun hand. Coming up short on the reach, Choy got a piece of Hoodie Two's hand but not control and landed instead flat on Finkelman. Caught off guard by Choy, Hoodie Two slammed his gun hand through the back-seat window and damn it all, another shot rang out. This time McFrank dropped to the ground. It was not clear to Yamanaka who had popped the trigger — Hoodie Two or Choy — but it was clear that McFrank was not going to make it.

His hand shaking, Hoodie Two tossed the gun to Hoodie One, shifted the SUV into gear and pulled away as quickly as it would accelerate, planting skid marks on El Camino Real. The extra seconds had counted, local law enforcement arriving on scene too late to do anything but attend to the afflicted. The SUV was gone, another department's chase if it could be found.

Yamanaka stepped forward through the gate and Riley ran to her thrashed husband. The Professor gazed at McFrank's splattered sport coat torn to shreds, a collage of acquired business cards from the day scattered on the pavement. The afternoon's hijinks were complete. The tally? One dead Banker, one beaten and unconscious Investor, two accidentally kidnapped Operators, one of them badly wounded. Not your ordinary Silicon Valley social affair, this one would deliver vast unwanted headlines.

Yamanaka would be the first witness interviewed by the Atherton police, knowing the investigation would soon be escalated to state or federal authorities. For whatever reason, the only thing going through his head was that yesterday he had filed a disclosure and placed an order to sell ten thousand shares of EnvisionInk in the upcoming open window for insiders. The stock had closed Friday at $135, with a still coveted price-earnings ratio, a P/E of fifty-five. Clearly he was not going to get that price.

$ $ $ $

1.2
It's Terrestrial

"Get ready to bleep me."

Kimo Balthazer was not having a good day. Or maybe he was, it was always hard for him to know. Was the anger his path to the limelight, or was it real, a dark gift that had kept him employed much of the past twenty-five years? It had become impossible to keep that straight in his head, what was the act and what really bugged him. Market tastes ebbed and his desire to push the envelope found new edges, but valiant noise always seemed to work. Light a bad dude on fire and oh, would they listen. Blend in some honest heat and they would scream right back, but they would never change the station. Mission one could not have been clearer.

"Kimo, be cool. We're on warning here. I don't want to lose this job." The words flowed through the studio monitor; Producer Lee Creighton was already perspiring. They had been on the air twelve minutes and already Balthazer was bringing it. "Kimo, kids in private school, the ex will drag me back into court if I miss one support check by an hour. Last time we were out almost five months. I'm at monthly minimums with Visa. Did I complain when we had to move from LA to Fresno? No, I said how nice, we'll spend weekends in Yosemite. Did I mention I hate bears and granite cliffs make me hyperventilate?"

"Pussy," chortled Balthazer, carefully muting the mic with the ignore button. "We're syndicated. It doesn't matter where we broadcast, as long as we have a tower." It was a partial truth. Syndication was the right business model, but LA got you four hundred affiliates, Fresno maybe sixty. Not poverty, not obscurity, but the wrong side of the ladder with the bottom unclear. Balthazer opened the mic and the words flowed like drain ditch run-off.

KIMO: Let me be clear, Rush Limbaugh is a monster fat ass, ugly as an inflamed wart on a circus freak, enlightened as frog excrement, who spews plague and wipes his ass with fifty dollar bills brought to him in barrel loads by semiliterate, emasculated sponsors. His listeners are limp-limb bullies, his financial backers are modern day fascists, and if the nation goes up in flames it's on his conscience, although he's so sedated on narcs he probably won't even notice the smoke.

"Kimo, wise up, play smart," pleaded Producer Lee Creighton. "Some of his sponsors are on our show."

KIMO: So my shivering nail-biter producer tells me some of Limbaugh's sponsors are on my show too, right here, on *This Is Rage*. What are they, Communists? Deviants? Didn't anyone tell them who hosts my show? They can't have it both ways.

"Kimo, you're headed over the top," added Creighton. "A touch more gentle as she goes, so perhaps we can come back tomorrow."

Each and every day at drive time 4:00 p.m. Kimo Balthazer—his last name pronounced with an awkward hard accent on the second syllable, such that the end phrase rhymed with laser—held court with an audience of one, Producer Lee Creighton, plus about a million loyals who still tuned in on one form or another of stone age radio. Sports, News, Traffic, Spanish headlines, and Talk, that was all that was left of AM. High-def tried to save it, but the Hail Mary had come up short for all but a chosen few who still had reach, most of that club so right wing they would have sent Ronald Reagan back to a union job. Satellite radio, internet radio, iPods, MP3s, Bluetooth, you name it, terrestrial radio had been shellacked by every technology a spurned Luddite could mutter. Anyone under the age of twenty barely knew it existed. The AM dial spectrum was a Trivial Pursuit question with a higher value than the benefits of eight-track tape a generation before. It was dead to all but the ancients—commuting middle agers, addicted politicos, and the rest of the graying boomers who could not bring themselves to think of

Pandora as something other than an entombed myth. For those who held on, it was ticktock ticktock, but there was still time to fund the 401k before they pulled the final plug. A few health salaries remained for the survivors who could draw, anyone who could suck ad dollars for the merged conglomerates, but fewer listeners were split among the fading stars. No one could predict how little time was left, but you could smell the body even while it was uttering soulless retransmission.

Balthazer knew he was among the last of his kind, not only the end of the line for broadcast radio blather, but a last stand for the left in largely ceded terrain. When he remembered to be amusing, he could rise above the best of logical argument, unpredictable as a core virtue, offbeat to the point of discomfort. To despise him was easy, he made it that way, all you had to do was see the world even slightly differently and you were cannon fuel. He was all mouth, no camera candy, and like his peers who could never make the TV cut, he learned to like himself that way. Squat but not enormous, maybe twenty-five pounds over fighting weight for his five tenish frame, Balthazer locked his hair style circa 1974 which kept the upper thinning crown mostly hidden from frontal view. When *The Rocky Horror Picture Show* came out in the mid-1970s, he had been mistaken at a screening for Meatloaf by fishnet fans and he kind of liked that, later leaning on the moniker "Bat Out of Hell" as his cheeky own. The trucker's goatee was a relatively new addition to his website headshot, not with him more than five years but bringing him a simultaneous texture of thought rebellion and beer hall, a perfect accent for his gruff baritone and the themes of civil fairness forever stapled in his playbook.

Liberal talk radio never made any sense to the programmers. Air time on the right was served by followers and dissenters alike — the left always had to know what the enemy was thinking, so naturally they doubled the audience, good for selling cars at local dealerships, true bipartisan opportunity. The right could not care less what someone like Balthazer had to say, not even the vaguest of interest, he and his sad circle just did not exist.

Liberal talk was a loser, always was. To make it work at even modest scale, you needed a ploy. That's where Balthazer was good, he could bottle wrath and sell it in a rainbow of flavors, only he knew what was in the rainbow, and that kept him going.

This Is Rage had started out authentically enough, an answer from one raucous voice in the wilderness to the nationwide fascination with moral superiority. In the beginning, Balthazer wanted to he heard. Then he wanted to be funny. Then they started paying him real money. He always knew if he lived long enough, he would become what he most feared, and that was the step twin of the evil mirror he once wanted to shatter. Power was the enemy, but power was nice to have, particularly if you could be self-effacing about it. Balthazer had become oh so complicated, but like the enemy, he had also become thin; not in the waistline, quite the contrary, but in the construct of argument. Facts did not sell air time—spoken word ads had become the province of online subscription dating sites, orange oil fumigations, and risky high priced medical weight loss surgery. The numbers game of radio was simple, smaller sales conversions meant bigger numbers needed to get ad spend return on investment. If you could put up big numbers, you got more air. If you could put up really big numbers, you could have drive time. Stay in drive time and syndicate, you'd pull down seven figures. Lose the numbers or piss off the wrong people, well, you'd always have Fresno.

Not a half a year earlier, Balthazer had been a seven figure guy, afternoon drive time in LA with the big network of affiliates. He had taken the show a different way, it was mostly why women were so good at ruining men, and how the male species could best beat the odds by not playing nice. Decent numbers, no question, but the quality of ad buys was slipping. Restaurant chains became truck stops, discount airlines became bulk condoms, cell phone service became salacious mobile apps. The station owners, truly nice corporate people who owned most of the four hundred stations and would have broadcast Fidel Castro if he could put up numbers, told Balthazer to clean up his act. Balthazer told them it had taken a lifetime to dirty up the act, what Sam Kinison died trying to commercialize he had stolen from the grave and turned into cash. The station owners, truly nice corporate people who once had one of their own alcoholic DJs arrested by rent-a-cops and dragged to the desert until he dried out in an outhouse, told Balthazer unless the material warranted national sponsorships, they would not just fire him, they would sue him for the last three years of salary he had taken from them in the form of negative return on investment. Balthazer thought about that, went on the air, and kindly suggested that the owners were part of a spouse-swapping cult, that they had secretly formed their own religion and made it a sacred practice to mainline erection enhancing pharmaceuticals with coupon discounts to achieve extended ritual enlightenment. The libel suit that followed cost Balthazer three years of back wages, plus a new Guinness Record for a radio host in attorney's fees. His third wife used the opportunity to walk out with the unleveraged equity remaining in his Brentwood home. Almost ten years doing drive time in the number two media market in the nation and he was broke. Again.

So Fresno was looking pretty good this fine afternoon. The mic was hot, the tower put out a signal all the way to Merced, and there was even an expense check in his mail slot for last week's live remote ribbon cutting at the Steer 'N' Ale. The act had reverted to plain old ranting news talk, his choice from the day's headlines, with a progressive tilt toward workplace cruelty and confession. As the only entertaining voice on the left since Al Franken had gone to the Senate, it would seem he might become a little less angry, but the office suffering angle was building a curious following, and even more, was pushing a pin in his forehead, anger as its own catalyst.

KIMO: So Jumbo Limbaugh believes there's nothing wrong with the current tone of the discourse in America, that the lunatic drivel he concocts is all in the name of democracy, and if he wants to trash the president, a nominated Supreme Court justice, or just about anyone who is not his own flavor of sadist running for office then that is his ordained American right. If we don't like it, we should just rally against the First Amendment and see what the ACLU is really made of. Okay, Rush, I'll give you that, the arguments on the airwaves are fine, no one has to be accountable for anything they say, and if leaders on one side of the aisle can get others removed solely through invective then so be it. I have an idea, let's turn it on you. Let's get everyone saying that you and Glenn Beck are working in earnest on a secret science experiment to reproduce to perfection by combining your DNA. I'm not saying you're gay, let's presume there's a petri dish involved. So you add your drip, Beck adds his, and for real laughs, let's get some Hannity in there, too. Call it a right wing reproduction gang bang, and once that diseased beast is fully baked who knows where you'll send it to burn down a library. You think that's extreme? Imagine a woman, an actual woman, who would have sex with one of those self-aggrandizing mind scavengers. I can't. So let's take a caller. Robert from Boise—Welcome, *This Is Rage*.

Balthazer waived through the glass daintily with three fingers to Producer Lee Creighton, who had to know this was not going to be a good-good night. The studio was getting hotter. Around the corner, behind Creighton, Balthazer saw lurking the chief local representative of the nice corporate people who owned the sixty stations. Her name was Sheri Stiller, but to everyone with a pulse over whom she was destined to crawl, she was addressed solely as Ms. Stiller. Wading down the hall, she peered through the glass at Balthazer. He tried to ignore her, but she knew he saw her. Producer Lee Creighton translated, mouthing the words, "For the love of god, tone it down." Balthazer collapsed two of his three fingers into the well-known salute, then smiled at Ms. Stiller to make it clear he was not giving her the finger, although to anyone who knew him, he was. Her stare was fixed, mechanical limbo, a humorless idle. She was waiting for anything fatal.

CALLER ROBERT: Kimo Balthazer?

KIMO: Goodness gracious, it's Albert Einstein, calling from the grave. Yes, Albert, it's me, Kimo. Let's try for a dialogue. Take Two: Welcome, *This Is Rage*.

CALLER ROBERT: No, my name is not Albert, it's Robert. Do you copy that, Kimo? Robert.

KIMO: Even better, it's Albert Einstein on a CB Radio, narrow casting from 1977. Robert, we are on the air. Why did you call? What's troubling you, trademark violation? Come on, you're dead.

CALLER ROBERT: I don't think I'm dead. Hey, the reason for my call . . .

KIMO: You're dead.

Balthazer cut the line, zero tolerance for the flat of thought. Not surprisingly, that was starting to become a problem, because when a talker is as abrasive as Balthazer, he needs to have a few friends for all the varied enemies. Friends now were too often in short supply, specifically when he kept hanging up on them. Producer Lee Creighton shook his head, held up his wallet so Balthazer could see it and opened the pouch to show no cash. Balthazer grinned as Creighton put a text message on his screen — MAURICE, FROM JERSEY, PLAY THE GOOF — tossing him the call. Balthazer noted Ms. Stiller without reaction, sideline drifting in her own world, likely hungry for contract infringement.

KIMO: Okay, we have Maurice, somewhere on the turnpike in New Jersey. Maurice—Welcome, *This Is Rage*.

CALLER MAURICE: Kimo, thanks for taking my call. Can't believe I got through.

KIMO: What's on your mind, Jersey Boy?

CALLER MAURICE: General Electric. Price-earnings ratio looks too tasty to leave on the table. What do you think, undervalued?

KIMO: You must be a first-time caller, Maurice. I don't do stock tips. Retail trading is for morons and losers. Which one are you?

CALLER MAURICE: Got the code speak, big guy, you don't like that one. Me either, that was a test, you passed. So how are you feeling these days about Cisco? I know, it's unexciting, a bell-wether, but I'm liking it for its boringness, solid fundamentals. How about a listener poll?

KIMO: Maurice, if you must incinerate your money, try Atlantic City. At least they give you free drinks while they pick your pockets. Eye candy there isn't what it used to be, but I'm guessing it's in your price range. Anything more interesting we can discuss, or can I move on? Don't leave my listeners hanging.

CALLER MAURICE: I'm thinking maybe I short the e-commerce sector, then go long on commodities. Talk to me, Kimo. Am I making good sense here?

KIMO: Do I sound like Cramer? Not a fan, he lies for ratings. If you want his crystal ball genius, go buy a subscription to Idiots Gone Wild. I'm going short on you.

Balthazer dumped Maurice, waived his open palms at Producer Lee Creighton with a wide-eyed look as if to say, "Are you trying to take me down today?" Creighton tapped his head in frustration, then mimed the outline of a smile, trying to lighten Balthazer's demon mood. Balthazer signaled for the next call without additional expression and Creighton texted another message on Balthazer's screen: ANNABEL, CRYING, KEEP THE BAT OUT OF HELL IN THE CAGE. Ms. Stiller stared. Waiting, still waiting.

KIMO: Let's take another caller, perhaps someone with an actually functioning frontal lobe. We have Annabel, and she's sad.

Annabel—Welcome, *This Is Rage*.

CALLER ANNABEL: Kimo, thanks for taking my call. I lost my job today.

Her tears were real, anyone listening with even the least human sensitivity could feel them. Balthazer tried to soften, he knew there was something of substance here, but his words leapt ahead of him.

KIMO: So you got fired today?

CALLER ANNABEL: No, I didn't say I got fired today. I said I lost my job. It's different.

KIMO: Can be. Let's talk about it. The economy hard at work?

CALLER ANNABEL: I guess. My department manager was given a target for cutbacks. I was a cutback.

KIMO: What do you do, Annabel?

CALLER ANNABEL: Insurance claims. I process payments. I mean, I used to do that.

KIMO: So you were one of those people who comes out to look at my car to see if I really hit something, then tells me you're only going to pay four hundred dollars when the body shop already quoted me three times that?

CALLER ANNABEL: No, that's a claims adjuster. I don't leave the office. I check their math and send the paperwork to finance, so you do get a check. You should like me. I am one of the good people who make sure you get paid.

KIMO: Got it, so if they cut back you, payment slows down. Everybody's happy. Except me.

CALLER ANNABEL: Exactly, they get a double win. My salary

goes to the bottom line. Fewer checks get processed, the company picks up momentum for a few months.

KIMO: Outstanding, criminals across the board. Can you tell us the name of the insurance company?

Producer Lee Creighton was on his feet, shaking his head No No No! Ms. Stiller looked his way, then back at Balthazer. She wagged her finger, like the very first school teacher who had jettisoned Balthazer from the classroom — like every teacher who had booted him to maintain sanity.

KIMO: Wait, don't say it. I'm getting a lot of negative energy from my producer who doesn't want me to name an insurance company on the air, in case one of them happens to be an advertiser.

CALLER ANNEBEL: It doesn't matter, Kimo, they're all the same. It's one big game. You file a claim, the insurance company says no. You file more documentation, they lowball you. You get a written estimate, we accidentally lose it. You file it again, we ask you if you'll take less. It goes round and round until you're worn out.

KIMO: So the point is, if you want your money, you have to hang in there long enough to get it? The ones who give up pay for the ones who are stubborn and get what they're owed.

CALLER ANNABEL: Kimo, we all know you'd get all your money.

KIMO: All my money. Every single penny of *my* money.

CALLER ANNABEL: And you're right, most everyone else will settle for less, because they have to get something or they can't get their car back and get to work.

KIMO: Got it. And you got canned why?

CALLER ANNABEL: I told you, I didn't get fired. I got laid off.

KIMO: You know, Annabel, I'm hearing something different. Let's go for some honesty here.

CALLER ANNEBEL: You think I'm hiding something from you, Kimo? Why would I do that?

KIMO: I don't know. Why did you call today? You're on the radio with a million of your closest friends, only you don't know a single one of them, and you don't know me. So why did you call into a talk show after you got laid off? Seems like there were a lot of other ways you could have spent the afternoon.

CALLER ANNABEL: Okay, I'm not happy about this.

KIMO: Yeah, I got that. What's the deal? Did you go to bat for someone, is that why they deep-sixed you? Because you tried to help someone do the right thing?

There was a pause on the line. Not quite the dreaded dead air that every host and owner fears, but something approaching that. Caller Annabel was choking up. This would not have been a great time to hang up on her, even Balthazar knew that. Producer Lee Creighton gave him a "move it along" hand gesture. Ms. Stiller now seemed bored, reading a magazine, thumbing through the thin headlines. Annabel's tale could not have interested her less.

KIMO: Annabel, you still with me?

CALLER ANNABEL: Yes, Kimo.

KIMO: You want to tell us something, don't you? Because you really feel awful about what happened, because you know how unfair it is.

CALLER ANNABEL: How do you know that?

KIMO: It's what they pay me to do.

CALLER ANNABEL: You're a psychologist?

KIMO: I'm an entertainer. Tell me what they did to screw you 'til you purred.

Producer Lee Creighton grabbed the studio mic: "I bleeped that choice phrase, Kimo. Come on, think of the mailing address—farmland and steeples."

Ms. Stiller looked up from her magazine, then set her eyes on Balthazer. He knew she could not believe any sane advertiser would want to be associated with this daily fracking fest, but the paying ones they had, she had been instructed to keep without fail. Balthazer suddenly had her on edge, fingernails silently digging into each other, swelling feet soon to stretch out her shoes. Really good laughs like this for him were rare.

KIMO: What'd they do, Annabel? Why'd they eliminate your position?

CALLER ANNABEL: I gave them a proposal. I showed them how much money I thought we were wasting making people submit the same claim four, five, six times. Then I tried to figure out the potential value of the good will we were losing with customers by rejecting their claims. I tried to explain to my boss how happy customers were when we did the right thing, and how many new customers they might bring in by word of mouth if we just played fairly.

KIMO: But you're not the CEO, Annabel. You know that. You're a claims processor.

CALLER ANNABEL: Not anymore. They fired me, remember.

KIMO: So they did fire you!

CALLER ANNABEL: I don't know. They said it was a layoff, just a routine layoff to cut some costs. But when I asked them who else was getting cut, all they said was lots of people. And when I went to HR, they asked me to sign this piece of paper saying they would not block my unemployment claim if I signed it. I'm really confused.

KIMO: Please tell me you didn't sign it, Annabel.

CALLER ANNABEL: Yes, I signed it. I had to sign it. Otherwise they said that I was fired, for cause, and I wouldn't get unemployment. I'm a single mom, two kids, and I didn't go to college. This was a good job for me. What do I do now?

KIMO: You didn't go to college, but you know the difference between pissing on customers and word of mouth advertising. I'd say you're going to do fine. I just wish you hadn't signed that release. They got you in a weak moment.

CALLER ANNABEL: That's right, Kimo, they got me. They got me just like they get everyone. They know what they're doing. You should see how they figure bonuses.

KIMO: Bonuses are paid to club members, Annabel, in exchange for silence. It's always been that way. If they all hold hands, no arms get broken. The pain begins when you don't hold hands. Now tell me why you're really calling, Annabel. Come on, *This Is Rage*.

CALLER ANNABEL: I'm calling because . . . because I think you really want to help people like me. That's what I always hear you do. Can you help me?

KIMO: You know, Annabel, I think I can.

Producer Lee Creighton looked deep into the glass separating him from Balthazer in the booth. Balthazer saw he was worried now, this call was shifting into turbo boost, the kind of call Creighton hated but made Balthazer big. Ms. Stiller cringed as she restlessly turned another magazine page. This time she tore it a little — more than a little.

KIMO: Annabel, we need to get that insurance company to give you back that liability release. Then you need to get an attorney. Then it's all about the American way.

CALLER ANNABEL: But I'm locked out, Kimo. How do I get the paper back?

KIMO: We get them to give it to you, Annabel. Just like that. For that to happen, we need to play a little game. Would you like to play a game, Annabel?

CALLER ANNABEL: Not exactly in the game playing mood, Kimo.

KIMO: Sure you are. Here's how we play. We need for the insurance company to be known to the public for the abusive, appalling, viciously amoral pox on society they are. Sound like fun?

CALLER ANNABEL: That would be all insurance companies, Kimo. Trust me, I have worked for three of them and it always ends the same way. Whoever improves throughput gets sent home.

KIMO: Throughput, I love it. You should be CEO. But we aren't talking about all of them, Annabel, just the one that set out to ruin your life. And once a million of our friends know who that is, you're going to have a much easier time getting back that piece of paper, and I'm guessing you may never need to go down to EDD. Let's play the game, shall we?

CALLER ANNABEL: What's the game, Kimo?

KIMO: The game is, I say the name of an insurance company, and you say Yay or Nay, so we know who did this atrocious thing to you and your two children. What say you, shall we try?

That was enough. Ms. Stiller flung the ripped magazine onto the mixing board and grabbed the studio mic from Producer Lee Creighton. "Knock it off, Balthazer."

KIMO: Listen carefully to the choices now, Annabel. Was it Allstate?

There was silence on the line, brief dead air again. Ms. Stiller still had the studio mic. "Balthazer, you are going to get this station sued."

KIMO: Okay, let's try again. Perchance it was Farmers?

Producer Lee Creighton looked at Ms. Stiller, her eyes ablaze, then opened the studio mic. "Kimo, she wants me to drop the call."

Balthazer shook his head adamantly. Ms. Stiller was blazing down the path to seeing bug-eyed, yet with textbook training she was forcing herself to maintain her ground. She leaned over Creighton to the studio mic. "Balthazer, at the moment you're still employed, you haven't said that it wasn't Allstate or Farmers. Get a clear negative on both of them so there's no implication, especially for the network. Even if they don't sue us, we're going to lose advertisers if we don't show respect for their brands." Ms. Stiller seemed new at this, or maybe she was just better equipped for the previous station format, Latin Top 40. Either way she was going head on with unchained talent on a live daylight broadcast. For Balthazer, that was better sex than sex. No killing this call, not a chance.

KIMO: Okay, the choices thus far are Allstate and Farmers. Let's try another, maybe was it State Farm?

CALLER ANNABEL: Kimo, I appreciate what you're trying to do for me, but I really don't want to get in trouble. I need my unemployment check. I need to work.

KIMO: Annabel, listen to me. The Man just did you in. You don't need an unemployment check. You don't need to work. You need a settlement—a nice, healthy, high six figure settlement.

Ms. Stiller was starting to sweat. Producer Lee Creighton reached for the Kleenex but she batted it away. "Balthazer, you bottom fisher, you are going to lose your slot. You are baiting that woman and that's not going to happen on my air. Tell her you are clear it's none of those three companies and get rid of this caller."

KIMO: Annabel, they stuck it to you, you need to stick it to them. Everything about this is wrong. You tried to help, they canned you. You cared about customers, they sent you packing. Who was it? Allstate, Farmers, State Farm, perhaps GEICO? Was it those lizard people at GEICO?

"One more brand name on my air and I kill the call, Balthazer. You are over the line. You think this station is beneath you? Imagine where you'll get air time if you get blown out of Fresno. Think Sarah Palin's Alaska, then head north." Balthazer was not sure if Ms. Stiller was bluffing. Ratings always triumphed in minor skirmishes, but he knew she desperately needed a live retraction from him on air to stay clean. If the corporation got sued for slander on her watch by a national insurance company, she would lose her job as well. Replacement jobs for radio executives were about as plentiful as launch pads for new talent. Everyone needed this gig, but Balthazer wasn't much into cooling the reactor core.

KIMO: We're running out of time, Annabel. We're going to have to go to commercial. What I really want to do is play a commercial for an insurance company on the next break, but it will be much more pertinent if we know which criminals were responsible for this injustice. You have to tell me, I can't guess. Allstate, Farmers, State Farm, GEICO? I need you need to give me a name, Annabel.

CALLER ANNABEL: Okay, Kimo, I trust you. I have no choice but to trust you. This afternoon I got fired by . . .

In a nimble fast cut to dead air, she was gone. Producer Lee Creighton had been quick on the draw, faders slid to zero, nothing Balthazer could do to bring her back. More than twenty years together had wired his producer's instincts for survival, to move the call to vapor so the show could go on, but that was not how Balthazer saw the game, not how he got to the top. He glared at Producer Lee Creighton, who grabbed a hand towel and took a champion's breath.

Balthazer was beside himself: "You killed my call, right before the punch line, you jerk off? You are a tier-one dick weed, shit coward, Cro-Magnon cocksucker!"

Unfortunately, both paws on the hand towel caused Producer Lee Creighton to miss that string. He had saved the GEICO lizard and all his logo pals, only to take his hands off the console in the seconds of relief that followed. Balthazer had slipped, and now so had Creighton. Balthazer heard his own foul mouth echo through the monitors, a broadcast outburst that would cost him everything. If it had not been his homeboy on the board, Balthazer would have thought it was a set up. It was simply an error following a save, but the error was unrecoverable.

KIMO: We'll be right back, after this word from GEICO—or one of its reptile competitors.

Balthazer switched to commercial, activating the recorded auto play sequence on his panel, freeing himself of the headgear. Then he let loose on Producer Lee Creighton. "You cut her off, but you left me live? What is that, friendly fire?"

Despite the day's ordeal, Ms. Stiller seemed almost gleeful. "Pack up, Balthazer. We'll finish the shift with Latin Top 40."

"You're firing me, over some blah-blah on insurance? Come on, Limbaugh serves up worse on his first cup of coffee."

"The insurance is for openers, Balthazer. We'll see if they sue. But those last lovely words, that sign off will cost you your license."

"Creighton, why didn't you bleep me? I told you when we started today, be ready to bleep me. I smell assassination."

"You think I'm conspiring with her?" shot back Producer Lee Creighton. "After all these years, you think I would purposefully take you down?"

Balthazer grabbed the mic cord and began to wind it into a

hangman's noose. "I don't know what to think, Creighton. You know what? Get the hell out of here. I'm done with you."

Exhausted as much as incredulous, Producer Lee Creighton looked hard at Balthazer, grasping for normalcy. "Kimo, I can't do this anymore, not again."

"I get it, Creighton. You're a pussy. Now do what I said. Get out of this studio, get out of my shadow. I'm not carrying you anymore. Get out!" The corded hangman's noose had become a lasso, and Balthazer was swinging it back and forth.

Producer Lee Creighton took a step toward Balthazer, worried, not seeing him quite this far gone before. "Kimo, you're going to need help. This round is not going to be the same."

"Get. Out. Now!" Balthazer released the lasso and the mic flew at Creighton, who quickly stepped out of the target zone. The makeshift missile knocked an old faded picture of the two of them at the Talkers Awards from the wall, smashing the frame, all that was needed to get the job done. Creighton had taken in enough drama for this tour and exited stage door right.

Balthazer was out of the chair, half way to the door, heading for Ms. Stiller. "Latin Top 40, you corporate criminal?"

Ms. Stiller was having none of it. "How far do you want to take this, Balthazer? Job? License? Jail?"

Balthazer re-roped the lasso, tossing the cord in Ms. Stiller's direction. She ducked it.

"You're going for assault now, Balthazer. Losing your career isn't enough? You really want to do prison time as well?"

"Here's what I want," said Balthazer. This time the noose landed on her hands, as if he had done this before. All in one move, he had her hands tied in the mic cord and started to wrap the slack around a loop in the control board.

"You're beyond crazy," she blurted. "You think this is somehow going to be okay?"

"I think it's going to be what it needs to be," Balthazer smirked. "Here you go, you cut costs to the bone. Afternoons — just me, Producer Lee Creighton, and you. Now Creighton is gone, and from what I can tell, you don't like the talent programmed for the hour."

Balthazer fixed the cord to the control board. Her hands were locked, she could not move. He slid the microphone boom directly in front of her and put the windscreen a half inch from her lips. "We're coming back from break now, ma'am." Balthazer reached for the control board and pushed the volume sliders live. "Commercial is over, Ms. Corporate Criminal." Ms. Stiller stared into the windscreen. On the wall of the studio, the red neon letters could not have been clearer: On The Air.

She tried to free her hands. Could not.

She tried to find a few words to say. Could not.

Balthazer wondered how many people might still be listening, and for how long. He left Ms. Stiller at the console, strode to the glass door, locked it behind him, then walked on down the hall and departed the studio.

No more valiant noise.

No more callers or commercials.

Dead air.

$ $ $ $

1.3
Never Bet Against the Bozos

Hoodie One had a name, it was Dennis Swerlow. Hoodie Two had one as well, it was Sam Kisinski. As if it were not clear enough from the job they had just botched, neither was a professional criminal. Up until a few weeks ago, they were just part of the Silicon Valley bullpen. Now they had killed a man and taken two others hostage, neither of whom they had set out to nab.

Four hours following the Steyer soiree they were parked at a rest stop off Highway 101 about one hundred miles south of San Jose, on California's central coast. Finkelman had regained consciousness but was still bleeding heavily, too weak to make any noise at all. Choy had been gagged and told by Swerlow to remain silent or Finkelman would be left roadside. Swerlow had been waiting for over an hour for his disposable cell phone to ring, after he had dialed the number for another disposable phone on the other end to let his number be captured. Now it rang, delivering a voice known only to him as Howzer.

"Howzer, what took you so long?"

"You're not the only job we're working," said Howzer. "You got him?"

Swerlow hesitated, this was the question he had been dreading all afternoon. He steadied himself, took an even breath, tried to ease into it. "Well, what if I tell you we have something better?"

"We didn't ask you to be creative," blurted Howzer. "We asked for something specific. The deal is tied to that specificity. You have it or you don't."

"I'm telling you, what we have is better," said Swerlow, sweeping into full sales mode. "Completely better."

"Champ, we don't have much time here. Your plane is

gassed and waiting in an almond grove with the money onboard. If you're where the GPS on your cell phone tells me you are, I can have you in the air in thirty minutes, then a plane change outside LA and you wake up in Hong Kong. For that to happen, I need Steyer. Do you have him?"

"It didn't go quite as planned," answered Swerlow. "We had him, but someone stepped in the way. We sort of killed him."

"You killed Daniel Steyer, you imbecile? That's our ticket to $20 million cash money. His wife would pay that by morning. You're telling me he's dead?"

"No, Steyer is alive. A little beat up, but he's fine. We accidentally killed another guy who got between us. I mean, maybe we killed him. I mean, he's dead, I'm pretty sure of that, but not so sure it was us who did it. It could have been. Hard to really know."

"Excellent, now you have a murder rap to beat. If I were you, I would tell me that you are about to deliver Steyer to me, because you really need to get out of the country now. And you probably want to go to Singapore, easier to disappear there, we can get that done. Do you have him?"

"Like I said, we have something better," continued Swerlow. "Two for the price of one."

"The price was for one — Daniel Steyer. That's who we want. That's who we can exchange quickly and without a lot of hassle. If you don't have him, we're done."

"Choy and Finkelman, we have both of them. They're yours. Same price, no increase. All yours."

"Your brain cells are without electrons," said the voice of Howzer. "The founders of EnvisionInk, what the hell do you think we can do with them?"

"Same thing you'd do with Steyer," replied Swerlow. "Only you pay once and get paid twice. Look at the margin improvement."

"You may be the single stupidest person we ever hired off Craig's List," said Howzer. "This was a simple job. You grab a backroom player worth a ton of dough whose wife loves him, you deliver him to us, we make the trade. Choy and Finkelman are public figures, they aren't married, and we don't ransom kids back to their mommies. Good luck, asshole."

"Wait," begged Swerlow. "Half price. They're both yours for a million. If you don't want Finkelman because he's bleeding, we'll leave him here in the park."

"Champ, we're done, off you go. Thanks for playing."

"Okay, last and best offer, both or one, yours for free, just fly us out of here. We really need to get out of here. You've got the plane. We'll even pay for the fuel, we'll work it off on a future job."

"You screw this up at this level of insanity and you think we want you on another job? You're not pros, you're not even amateurs. You're dunces. Good luck."

The line went dead. It was clear that Choy and Finkelman were not in the same work-for-hire demand that had come with the much failed assignment for Daniel Steyer. It was time to improvise.

"We can't stay here, Dennis," said Kisinski. "This is a rest stop, Highway Patrol comes by, they expect people to move along. And we gotta do something about this guy's leg or he's not going to make it."

"Mexico," replied Swerlow. "We're about eight hours from the border. We can get a doctor there."

"We're going to cross the US border with two hostages, one bleeding to death? I don't think so."

"Okay, let me think."

Swerlow and Kisinski were not just friends, they were cousins. Their mothers were sisters and still lived in their home state of Oregon, in a working class suburb outside of Portland. Swerlow was five years older than Kisinski, punching in at just under twenty-eight years old. Kisinski had graduated about a year ago from the University of Oregon with a bachelor's in computer science and should have had a promising career ahead of him. He had interviewed via Skype at Microsoft and was offered an entry-level job in quality assurance on the next generation operating system team, which with his talent would have likely catapulted him to full developer status in a year. Cousin Dennis had told him this was an insult, if Microsoft thought so highly of him they would have hired him as a developer outright, just as they had hired him when he almost graduated from the University of Oregon, pending only a set of final exams that he refused to take on principle because in his mind they were unimportant and a cave to validating industry norms. Bill Gates, Steve Jobs, Mark Zuckerberg, none of them had college degrees. Worker bees had college degrees—along with students who actually attended their classes, and did not spend senior year day trading their student loan money until it amounted to zero, which is how he had chosen to end his college career.

What cousin Dennis also had failed to tell Kisinski was that three months after Microsoft had hired him those half dozen years ago as a developer without any degree whatsoever, they had fired him for lack of talent. Sun and Oracle had done the same shortly thereafter on a similar timetable. Swerlow had also been let go by two start-ups in high ramp mode that hired him on impulse right in the middle of his interviews without even taking the time to check his references, only to discover that he talked more than he typed, and what he typed appeared elegant on surface review but never fully compiled. True to the mold, Dennis Swerlow was a classic ninety percenter, competent enough to get his resume to the top of the pile, but not a detail guy, never able to deliver the goods no matter how convincing he sounded. In this respect he was consistent, and indefatigable. He almost always smiled, he never ran out of concepts to pitch, and he was resilient to a fault without any regard for learning from his mistakes except to sell harder and faster. He never had anything approaching Sam's gift for programming languages, but he had learned most of the high notes of the money song. This made him an excellent candidate for the role he had proudly proclaimed himself: Entrepreneur.

Trouble was, Swerlow was not much better at being an entrepreneur than he was a coder. Sure he played back the jargon well enough, but in the same way his code never quite compiled, his company pitches had a sad way of always falling short. His first company idea had been for a set of fully customizable printer drivers that could be downloaded and configured in real time over the Internet and address any printer on anyone's desktop anywhere in the world instantaneously — you would just go to this destination and clink "Fix My Printer" and it would. Sounded good enough, but it didn't work. After start-up job two dumped him jobless in Fremont, Swerlow had succeeded in getting a group of young programmers in the East Bay to work on the problem for nearly a year without salary in exchange for equity, hoping to quickly sell the company after he demonstrated its potential to the right acquirer. The small team of coders got to about a dozen driver examples, but when each installation inevitably failed when anyone who did not happen to have one of the dozen leading printers on the market tried to detect their printer, the subsequent system crash was enough to send interested parties scrambling. Swerlow referred to this as a "nit," something to be worked out downstream by an acquirer with vision. When his programmers quit, he blamed the failure on lack of conviction and moved on.

Swerlow's next start-up displayed equal moxie. Now based in Gilroy, he envisioned a set of music videos that would edit themselves. Any musician or would-be auteur would simply upload his song to a remote database, select a set of visual themes and queues, and voila, storytelling heaven. The incomprehensible mishmash that would output made no sense to anyone, the streams were less interesting than randomized screensavers. Meanwhile video sites across the Internet were taking shape with every form of easy editing tool available as shareware. Swerlow had talked his mother out of $50,000 for this venture, which he spent on brochures and a tiny MacWorld trade show booth at Moscone. When he failed to get more than a few passersby to take his brochure or demo disk, he realized he might be a little late to market and again moved on. Mom was not happy. He had promised her a minimum twenty-five times return on her home equity loan withdrawal in less than two years' time, and the odds had become clear this was not going to happen. It was time for Swerlow to move up the ladder, and besides, he knew the place to raise real money was Sand Hill Road. He was kidding himself if he did not make the full commitment, go to the real Silicon Valley and put down roots.

One thing Swerlow was good at was talent recognition, and looking at the architecture of his cousin's senior project, he knew Sam was strong. By the end of his junior year, Kisinski had essentially completed his major in the computer science program, so he embarked on extra credit. Without anyone asking him, and without any thought to seeking permission or front door access, he had re-envisioned the entire university's database environment. Late one night for giggles, he launched an overwrite of the university's historical archive and back office. Swerlow had never forgotten the night his cousin called to tell him what he had in mind, as if seeking Swerlow's blessing, which Swerlow was only too happy to offer. Unfortunately, Swerlow was too dense to see the looming flaw in Kisinski's logic. Since Kisinski knew what he was doing, he had not seen or touched anyone's data or personally identifiable information, that would have been a crime, but he had de facto made it inaccessible by putting his program in front of the existing program and making it the default. Proving that his program could access the safely protected data without ever having been part of its encoding, Kisinski had inadvertently made all campus data inaccessible to anyone on campus except himself, and he had no authority to access it without breaking the law so it was in fact "on ice," a brilliant if largely academic proof of concept that baffled the school's IT department with an impenetrable virtual firewall that was nowhere documented. When campus security showed up the next morning to request Kisinski come answer a few questions, he asked for a moment to log off, grabbed his mobile phone, typed one line of code and switched everything back. The university had been unable to tie the hack back to Kisinski, and a year later, after a thorough investigation, he graduated with honors.

Swerlow was so impressed with Kisinski's ability to load and unload database systems on the fly that he helped his cousin file for a patent, sharing name ownership of the patent in exchange for his help in drafting the documents. Convincing his cousin that Microsoft's insulting offer was outrageously beneath him, Swerlow led Kisinski and his source code to a seven-hundred-square-foot apartment in Sunnyvale, which they dubbed World Headquarters of DB-SAAS-SYS. They shared a split shift at Starbucks to keep the lights on—Swerlow played barista while Kisinski flushed out the architecture, then Kisinski knocked out cappuccinos while Swerlow drove his rusting Accord up and down Sand Hill Road knocking on doors for a meeting. After a year on the fundraising trail, there was no money, no interested parties, and the manager at Starbucks was losing patience with the endlessly tepid Grandes. Kisinski was making noises about calling back Microsoft and begging for the job. Swerlow begged him to be patient.

Swerlow knew he did not have much time. He had to raise some money or he was going to lose his mission critical partner, probably just as the patent would come through. No path was too desperate for him, and when he found a post on Craig's List that suggested a seven figure payday for an afternoon's work, it was music to Swerlow's ears, sans video editing. The fact that the job listers wanted someone to "quietly kidnap" the renowned venture capitalist Daniel Steyer did not seem terribly outrageous to Swerlow. What he worried about most was how he would be able to operate after he snuck into a Silicon Valley party, abducted one of tech's most powerful finance guys in broad daylight, swapped him for a pile of no-strings-attached cash, and then opened shop with an ongoing need for Bankers to do his IPO. The fellow who wanted Steyer, known to Swerlow only as "Howzer" via a cell phone number that changed at the end of every previous call, told him not to worry about it. In addition to paying for the safe delivery of Steyer, they would relocate Swerlow and Kisinski to Hong Kong, pin the crime on another pair of guys who looked like them, and then when the coast was clear bring them back to the US and fully capitalize their company. Maybe it was because he was an eternal optimist, or maybe it was because he just wanted to believe, but to Swerlow, it all sounded credible. His focus had been first on convincing his cousin this was doable, and second, on convincing himself how it was doable.

Any notion the entire plan could go upside down never occurred to Swerlow. It all was quite simple. He and Kisinski would walk into the garden where they would be confidently at home and unsuspected as scrubby up-and-comers, wait for the right moment to grab Steyer, and then with the utter chaos around them, drag him out and drive away in their own car, which had been gate checked. Swerlow had been right about one thing, that in the shock of the moment no one was likely to stop him. What he had not factored was what would happen if someone with a sprinkler handle did try to stop him, how he would overcome the obstacle, who might get hurt, and what would he do if he could not get Steyer in the car. Strangely, for the briefest of moments, he had actually convinced himself that he had traded in a scratch off lottery ticket for the Super Lotto Mega Prize when he left Steyer in the sculpted bushes and ended up with the titans Choy and Finkelman. If Howzer was willing to pay seven figures for Steyer, imagine what he might pay for Choy and Finkelman.

He had since learned the answer was zero.

"Come on, Dennis," pushed Kisinski. "We're losing Finkelman. We're already responsible for one murder. I really don't think we want another one."

"Stop saying that," said Swerlow. "We don't know who killed that fat guy in the wet blazer. There was a struggle. It could have been anyone."

"Right, it was our car, our gun, we were trying to get the hell out of Steyer's driveway with his two best executives. It really could have been anyone."

"Maybe it was Choy. He forced his way over the seat. How do we know he didn't pull the trigger?"

"Fine, he pulled the trigger. What do we do now? We have no contract, no phone number, and a bleeding guy in the back of our car. Where do we go? And if you say Mexico again, I may kill you. What do I have to lose?"

"This is going to be okay, Sam. We just have to figure it out. Let's look at the facts."

"The facts are we are in way over our heads. We should leave these guys here, dial nine-one-one, and get as far away as we can."

"And then what?" countered Swerlow. "We can be visually identified from the party. You have to believe they have images of us from every angle on Steyer's security cameras. With no help, how do we get out of the country? How do we make a living? How do we get an identity change? We don't have any choices here."

"What are you suggesting?" asked Kisinski.

"Again, the facts. Steyer was worth over a billion dollars, a $20 million bounty from his wife was an easy ask. That's less than two percent of his net worth. What do you think Choy and Finkelman might be worth? Three times that, six times that?"

"Who cares if they're worth a hundred times that? We don't know how to do this. We're software engineers. What do we know about ransoming millionaire executives?"

"Did you ever think that maybe we already did the hard part?" asked Swerlow. "Think about it. What did Howzer hire us to do? To get him bait. We pulled that off. We walked into a party and exited with a pair of super high net worth individuals. Not one, but two. And not a mystery venture guy, but two guys who make the front page of the *Wall Street Journal* at least once a week. This has to be gold."

"But Howzer didn't want them," argued Kisinski. "This is his livelihood and he passed. What part of this aren't you comprehending? We screwed up, major league big time. We just screwed up."

"You keep seeing the downside in this, Sam. Try to see it from a different angle. Sure, Howzer and his guys are pros.

They trade bodies for cash all over the world. They knew how to make exchanges, but they still need the targets. They aren't the only buyer on the market."

"They seem to do just fine hiring an endless stream of idiots like us to go get their targets," said Kisinski. "On the supply and demand curve, subcontractors like us seem to be in abundant supply. For god sakes, we found him on Craig's List. He fronted us zero dollars and we said yes. Now we're going to play hardball?"

"Targets are currency, and we have a prime pair—two genius tech execs who run one of the most profitable and highly valued companies in the world. They are irreplaceable. Howzer has no vision. We don't need Howzer. He's just overhead."

"I can't believe you're going there. You think we're going to negotiate directly with EnvisionInk for the return of their founders? Are you losing blood that I'm not seeing?"

"Of course not, negotiating with a Fortune 500 company would be absurd. We're going to negotiate with their insurance company."

"Dennis, there's no longer a wired brain between the top and back of your skull," said Kisinski. "I didn't need to be a millionaire. I wanted a job coding at Microsoft. Now I can't do that because I'm a murderer."

"I told you to stop saying that, Sam. You have to stop saying it or you are going to start believing it."

In the back of the SUV, Choy was tapping his head against the rear window to call their attention to Finkelman. It was just past sunset now, so it was harder to see through the windows, but it was clear that Finkelman was not getting any better. They had to do something or they were going to lose him.

"Do you know any doctors we can trust?" asked Swerlow.

"Trust, as in, will operate on a gunshot wound and then just let us walk away with the patient when they're done?"

"Precisely, that's what we need."

"Doesn't exist," said Kisinski. "We need to take him to an emergency room. When we get there, they are going to ask questions. Those will be followed by police questions, which will be followed by our arrest."

"So the answer is no, I got that. So the doctor has to be working with us, not against us."

"Are we going to kidnap a doctor now? Dennis, we are the worst kidnappers on the planet. How bad can you make this?"

"Let's get back to the payday. In exchange for Steyer, we were due $2 million, a hundred percent on delivery, plane to Hong Kong waiting at the exchange site, no consolation prizes. Right?"

"So what?"

"Howzer's take was $20 million, ours was ten percent of Howzer's. We're talking way less than a quarter percentage point of Steyer's net worth, about twenty basis points all in."

"You're negotiating with yourself. Finkelman is bleeding. How does this help?"

"Presume Choy and Finkelman are collectively worth several billion dollars. I think I'm being conservative here." Swerlow paused to run a quick search on his smart phone. "At Friday's trade and a six month average P/E in the mid-fifties, the company has an enterprise value of about $36 billion, plus or minus."

"And . . . ?"

"A hundred million dollars is nothing, it's a bargain. That's our current valuation, what we can use for leverage."

"To do what, Dennis? To do what?"

"To get help. If Finkelman dies, they lose a hundred million in market cap on the first trade down, that's in a millisecond. By the end of the first day, they could be off ten percent, that's more than $3.5 billion. Wouldn't you pay $100 million to save $3.5 billion? Of course you would, especially if it's insurance money. It doesn't even register as a fractional statistic."

Kisinski paused. Swerlow was breaking through. Swerlow was good that way, relentless, not one to stop talking until the other side started hearing or otherwise begged for silence. Kisinski held up a hand to acknowledge he needed a breath. He took a few steps away from the SUV, toward the cinder block restroom structure, his eyes fixed on the highway traffic racing past the off-ramp, headlamps beginning to pierce the twilight.

Yep, Swerlow was sure he had him.

$ $

Kisinski exited the restroom, his hands only half dry from the eco-friendly wall blower. He retrieved a Mountain Dew from the vending machine beside the parking lot, surrendering one of the final dollar bills in his wallet, then another, the second can in his pocket. Was his cousin making any sense? The equation couldn't be that logical. If it was, why hadn't Howzer thought of it? Swerlow was taking all the emotion out of it, making it a transaction. Ransoming back Steyer to his wife, that was emotional. This was not Howzer's style, he thought, it was something else. Pure Dennis, a Swerlow Special.

When Kisinski returned to the SUV, still quiet, he knew the decision was his. Swerlow could not do this on his own, he was only half the code library, probably less than half. He handed the open Mountain Dew to Swerlow, who smiled and took a sip.

"How do you propose we go about this?" asked Kisinski, his interest if not his confidence on the rise.

Swerlow continued on his methodical path. "All we need are a few people to help us, and they have every reason to offer their help. No backroom secrets, all daylight. It's just business."

"You're always so sure of yourself, Dennis. Everything to you is a deal."

"My confidence is grounded, Sam. The two gentlemen in the back of our SUV have extraordinary incentive here. We tell them what we need—starting with a doctor—they make a few calls, we move the dialogue along."

The unending day was getting to Kisinski, exhaustion was taking its toll and time for recalibration was not on the evening program. That morning they had downed their lattes as aspiring criminals, with hope energizing ambition. By nightfall they were failed criminals, yet actual criminals nonetheless. Kisinski was not sure if Swerlow was making sense, or if he personally had crossed the logic barrier and was allowing desperation to overtake his good judgment. But what real choice did they have? If they abandoned Choy and Finkelman at the rest stop, it was entirely possible that Finkelman would die. While they were accidental murderers, this would be a fully conscious decision, one they could never escape in actuality let alone mind. With no money and no plan, life on the lam held little appeal. Not getting some help was a path that could not possibly end well.

"Suppose I buy into this," said Kisinski. "Walk me through it."

"I don't have it all figured out yet, but we get Choy to call Steyer, set up an emergency room doctor for us, wire us some cash, and then we tell them to wait for instructions."

"And you think they're going to wait? What makes you think that?"

"You have to start trusting me, Sam. I managed to convince Howzer we were Valley insiders, didn't I? That we could slip into Steyer's backyard undetected and slip out with Steyer unnoticed. So we didn't pull it off, so what? But I did sell it."

"And your point is?" asked Kisinski.

"I can sell this," said Swerlow. "I know I can sell this."

"I want to believe that, Dennis. I really want to believe that. But you have been wrong about everything."

"With learning comes experience, and with experience comes better decision making. You have to admit, we're in a better place now than when Howzer hung up on us a half hour ago. That's progress."

"We've made a terrible mess, Dennis. We have to find a way out."

"We have to get into a negotiation. Once we are in a negotiation, we can ask for anything: money, forbearance, safe passage. EnvisionInk has to want these guys back. They're rudderless without their CEOs. Without a rebound story by the end of this weekend, come Monday morning the share price of EnvisionInk has to slide. Their board can't let that happen. They need Choy and Finkelman on the job, safe and sound. We're mouse-nuts at $100 million. We just have to get into position to make the offer."

Kisinski looked into the back of the SUV and saw the condition of Finkelman continuing to slip. It was dark now, and on the corner of the rest stop parking lot they were quite alone.

"Let me talk to Choy," said Kisinski. "I'm a programmer like he used to be. He might listen to me."

"No ego, no pride of authorship," said Swerlow. "We each do what we're best at. We're a team."

"I wish it were otherwise," snapped Kisinski as he stepped away from Swerlow and opened the back of the SUV. Kisinski looked into Choy's eyes. Choy was silent, still gagged, not appearing afraid, but Kisinski could tell this could go either way. "It's Calvin, right?"

Choy nodded. His stare was fixed, impossible to read.

"Calvin, we don't want anyone else to get hurt," said Kisinski. "Or more hurt. We want your friend to get some help. If I take off the gag, you promise not to make a lot of noise?"

Choy nodded. Kisinski looked at Swerlow for reassurance. Swerlow seemed confident that Choy was sincere. Kisinski took off Choy's gag.

"I know this is going to sound strange, but we're not really good at this," said Kisinski. He reached in his pocket and handed Choy the second can of Mountain Dew.

"My friend is going to lose his leg if we don't get him to a doctor," said Choy, holding the sealed can in his bound hands.

"In fact, and you might find this ironic, we're programmers," continued Kisinski. "Well, I am, my cousin not so much." Kisinski opened the soda can for Choy, who took a needed gulp.

"You looking for a job?" asked Choy, his sarcasm clear to the core. "Stephen and I run a very successful company. Maybe we could work out something. But he has to live."

"Yeah, I'm guessing we're a little far down the path for that," said Kisinski. "But thank you, it's a kind offer. This situation, you can probably tell, it's not what we intended. We're going to need some help."

"I can do that," said Choy. "But you have to take my friend to a hospital. You have to do it now."

"Right, but we're going to need you to make a few calls for us," said Kisinski. "Does that work for you?"

"Do I have a choice?" asked Choy.

"None of us do," said Kisinski. "We're sort of in this together now. At least until we're not."

"Who do you want me to call?" asked Choy.

"That teacher of yours from Stanford, the one we met at the party," interrupted Swerlow. "He's on your board of directors, isn't he?"

"George Yamanaka?" asked Choy. "Yes, he's on our board — audit and governance committees. He chairs governance."

"Yes, Professor Yamanaka. Let's start with him," said Swerlow. "Governance, perfect."

$ $ $ $

1.4
Let's Get Small

Balthazer's head hurt. It had been a long week. Or month. One of those. The days without a live shift and minimal human contact before happy hour were isolating and redundant. Discretionary cash was in short supply, and along with it, discretion. Cheap tequila remained plentiful, limes grew on trees. Somehow Balthazer knew this was not a recipe for reinvention.

Balthazer sat alone in his almost empty apartment, his laptop open to his own home page, not a lot of action there. As he searched random destinations and distances on Google Maps, his mobile rang and the smart phone recognized the caller. It was now Ex-Producer Lee Creighton, there in alphanumeric clarity on the tiny digital screen. Balthazer had not spoken with him since the incident, did not even know where he was. This was uncomfortably strange. Prior to separation they had been together for over twenty years, on the air in a half dozen markets, untold personal appearances in venues ranging from community college bars to third rate rodeos. They had spoken every single day of their working lives, but not since the incident. Balthazer did not want to answer the call, but he knew he could not do otherwise.

"Traitor pussy," said Balthazer, biting open the discourse.

"Thanks, Kimo, how could I have expected less? You okay?"

Balthazer figured Creighton knew better than to come back viciously at his jugular. It seemed as though his ex-producer had a pretty good sense of what he was dealing with. "I am a reflection of delivered evolution," answered Balthazer. "Unemployment doesn't suit everyone quite so well in spirit, but for me, it's a natural fit."

"Kimo, what are you still doing in Fresno?" continued

Creighton. "You have an ugly trail there, and you're not making it better. You need to leave."

"You must have some intelligence machine," said Balthazer. "Are you stalking me? Where are you, anyway?"

"Back in LA," answered Creighton. "I used all the political capital I had left to get a show. I'm at KFI."

"Outstanding, KFI, fascism for dough!" replied Balthazer. "What political capital? You mean you blew one of those right wing flunkouts for a gig?"

"Yeah, Kimo, I begged. I'm doing the overnight. Some rookie they're trying to break, a young Hannity, but he's smarter, which takes so little. They think he has legs, but he needed a vet to make sure the right calls were put through. It's a job. It's a health plan. It was this or telemarketing. We aren't trained for much outside the studio."

"Three decades in the business and you're producing the overnight as Satan's tutor. That's a career move."

"You're talking career moves, Kimo? It's a major market and a paycheck. Remember what that woman Stiller said, where do you go after Fresno? Well, I found mine."

Balthazer said nothing, leaving Creighton to break the brief silence at will. He knew Creighton had more to say, it just had to be extracted, no different than on-air torture.

"Something else," continued Creighton in a weaker tone. "I think I'm getting back with my ex. She said as long as I don't work for you, she'd give me another chance. It beats the cost of child support. She doesn't hate me as much as she used to."

"Why are you calling me?" asked Balthazer, unmoved by the confession. "Great, you're working, I'm not. You're back with your ex. Send out a press release, party at the Self Realization Center. We were done when I threw you out. You let me say cocksucker on the air, among other choice utterances. Did you tell your new boss Son of Gingrich that?"

"I didn't have to, he read it in *Talkers*. Now he has the clipping on his Wall of Death, right next to every other cancelled bleeding heart who's tried to stick in LA He's got you up there twice now, Fresno is an honorary kill. I'm just calling to tell you if you haven't figured it out yet, you need to be out of there, gone now. Where were you last night?"

"A bar, Creighton, is this News Talk? It's where I've been every night. And don't worry, I'm packed. I just gotta figure out where to go."

"Some guys from the station saw you last night. I'm guessing you started at afternoon Happy Hour and closed the place before sunrise?"

"Free nachos and they let me run a tab. Sounds like home to me. Sometimes you just hang out."

"The guys were surprised to see you still around. The FCC has been all over the station, and the station says they aren't paying the fine, it's your problem. You can expect visitors, I'm guessing soon."

"My problem," barked Balthazer. "Was I running the board? You pay the fine. You're the putz who left me loud and naked."

"It doesn't work that way, Kimo. You know the game. The guys also told me your landlord called the station looking for the rent when you stopped answering your door. Now he knows you're unemployed. I'm telling you as your friend, go somewhere now."

Balthazer thought about it, relieved to know that Producer Lee Creighton cared enough to tip him off. "I appreciate the call. You know what? I miss working with you. I don't miss you, but I miss working with you."

"Same here, Kimo. Call me when you get something going. Just go somewhere." Creighton hung up.

Balthazer put down his mobile. Too many drinks, too small a town. He knew he was stupidly late getting on his way, but he still could not figure out where to go. Where do you go after Fresno? The concept had not been lost on him. Ms. Stiller was no visionary, but about this she was right. His wave had not only crested, it had flat-lined. Balthazer knew he was screwing the pooch when he left his boss tied up with her mouth in front of a live mic on afternoon drive time. There was charming, there

was stunt-like, and there was line crossing. These three gradi-
ents may not have been fully differentiated in the life of a radio
talk show host, but he still knew when he discovered a new extreme. *Talkers*, the trade magazine of his chosen profession, had
offered a special extended celebration of Balthazer's "Afternoon
in Fresno," which normally would have been as much resume
fuel as any jock could want. Yet Balthazer had gone the distance
now: fired in Los Angeles for humiliating his station owners,
fired before that in New York for less than patriotic discourse
following 9-11, and now a triple crown—on air named sponsor
bashing, a live string of expletives, and assault on female personnel, all in half a shift. Even if he could get an offer, and he
couldn't, there were legal battles in his rear view mirror, and
that nasty nuisance of getting his broadcasting license reinstated
following a hearing, where he would have to have a really good
reason in a judge's eyes why he did what he did, and even he
couldn't imagine what that might be.

Perhaps the only thing going Balthazer's way was that Sher-
ri Stiller had elected not to press charges, thinking the public
embarrassment of losing control of a station under her direction
was unequalled in value by the satisfaction of seeing Balthazer
do time. She also knew that since he had not really physically
hurt her, incarceration would be brief, and the attendant pub-
licity would be more valuable to Balthazer's reemergence campaign than any further detriment to his hiring. She had gotten
what she wanted across the board. In the wake of the on-air
fiasco, corporate had agreed to a program shift that reverted her
format to Latin Top 40, with almost zero cost of talent replac-
ing an entire line up of talk hosts, ensuring her better year end
profits and a commensurately improved bonus. Balthazer was
as unemployable as she could imagine for as long as she could
imagine, so retribution was satisfied by taking from Balthazer
what he most wanted, an audience. Clearly her corporate bosses
were pleased that she was willing to take it on the chin for the
company and get back to profit making. It was not a terribly noble change of events, but in that good corporate way, it worked

for everyone at just the right level of sell out.

In retrospect, Balthazer was not sure why he melted down over so little. His hot head had always been an asset, the unique entertainment value he conjured four hours each day out of otherwise sad silence, but he had always played like a pro and known where to pull it back. The past year had not been ordinary times, but he could not pinpoint what had changed. What had pushed him over the edge in LA and then Fresno? What was so bothersome that he could not separate the act from the identity? Something was different, maybe it was the tone of the calls, or the tone of the corporate owners. It was irritating angst without answer, painfully intangible, metaphysically impenetrable, but materially present—like a pimple under your chin you could neither see, nor stop from forming.

What Balthazer did was a dying profession; it just did not have to die now unless someone forced it. Nearly every major radio station in the nation was in the hands of a very few media empires, mostly remaindered in terminal value extrapolations by shrewd private equity quants. While that might not have been great for emerging talk talent still finding a voice, the proven money machine line-up owned a chokehold on the podium. Major markets came with built in syndication, because owners could pay salaries once and monetize as many times as made sense. It was just so easy, so economical. All hosts had to do was draw an audience and stay on the air and they could literally die in the chair when all the air was gone. Balthazer knew this, he knew it was to his advantage, yet he chose to impale himself, spontaneous combustion without a traceable spark. It was that tone, that awful tone coming from below and above. A live call the week before he imploded sat long on his consciousness—a middle-aged sales rep for payroll services who covered remote towns in New England named Todd.

KIMO: Welcome, *This Is Rage*. We're on with Todd.

CALLER TODD: Kimo, you got me fired.

KIMO: I got you fired? That's a lot to put on me, pal.

CALLER TODD: You told me to be honest with my boss. I was honest. Now I'm on COBRA.

KIMO: Easy, pal, I'm just doing a show here. What exactly did you say to your boss that got you a walking package?

CALLER TODD: I told you when I called the first time. My company wants more accounts. They don't care how I get them. I'm just supposed to get the accounts.

KIMO: Yeah, that's called business development. As I recall, that's what they pay you for.

CALLER TODD: Right, and do you recall what else you told me?

KIMO: Todd, I do about thirty calls a day, you're going to have to help me here.

CALLER TODD: I sell online accounting packages, software as a service. I meet with small companies, figure out their staff costs to produce their financials, then give them a proposal for a package that saves them fifty cents on the dollar.

KIMO: I remember now, fifty cents on the dollar, every time. And that savings lasts for a good six months before the first change order, right?

CALLER TODD: There you go, your entire memory isn't fried. So no matter what data they give me, I beat the price and tell them to fire the staff they have in place. So they do, and then strangely enough, their systems hiccup and we have to fix them. The costs go up quickly to get everything back to normal. By the time the client figures out they're paying us more than they were before they cut the jobs, we are so deeply wound into their system, the switch back cost is more than they can afford. Besides, at that point all their people are gone. Switching back is not an option.

KIMO: And you were going to suggest to your boss that you only close the clients where you really could save them money, so you could feel good about yourself again, or at least good enough that the only people getting fired were people who really were obsolete?

CALLER TODD: Exactly, full honesty. I wanted to do the right thing, so I followed your advice. Now I'm writing a resume.

KIMO: So take it to the FTC, screw the lying bastards. Worst case you have a wrongful termination. Lawyer up and threaten to go to the feds. They'll settle.

CALLER TODD: Kimo, I don't want a settlement. I want a job. I like sales. I want to work.

KIMO: So what do you want me to tell you?

CALLER TODD: I want you to start giving people much better advice.

KIMO: Pal, this is a radio call-in show, not clinical therapy. Did I ask to run your Blue Shield card? You take what you want, you leave what you want. It's a buffet, no one asks what's on your plate when you take it from the cafeteria.

CALLER TODD: That's BS, Kimo, and you know it. You sit there in that studio, people call in, you tell them what you think and they do it. I did it, now I'm jobless. That's what I get for being a loyal listener.

KIMO: You can't lay that on me, Todd. I'm a radio guy. You pay nothing for the call. You do with it what you want.

CALLER TODD: You've lost touch, Kimo. It's rough out here. You can't just use us for ratings. You want to give advice for a living, expect people to take it. Words lead to actions, actions have consequences. What you say on the air has consequences.

KIMO: You think I should be doing this differently? You sit in the chair. You get the ratings. You tell the schmoes I work for it's about consequences. I create audiences, they sell ads, you get a free call-in show, that's the contract. What I say has no consequences unless you stop listening. I say things to keep you from changing the channel.

CALLER TODD: You can't just say things, Kimo. You're supposed to be helping. You're not helping.

Caller Todd was gone. Balthazer went to break, finished the show, but the call stuck like gum in his ear canal. He wasn't helping, that's what Todd had said. Balthazer had always thought he was helping, but maybe he wasn't. Before Todd was Caller Todd, he was employed sales guy Todd. After the call, he was out-of-work Todd, because Balthazer told him to do the right thing, and he did. The right thing was the wrong thing, and it had not even been that entertaining, hardly even memorable. That was not *This Is Rage*.

No matter how he tried to shake it, there was something about the Todd call that would not settle with Balthazer. There had been others like it, though not as direct; but the anger was out there, too much anger, too many people hurt. Balthazer's real job was to turn it into background noise, he knew that, but at a certain point all the advice could not be the same — hang in there, let it roll off your back, roll with the punches, the orchestra of passionless clichés. Frustration and failure were everywhere; he saw it in his own company, he kept hearing it from his callers. No one could tell the truth, no one could be themselves. Keep the job, keep the taxes paid, keep the health plan, keep the mortgage current. That was it for working America, he needed to tell them otherwise, but he kept making a market in hope, not reality. Balthazer needed to keep spinning, but he was spinning. How to turn it, how to work it? You had to take a stand, be honest, do what was right and yeah, that had consequences. Selling short was not what the show was supposed to do, it was supposed to help people do better, not send them scrambling, no more victims. If the show was not working, Balthazer had to make it work. That ate at him until it pushed him to defy his own comfort limits. Then with just a few bad decisions, it was over.

Fresno was not where Balthazer envisioned his career ending. The question remained, where to now? He had to stay ahead of the landlord, ahead of the FCC, ahead of three ex-wives hounding him. He had to find a way to reboot. The little savings he had could keep gas in his tank for a while, but he needed a plan. Emailing MP3 samples to third- and fourth-tier markets until some station called him back, hoping they would not check references, that was wafer thin. Besides, he had gone national already and the grand episode in *Talkers* was going to make it tough to hide from infamy. Maybe it did not matter, he just needed to hit the road and see where it took him—ABF— Anywhere But Fresno. Road trips were good for the leveraged soul, good for the creative spirit, and a sure way of collecting new material in each passing town in the unlikely event he ever again got a contract.

One thing Balthazer had done right was keep ownership of his website, despite the network's demands in every negotiation he had fought since 1995. Balthazer was never entirely sure how valuable www.ThisIsRage.com might be someday, but he knew enough about "his own personal brand" that this was the one constant that traveled with him. In New York, the show had been *This Is Rage*, about politics and government abuse. In Los Angeles the show had been *This Is Rage*, about visceral extortion from wives, and ex-wives, and girlfriends. In Fresno the show had been *This Is Rage*, about how companies screw employees, and about how employees need to survive the system the best they can. Of the three latest incarnations, the third had been the least successful, but Balthazer found it the most interesting. He did not have many regrets, but about this he felt incomplete. Failing or not, the third generation voice for *This Is Rage* was just starting to come around when he managed to get himself yanked off the air, yet he still had the sense he was onto something. There was pain, and longing, and suffering, and injustice in cubicles all across the country. If he could somehow unleash that energy, it would be like splitting the atom, the nuclear explosion that would follow could be life changing, society changing. He had not cracked the code, and he wondered if he ever would—what that freak show genie would look like pouring out of the earnings bottle, and whose bottom-line butt it would kick when it was set free to do battle.

With his leased Infiniti M readied out front with the clothes he was going to take, along with the remains of his cheap tequila and a box of CDs dating three decades, Balthazer sat alone in the apartment he was about to abandon, staring at his website — the website that had been an endless struggle of contract war, but a website that was still his. What was it about this website that meant so much to him? He had left money on the table with every contract to keep it, and now it sat there before him, all but worthless. Right below the title, *This Is Rage*, was the subhead: Talk Shop with Kimo Balthazer. Below that: "We are temporarily off the air, but we won't be gone forever." It might have been wishful thinking. That was all the optimism Balthazer still had.

Balthazer had built the first version of the site himself, a single digital page when it launched, registered the web address and fiercely kept the account info secret from everyone. He paid the registration fees years in advance, and each month paid the modest hosting fees on a recurring credit card cycle. Over time, other webmasters would come and go, run the site for him and add fanciful features, but the log in info was Balthazer's alone, he kept it to himself and made sure he was always in control. There were his historic podcasts, there was his affiliate station list, and there was his email army, more than four hundred thousand names collected over the years and not one ever deleted — which meant sure enough a lot of them were bad addresses, but Balthazer liked the notion of "approaching a half million" names in his database, so that was the number. He emailed them weekly, but his last email had been a month ago, his farewell. He wondered how many of the approaching half million were still with him, how many had given up on him, how many even cared what happened to him. Balthazer was not naïve. He knew the law of media — go off the air and you really are gone. It would happen to Rush if he went off the air. Howard Stern simply went to satellite and that was pretty much the last time anyone outside his few million purposelessly devoted refuseniks ever heard his name.

For a strange moment, Balthazer wondered how many might be on his web page now, right now, this very millisecond he was looking at it. Twenty? Ten? Hundreds? There was no reason for anyone at all to be on his page since he was off the air. No new posts, no new podcasts, just the farewell message. What if someone was there? What if someone was looking at the same empty screen imprint he could see right now, could he say adieu? Could he be less than alone? It was a morbid thought, and of all things morbid, internet radio was probably the most morbid notion of all. If he thought Fresno was undersized, imagine how submeasurable an internet audience might be, if it was even there. Balthazer could not help but wonder. He was ready to go, but he needed closure. He needed a live goodbye, just to someone. The streaming app was still there on the home page, dead as it could be, the microphone icon grayed out since the Fresno station signal link was shut down.

Only a live mic could change all that. Conveniently enough, no radio host — working or not — would be caught dead without one. Balthazer's was standard issue Bluetooth, upgraded with studio quality headphones and a Madonna style wrap-around windscreen. Just clamping it on put Balthazer back in the booth, he was right there where he was supposed to be, the fantasy image 32-bit color, dream clear in his mind. A few mouse clicks in the control panel and it could be live. So could the chat box where his listeners used to bombard him with asinine text questions. Oh how he longed for an asinine text just about now. It was tempting, too tempting. He switched it live.

KIMO: Hey gang, Welcome, *This Is Rage*. Well, it was. I think I took the label a little too seriously. But it's me, and yeah, this is pathetic. I'm about to leave town. You probably thought I left already—or maybe you didn't think anything at all. What the hell do you care about an ex talk guy on broadcast radio? You're probably listening to Latin Top 40, more fun than my big mouth, anything has to be. That's why they put more backbeat on the air and took me off. Well, sort of. I could tell you the whole story but you wouldn't find it that interesting.

Balthazer paused. Sanity was draining without combat. He was sitting alone in an empty apartment, talking to his laptop, pondering if anyone alive might be listening to the farewell broadcast he never got to do. He was doing this of free will and at extreme risk, knowingly delusional. He knew he needed to be gone, before his landlord blocked his escape, before he was served to appear before the FCC, before any of his ex-wives had their attorneys hunt him down and restrict his freedom to evade. Even if anyone was listening, it would be counterproductive—whatever mystique still existed around him needed to be preserved so that he could someday ride again. Everything he was doing was wrong, except for the part where he needed to give better advice. There were consequences, words had consequences. He was supposed to be helping. So he continued.

KIMO: Like I said, I'm about to leave town, and I'm looking at my website, you know the address. I guess I should say our website, because it was created for all of us, where we got together. I think I gave some of you bad counsel. I'm sorry about that. That was not what this show was about. If I let you down, you need to know, I carry that with me. If I do get another show somewhere down the road, I won't let you down again.

Balthazer knew his time was limited, and he did not have much to say anyway. It just felt good to be talking again. That was what he did. He talked, people listened, and every once in a while it was more than that. Yeah, he had led Caller Todd in the wrong direction, now both of them had lost their jobs. What about all the others? How many had he helped ask for a raise, stirring their courage to go to their bosses and insist on what they were due? How many had he helped set new goals, commit themselves to doing their best work, have the courage to look for a new job when everyone around them told them they were not good enough. He could help, he just had to control the tempo, keep the muse even, bring the listener from nowhere to somewhere. All that he needed was some dialogue, someone else present for an exchange. He stared at the chat box, the single flashing cursor inert, locked in place, dormant to the cosmos. If anyone was out there, if anyone made it move, that was all he needed, any nanoscopic indication that someone wanted to listen.

KIMO: Okay, gang, I know we've seen better days, maybe we'll see them again. You have to know this, I really liked doing this show. Radio was all I knew. Who else would pay me to talk? So I let you down. I gave you bad advice. I got myself fired and now I can't help you at all. But let me ask this, if anyone is out there, if anyone can hear my words right now, that means you've got the stream on *This Is Rage* dot com. There's a chat box on that page, where you used to text me when you couldn't get through on the phones. If anyone is out there and wants to say goodbye, go to the chat box and let me know. Just go to the chat box and type whatever you want. Then we'll be done.

The chat box remained static. He had tried, he had reached out, he had said what he needed to say, but no one was listening. Balthazer knew what that meant. The cosmos had moved on. How about that?

KIMO: Well, we gave it a good shot. It was a decent enough run. You'll hear me when you hear me, or maybe you won't, but I'll hear you every day. If I make it back, you have my promise, I will only say things that matter. Just good advice. It's not like that wasn't what I was trying to do before, but I'll do better. I will do better. Until then . . .

Just as he was signing off, the cursor in the text box moved.

CHAT TEXT: Welcome, *This Is Rage*.

Balthazer wondered, was it a phantom blurt, some prepro-grammed text left stagnant in the system? It had to be, just a screensaver, some old scrolling promo text. Then it moved again. Actual words appeared, a letter at a time.

CHAT TEXT: Kimo, I'm cool with you.

Balthazer blinked. Someone was listening. Someone out there, an actual verifiable human with a heartbeat, conscious and alive somewhere in the known world, was on his web page and listening to his voice.

KIMO: Gang, you aren't going to believe this, but the chat box is active. Who is that?

CHAT TEXT: Missy, in Southern Illinois. You told me a few months ago that if my coworkers didn't take me seriously, that was their problem, not mine.

KIMO: What's the story now?

CHAT TEXT: I'm department manager. That wouldn't have hap-pened without you. Thank you, Kimo.

KIMO: That's incredible. Congratulations, I think you got that one right, solid progress. Anyone else out there?

CHAT TEXT: Hey there, Kimo. This is Ed in Miami. I check this page every day to see if you're coming back. You told me not to be afraid to take a relo offer, and I listened to you. I moved here with my family from Raleigh. I kept my job and it's working out.

KIMO: Outstanding, Ed. Good luck to you! Anyone else out there who can hear me?

CHAT TEXT: Balthazer, you're an asshole.

KIMO: Ah, a true fan! Where are you texting from?

CHAT TEXT: This is Justin in Boise. I thought we were done with you. You have nothing better to do than babble on the Internet?

KIMO: You're listening, aren't you? That's a good sign. What are you doing on my dead web page in the middle of the afternoon? Are you that engaged at work that you're surfing mothballed web pages?

The text box went dead again. No more Justin in Boise.

KIMO: Okay, so I have an audience. This is a miracle. Who else is out there? Is anyone else out there?

No cursor movement. The chat box was dead.

KIMO: Come on, gang, *This Is Rage*. Make a case for internet radio. Give me a reason to try. Don't make me opine on my own, you know where I'll take that. You want to hear what I think, maybe about Malcolm Gladwell, that endless *New Yorker* crap about a tipping point? One paragraph, one Poindexter blog entry and he turns it into a published book and makes millions—vapid tin pan rubbish masquerading as meditative thought. Come on, don't let me make this a monologue. Interrupt me, text me. Tell me we are still in business.

Nothing. Balthazer waited. That was it. An audience of three, texting on his home page, but that was enough. He had started the dialogue again. *This Is Rage* was still on the air, the tiniest, most insignificant audience in the world, but he still had one. There was hope. And now there was a path.

There was also the sound of footsteps coming up the back stairs of the apartment complex. His landlord must have seen the packed Infiniti and was coming for the rent. Or maybe the process server from the FCC. It did not matter. Time to go.

Balthazer powered down the laptop and flipped closed the lid. He took it under his arm, flew down the stairs and tossed the laptop onto the passenger seat of the Infiniti. Sunglasses mounted, he took his place behind the wheel and headed out of town, north from Fresno on Highway 99.

$ $ $ $

1.5
No Such Thing as CEO School

It was early Monday morning in the boardroom of EnvisionInk. Daniel Steyer sat at the head of the table, as usual the
first to arrive, his fellow board members assembling around him.
As chairman, he would momentarily call the emergency meeting
to order. The raw stinging in his wired jaw was too fresh to ignore, but nothing he would acknowledge. There was too much
else on his mind, despite the pain killers causing him some mild
disorientation.

Personal net worth was never the yardstick by which Steyer
wanted his life's work measured, but it had helped him accomplish much in the way of lasting influence, which mattered increasingly to him. He never considered himself as a visionary,
rather he was the guy who identified visionaries long before
others wrote about them. He enjoyed being credited for backing
product breakthroughs so many others had missed, and launching careers that would have gone undiscovered. He was a fa-
cilitator, but never thought of himself as a manipulator. Party
politics had been terrain he historically avoided. Certainly he
had opinions, but like religion, his leanings were a personal matter—not because he had any cult-like convictions he needed to
hide, but because expressing any polarizing opinion was seldom
good for business.

Steyer believed money was agnostic. In raising a fund, he
wanted to be open to money of every persuasion. Companies
in which he invested undoubtedly reflected any number of
philosophies and factions. Talent was what mattered to him. He
contributed to the PACs of both Democrats and Republicans
because it was smart to have friends at all tables, but he would
not endorse any candidate running for office in California or

otherwise. He had served on the economic advisory councils for Presidents both Democrat and Republican, and it was unclear to which, if either, major party he held loyalty. He had dodged an inquiry to serve in the Treasury Department—a potential path to Secretary was even kicked around—but Steyer saw the opportunity cost as too severe. He liked what he did, it paid implausibly well, and he believed that venture investing had a more profound impact on society than policy making ever could.

When Steyer graduated from Harvard, he had thought that government service might be his career path. Growing up on the outskirts of Oakland in a comfortable but simple middle class home, he considered himself dedicated to improving the community. He was an only child of financial necessity, his father a journeyman carpenter and his mother a middle school science teacher. Both his parents worked hard, always putting commitments ahead of luxuries, but in meeting their obligations they could never hold onto much in the way of savings. When it became clear to Steyer on his near perfect SATs that his gift of memory would land him a full Ivy League scholarship, he remained convinced his future would return him to the Bay Area where he would work his way up the political ladder to an elected position. There he could have a positive impact on society, to help people like his parents who played by the rules, but never got anything for it other than endless unsolicited offers for revolving credit at double digit interest rates.

With a BA in economics, magna cum laude, Steyer went where so many idealistic young people went in those days before attending law school: two years on Capitol Hill as a congressional aide, first for a Republican, then a Democrat, to ensure he had the full picture of his potentially chosen profession. He quickly discovered the fine line between campaigning and governing was not fine enough. It occurred to him in the year he served on each of the different staffs that the common ground in any elected government job was fundraising, and it was almost always Job Number One. Members of the House had to run for office every two years, which meant they were raising money all the time. If they were not running for reelection, they were eyeing the latest Senate seat that had opened due to death or dishonor, or preparing a home state run for governor, or, with enough cheap well drinks in them at a Connecticut Avenue Happy Hour, tossing about the wild notion of a someday run for POTUS perks. Their ambition was not the problem. It was their time management that bothered Steyer, their use of resources that distracted their staffs from the vital work of the people. Perhaps it was reality setting in, perhaps it was the way all idealism erodes over time, but the cycles consumed by fundraising activity were, in Steyer's eyes, daunting and deplorable. When an event was not on the schedule, there was always a donor, or support group, or lobbyist who needed hand holding, every unblocked hour in the daybook without exception. Steyer had been proud to understand his role as a legislative analyst, which sounded great, until he realized that his real job was to inform his colleagues how an elected official's point of view on any given position might poll, then did poll, then how it might have an impact on fundraising and the next election. Teasing apart policy and fundraising was impractical, not at all strategic. Ties went to fundraising, which made the noble aspirant Steyer a de facto telemarketer.

Steyer had been thankful for his two years on the Hill, because it talked him out of law school, another credential most of the high-ranking Entrenched seemed to have for brand distinction, rather than application. Steyer concluded that if he was going to be a fundraiser, he might as well be a for-profit fundraiser. When he was accepted at the distinguished Stanford Graduate School of Business, about an hour's drive from where he grew up, his choice was easy. It had been a good decision for Steyer on multiple levels. He had been able to spend a bit of time with his father before he passed away during the spring of his first year in business school. He also met Riley, a dynamic Stanford undergraduate in the creative writing program who would become his wife, life partner, and forever perfect companion. Then in the summer between Steyer's two years of business education, he was offered an internship as a statistics wrangler at a local venture capital firm in Menlo Park, just as Silicon Valley was beginning to heat up with the dawn of the personal computer.

There had been no turning back for Steyer once he saw what Silicon Valley would do for the world. Most important, it put motivated people to work in good-paying jobs. Steyer could see no more effective way to improve the human condition than through boundless investment and wealth creation. The fantastic advances in accelerated technology emerging from risk embracing start-ups were mind-boggling. The new wave of tireless engineers was not just talking about changing the world—they were making people's lives better by ending rote tasks and unlocking the computational power of Moore's law, allowing exponential creativity to blossom. Not only were they creating jobs and unprecedented new tools in every form of application, they were putting America on the map in a positive reflection post Vietnam, as a world leader in innovation beyond the defense industry and the endless export of trite popular culture. That made Steyer proud to be an American, proud to be an innovator, and worthy—in his own mind—of the prosperity that would come, his share as well as that of others. It was a lifestyle far more consequential than government, lucrative and legally defensible, a platform where his flair could shine and make a permanent mark.

Steyer never thought twice about public life once he got going in venture. He forever avoided the tentacles of politicians and the media that followed them, building up heroes one day and destroying them for headlines the next. He and his wife never had children. With the all-consuming competition of his rivals, he was convinced he would be no good as a father, and after Riley's first bestselling historical novel on the shifting power structures of medieval Rome, they never much discussed kids. He had made good choices, and he would continue to make good choices, even as his agenda for improving the community faded into the background as compounding returns pushed his bar higher. What Steyer was doing was helping matters, he always thought that, and even when conflicted, he never second guessed his own motives. Defining the line between noble and exploitative was poetic, not practical, a distraction from incomparable achievement.

"Are you ready to call the meeting to order?" asked George Yamanaka, the last to enter the room, diplomatically bringing back Steyer from his momentary contemplation.

"Yes, of course," said Steyer, refocusing on the live digital stock ticker above the clear glass wall. EnvisionInk was trading down, off 6% this morning in a reasonably flat market, almost a gift to shareholders considering what could have been. The Street was being patient, waiting for a statement from the board meeting that would not be released until after the market closed at 4:00 p.m. EST / 1:00 p.m. PST.

Steyer surveyed the room, without need for ceremonial roll call. Of course two of his board members were missing, thus seven of the nine board members had made themselves available, a somewhat unexpected occurrence given that required notice had gone out so late the previous night. To Steyer's left was Yamanaka, the much respected Stanford professor and mentor to Choy and Finkelman, who had in fact received an unexpected phone call the night before. Yamanaka pulled double duty at Stanford, a tenured PhD in computer science who also lectured on best practices at the prestigious GSB, the Graduate School of Business. Next to Yamanaka sat Rebecca Gutierrez, executive director of the Human Potential Project, a San Jose non-profit funded by a broad consortium of tech firms to identify and champion minority talent in engineering that would quite likely otherwise go unrecognized.

To Steyer's right sat Dr. Philippe Francois, a native of Switzerland and onetime world renowned neurologist, now CEO of The Wellness Collective, one of the nation's largest and most profitable roll-ups of for-profit hospitals and medical clinics, notoriously at war with the health insurance industry and historically successful in litigating against their obstruction to high premium claims. Beside Dr. Francois sat Melissa Stanton-Landers, most recently CEO of eProxent, a $400 million back-end enterprise payment engine for mobile devices that had sold for over $2 billion cash in a private sale. She was now CEO in Residence at Hartwell Investments, which meant when not attending high profile board meetings like this, she read business plans and went to partner meetings while trying to figure out her next gig.

At the opposite end of the egg-shaped conference room sat Barton Throckmore, representing Tehama Capital, the other venture firm that had bet heavily on EnvisionInk in its second private round, allowing the initial round led by Steyer's own SugarSpring Ventures to price up nicely. Throckmore was a former All-American wide receiver at Cal, top of his MBA class at UCLA Anderson, and a key leader of the California Democratic Party African-American Caucus, which he considered an avocation that offered him time to relax. On the conference table polycom from the East Coast was the Honorable Mitchell Henderson, five-time Senator from the great state of Florida, recently retired from government work and now an independent technology consultant as well as a renowned and handsomely compensated public speaker, much in demand around the globe.

They were joined in the boardroom by EnvisionInk executive officers, but non-board members, Sanjay Basru, the company's CFO, and Sylvia Normandy, the company's general counsel, who would keep the minutes. Steyer, Throckmore, and the two missing CEOs constituted the insiders, those with substantial personal involvement and financial interest in the company accompanying their responsibilities of governance. François, Gutierrez, Stanton-Landers, Yamanaka, and Henderson were deemed independent directors, specifically so that they could outweigh any caucus of insider influence, although with Steyer in the room, it was never a fair fight at one to eight let alone four to five. Predictably, no vote on any board action had ever polarized to that level, not even close. Board meetings historically had been pleasant affairs, if somewhat boring. The company had been public for just over six years, and until a year ago had been roughly doubling revenues every nine months. Now at a run rate of $6 billion topline for the year with earnings above $1.5 billion, the company had seen growth slow somewhat as it fairly well marginalized its last serious competitor and stabilized with just over 65% market share, annualizing at a mere 30%. For most companies that would have been heaven, but for a company that was trading at a valuation of $36 billion and a price earnings ratio above fifty, the flattening had become a modest cause of concern. Modest, that was, with the independents. The insiders felt differently in that they had much more at stake, with their own net worth largely tied up in stock options that could only be sold in a trickle at preordained open windows. Any major correction in the stock to a more reasonable growth P/E of, even thirty-five, could reduce all of their personal net worth by hundreds of millions of dollars. On this point, although Yamanaka had so much less in his portfolio, Steyer knew he was with the insiders. Steyer could count on Yamanaka to understand EnvisionInk had to stay a growth company, no matter what, even if a really good new idea had not emerged from the brain trust since the IPO. It could not have been more obvious to Steyer, this was Yamanaka's one shot, his two miracle students at the helm after a career of waiting. It was growth or nothing.

Steyer refused to concede any discomfort, unquestionably aware he did not look too good. Half his face was in a fiberglass cast, not so much that he couldn't talk, but enough that he looked like the Phantom of the Opera inverted, plus widening bruises and scrapes mending in fresh accent. How he had made it to this meeting after the incident at his home yesterday and an intense night with doctors under bright lights made no sense at all, unless you knew Daniel Steyer. He was not just tough. His resilience was a reflection of ambitious imbalance, focus beyond rationale. That photographic memory was only one of his attributes. His real talent was endurance, a trait he admired on par with intellect and sought to mirror in those he backed. No one could quite look him in the eye this morning without wincing, which he noticed but did not acknowledge as he proceeded to the day's business.

"Thanks, everyone, for being here on such short notice," began Steyer. "Let the minutes reflect that all board members are present either in person or via conference call, with the exception of our co-CEOs Choy and Finkelman, who are the subject of today's meeting. I apologize in advance for not publishing a more formal agenda, but either George or I have spoken with each of you individually in the past twelve hours to advise you of the events at my home yesterday, which I'm sure you appreciate have left us in a difficult situation."

"How you doing, Daniel?" came the voice from the phone, former Senator Henderson. "Sounds like you took a beating. You okay to be on the job?"

"Thanks for asking, Senator. I won't kid you, it was not the greatest afternoon of my life, and I was only released from the hospital a few hours ago."

"You weren't released, from what I heard," interjected Throckmore. "You walked out the door half-bandaged and told the doctor you'd get back to him when you could."

"There may be some truth to that," returned Steyer. "Candidly, I think they were glad to be rid of me, they have rules about phone use, and as you might expect I wasn't very good at adhering to them. For the record, I'm fine. I have two broken teeth, a partially fractured jaw and some damaged cartilage in a few limbs that dragged on the ground. I'm going back for some more tests today, but it's mostly cosmetic. This meeting was too sensitive to conduct from a hospital room."

"You are one invincible soldier for the cause," said Melissa Stanton-Landers. "Not many Operators would show up for work for weeks after what you went through. Most would take a leave of absence. As a board chair, you just set a new leadership standard for shareholder care."

"Or psychosis," added Throckmore. The ribbing between rival venture Investors was too irresistible for him, regardless of the circumstances.

"Thanks, Barton, I'm sure you will help the story evolve nicely over time with your partners. In any event, while I was being looked at last night, our colleague George Yamanaka received a call, which it makes sense for him to summarize here. George, you have the floor."

"Thank you, Daniel, and may I say, as the only other board member on site for this mishap, our chairman is quite understated about the altercation he endured. You are indeed a hero, Daniel. I truly am surprised, but not really, to see you here today."

"I hope you received the best medical care the peninsula has to offer," said Dr. Francois. "In the event there is any specialist you might benefit from seeing, I will enable that without delay. But I have interrupted our colleague, Professor Yamanaka, please do continue."

"Thank you, Philippe. If Daniel does not take you up on that offer, I will see to it that his wife is in touch with you. Now then, last night I received a call from the abductors, whose true names we still don't know, but they have suggested using the monikers, Ben and Jerry. Forgive the dark humor, theirs not mine. While Calvin was doing reasonably well, they expressed grave concern about Stephen. As you should be aware from the briefing memo that was emailed this morning, in the struggle, Stephen suffered a massively damaging bullet wound to his left leg. As the evening progressed, we are told the bleeding became increasingly severe. The two adductors became concerned that if they lost Stephen, whatever plans they had formulated would be compromised further. To be clear, we do not appear to be dealing with polished criminals here."

"What about that investment Banker, Charles McFrank?" asked Rebecca Gutierrez. "Are the individuals we're dealing with now being sought for his murder?"

"They are, quite definitely," replied Yamanaka. "I have been in touch with local authorities, as well as the FBI, several times through the night, and in addition to a kidnapping, this is a murder investigation as well."

"I've fired off a half dozen emails to the DOJ this morning," came the Senator's voice. "I don't suspect we'll have any shortage of their attention. FBI should pick up the case in California shortly."

"Much appreciated," said Steyer. "If anything, they are a bit eager to be helpful. We need to slow this down some. Right, Professor?"

"I believe that will be a more beneficial approach," continued Yamanaka. "Here is where we are. As I mentioned, there are two abductors, Ben and Jerry. First I spoke with Calvin to be assured of the situation, which he corroborated. Then I talked to Ben, I think he is a bit older than the other fellow, if memory serves from the party. I did meet them before they let loose. Ben told me they did not want Stephen to die, that he needed us to use our influence to arrange for medical care in the area. I did the best I could to consult with Daniel, Dr. Francois, and Senator Henderson as I could reach them. With everyone's cooperation, we were able to secure an isolated emergency room at Salinas Valley Memorial Medical Center, just off the 101, east of Monterey. Ben, Jerry, Calvin, and Stephen made their way there, and last I heard, Stephen was receiving excellent medical care and they were likely to save his leg."

"That is correct," added Dr. Francois. "I just received a text from hospital administration in Salinas. Stephen has progressed to stable condition. The bleeding has stopped. This is one of our hospitals and fortunately they were not far away. We were able to make timely and critical arrangements."

"I apologize," interrupted counsel Normandy, "I know I don't have a board role in this discussion, but may I ask a question?"

"Of course, Sylvia," said Steyer. "You know we don't stand on formality here."

"Terrific, so I am confused. We have our chairman nearly removed from his own home and beaten within an inch of his life. We have a dead—hang on, murdered—investment Banker. We have our two senior-most executives kidnapped, one with a near fatal gunshot wound. And we arranged a private medical emergency room through a network of legal and medical connections where our happy family of dysfunctional, band on the run, yin and yang renegades is holed up? I'm trying to get a clear picture."

"That's a pretty clear picture," pounded the voice of Henderson. "We have them pinned down in Salinas, behind a locked door. Our boys—and girls—are on site, on the other side of the door, but on their side they have a loaded semi-automatic pistol, I believe a Walther P22 from the reports I'm getting, but don't quote me on that."

"Excellent, I was just checking to make sure our minutes were complete and accurate," said Normandy, her tone not lost in its contempt.

"Please keep the minutes high level, Sylvia, would you?" deflected Steyer. He had little appetite for sniping and once again controlled the room.

"I was attempting levity, Daniel," countered Normandy, ever incredulous. "Lawyer humor, on par with programmer humor. So what happens now?"

"That depends on the will of those assembled here," said Yamanaka. "The other request we received last night from Ben and Jerry was to engage in a brief conversation with the board at its next meeting. They are awaiting a call from us at the hospital if we are willing to place it."

"They aren't as stupid as we think," offered Stanton-Landers. "They have some understanding of business protocol. They obviously knew the board would be convening under emergency circumstance. This may be a better planned sequence than we think."

"With all due respect, Melissa, you don't have to be Larry Ellison to know the board of a public company would promptly meet upon the abduction of their co-CEOs," shared Gutierrez. "I may not be in the public sector, but even criminals can have common sense." Steyer noted her comment as another in a continuing theme that had toiled without excuse over the years. The competitive tension between the two women on the board was palpable.

"May I ask a question?" said the CFO, Sanjay Basru, his tenor unassuming, unchanged from any other day.

"We already established a lack of formality, Sanjay," said Steyer. "What's on your mind?"

"Are we going to be discussing Atom Heart Entertainment today?"

The air had been sucked out of the room. Basru was as soft-spoken as he was matter of fact, with a complete lack of people skills and the perfect ability to say the wrong thing at the wrong time.

"Honestly, Sanjay, that is about as insensitive a remark as I could imagine given the circumstances," declared Throckmore. "Even a schmuck like me knows when to backburner business over more critical issues."

"Unfortunately, it's all business," replied Steyer. "Yes, we will have a brief update toward the end of the meeting on Atom Heart."

"That is good," said Basru. "I have received five texts from Sol Seidelmeyer since you called this meeting to order. I believe he wants an update on our intentions so he can plan accordingly."

"Yes, that's right," said Steyer. "So the motion before the board is whether we wish to engage in a verbal discussion with Ben and Jerry to hear what they want next. Or I suppose I should say, how much? Any response is going to be problematic, especially with the media gathering outside. I see little downside in the conference call, but I don't want to pressure or lead the board. Counsel, any opinion?"

"It should be an executive session, especially if you intend to have the call without police participation," said Normandy. "Board only, action minutes, which should be none. I offer no other opinion. There are greater minds than mine to decide if Ben and Jerry are phone worthy."

"As chair of the governance committee, I think it only responsible that we hear from them directly, as I did last night," stated Yamanaka. "What we do next could be directed as much by the style as the content of their communication."

"I concur," said Stanton-Landers. "Style is content. So moved."

"Second," came the Senator's phone voice.

"Discussion?" asked Steyer. There was silence. "All in favor?"

Seven ayes, none opposed. No surprises, the same way Steyer architected all shared decision making. Basru and Normandy got up to leave.

"Please call us back when you reconvene on the topic of Atom Heart Entertainment," said Basru. "I appreciate the timing is not good, but I think the potential activity under consideration is now of even greater importance."

"What's the stock doing?" asked Throckmore, reaching into his bag to replace the dead battery in his fully-consumed mobile.

"Hasn't moved since the open," said Normandy. "Still down six percent. I'm guessing it will close there today. We need to issue a statement at market close."

"Thank you, Sylvia, we will get that done. Also please note for the record that the board has been reminded of its fiduciary duty. Any discussion or decisions today as always will be made with the interests of our shareholders first and foremost."

"That's why you're the best," said Normandy as she jotted down the note and left the room, CFO Basru immediately following her.

When the boardroom door closed, Steyer looked around the table to ensure he had the control he presumed. Slight nods confirmed implicit concurrence, as was the group's behavioral norm. After a moment to allow all participants to put down their mobile devices following a quick check, he reached for the polycom.

"We are in executive session," said Steyer. "Let's place the conference call."

$ $

Pain has an odd way of expressing itself in the acts of business. No matter how many setbacks a leader might experience, there always seems to be a new opaque watermark of endurance

testing, invisibly triggered for erratic combustion in each compounding decision. Every CEO in the world knows this, yet few
have the good sense to walk away from the table when their
cards are hot. Why win in Act Two when a comeback in Act
Three gives you a longer biography? Ego is not so much about
immortality as it is about demonstrating stately resistance to
nightmarish attacks in public forums. Any good smack to the
head is a continuity wake up call, or at least another invitation
to be interviewed by Charlie Rose.

That largely summed up what Calvin Choy and Stephen J.
Finkelman had learned after nine years on the job as co-CEOs
of a moon shot. Perhaps their only real regret to date was that
life itself just did not seem long enough to learn everything you
needed to know to stop making huge, embarrassing mistakes. It
always seemed to them that any reasonable human being would
need to be a CEO twice, the first time to figure out what it was,
hopefully without burning up too much risk capital in the process, and the second to deliver a winning game. No reasonable
human being would ever want to do the jobs they had, for as
much wealth and power as they brought, the personal cost never
seemed to balance the equation. They had never intended to be
CEOs at all, the past six years leading a public company and the
prior three founding it out of a Stanford dorm room. Everything
was a test, and no score could ever be passing because the curve
was set by the moving market itself. They had to be decisive, but
every decision was a self-contained paradox of personal values,
competitive will, and collective outcome. They learned to make
trade-offs quickly, definitively, and without enough information,
but they were always trade-offs. Someone had to be left unsatisfied for any agenda to be moved forward. They learned to live
with it, but they never learned to like it. Now they wondered
if anything at all they had learned could help them craft a path
from gunpoint back to their desks.

Calvin Choy and Stephen J. Finkelman were, at heart,
geeks of the first order, extremely good at the art and science
of the algorithm; business leaders by default rather than choice.

Unlike Daniel Steyer or any of his board colleagues, whom no one beyond the *Wall Street Journal* readership could pick out of a police line-up, Choy and Finkelman were near household names. They were prodigies, real rather than manufactured. They made national headlines on a regular basis whether they earned them or not. The story of EnvisionInk was mythic in a way that almost defined Silicon Valley for people east of the San Andreas Fault, who probably could not point to it on a map — which was not hard to miss, since there really was no such place called Silicon Valley. Perhaps the only way you could define Silicon Valley as geography was to say it's kind of between San Jose on the South, Oakland on the East, San Francisco on the north, and the Pacific Ocean to the west, pretty much anywhere in that polygon where society-altering technical innovation happened — unless it happened anywhere else in the world with financial backing that came out of that turf, or if the non-local money backing some tech success just as easily could have come out of that turf. Silicon Valley took its lead from Hollywood — if it sounded like it came from there, good enough. It was a state of mind, a consciousness, an adjective more than a locale, but a place nonetheless that defined the resurgence of the economy in something called the post-manufacturing Age of Information.

Choy and Finkelman had impeccable timing on their side. EnvisionInk was a company that needed to be invented. Its financial backers were on the rebound after Crash v1.0. The original dotcom implosion was their approximate birth date and their IPO surged into the rebound that preceded Crash v2.0, the Great Recession, which they never at all felt. In the crossfire of the Flubbed Search Engine Wars, which followed the brief peace left after the vast wreckage of the Settled Portal Wars, the great leveler called Search Engine Marketing was changing the media landscape in record time, laying waste to radio, magazines, and newspapers, with television in its cross hairs. This very simple thing, the tiny text ad, was the germ warfare that was stealing dollar share from every Fortune 500 advertising budget on the planet, shifting every advertising agency still in

business to retool client budgets to bid for keywords, those super highly targeted phrases that became hot links that led customers to destination sites. Now when you plugged virtually any
word or phrase into any search box on any screen, toolbar, mobile device, or the like, no matter what the word or phrase might
be, the legitimate "organic" search queries on the screen would
be surrounded by paid insertions. It was so simple it made you
want to cry, search for Orange Peel Scented Linen Napkins and
every company on the planet that sold them would bid to see
their advertisement on the screen, "Buy Orange Peel Scented
Linen Napkins Here!" Click on that, and wherever it sent you,
someone was paying the search engine for that click—and not
just any agreed price, but a fluid, variable fee set by a perpetual,
real-time auction that had no beginning or end. Today at 11:00
a.m. that click might cost you a dime, tomorrow at 4:00 p.m. a
quarter—you could not control it, you could only say how much
or how little you were willing to pay for that click, and how
high up on the page you might want it at a premium. Depending
on what other companies in the secret auction were willing to
pay, that was the competition that set and moved your price. It
was genius, it was ubiquitous, it was effective, and it was more
efficient and measurable than anything compared to it. For the
auction house, it was nothing less than a global cash factory.

It was also obnoxious, one-sided, and frighteningly addic-
tive. The genius of Choy and Finkelman was their foresight
into the unfairness of the mass blind frenzy. No one had taken
a mathematical opposition to the steamrolling search machine,
and in this they saw opportunity. If only they could write an algorithm that, in real time, would back the advertiser's bid off the
screen when they were about to bet stupidly against weak or little competition, they could save their advertisers billions of dollars. They knew they could not reverse engineer the search algorithms for profit, that would be an illegal invasion of intellectual
property rights, but if they could simply analyze the search environment in fractions of milliseconds and get an upstream packet
to the ad server before the ad was served when the bids were too

high or unqualified, that would save advertisers from buying the clicks they never wanted. The old adage of half your advertising spend always being unnecessary was not lost on the shift to digital, to the contrary it was alive and well, and of profit to the search engines. Choy and Finkelman attacked that problem as an engineering conquest, not a media crisis, then fashioned their business on a percentage of dollars saved by improving their clients' bottom line performance. These calculations of actual dollars saved on measured and improved return on investment was their secret sauce, and it worked. They were not the first to go after pay for savings as antidote to pay per click, but they were the very best. The search engines pushed the price of clicks up through obscurity, EnvisionInk pushed them down through strategic abstinence. Advertisers finally had a real ally to save them from their "marketing partners" who had, in turn, saved them from traditional media before fashioning the mother of all shakedowns. The target was ever moving, and so was the algorithm. This was all that mattered to Choy and Finkelman, keeping the algorithm nano-fractional notches ahead of the search engine triumphs, so their favorably priced software as a service would always be in demand.

The fact that they had to run a company based on their math was a necessary evil, not a step up. That they then had to use the cash stockpile they generated to buy other companies that produced incremental cash flow was more distraction than intellectual mandate, but to keep that stock price moving, they were driven by task-masters like Steyer and Throckmore to aggressively buy topline and relentlessly shred costs. They had considered stepping down any number of times to devote themselves religiously to the algorithm, but there were too many stories in Silicon Valley of the suits getting power over founders and their vision of changing the world disintegrating into a singular vision of cash management. There was no way to let go without risking the whole show, so they stayed in place, learned to hire CFOs and attorneys and sales managers and marketing types, and did their best to create positive headlines. In the early days they hired more wrong than right, muffed interviews, cut short earnings calls, let too many lawsuits get filed and not the right ones withdrawn. Yet every day they made sure the algorithm got better, and in so doing, much to their chagrin with lady luck profusely kind, they figured out their job descriptions and built EnvisionInk into a leviathan without peer. Professor Yamanaka wished he had taught them all this at Stanford, but he knew better.

Timing, they knew it had all been about timing. A few years earlier and no client would have been angry enough to give them a try. A few years later and two other guys would have invented it, maybe Ben and Jerry. It was all locked up with the fates, circumstance, the unknown and unpredictable, all of which a CEO had to be ready to absorb without warning, notice, or emotion. They thought about that a lot in their sealed hospital room, which they somehow saw as not that different from picking the date and terms of their IPO. They were by no means in control, but they had more at risk than anyone, which made any outcome their personal responsibility. Market forces had emerged and required response. Ben and Jerry were market forces of a different flavor, but no more or less real or worthy of second guessing. Sure, if Choy and Finkelman had only stayed at the office and coded that weekend, they would not now be under the thumb of two poorly armed, but no less dangerous, numbskulls. Had they learned anything on the job that could be applied here, with the stakes being their own lives? It did not appear so, no algorithm of detachment standing ready in the reams of documentation, but that did not mean much. The had not created global wealth doing the obvious. The obvious led only to mediocrity, a bad memory at best.

$ $

It had been an excruciatingly long night. Finkelman had lost consciousness several times, but was stable now. Choy's minor injuries had been bandaged. They sat in a private, windowless hospital room where they had been told by Swerlow and Kisinski, also known to them as Ben and Jerry, to wait, do nothing, graciously accept medical care. The door would open when Ben and Jerry had something to say.

On the other side of the door, in an adjacent windowless room that had been provided upon request, were Swerlow and Kisinski, about to dial into the EnvisionInk boardroom.

"We've got them," said Swerlow. "They wouldn't be taking our call if they didn't want to make a deal."

"You do realize we have zero leverage, none of any kind," countered his cousin.

"What are you talking about?" argued Swerlow. "They gave us everything we wanted, absolutely everything. They have no reason to stop. They want Choy and Finkelman back. It's a submeasurable amount for them to pay. The stock was down six percent today, that's more than $2 billion in market cap. They provide us a tiny bit more of what we need, they get back that $2 billion with a press release, maybe a good faith premium on top."

"Right, mouse-nuts, like you said," snipped Kisinski. "No complications. You have it all figured out."

"I'm improvising, not perfect, but we'll get there. Let me do as much talking as possible," said Swerlow. "Remember, at the end of this, your code will go to market, big time."

"Right, either that or they base Thelma and Louise II on us. It will be called Ben and Jerry Die in a Murderous Financing."

The disposable cell phone rang on schedule. Swerlow smiled, full confidence brewing.

"I told you to stop using the term murder," said Swerlow. "It won't help us."

The disposable rang again. Swerlow waited.

"Dennis, these are serious people we are dealing with. We have one gun and by now the building has to be surrounded by SWAT. Get this right or we are Thelma and Louise."

The phone rang yet again. This time Swerlow answered it and put it on speaker. "EnvisionInk boardroom?"

"Yes, this is Daniel Steyer. We met briefly yesterday at my home. Do we have both Ben and Jerry?"

"Yes, you do," answered Swerlow. "Let me first say, thank you for the arrangements you have made thus far. It is not an exaggeration to say that Professor Yamanaka's decisive actions allowed Mr. Finkelman's life to be saved. He is doing quite well."

"We know that," interjected the voice of Dr. Francois. "We are in constant communication with the hospital. I own that hospital. Or I should say, the corporation I oversee owns the walls around you."

"Thank you, sir," interjected Kisinski. "This is Jerry. We appreciate your sphere of influence." Swerlow shot him a dirty look. Kisinski was not supposed to be talking, but clearly he was not going to trust his cousin to fly solo on something this delicate.

"Can you bring us up to speed on your view of what is going on there, and what you may have in mind for it to end peaceably," prodded Steyer.

"I'll do my best," replied Swerlow. "Last night we phoned Professor Yamanaka, told him of Mr. Finkelman's condition, and reported that Mr. Choy was for the most part unharmed. We told him we needed to get Mr. Finkelman immediate medical attention. He got back to us shortly, told us to proceed to Salinas Valley Memorial Medical Center where private quarters were arranged. Mr. Finkelman received initial treatment. He is resting in the room adjacent to this one, with a door only to our room. We are locked in here and of course believe you have surrounded the medical facility with armed authorities. Are we on the same page so far?"

"Gentlemen," boomed the voice of the former Senator. "You don't know me and I don't know you, but I served five terms in the United States Senate, three as chair of the Armed Services Committee and one and a half as chair of Intelligence. I sing Christmas carols at Langley and have July 4 barbecues at Quantico. Trust me when I tell you, there is no way you can walk out of that hospital. You can't be very good at this. You boxed yourselves in, one bad move to checkmate."

"Let's call it check," said Swerlow. "We still have the king and queen. We don't intend to walk out. We intend to be escorted by well-trained servicemen."

"What's the ask?" said Steyer. "You aren't going to get it, but tell us the ask."

"One hundred million dollars in a Shanghai account, an

EnvisionInk overseas R&D fund which we will manage on your behalf. Plus thirty-six hour use of the company's G550 to fly the four of us there, and Choy and Finkelman back."

"What can you possibly expect to do in China with $100 million and a cloud hanging over you?" asked Steyer. "And you want to take our co-CEOs for a joy ride?"

"You'll have them home quickly enough, sir," said Swerlow. "We plan to start our own high-tech company. It will be formed as a wholly owned subsidiary of EnvisionInk, which we will establish for divestiture. We had hoped to do something similar here in California and create a lot of local jobs without EnvisionInk's backing, but our plans had to change, rolling a bit with the circumstances. We think it will work in China, but hopefully when we go public, we'll still trade on US exchanges."

"You seem to be rolling quite fluidly," said Steyer. "You came to my house for me, and left me with a few less teeth than I began the day. Then you stumbled, took Choy and Finkelman, and shot McFrank. In the middle of the night, you called one of our board members for help, to save yourselves from a second murder charge, which was the first smart thing you did. Now you want a $100 million reward, a job, and a free ride to Shanghai. Do we have the full ask now?"

"Not a reward or a job," said Swerlow. "It's an investment, where you will reap the rewards at a far greater multiple than we will when we spin off, given your stake at current valuation."

Steyer was speechless. Swerlow tried to imagine his calculus. He was well aware Steyer had heard every pitch imaginable, and this was a term sheet beyond compare. Swerlow grew antsy as the silence continued, but he knew whoever spoke next lost. It could not be him. Who was Steyer looking at in the room? He had to be anointing someone to continue the dialogue at some level of sensibility. If no one obliged, Swerlow's next move would be unrecoverable. The room was bigger than Swerlow, maybe bigger than Steyer. No answer would be final. Swerlow waited, the big boys' game, the no limit table to which you invite yourself. Then he heard words, and felt redux behind his tonsils.

"Hey Ben, this is Barton Throckmore. I'm a venture guy like Steyer. I used to play a bit of D1 football, I get the coin toss. You seem to be a clever fellow, you've read a blog or two on investing. Suppose for an extraordinary moment we were to consider this, which we are not. How exactly would we position this with our shareholders?"

"As yet our names are unknown to the public," let out Swerlow, his game voice forcibly conditioned. "You let a little time pass, then you announce the new venture with us running it. No harm, no foul."

"Would you mind if I muted the polycom for a moment?" asked Throckmore.

"Not a problem," said Swerlow, believing the agreeable a decent ploy.

Throckmore instead left the polycom line open, addressing his colleagues. "Well, here's what we know, this guy was probably trained at Microsoft. Either that or he escaped from a mental hospital and is stupid dangerous beyond any sentient level of comprehension. We remain in executive session."

Swerlow was baffled. Did Throckmore know he had not gone on mute? Of course he did. Damn, these guys were a different class.

Throckmore continued, no longer feigning the mute. "Sorry about that, Ben, conferring with my colleagues, this is still Barton. You are indeed a clever fellow and have fully thought this through. A few more questions. Presuming that we did this, and you were in fact guilty of a crime, our board would become complicit in that crime. Again, these are all hypothetical presumptions. How might we handle the matter of Charles Mc-Frank, whom you killed? Is that crime to be forgiven? Shall the Senator quietly arrange a Presidential pardon?"

"We don't believe we did that," said Kisinski, holding the new company line per Swerlow's direction. "There was a struggle, for all we know, Choy shot him. We suggest you help to have it buried as an unsolved crime. It's a tragedy, certainly not what we intended."

"Jerry, are you aware that we have a Constitution?" barked Senator Henderson. "Are you and Ben aware of any laws at all?"

"Senator, we are quite aware of the law," said Kisinski. "We do understand we have broken some laws. We are trying to minimize the damage at this point, if we can."

Throckmore seemed to be out of gas, same as Steyer. Melissa Stanton-Landers picked up the thread. "Gentlemen, my name is Melissa Stanton-Landers, I was formerly a small cap CEO, so I do understand your passion for the entrepreneurial. You are clearly not fools. Let me ask this. Suppose we send you to Shanghai with Choy and Finkelman on the G-5. You get off the plane, the plane comes back with Choy and Finkelman. You have given up your trump card. How exactly do you get your financing and your sign-on announcement?"

"I'm glad you asked that," said Swerlow. "Once you send us on the Gulfstream, we believe you are all in. As your colleague noted, if there was a crime and you were complicit, you are in much worse shape than we are. All we need to do is play back this recording for CNBC. Since China has no extradition treaty with the US, our worst case is that we are free and out of the country. China has no beef with us, we change our identities and disappear. Your worst case is that you destroy your company, ruin your personal reputations, and probably do some time. So we're confident at wheels up that we'll have a solid deal."

Swerlow was running the table and had taken out Melissa. Just like that, all the chips coming his way. Luck, precision, he didn't care. He was on a roll, all the way to the banker's cage. No mistakes now, just the close.

Gutierrez was up next. "This is Rebecca Gutierrez, and I believe this is the last question. Suppose we don't get to wheels up?"

"We simply have to get to wheels up, or we will have to commit two more truly regrettable crimes, knowing the servicemen surrounding this hospital will kill us," threatened Swerlow. "Should that happen, EnvisionInk undoubtedly will be worth a lot less than it is now—perhaps nothing at all, without the visionaries who founded it. We want the money moved, verification provided, and the company jet ready by 6:00 p.m. tomorrow. I think we're done."

"Ben, you aren't giving us much time for something so unprecedented," reengaged Steyer, taking back leadership of the opposition. "Talk it over a bit with Jerry. We may need more flexibility to get to a good outcome."

"We speak with one voice, that's our proposal," said Swerlow. "You have our contact number. Let us know what you decide. If we haven't heard from you by 6:00 p.m. tomorrow, we will consider ourselves convicted and do what we have to do."

Swerlow clicked off the phone and tossed it to Kisinski, who had broken out in a cold sweat. Swerlow walked passed him to the door that joined their room with Choy and Finkelman's and opened the door.

"Guys, we just had our phone conference with your bosses. In all candor, I think it went well."

"What happens now?" asked Choy.

"We're in a holding pattern for the evening. Tomorrow an all-nighter. Tell Finkelman to pick out a favorite doctor or two, preferably ones who won't mind crossing the international date line twice in the same day.

$ $ $ $

1.6
Live from the Boulevard of Broken Dreams

FOR IMMEDIATE RELEASE
SANTA CLARA, CA
ENVISIONINK WILL NOT NEGOTIATE
IN CO-CEO MATTER

(1:00 p.m. EST) EnvisionInk Systems (NAS-DAQ: ENVN), a global leader in digital advertising platforms, today responded to news reports of the abduction over the weekend of the company's co-chief executive officers, Calvin Choy and Stephen J. Finkelman.

"Our board of directors is working with legal authorities in all proper respects," said Chairman Daniel Steyer. "While it would be unwise at this time for us to comment more specifically on our actions in order to best protect our colleagues, it is the unanimous opinion of the Board that no ransom will be paid such that it might reward criminals for their undertaking."

The company acknowledges the presence of two unnamed, uninvited men who attended a party at the home of Board Chair Steyer over the weekend, and, following an altercation, their departure from the residence with Choy and Finkelman. The company confirms that that the basic well-being of Choy and Finkelman has been verified, and a dialogue exists between the company and the abductors around their release. In keeping with the spirit of necessary confidentiality to maintain the safety and optimal outcome for all involved, the company must offer no further information on the location or comment on any other circumstances surrounding the incident.

Company management remains unchanged
with a strong senior executive team in place.
More formal succession planning at this time
has been deemed by the Board unwarranted.
Government and legal bureaus remain fully apprised of the matter in consultation with board
and management.

In an unrelated matter, and in the spirit of
relevant disclosure given current circumstances, the company also acknowledges preliminary strategic discussions with Atom Heart
Entertainment, a Los Angeles based media
conglomerate under the executive management
of CEO Solomon Edward Seidelmeyer, which
has approached EnvisionInk to consider the
merits of an amiable combination. No definitive
agreement between EnvisionInk Systems and
Atom Heart Entertainment has been reached,
nor is further statement on this matter likely
before the expected safe release of Choy and
Finkelman.

Commentary in this notice may contain forward-looking statements within the meaning
of Section 27A of the Securities Act of 1933,
as amended, and Section 21E of the Securities
Exchange Act of 1934, as amended. Such statements may use words such as "anticipate," "believe," "estimate," "expect," "intend," "predict,"
"project," and similar expressions as they relate
to EnvisionInk Systems, Atom Heart Entertainment, or the respective management of
either or both. When we make forward-looking statements, we are basing them on our
management's beliefs and assumptions, using
information currently available to us. Although
we believe that the expectations reflected in
the forward-looking statements are reasonable,

these forward-looking statements are subject
to risks, uncertainties and assumptions including those discussed in our filings with the
Securities and Exchange Commission. Both
EnvisionInk Systems and Atom Heart Entertainment extend caution not to place undue
reliance on its forward-looking information as
a number of factors could cause actual results,
conditions, actions, or events to differ materially from the targets, expectations, estimates,
or intentions expressed in the forward-looking
information.

$ $

Kimo Balthazer was parked outside a McDonald's in Stockton, reading the press release on his laptop. The gift of free wireless from McDonald's was much appreciated, as was the tremendous improvement of late in their coffee. If you didn't have
an office and didn't speak Starbucks, which Balthazer didn't,
McDonald's had really come around these past few years, especially if you stayed away from the children's climbing equipment, a survival strategy.

The press release was now almost a day old, though not
quite, this fine Tuesday morning after its distribution the day
before. Balthazer looked at the hot stock listings on his home
page and noted the stock of EnvisionInk was trading up 17%,
an increase from the previous day's decline of 6%. Balthazer
was not much of an active stock trader, but common sense told
him that if the founders and co-CEOs of a company were kidnapped, their stock price might be expected to remain in a nose
dive. Perhaps the company was getting credit for "refusing to
negotiate with terrorists" as the government was fond of lying
about, but that would hardly seem solace for Investors in a company so closely tied to the personae of Choy and Finkelman,
names known to Balthazer through front page headlines, financial as well as news and lifestyle. More likely it was optimism
and expectation of a premium anticipated in an acquisition of
EnvisionInk by Atom Heart, although that seemed strangest of

all, to confirm a rumor of a potential corporate merger but provide no more details, not even identify formal discussions. Yes,
to Balthazer that did seem strange, an almost deliberate attempt
to put some good news out there with the bad, presuming you
thought a merger of EnvisionInk, a tech giant built on a single,
albeit windfall, premise, and Atom Heart Entertainment, a fully diversified old world media giant with big profits but little
digital DNA, was in fact a good idea. They were both lumber-
ing assemblies of fat cells, both once inspirationally great, both
still mammoth cash cows. Two generations center stage at the
dance, one old school and one new school, one with its acerbic
but enormously successful CEO still at his desk, possibly con-
templating merciful retirement, the other with two celebrated
but long term unproven thought leaders swept away in captivity. Maybe Sol would run the NewCo for a while, maybe the
adolescents would be released tomorrow and they would prove
their true genius running it. Maybe it was a good deal, maybe as
moronic as AOL Time Warner. Honestly, Balthazer had no clue.
The only thing that mattered to him was he now had a killer
topic for his internet debut.

In the last twenty-four hours, Balthazer had suddenly become focused on rebirthing his career, with a determined, if unproven, path now fixed in his mind. Turning to pure play internet
radio as a creative outlet was no doubt an act of desperation, but
he had learned repeatedly that self-delusion was often the key to
longevity in the media spotlight. Anyone with a brain would tell
you the idea of becoming internet radio's first breakout star was
so outlandish you would have to be staring down the hangman's
noose to bet what was left of your name on it. The level to which
this was absurd did not escape Balthazer, not long ago a much
sought and highly followed radio talk show celebrity syndicated
coast to coast and on US military bases around the world. His
signal had for many years been streamed online, but the aggregate of all those streams on any given day did not even add up
to a small redevelopment zone on the outer edges of Fresno.
In any given week, all the streams and podcasts together did

not goose ad rates even a penny, it was just nothing, nothing at all worth mentioning even at a buffet happy hour. Original programming for internet radio had no traction, no commercial scale, there was no apparent reason for it. Stations and branded channels were nihilist remnants of another age, fragmented beyond recognition, remaindered bits of forgotten noise for baby boomers. Listeners today no longer thought in terms of channels or themes. They thought in term of personalization and I want what I want, assemblies of Pandora predictions and Spotify collectives, not return destinations. Hyper niche was an amateur hidden URL spitting out pennies, and hyper local was a fire pit for small fry cash. The brand was the listener, self-absorption that trumped opinion. Internet radio signals were repurposed air fillers, intended for surviving station managers who wanted to tell their bosses they "got it" when it came to digital destruction. Internet radio tuned to retransmission was beyond geeky, there was almost no one listening, and no one at all who mattered to the ad mob which was all the more disheartening. If anyone alive still cared about old fashioned talk radio, they would listen the old fashioned way, in their car, directing that thing with knobs in the dashboard. The rest of the mobile world could care less. Digital distribution qua internet radio should have held all the potential in the world, but to date it reflected no measurable audience share worth quoting.

Balthazer was determined to change that. This was his answer to, "Where do you go after Fresno?" It was simultaneously an act of need, fantasy, speculation, and prayer. If there was an audience to be had, he was going to find it now or disappear forever. His email list of almost a half million was a good enough place to start. Last night at the roadside motel, which he picked from a crumbling sign for its generous free Wi-Fi and acceptance of cash without questions, he had blasted an announcement to his loyals that today was his launch. No anxiety, no apprehension, he thought it up and did it. Now, live from this McDonald's parking lot in Stockton, which kindly offered free Wi-Fi, he was going to give it the first test. His laptop drew power from the cigarette lighter dock of his Infinity turned studio. He had enough bars on the connect gauge to move voice upstream and down. His Bluetooth headset and mic were comfortably fitted around his skull. The basic version of Skype was free. He tilted back his leather seat and took a deep breath, redemption hour was on deck. *This Is Rage*—real, unadulterated, pure, internet exclusive, going on the air, and his day one rant was ready.

The signs were good. The Chat Text box had been populated since dawn. Feedback was flowing without pause, great comments from the many loyals who had received the email and found him:

"Kimo, can't live without you. Mega glad you're back."

"Internet radio is a loser, Balthazer. You're a loser. But you're our loser. Count me in."

"My boss was a prick when you were in New York, LA, and Fresno. She's still a prick. I need you, Kimo. Help me from doing something I'll regret."

"There is only one Kimo Balthazer. One mouth in a billion."

The comments kept scrolling, it gave him pause, a hell of a pick-up from his first discovery of just three in the box. When he went to sleep the night before, he thought if he got a hundred today, he would call it a walk-off win. If he got a thousand, he would call it the Pennant. He looked at the ticker widget on his home page—over five thousand people had checked in! Five thousand internet listeners, a 1% response rate from his half million emailing! In Fresno, an audience of five thousand would have you sweeping floors at the Slovakian broadcast co-operative. For Balthazer, these five thousand were a new world, the chance at a comeback. He was ready to go, voice to voice, as long as McD's bandwidth held up. His listeners would hear him and he would hear them. Just minutes to broadcast and *This Is Rage* would be back on the air. There were risks, so many risks. Could he get a decent caller without a screener or would he have to take whatever would come? Would this first show be enough to go viral? How far did he need to go to get listeners to push the forward button on their emails? Could he keep his promise and not hurt anyone this time, but still be entertaining? Could he balance the edge with a sample of so few?

It would all come down to today's subject matter, his first run at this vacuous new world. He needed a hype story, momentum that could not melt. That EnvisionInk press release was packed with lies, pure brain pollution, a gift of masked pain forged by the company's counter intelligence propagandists. Their sins were his onramp, no judgment, a business proposition inviting entry. Thank god, thank god for EnvisionInk—those joyously corrupt, awful, scumbag, horror freak show criminals running EnvisionInk.

The self-imposed air time moment had arrived, Balthazer's last stand.

On The Air.

KIMO: Welcome, *This Is Rage*. I am back, your host, Kimo Balthazer, one hundred percent commercial free, you have my promise on that. Live on internet-only radio from . . . I can't tell you that. Too many ticked off people looking for me, and I don't see a reason to tip them off. I'll be on the move for a while, but when I am on the air, I'm all yours. So let's get angry. Let's talk about things that matter. I need your important calls more than I've ever needed them before, because this show is about us. It's our show. We need to prove that. What's going on in your company that hurts you? How is your greedy, soulless employer bringing you down? There's a bit of news on this in the headlines—seems everyone's favorite lovable, huggable, digital teddy bear, EnvisionInk, has a mighty mess on its hands. Have you seen any of this soap opera? Their superstar billionaire CEOs—they have two of them, you know, when you're minting that much coin, why compensate one gazillionaire when you can double the cost and have co-CEOs—well, it seems they were kidnapped over the weekend. You can't make this stuff up, gang. This is the stuff of legends and it is real, real, real. According to news reports, Mr. Calvin Choy and Mr. Stephen J. Finkelman were whisked away from a party at the home of their board chairman, Mr. Daniel Steyer, who might be the wealthiest man in California. Steyer is what's known as a venture capitalist, a mega high risk, super self-important investment addict. What he does is collect mountains of money from other rich people, kind of like a loan to buy whatever he wants after he takes out a two percent annual fee, and then he bets it on rising stars like Choy and Finkelman. If it's a good bet, he gets to keep twenty percent of the winnings and the rest goes back to the rich people so they get, you know, richer. If they burn it all up in an oil drum, well then, it's a tax write off, not many tears shed. Now in this particular case, unless you have been counting your savings on an abacus, you probably know the bet paid off, Lotto Style! EnvisionInk Systems is one of the most successful technology companies ever, and I wish I could tell you what they do, but as clearly as I understand it, they tell companies like Macys and Amazon when not to buy advertising on sites like Google and for that they have been tremendously rewarded. I don't much get it, but then, I don't get Google either, so let's just say Yin found a Yang and the legal money keeps on coming. So now the co-CEOs of EnvisionInk are holed up somewhere, they can't tell us of course or they'd be swimmin' with the fishes, but what we do know from an EnvisionInk press release is that whoever took Choy and Finkelman must have requested a super oozing vat of moolah, because all the press release says is they aren't serving up a cent. I'm reasonably sure that's not going to be pleasantly received by the mean old monsters who took Choy and Finkelman, whoever they are, so pretty soon we're all going to find out what the hell is going on here. Okay, here's my question for the, wow, 16,572 of you who are now checked in and listening to me—and thank you for that, you have no idea what that means to me—but what I want to know is, if you were on the EnvisionInk board of directors, would it make good sense for you to shell out some dough to get back your top dogs with all their limbs still finely tuned, or would you trust our government—which has such an amazing track record on these sorts of showdowns—to get your founders home safely?

In those very few moments, Balthazer had recouped his groove. He might as well have been talking to himself, for all he knew he was talking to himself, save for that ticker widget on his monitor that kept ticking up like an energy meter in summer. It was fluid now, the numbers were turning steadily. Somehow people were finding him. Perhaps he had been wrong about Malcolm Gladwell, maybe *The Tipping Point* was not a pointless expression of the obvious masquerading as a book. What was also quite real was the sound of his voice. Outside the Infiniti M in the McDonald's parking lot, you could almost feel the bass notes booming through the windows. Balthazer did not even notice that civilians, kindly families with lively young children, were pulling into the lot all around him on Big Mac retrieval missions and could not help but notice the funny looking fat man with the headgear bantering away at full volume. Of course the french fry adoring passersby likely assumed he was just on a mobile call, but mobile calls had beginnings and endings and were not usually accompanied by wildly waving hand gestures and drama queen bits of steam forming on the inside of the rolled up auto windows. If you did not know better, and no one had reason to know better, you might think there was a mad man raving uncontrollably in his luxury car, either talking to himself or freaking out whoever might be on the other end of the line. In some senses, you'd be right, and you might even bring it to the attention of the McDonald's dimple cheeked manager inside. Host Balthazer was oblivious, he was fully alive and again in his glory. This was plain clothes therapy, now with 29,419 therapists on his virtual frequency. Or were they the patients and he the head shrink? It didn't matter, he was rolling.

KIMO: Well, it seems we have a nice list of willing participants teed up in the bullpen and ready to play today. I see your "screen names" on the Skype grid and if I click on you then you will be on the air with me. Warms my heart so many of you are here, but to be clear, a few ground rules—this is uber low budget, I don't have a screener anymore, so I'm going to be guessing when I bring you live. If you are dull or pointless, I'll have to dump you with even less patience than usual. So be angry, but be interesting. Otherwise you're gone. Dracula XY—now there's a handle—Dracula XY from Benton Harbor, Michigan, Welcome, *This Is Rage!*

CALLER DRACULA XY: Dude, you're back. And I'm caller number one, how cool is that?

KIMO: Depends on how attention-grabbing you are, Drac. Try me on.

CALLER DRACULA XY: So, like, I don't know much about all these rich guys in San Francisco and that technology of the future stuff, whatever they call it, the vision thing. I just work in a tire shop, you know, like, fixing tires. But I'm like wondering, like, maybe they kidnapped the guys themselves, like, they didn't like the CEOs, so they got rid of them. 'Cause I've thought about doing that myself, you know, because our CEO is such a douche bag, he tells us we've gotta tighten our belts, but all he does is keep taking all our money. So if I could, I would definitely have him kidnapped, wherever he lives, you know? He needs to suffer.

KIMO: Swing and a miss, Drac. Already got a story about kidnappers, don't need another. Stay away from the sun light, you'll stay out of jail longer without human exposure.

Not at all what Balthazer was looking for, he dropped the call. This was undoubtedly going to be harder than he imagined. Inside the McDonald's, he was starting to draw more attention. Kids were watching him through the windows, their breathing fog on the glass panels starting to rival his in the car. The playground was becoming an unsupervised observation deck, children hanging backwards with their legs wrapped around the climbing bars, eyes fixed on the Infiniti and its very strange driver.

Balthazer looked at his screen, and to his delight the ticker widget crossed thirty-seven thousand. He was ready to go again, mouse click on.

KIMO: Alien Bean, from El Paso, Texas . . . That's Bean, rhymes with mean, not Being, that'd be too on the nose. Alien Bean, Welcome, *This Is Rage*.

CALLER ALIEN BEAN: Good thing you're not on regular radio, Kimo. You'd have to report that vampire creep for threatening a crime. The Internet is so much better, don't you think? No rules, no FCC, just let it out.

KIMO: Don't make me do to you what I did to Dracula, Ms. Bean. What do you think—ransom, rescue, or no rescue?

CALLER ALIEN BEAN: I don't know about that, but let me tell you this about EnvisionInk, Kimo. They're a bunch of bullshit fascists. That's so chill, this is like HBO. I can say bullshit on the radio.

KIMO: You're not on the radio, Alien Bean. You are talking into a tiny chip in your computer and we're on the Internet with, how about that, 48,358 of our compadres and still climbing. I tell you what, we get to one hundred thousand, this digital sideshow act could make headlines of its own. So what's your problem with EnvisionInk?

CALLER ALIEN BEAN: Used to work there, Kimo, back when it was a start-up. It was a cool place then, maybe seven or eight years ago, before it was all about the money. Choy and Finkelman were normal guys. They were way smarter than the rest of us, but they weren't assholes. Oh, that's just so cool, I can say asshole and you don't make me stop. Love this. Then it got weird, after the company had its IPO, that's an Initial Public Offering, you know, where they sell stock to people and people start watching the stock price everyday . . .

KIMO: I know what an IPO is, Alien, and I'm guessing most everyone else listening does too. I don't know, maybe not, let's not forget Dracula. What exactly happened after the company went public?

CALLER ALIEN BEAN: Oh, crap on me, everything changed. We moved from these cool digs where everyone worked around a couple of tables to this football field office park. They stuck all of us in rat box cubicles and gave us job descriptions that no one with a PhD could translate into human speak. Choy and Finkelman moved into these steel vault offices and we couldn't talk to them anymore without an appointment, which was impossible to get from their horrid bitch secretary unless you sent an email that was about how you could make the stock go up. Then it got even weirder.

KIMO: Weirder, how?

CALLER ALIEN BEAN: Choy and Finkelman, it's like they weren't focused anymore, they got spooky. They turned our courtyard into a biodynamic micro-vineyard with a signpost that said, "How green is your pasture?" They started caravanning every year to Burning Man—I mean, Choy did, Finkelman went once and thought it was a sick joke; he was more into extreme wind-surfing on the bay. They'd review milestones while doing yoga on the lawn, invite Russian poets to give lectures in the cafeteria on making variables more beautiful—except almost no one in the company speaks Russian. They'd raffle off seats as recruiting incentives to watch the sunset and down mixology blends on this ginormous party jet they bought. Meanwhile it was all, make the stock go up, make it go up more. Don't get me wrong, our software was selling like cheap crude oil. Our customers loved us because we were saving them money when other companies were stealing it, but all the money we made, it went to Choy and Finkelman and a few VPs and the board, and no one else could get noticed. And if you told anyone in management maybe you had a better idea, you got yelled at.

KIMO: Choy and Finkelman didn't share? That is a bit of weirdness. I thought they were such jolly, model visionaries.

CALLER ALIEN BEAN: Image police, dude. I mean, what do I know, I don't even think they make those calls, who gets the money and who doesn't. That's not their thing. They're big picture, front office, at least that's what happened after the IPO. They surrounded themselves with handlers, and the handlers knew every dollar we got was one less dollar for the handlers.

They tossed around a few pennies to prevent a revolution, fed us free trade coffee and USDA lamb shanks, but the big money, hardly any of the worker bees could even trade up their condos.

KIMO: So you left for greener pastures?

CALLER ALIEN BEAN: Texas, dude. I did better than a lot of people, cashed in enough to live on for a few years to study rodeo. At least I didn't have to stick around with the grind of doing the same thing every day while the handlers took all the money. I don't like being bored, or getting yelled at.

KIMO: You studied rodeo, fascinating. What are you doing now, Alien?

CALLER ALIEN BEAN: Calling you, Dude, aren't you paying attention? I'm just messing with you. I'm hacking, what else? I'm going to tap into their system and crash it. I've been at it for two years now. It's a pretty good system, that's for sure, but when I break through, it's coming down and I will be immortal. That'll kill their stock price, huh? And don't you think it's weird their CEOs have been kidnapped and the stock is going up? There's got to be some kind of conspiracy there. Maybe Dracula was right.

KIMO: Thank you, Alien Bean. We'll call that the JFK angle and keep an eye out for J. Edgar Hoover fashionistas roaming the halls on casual Fridays.

Balthazer dropped the call and saw the counter roll past sixty thousand, incomprehensible for a first day stat. He wondered if the ticker widget might have a virus, if someone really was messing with his mind and moving the decimal a place or two in the background. No, he triggered a quick background scan for malware. His system was clean, the tally appeared to be good. He had only been on the air a few brief moments, and with no expectations, he was on his way to a verified audience of one hundred thousand. Call letters or not, he could still draw.

Internet stardom seemed possible, he just needed to lower his expectations to a milder definition of star, and with all that had transpired that was not so hard. He noticed his callers were more themselves here—more anonymous meant more raw and unformed, but also more candid and engaging. What he did not notice as he took the next call was the iron-willed McDonald's manager, who had noticed his antics and was trying to calm his customers, all at once starting to leave the store.

KIMO: Dark Thunder from Santa Clara, California, Welcome, *This Is Rage*.

CALLER DARK THUNDER: Hey there, Kimo, thanks for coming back. We missed you. On the job, nothing like your voice to pass the hours.

KIMO: I think that's a compliment. Beats working for your paycheck. Let's see where you take us.

CALLER DARKER THUNDER: I'm an EnvisionInk employee too, still on the job. I think the most interesting part of the press release is what you haven't talked about yet, the part about Atom Heart Entertainment.

KIMO: Yeah, I thought that was on the creepster side. Why'd they throw it in, any insights?

CALLER DARK THUNDER: I actually have some inside information, and I'm just pissed off enough to tell it to you and your listeners.

KIMO: All 77,921 of us now?

CALLER DARK THUNDER: Yeah, whatever you got, maybe that's enough to spread it, because it needs to be spread.

KIMO: Let me make sure I have this right. You are at your desk, at EnvisionInk Systems in Santa Clara, and you are going to drop some inside information right here, on *This Is Rage*?

CALLER DARK THUNDER: Kimo, I'm not stupid. I'm not going to lose my job on their time table. No, I'm not at my desk where they log every keystroke. Let's just say I know how to route internet packets so they can't be traced. I know the EnvisionInk platform forward and backward, but that's not the point.

KIMO: Sure are a lot of angry people inside that happy camp everyone likes to put on their resumes, where the second tier brass isn't willing to pay a dime to rescue your founders. Guess all that free food in the cafeteria isn't as tasty as it once was. What exactly is pissing you off in paradise?

CALLER DARK THUNDER: The Atom Heart deal is going to happen. There are definitely people here who want to do it, not Choy and Finkelman, but others who call the shots. That's why the stock is up. The take out price when they get to a tender offer is going to blow your mind. They aren't betting the farm, they're auctioning off the county.

KIMO: I don't know, Dark. You're awfully confident for guy on a call-in show. You sound like one of those blah-blah guys on the finance bulletin boards, a virtual talking head. How do I know you're not some big mouth trying the run up the stock and dump it?

CALLER DARK THUNDER: If that were the case, why would I call you? No one who listens to your show has a brokerage account. Look, no one cares about Choy and Finkelman anymore. We've squeezed all the profit we can from the EnvisionInk enterprise, the smart money knows that. All we have now is a ton of cash, and no one with a checkbook trusts these guys to keep using it for our own acquisitions, they're too soft. So instead we'll let ourselves get bought by a big, stupid, analog entertainment company who wants to pump content through our engine, get advertisers to up their buys on search, and use our system to save them money. The pie gets bigger, the size of our slice balloons with the pie.

KIMO: I don't see the bad part.

CALLER DARK THUNDER: Layoffs, Kimo, enormous cuts at both EnvisionInk and Atom Heart after we integrate. That's how they pay for it, bigger profits from labor savings, wash away the overlap in one quarterly charge. Hello cash flow, hello misery.

KIMO: Seen that one before, haven't we?

CALLER DARK THUNDER: Not on this scale, it's an asteroid crater, and it's a nasty secret. Well, it was until a minute ago. For all I know, that's why Choy and Finkelman vaporized. Might even be someone on our own team, like your other callers said. Morale has been way low here, and that was before Choy and Finkelman were grabbed. They keep telling us there's no more organic growth, all of our ideas can't move the needle. So they just buy things and try to take out costs, but they don't take out enough because they don't want to be bad guys, they don't fire enough people from the companies we buy. This deal is different. Sol Seidelmeyer will have no emotional problem strip-mining costs.

KIMO: And you know this because you're an engineer at EnvisionInk and you don't want to see it happen?

CALLER DARK THUNDER: Me, an engineer? That's funny. I mean, everyone at this company can code, that's how you get in. No, I'm in human resources and I helped evaluate the initial elimination plan—until I saw the latest draft, which had my name on it. Choy and Finkelman haven't even seen it. The jump in earnings is staggering. No, I'm in a conference room at one of our competitors, waiting to interview for a new gig. Good luck, Kimo, keep it honest and don't ever sell out. We need you.

The caller was gone. Balthazer was not sure what to make of him. He might have been legitimate, but maybe not. The listener count kept building, now a magnificent 89,113. Balthazer looked up and noticed the side door to the McDonald's opening, a focused young fellow with a manager's nametag starting to make his way across the parking lot for his car. For the first time, Balthazer realized he might be making a spectacle of himself. The windows of the Infiniti were thick with steam, but not so much that he couldn't see so many mom eyes were on him. This would not be an extended debut, that was for sure.

KIMO: Well, we are having some first day with this new way of talking, aren't we? We are over ninety-two thousand listeners now, and you know, I would be further humbled to reach one hundred thousand so I can put that bragging right in my pirate radio email to all of you tonight, which I invite you to look for in your in-box. I promise, we will continue tomorrow, so stay tuned for my announcement of the specifics. I think we have time for one more call, but let me say in advance, if I have to drop the show suddenly, there is a very good reason, so please come back tomorrow. Ben E. Arnold, Gilroy, California, Welcome, *This Is Rage*.

CALLER BEN E. ARNOLD: Kimo, sounds like you're in a squeeze, I don't know if I can make this quick. I have some information your audience will find valuable. I just don't know if I should tell you.

KIMO: You're conflicted, Ben. That's understandable. Start in the abstract. Tell our 94,626 listeners in the broadest strokes what you have. And please don't take too long.

CALLER BEN E. ARNOLD: What I have is the location of Choy and Finkelman.

KIMO: Is this internet bonanza day or what? First we get the inside scoop on the Atom Heart deal, now we get to know where the co-CEOs are in captivity. I so love the grid. Any credential sharing you wish to offer so we know you're not a crackpot, Ben?

Balthazer peered across the parking lot. The Burger Meister was coming, followed by a posse of disturbed mama warriors and their sugar infused children—ketchup McNuggets and apple slices with caramel on parade. Balthazer was going to have to wrap up this show pronto.

CALLER BEN E. ARNOLD: How's this—I have a relative who is a captain with one of the police departments called for back-up. If I tell you any more, I might cost him his badge. Unlike that HR geek who called before me, I'm not much with a keyboard, so I'm probably leaving a trail. Luckily I'm at Best Buy, shopping for a new tablet, no one even notices I'm here, show-rooming rules. I'm just not sure if telling everyone is the right thing to do.

KIMO: Very helpful, those bright polo shirts at Best Buy, easy to find since they never find you. I'm sure you realize, if you do tell our 97,304 listeners where Choy and Finkelman are holed up, it's going to draw a crowd. That could be helpful, bring the right things into focus.

CALLER BEN E. ARNOLD: They're already drawing a crowd, Kimo. There's FBI all around the place, plus cops from every neighboring district. If this goes on much longer, we can probably expect National Guard, maybe soldiers from one of the bases.

McDonald's Finest was at now at car-hop position, tapping on the glass of Balthazer's car window, looking much like a school principal annoyed by a spit ball war. Coupon moms surrounded the vehicle, and kids armed with dipping sauce were finger-painting the Infiniti. Time was of the essence.

KIMO: Ben, I know you're struggling with this, but as I mentioned before I took your call, this first internet radio show I'm doing is experiencing a few technical difficulties. There are two things left on today's agenda: getting to one hundred thousand online listeners which you are helping me with, and letting our audience know where they can find Choy and Finkelman if they want to get to the truth about EnvisionInk. Can you close the loop for me and we'll call it a show?

Mayor McCheeseWhiz was becoming more irritated that Balthazer would not acknowledge his existence. His tapping was translating into an echoed thumping that astute listeners could pick up on the webcast. The sound of children whining began piercing the soundproofing of the Infiniti, finding its way past the windscreen on Balthazer's mic. Gobs of caramel were dripping from the car's hood.

CALLER BEN E. ARNOLD: Okay, Kimo, I'll trust you. If you say people need to know, they need to know. There's a crowd outside Salinas Valley Memorial Medical Center. There's a reason. Choy and Finkelman are being held inside. Now that it's clear EnvisionInk isn't going to pay up, who knows what happens next. Maybe your listeners can help.

KIMO: Ben E. Arnold, you are a prince. And you know what else? We are at 99,865 listeners, and as much as I hate to stop shy of a goal I think we're going to have to call this milestone incomplete. The good news is, tomorrow I promise I will have a better set up. Tomorrow, we reconvene. As always, *This Is Rage*.

Balthazer snapped down the laptop clamshell, pulled off his headset and gave the McDonald's manager the finger. Without otherwise telegraphing it, Balthazer hit the ignition and revved the engine. Startled by the pulsating motor, the sugared kid pack jumped away, their doting mothers following after them. The McDonald's manager returned the favor of the finger and pointed to the driveway with it, standing between the families and the Infiniti.

Balthazer put the car in gear and tore out of the parking lot with a sly smile affixed. He was headed south out of Stockton, en route to synch up with Highway 101. In a matter of hours, he would be in Salinas.

$ $ $ $

1.7
The House Checks and Raises

"Who the brain dead hell is Kimo Balthazer?" bellowed Daniel Steyer.

The language seemed unusual for a poised fellow like Steyer. He was on the phone with FBI Special Agent in Charge Kaamil Hussaini, a summa cum laude graduate of Princeton who usually specialized in counterterrorism. Hussaini was mighty upset to be yanked off a classified case of national importance and dispatched from Langley to Salinas when the call came Monday morning from the office of former Senator Henderson. Hussaini did not much consider it an honor to be made EnvisionInk direct liaison for the balance of the incident, but from what he could tell, he would be back at his desk by the weekend. There was not much to this—wait for the Director to call with the green light, send in the fire strike, mop up whoever was left and avoid all reporters. He could not tell Steyer this, but he gave Ben and Jerry about a 5% chance of survival, with Choy and Finkelman a point or two ahead of them. Those odds had been locked when he learned of Kimo Balthazer's webcast debut earlier in the day, the joy of which he was now relaying to Steyer.

Hussaini's briefing file had told him to expect a reasonable fellow in Steyer, classically stoic throughout a career of navigating bubbles, never one to let emotion cost him a deal point. At the moment, this was not the case. Steyer was a hair-on-fire Field Marshal, and the cliché hyperbole transmitted over the secure line seemed to be muffled by the thick bandaging around his chin. This Balthazer character had proven out of the gate he could have a disorienting impact on the otherwise controlled Steyer. For all Hussaini knew, Steyer would be as unknown to Balthazer as Balthazer should have remained to Steyer, but in an instant that was no longer possible. Steyer would have zero interest in a repackaged street performer like Balthazer, even less in his sad audience, but Hussaini had to make it clear the luxury of that ignorance had evaporated in internet time. The last thing Steyer needed at this strategic inflection point was to be on a collision course with a flunkout talk show host, and yet, the market forces had acted without his permission.

Despite his distaste for the assignment, Hussaini knew he had been the right call by Henderson. Counterterrorism had taught Hussaini the unyielding power of packet transfer, how quickly data moved, how much of it was flawed, and how un-scientifically the public would react to media snacks. Hussaini was a polished thinker, he knew that content had a life of its own, and he understood more than most of his peers that speed was everything in reducing a potential catastrophe to a news cycle crisis. Within minutes of Balthazer's sign-on—reported to Hussaini by his data center when first mention of the Envision-Ink tag triggered a keyword alert—Hussaini had ordered all the driveways and entry paths barricaded around Salinas Valley Memorial Medical Center. A half hour later, a parade of cars hauling in the spectator traffic he had anticipated were backed up into the surface streets of Salinas. In just over an hour, the freeway ramps leading to the hospital in both directions had to be closed and road traffic was being police directed to bypass the hospital for anything but a demonstrated medical emergen-cy. That only served to push the crowds on foot to approach the hospital, and that required Hussaini to call for more local police to hold them back. Balthazer's online antics had gone vi-ral, igniting a free for all that invited all those within fifty miles of the vicinity with little better to do than come watch the live cop show.

Hussaini knew that on a better day Steyer might have ad-mired how much he understood what he was dealing with, but he could appreciate that Steyer had reason to be on edge, await-ing response from Ben and Jerry to the company's refusal to pay up. In their introductory exchange earlier that day, Hussaini had told Steyer to expect that Ben and Jerry would refuse to answer any further phone calls following the press release yesterday, until the very last moment as they approached the 6:00 p.m. deadline. That was how amateurs would play it, and from all the data he could observe, Hussaini was certain he was dealing with lightweights. That had not given Hussaini reason for comfort, true to form, the more foolish the criminal, the more havoc they could create. High stress and stupidity were as bad a combination in crime as they were in business. No question about it, with this much inexperience in play, speed was going to mean everything. The faster the strike force was allowed to move in, the fewer lives would be lost.

$ $

Steyer's temper had been worsening as the clock ticked. It was only a few hours to the 6:00 p.m. ultimatum, and he had no idea what might happen next. He had been told by Hussaini, Henderson, and every subject matter expert he trusted that the board made the correct decision not to negotiate, that Ben and Jerry would inevitably break down with no other alternatives. As soon as they showed weakness, the FBI would pounce. Of course all that was before Balthazer had made the location public, welcoming the media circus that arrived on cue.

Steyer was in his understated but refined garden office suite at SugarSpring Ventures, two blocks off University Avenue in Palo Alto, about half an hour from EnvisionInk's offices in Santa Clara. Most of the Silicon Valley Investor Class made camp in a renowned axis of low rise clusters along Sand Hill Road in adjacent Menlo Park, but Steyer always wanted SugarSpring to be a little different, physically annexed to Stanford's academia, a less traceable place for entrepreneurs to be seen coming and going with their endless pitches. Sitting across his new world composite desk when the Balthazer advisory notice came from Hussaini was Atom Heart Entertainment CEO Sol Seidelmeyer. Steyer had not planned on Seidelmeyer's visit, he just happened to drop by a few minutes after the studio's Falcon 2000 landed in San Jose and a town car delivered him unannounced to SugarSpring's beveled glass door. Steyer knew that to turn him away upon his unscheduled visit would not have made for a more productive dialogue—full service private jets these days, with operating costs above $5,000 per hour, had to be justified, even by CEOs—but he needed to consider what lines he might be crossing having Seidelmeyer on his sofa when the call came from Hussaini.

"We share this mishegas, put him on speakerphone," said Seidelmeyer, gazing around Steyer's unadorned working space, likely looking for anything that might be useful. "I promise to stay quiet."

Steyer looked past his own bruises at Seidelmeyer's primal, piercing eyes. What else could he do? He took the call with Hussaini live, but did not announce Seidelmeyer's presence.

"So a fully masked worker bee blurts out the location on internet radio, just like that?" continued Steyer into the polycom. "Aren't there laws that stop that sort of thing?"

"You know the Internet as well as I do, Mr. Steyer," said the special agent, his tone of displeasure professionally ambiguous. "You're aware we can't enforce laws if people are anonymous. That caller is long gone from Best Buy, which is as far as we could trace the IP."

"What about the moron host, Balthazer, where was he?" asked Steyer.

"As far as we can tell, at a McDonald's in Stockton," answered Hussaini. "We haven't completely tied down that piece, but we're working on it. We do know he was fired from his last radio job in Fresno over a month ago. He burned his landlord for the rent, has a hearing pending with the FCC, and drives an Infiniti M. But he hasn't really broken any law, certainly no federal statute that would let us bring him in. According to our lawyers, he's safely within his First Amendment rights, particularly as a journalist."

"A journalist, are you kidding me, where'd he study, the WikiLeaks School of Ethics?" blurted Steyer.

"Talk show hosts have the same halo," qualified Hussaini.

"As long as he doesn't incite violent action, he is within legal bounds."

"Outstanding," proclaimed Steyer. "When they bring out Choy and Finkelman sideways on a stretcher, you can tell their moms all about the First Amendment. What happens now?"

"It's their move, they set the deadline. If we don't hear from them by 6:00 p.m., the Director should give us the order to move in. We are readying for position on that. We have a well-trained team on the ground and will do what we can to keep civilian impact at a minimum, including your guys. My crew is tight and will be ready to do what they're good at. If we go in, it will be quick. Hopefully Ben and Jerry will negotiate and we'll talk them out, but that's their call. If they want to negotiate, they'll let someone know."

"Keep us apprised," said Steyer as he clicked off the poly-com. He probably had not noticed that he had said "us" instead of "me," but then, Hussaini likely presumed others were listening in, though not corporate competitors bound by SEC regulations. Steyer shook his head in derision after another unneeded jolt, looking to the sun-worn Seidelmeyer for anything encouraging.

"You got a tough situation on your hands," offered Seidelmeyer. "I'm not sure what I would do if I were you."

"After this deal, you are me," said Steyer. "Isn't that why you're here?"

"We don't have a deal," replied Seidelmeyer. "Last I looked we were about $6 billion apart, which I know in your world is not big money. Heck, you got almost half that on the lift this morning. My offer is still above market. The stock's adjusted to a price the Street can swallow. I'm doing better than that, the deal should be easy for you. If you want to tell me the gap is closed, we can talk about what happens next."

"Sol, don't try to use this string of events to tell me you're not paying the expected premium. That's unbecoming, even for you."

"I'm a showman, what do I know about asking for the wrong thing?" quipped Seidelmeyer. "You have a point of view and I have a point of view. The difference is, you have a problem and I really don't."

"Sol, you do have a problem. You're old, and your company is old. Without EnvisionInk, you have no growth story. Your board tosses you out, sells to someone else and blames you for blowing the deal. Your legacy will be that of a failed Neanderthal. No one will remember what you did to put that company on the map, all those movie openings, all those shows and networks, all those dividends. All they will remember is that you were brushed aside, bitter and dusty, because you missed the shift to digital. No one remembers obsolete."

"You're a putz," said Seidelmeyer. "You may have more money in the steel vault than me, but you haven't created anything lasting. Dollars come, dollars go, who remembers, who cares? My company touches lives and we make a fine profit."

"Sol, we can agree to disagree, or we can piss on each other, which isn't going to win you another Academy Award. You want an Act Three, we're your Act Three. You become chairman of a goliath industrial, my partners get liquidity and I go away, everyone's happy. You want to retire as a goat, walk out the door and leave me to figure this out on my own. Right now I can't even think about price. If I don't get those kids back alive, we have nothing."

"Funny, the Street doesn't see it that way," said Seidelmeyer, regaining an even tone. "The kids are tied to a bomb, you leaked our deal, and the Street is sending up balloons."

"That's because they're confident we will get them back, and get a deal. That's what we hinted. For big institutional holders to dump volume with Choy and Finkelman an unknown, and a clear path to a combination viable, that leaves money on the table, so arbitrage is indulging us. But we only have a few hours."

"Those bumpkin punks are bluffing," said Seidelmeyer. "The special agent has a mirror on the crown moldings behind their cards. They don't even know what game they're playing. This is ours to lose. You hold tight, they'll cave. I've played at this table before."

"You've had top executives kidnapped?" asked Steyer.

"I've been held hostage by the likes of you, not a lot different. We just have to figure how to get out."

Getting out had to be a concept well understood by Sol Seidelmeyer. At sixty-eight years old, he was both legend and target. He was a monument of the traditional, with more framed
top ticket one-sheets than wall space, but creative destruction
had thrown him big time. Steyer knew from public record that
Seidelmeyer had lost hundreds of millions of dollars on convergence folly, buying this and that inflated asset brought to him in
time-strapped auctions by friends, enemies, and Bankers. When
Seidelmeyer took over Atom Heart some twenty years ago, the
world was a simpler place. No one back then called movies and
television shows and magazines "content," an appalling descriptor that purposely lacked respect. Even the term "media" was
insulting to the old guard, suggesting undifferentiated, ephemeral stuff that was created to charge people admission or paste
up with ads. What Seidelmeyer and his teams created was Entertainment, another of America's greatest and singularly most
unique twentieth century contributions to the global economy,
after affordable motor cars and before computing power. The
twenty-first century had come with promise that this new "digital paradigm shift" would make the half dozen surviving show-
biz conglomerates even more at the hub of all knowledge transfer, as deregulation spilling over from the Reagan Revolution
allowed production and distribution to legally consolidate with
technology as the fulcrum that tilted the see-saw in favor of the
studios.

Unfortunately it had not worked out the way the pundits
called the breakthrough. Mergers like AOL Time Warner
proved to be much better PowerPoint decks than they were
companies to run. Young customers upon whom so much of entertainment's unprecedented margins depended found stealing a
much preferred alternative to paying. Fragmentation made audiences smaller, while talent manipulated the few big audiences
remaining to drive operating costs higher. Failing to navigate

this landscape had, as Steyer so gently articulated, destroyed more old world careers than it elevated, with almost all Hollywood obituaries now ending in sentences that said the subject had enjoyed a meteoric rise on the creative front but ultimately sunk to demise in the mash-up of digital carnage. Sol Seidelmeyer was the last old world body standing, and carnage would not be a concept he wanted in his obituary or backstabbing wine bar eulogies east or west of Rodeo Drive. He made it clear he never liked the idea of merging Atom Heart and EnvisionInk, but he liked every conceivable alternative less. In that spirit, the final chapter of his storybook seemed to be all he cared about, and in trying to draft those chapters he had become beholden to Steyer. Now for the briefest of moments, it seemed Steyer needed him, a carved path through the muck that he knew much better than Steyer, a place where surviving was winning and reality was interpretation.

"Daniel, I think a door just opened and we need to walk through it," continued Seidelmeyer. "First you have to see it."

"Tell me what I don't know, wise man," taunted Steyer.

"Kimo Balthazer might be the best thing we have going right now," replied Seidelmeyer.

"That blowhard? I suppose you know him from social circles." "Not personally, but we own about three dozen radio stations that carried him. I know his act, his ego, what he likes on the menu. If we feed him what he eats, he's our tiger in the cage. He can help."

"I can't believe we're having this conversation," said Steyer. "You think that lunatic is going to get Choy and Finkelman out of there?"

"I didn't say is, I said can." Seidelmeyer saw that Steyer really was listening, another door had opened. "I'll bet you the $6 billion he's on his way to Salinas this very second. He's a mud scavenger. He goes where the mud is and makes misery his triumph. It's an old formula, and it pulls big numbers."

"What are you suggesting we do?" asked Steyer, cautious but intrigued.

"Call back Special Agent in Charge Hussaini. Tell him when he sees the Infiniti to let it through."

"What good will that do?" asked Steyer, still not following. "You heard Hussaini. In a few hours the whole hospital will be up in smoke."

"Not a chance," said Seidelmeyer. "You may know about bits and bytes and be able to remember every equation Newton saw in his dreams. My business is built on the backs of lies. All of LA is a house of cards. To be a remarkable asshole in LA requires aspiration, because to be an ordinary asshole is accomplished by everybody. The two schmendricks that have your CEOs, they're bluffing. You keep your money in the pot, they will not plug your CEOs. No chance, not going to happen. I'll put my new last, best, and final offer, $46.5 billion, on that. I'm right and no one else gets capped, you agree. I'm wrong, I pay you a $2 billion breakup fee for the inconvenience. Fair wager?"

"I'm not betting with you, Sol," said Steyer. "And we're not going to break any securities laws discussing this out of process."

"I agree," said Seidelmeyer. "So do we have a deal?"

Steyer shook his head in disbelief, then yanked the polycom from the wall and reached for his desk phone. Whatever he was going to say to Special Agent Hussaini, he was not going to give Seidelmeyer the satisfaction of more than half the dialogue.

$ $

"It's kind of too bad the doctors saved my leg," said Finkelman. "It really isn't going to matter much when Ben and Jerry put us down."

"That's pretty advanced reconstruction work they started to let it go to waste, major league medical bills," replied Choy. "I told them while you were under if you weren't windsurfing again with the Stanford alums at Coyote Point this time next year, you were coming after the hospital for a refund. Of course to ask for your money back, we'll need to be alive. Call me an optimist."

"If they do pull the trigger, it's not like we'll die in obscurity," said Finkelman, pointing to the television with one hand while checking the sensory response of his healing limb with a digital pen in the other.

He and Choy were alone again in the inner room of the hospital suite, watching the media circus on their in-room TV, observing with overdubbed commentary events taking place not fifty yards from them outside the building walls of the medical complex. They had not seen daylight since Sunday afternoon. That night had been spent on the operating table with Monday in recuperation. Ben and Jerry had told them about the board call, strangely hopeful that Steyer would find a way to give them what they wanted, then seen their hopes dashed when the press release appeared that afternoon. That had been just over twenty-four hours ago, and they had been locked in the room ever since with only doctors and food bearing attendants appearing and disappearing briefly. Ben and Jerry currently had no more interest in talking to them than in talking to their board. It was a defensive posture of silence, which in their minds had only come to mean one thing. At the 6:00 p.m. deadline, the last line of their bios was likely to be written, and somehow they knew that part of the story might overpower most memory of what had come before.

The telephone had been removed from the inner room upon their arrival, and Ben and Jerry had not left them with an internet connection, a laptop, a tablet, or any mobile devices. Kindly enough, they had left Choy and Finkelman with the television intact, largely because it was built into the wall, but more so because the information it was likely to provide was hazy enough given the facts that had been released, and at this point Ben and Jerry's identity was still just that, unknown and unimportant. What had broken on the local news moments ago was something about a radio host on the Internet named Kimo Balthazer, which meant nothing whatsoever to them given their media preferences. The reporter onscreen had reported that the location of Choy and Finkelman had been announced but not yet verified, which Choy and Finkelman knew could not be of value to them. Choy and Finkelman watched the unfolding snippets on TV, as not only media trucks arrived on the hospital site, but ropes and cones were put in place to restrain the crowds of onlookers who seemed to be defying gravity by making their way to the crime scene climbing over anything in their path.

"That radio guy gave up our location," said Choy. "Someone at the hospital is going to verify we're here. Then this freak show is going to turn into a stampede."

"They're idiots," said Finkelman. "Don't they know by coming here they put themselves in the same danger we're in? Look at all those FBI vehicles, all the police, they've got more loaded weapons than Waco. They're waiting for someone to give the order, then they come in and it's over. Who knows what spills where? It's so stupid."

"There has to be some way to convince Ben and Jerry they're in over their heads," said Choy. "Come on, all the resources we have, everything we've built, we're locked in a room with a TV and no one will talk to us? We can't die like this. I'm guessing Ben and Jerry don't want to die either. They called it wrong, now they're frozen. We have to help them get unfrozen."

"How do we help them if they won't even talk to us?" said Finkelman. "I can't even walk right now with this brace on my leg and these things in my arms. We can't leave even if we wanted to. Either they make a deal or none of it matters."

"There's no deal to be made, Stephen. The only deal is they go to prison forever. If I were them, I wouldn't want that deal either."

"How do we help them?" asked Finkelman.

"Help them?" echoed Choy. "There's no helping them. We belong to them. This is their problem, not our problem."

"Calvin, let's think of this as a business problem. Brainstorm it, break the algorithm. Make it the kind of problem we are good at solving."

"I hear you," said Choy. "I guess we have to be smarter than they are. We can't let them solve it or everyone loses."

"Right," said Finkelman. "We have to help them solve it in a way that works for them first, us second."

"How do we do that?" asked Choy.

"Maybe we give them what they want," said Finkelman. "They want money to start a company and a flight to somewhere they can build it. We make that happen."

"But the board unilaterally rejected their request," said Choy. "They read us the press release before they went silent. The company did what we should have expected."

"Right, pretty much by law the board of a public company in a public spectacle can't negotiate with them," said Finkelman. "But we can."

Despite being pinned to a hospital bed with a decent level of painkillers running through his veins, Stephen Finkelman had deduced a key point. The logic was not lost on Choy, whose emerging apathy was suddenly replaced by a shared moment of understanding. Besides both being brilliant engineers, Choy and Finkelman had long ago discovered a rhythm with each other in their thinking patterns, a shared set of values that let them problem solve together in ways that were exponentially better than what either of them could imagine on their own, and what together they could implement in ways that made their competition repeatedly blink. This ability to riff had always been what made them not just good, but exceptional.

"I see where you're going," followed Choy. "Regardless of what the company can't or shouldn't do, we're still private citizens. What means we have is ours."

"We don't need the company's Gulfstream, we have our own plane," added Finkelman. "Ben and Jerry didn't see that in the 10K because it's ours. It doesn't belong to EnvisionInk."

"So if we want to offer them a ride, we just do it?" queried Choy.

"There is the matter of the FBI letting us leave the country. We're going to have to get the Feds onboard. As for the money, we take the offer up, we can each give them $100 million and neither of us will ever miss it. It's our own money to give away, or invest, whatever you want to call it."

"You're right, it's almost nothing, especially when you think about what we're buying," said Choy. "So you're thinking we just tell them they can have what they want, we all walk out of here together and fly to Shanghai, then we put them in business and come home? It has to be harder than that."

"Compared to being shot dead in the next two hours, I'd call it a plan worth trying," replied Finkelman.

"You're clearly the smarter of the two of us," said Choy. "Tell me, what's this crap about Atom Heart Entertainment? You and I nixed that months ago. It's a dinosaur lodged in a tar pit. What was that doing in the press release?"

"I'm not smarter than you, Calvin, that's why the company works. What Atom Heart is doing in the press release makes no sense to me. It's like Steyer and the board are running a shadow management roundtable. I know Steyer wanted the deal, but we didn't and we're the CEOs. I thought that was behind us."

"Guess we missed the wrong board meeting," commented Choy. "We're going to have to fix that, too. So how do we pull all this off? We are a bit restrained at the moment."

"First, we have to get Ben and Jerry to talk to us. You seem to have a built a relationship with Jerry. You need to take the first opportunity you can to get him talking to you, programmer to programmer."

"I can do that," said Choy. "Then what?"

"We're going to need to get them to let us talk to whoever is in charge of this operation. Somehow we have to get in touch with the outside. Some rules are going to have to get broken. That's going to take some smoothing over."

"Steyer?" asked Choy.

"Not this round," said Finkelman. "I'm having some trust issues with this Atom Heart override. Steyer has to be calling the shots, but who knows what his agenda is. After the two of us, he's the one with the most at stake, like $10 billion of Sugar-Spring's gains still tied up in EnvisionInk paper. For a path to full liquidity, I think he's playing for his own team."

"We need a lawyer," said Choy. "We need Sylvia. She's objective and she's unconflicted. Pure fiduciary."

"I think you're right," said Finkelman. "We need a wall between us and the board, before our investors lock in a point of view. We're supposed to be insiders, but right now not so much. We need to get to Sylvia so she can cut us a deal."

$ $

In the outer room of the hospital suite, Swerlow and Kisinski were pacing. Save for the closed door, they were all but showing their cards. They heard muffled bits of the conversation in the inner room, and had they wanted to pay attention all they had to do was crack the door open and they could have heard every word Choy and Finkelman were saying. They were uninterested, they had their own problem to solve, and not much time left before they lost all the leverage they had created. Kisinski was out of patience.

"They said no, Dennis. They didn't say maybe. The press release was definitive and public. What do you think we're going to do now, kill the two of them like you threatened? If that's your plan, I'm out. I'm walking up to the closest FBI agent I can find and surrendering."

"They've called us every hour since they dropped the press release," said Swerlow. "They want to negotiate."

"And you won't take the call," countered Kisinski. "To negotiate you have to have a dialogue, words go back and forth. That's not the message we're sending. In terms of negotiation, I think the only options left for us are death or prison. I'm not seeing a Boy Scout trail to the Shanghai Jamboree. I just know I'm not going to be part of killing anyone else."

"There's no proof we killed anyone, Sam. I keep telling you that. You fade in and out on me."

"Those are nice guys in there. They haven't done anything wrong. We have to let them go. No more blood."

"I'm almost ready to talk," said Swerlow. "I just need to get the approach right. On the next call, I'll pick it up. I promise."

"Outstanding, Dennis, an hour before expiration and at last you're ready to schmooze. What do you want to do now, offer a discount?"

"No, that won't work," said Swerlow. "They aren't playing this right. They aren't playing it right at all."

"You were so sure they would do it your way. What made you so sure, Dennis?"

"Because, damn it, it was a good deal. Good business people take good deals."

"Not from losers like us, Dennis. We've gotten ourselves trapped in here. The only thing that's kept us from being identified is that we're so irrelevant no one can even match the surveillance video from Steyer's house to any database anywhere we exist at all. Now we're on the evening news. As soon as that door opens, someone watching TV will call up and ID us for the high five—and the only thing my mom and your mom are going to be asking themselves is what went wrong with their parenting skills."

"We're not going to prison, I can tell you that," said Swerlow. "Guys like us don't do well in prison. There's no way this ends in a locked cage, not a chance."

"Fine, then let's let the CEO boys go and take the bullet and call this done. I couldn't write code again even if I wanted to. I'm fried."

There was a pounding on the inner door. Choy and Finkelman obviously heard their argument and wanted to get their attention.

"Maybe we get them on the phone with Steyer, make them believe we're serious," said Swerlow. "Those two guys can sell it. We gotta get them to want to work with us."

"We're not serious, Dennis, and even if we were, Steyer isn't negotiating. But maybe you're right about getting Choy and Finkelman to work with us. They're smart guys, maybe they can think of something. Maybe they already have."

There was more pounding on the inner door, a steady but insistent beat that would not stop. The co-CEOs clearly wanted to talk. Kisinski liked the idea of working them as an angle. It seemed his cousin was still trying to second guess their intentions, to control the moment and steer the conversation.

Swerlow was sweating heavily now. The phone would likely ring again in a matter of moments, and this time Kisinski knew if Swerlow did not answer it, a battlefield strike would be imminent. There was just over an hour left to their self-imposed deadline. This was Swerlow's last chance to spin it.

"Maybe Choy and Finkelman can get us immunity," said Swerlow. "They seem really scared. Maybe they can convince someone on the outside we're not full of shit and the FBI will have to hit us so hard it won't be worth it. If the difference between all of us getting killed and us getting out of the country is Choy and Finkelman selling the FBI, they could position it as an act of goodwill. Stranger offers have been made. We're going to have to scare them a little more though, you know. Shake them up so they have reason to fight for us."

Swerlow drew his weapon and approached the door. Kisinski hesitantly followed along as Swerlow reached for the door knob, opened it and walked through. Choy and Finkelman appeared almost surprised they had responded. There was a brief silence no one seemed quite sure how to overcome. Choy broke the ice.

"You two have been doing some talking," said Choy, directing his line of sight at Kisinski. "Sounds like you might not have a clear path from here to there."

"We know what we're doing," blurted Swerlow, embarrassingly unconvincing.

"Let me try, I have this," said Kisinski, adroitly cutting off his cousin, knowing that a few more wrong words from Swerlow would likely put them on an irreversible path to melt down. Kisinski could see that Choy was deftly reaching across the aisle, a young pro to his rookie sloppiness. Somehow he and Choy had bonded at the roadside rest stop. It was all quite strange, as if they had worked together developing a set of libraries and formed their own shorthand.

"You've been talking a bit in here, too," continued Kisinski. "Maybe you've thought of something we've missed."

"I don't think you want to kill us," said Choy. "I know you shot Stephen, and who knows what happened to that Banker, but it seems like that's just what happened. It wasn't what you wanted to happen."

"Don't question our intensions," interrupted Swerlow. "You guys want to get back on the job someday, you're going to have to step up for us."

"I said I have this, Dennis," reiterated Kisinski more firmly, for the first time saying his cousin's real first name in front of the others. Swerlow shot him a vicious look of contempt, like he had just blown it. Kisinski remained laser focused on Choy, who picked up the opening.

"We were thinking you might let us try a call or two, buy some time, work a little outreach," said Choy. "The 6:00 p.m. deadline is going to creep up on us pretty quickly if we don't stop the timer. Some folks might get antsy, read that wrong, and they have more guns than you do."

"We were thinking something similar," said Kisinski. "You think you can move this along so none of us gets hurt?"

"My partner and I have a fair amount of money that is our own," said Choy.

"We also have a Boeing Business Jet that's ours, not the company's," added Finkelman, pulling himself to eye level in the hospital bed. "It's pretty big and well-equipped with a private office, not super long range, but it can be refueled with a quick landing on a decent route."

Swerlow's eyes nearly exploded, visibly protruding from his head. He looked at Cousin Sam, who was in equal disbelief, doing everything he could not to show a response.

"Are you saying that you can give us what EnvisionInk can't?" queried Swerlow, waving the pistol back and forth.

"Well, technically, I suppose in the United States of America, an individual still has free will to do what he wants with that which belongs to him," said Choy. "There is still a question around any crimes that have been committed, getting those in authority to agree that letting us act on our wishes will provide the best outcome for all."

Swerlow and Kisinski stared at each other, incredulous. The moment drifted into a standoff, as they recalculated their approach silently on the spot.

$ $

Choy and Finkelman could not be sure what to make of the soft stalemate. Maybe they were wrong about their captors. Maybe the aforementioned Dennis and his partner truly were bad guys and thought this was a ploy. Maybe they would just shoot them in the next few minutes and be done with it. Finkelman was not willing to risk it.

"You asked EnvisionInk for an infusion of $100 million," said Finkelman from the hospital bed. "They said no, because given the circumstances, they really can't. Calvin and I think you're a pretty good investment opportunity. We're prepared to each put in $100 million. That's $200 million to get you capitalized. Provided someone out there has the authority to allow it, we'll fly you to Shanghai like you asked, on our plane. You just have to promise—promise—to let us go safely when it's done."

"Five hundred million dollar valuation," declared Swerlow, a non-sequitur if ever there was one. "We don't want to seem less than appreciative, but we need to retain control. You get forty percent of the NewCo, we get sixty percent. But you have my word, you'll do well on your return. And you'll walk away without fail when you get back from China, you have our categorical promise."

Finkelman looked at Choy and nodded his approval. Choy returned the nod without hesitation, though more subtle in gesture. It was all too surreal. They had a deal.

"How do you get us from here to the airport?" asked Kisinski, hanging slowly on each word. Before Choy or Finkelman could answer, Swerlow was building on the plan, drawing the disposable mobile from his pocket.

"This phone has rung every hour on the hour since we got the press release," noted Swerlow. "We haven't answered it since we talked to the board. When it rings again, it's your move."

"When it rings again, you tell whoever is on the line there's no 6:00 p.m. deadline, that you've extended it indefinitely and no one is going to be killed tonight," said Choy. "Then you ask whoever it is to put our general counsel and corporate secretary, Sylvia Normandy, on the phone. Tell them Stephen and I are asking for her, as her boss, and everyone else is instructed to leave the room as the call is privileged and confidential information. If she isn't there, and she will be, you have her call us back when she's alone. Then you leave Stephen and I alone to talk to her. Got all that, Dennis?"

Choy and Finkelman were taking command. Somewhere along the way it was clear they had learned what it meant to be CEO. They may not have had control of the entire situation, but they had gained control of the moment. For now, that was more than enough. Swerlow and Kisinski had the makings of a deal, which was worth a full $200 million more than it was fifteen minutes ago when they were simply playing for their own lives. It was blind, it was messy, but in business parlance, it was a hell of a win-win.

All Choy and Finkelman had to do now was sell it. That might not have seemed like such a great task to own, but compared to letting Ben and Jerry try to land their wreck in the river, they were practically packing their bags. They also had bought themselves 40% of a new high-tech venture in China. The day would end quite differently than seemed likely. Overtime would be added to the clock. No one in this wing of Salinas Valley Memorial Medical Center needed to die tonight.

$ $ $ $

<u>1.8</u>
If There Were Rules Who Would Listen?

Balthazer awoke to two emails flagged with red exclamation points, accompanied by the opening notes of Beethoven's
Fifth that he had associated with such urgency in his preference settings. The sun was not quite up, a sight with which he
was unfamiliar, particularly looking through the frayed, nearly
translucent synthetic white curtains of his Salinas motel room.
Surmising that Salinas Valley Memorial would be extremely limited entry following his show yesterday, he had planned
to get up early, to make his way to the hospital site before the
crowds combined with the cops created too much of an obstacle
course. Thus the predawn wake up salutation proved to be op-
portune, if not pleasant. There was also no love lost between him
and the local motel he had selected, amenities rivaling Motel 6,
again selected solely for its free Wi-Fi, willingness to take cash,
and not ask any questions beyond how many keys he wanted.
Balthazer imagined his listenership in this struggling agricul-
tural support town would not be tremendous, and was pleased
he could move about freely without being recognized. With the
exception of Limbaugh and Stern, almost any radio personality could enjoy the obscurity of their celebrity, whether local or
national, although a talk show host always risked an enamored
fan sighting, particularly after midnight in a suburban Denny's.
In Salinas, Balthazer was safe—until his remote webcast would
light up the grid in just a few hours.

The first of the two emails heating up his laptop screen in
bright block text was a dire warning from the Internet Service
Provider that hosted his website, demanding that he instantly
upgrade his billing plan or ThisIsRage.com would be dropped.
Balthazer had enjoyed the graciousness of McDonald's free

Wi-Fi from their parking lot, but he never anticipated the almost one hundred thousand concurrent visitors to his site, nor
the cost of bandwidth associated with real-time callers flooding their servers with dialogue. No problem, he logged into his
ISP, changed his plan to unlimited, even entered a backup credit
card in case his current one on file might be cancelled. What
did he care? He was not going to pay the bill until he had income again. If they wanted to charge him more for bandwidth,
he would carry it on a revolving balance and pay the minimum
monthlies until all his credit was exhausted. This was a critical
business expense, and the only thing that mattered to Balthazer
was that he was back in business.

The second email alert was much stranger, more intriguing,
but not nearly as easy to digest. In the From line appeared the
address Chairman@EnvisionInk.com and in the Subject line
were the words "Ben & Jerry Phone Number." At first Balthazer thought this was a hoax, someone messing with his mind,
or worse, a phishing expedition looking to steal his identity or
crash his system. Wary but unable to ignore the item in his in-
box, he took the bait and opened it:

Mr. Balthazer:

We don't know each other, but we both have
an interest in Calvin Choy and Stephen J.
Finkelman. My name is Daniel Steyer. I am
the Board Chair at EnvisionInk Systems. Our
co-CEOs were abducted from a party at my
home. When you dial the phone number (888)
555-6789 to get Ben and Jerry on the phone,
you will know this email is authentic because
according to them only we have it. They will
be surprised to get your call. We are hopeful
that you and your participatory audience might
be able to persuade them to walk out of the
hospital building in an act of willing surrender
before anything more troubling occurs. Our
belief is that the peer pressure of the crowd is

the best chance we have for this to end without
violence. The value to you, as I understand the
proposition of media, cannot be underestimated. Your popularity will increase exponentially,
and you may even set a new live event audience record for an internet talk show. Should
Choy and Finkelman be released as a result
of your dialogue, you will be lauded as a hero.
Please respond to this email if you find this of
interest, along with any needs we can provide.

Kind regards,
Daniel Steyer

Balthazer had no idea if this was a game of true and false
or truth or dare. To respond to the email could give the sender
confirmation that he had been authenticated, in which case his
computer could be subject to hacker attack. To ignore it was
his safest bet, but the outreach it offered if real could be outrageously opportunistic. Balthazer had originally imagined going
to the hospital site, collecting information locally, then coming
back to the motel for more free Wi-Fi. If the hospital could provide him with a wireless field connection, his show could be a
live on-site remote, and if Steyer's offer was real, include direct
communication with Ben and Jerry, maybe even Choy and Finkelman. The risk was absolutely justified. He hit reply.

Steyer:

If this is really you, and I'm not convinced it is,
forward a wireless network I can log onto from
the hospital area and an encryption key. Lock
the channel just for me so I have enough bandwidth for the broadcast. BTW, no commitment
of any kind on the content of my show, no
input from you or anyone else. Deal?

KB

Balthazer hit send and looked down the list of his "regular status" emails. There were hundreds, too many to read, but the subject lines all carried a bizarre, similar theme:

Subject: Maybe more CEOs should be taken hostage.
Subject: Give executives the same misery they create.
Subject: Corporate crime is crime.
Subject: Leave the criminals to the criminals.
Subject: Who cares about a couple of rich dudes?
Subject: Choy & Finkelman no better than Ben & Jerry.
Subject: Let them croak.

It was a reaction that Balthazer had not at all anticipated. He thought his listeners would despise the board and the corporation. He thought they would loathe the kidnappers. What they seemed to hate most was the victims. If anything, he had expected some empathy for Choy and Finkelman. The two young prodigies had been praised far and wide, across all forms of media for setting the tone of the new economy, for taking a more human approach to business, for creating jobs and treating employees differently. That may or may not have been the case, but there certainly was no goodwill with his audience. Instead the forum reflected retribution, a crude expression of digital street justice bucketing a universal dislike of CEOs, who—even if co-CEOs—embodied in title alone a basket of badness that included greed and oppression, even if these two really were not such bad guys. EnvisionInk might have been as good at manufacturing its own storybook goodness as it was saving its advertisers money. Even Steyer, if that email was from Steyer, seemed to think that public opinion would help him, to motivate the real criminals, Ben and Jerry, to give up their undertaking. At this point there was only one item of certainty in Balthazer's mind: today he was going to have an excellent show.

The four note intro of Beethoven's Fifth rang anew, and

with it came the re-reply from Steyer to the response Balthazer
had just sent. Someone was definitely hovering over that email
account with eyes on the inbox, so whoever it was had to be serious. Balthazer opened the new email with Subject: re: re: Ben
& Jerry Phone Number.

> Mr. Balthazer:
>
> You will have all the bandwidth you need on
> a dedicated network. We will send ID and
> password in an hour. The hospital site is locked
> down, but you will be escorted in when you
> arrive, just identify yourselves to the Salinas
> Police (please do not disturb the FBI). You
> will be provided full security while on site. I
> ask that you don't reveal this source, your jour-
> nalist's privilege applies. What time will you be
> on-air?
>
> Kind regards,
> Daniel Steyer.

Balthazer still was not certain if the correspondence was
real, but it was too deliciously tempting to ignore. Balthazer had
to take up the sender on this offer, Steyer or not. What was the
worst that could happen, he'd be arrested on arrival? For what?
He knew he had not committed any serious crime. Besides, a
public arrest after yesterday's show was more than enough to
put him back on the map. He almost hoped the invitation was a
fake, but not really. The opening, if real, was talk show heaven.
He hit reply again.

> Steyer:
>
> Live@noon PST. Do not piss on me or I'll
> serve you up. Believe me on that.
>
> KB

Balthazer hit send, noticing on his home page that as the stock market opened just then at 6:30 a.m. PST, EnvisionInk stock had jumped again, soaring up another 18%. Balthazer could not imagine how that could be. First the crowd was against Choy and Finkelman, now the Street seemed to be applauding their capture. There had to be piles of nasty poop being shoveled all through the night he did not know about, erased conversations to which he would never be privy. It barely made sense to him that the FBI—whom he had just been instructed to avoid—had not brought this thing to a close. He did not much care, as long as he could get on the air today and do what he was best at, turning conflict into entertainment. He closed his laptop, swiftly packed up the few belongings he had toted into the motel, and headed out to the Infiniti. No question about it, this was going to be a show like no other.

$ $

At a makeshift command post under a nondescript canvass framed by tent poles, Special Agent in Charge Hussaini was coming to the conclusion that he was not going to be home in Virginia for the weekend. Based on the phone call he had received yesterday just before 6:00 p.m. from the Director, he was also not likely to be back at his desk next Monday morning, focused on matters he deemed to be of significantly greater national importance. When the call from the Director had come in, Hussaini was convinced it would be the green light allowing him to take out Ben and Jerry, which with relatively uncomplicated ground coordination looked to be a no brainer. Ben and Jerry had cornered themselves in the windowless two room hospital suite. Even as amateurs they would know to come out of the suite with Choy and Finkelman in front of them, hands tied, their one gun trained on their captives. As soon as Ben or Jerry cleared the shallow doorjamb, there were any number of clean angles his sharpshooters could take that would safely avoid Choy and Finkelman. With the proper planning Hussaini had reviewed in a dozen rehearsals, all of ten seconds were needed to finish this.

All Hussaini needed was an okay from the Director to engage, and the suite door to open. He could have personally talked Ben and Jerry through the door, offering them anything they wanted in a deal meant to be broken, if only he had been given the authority to take over the direct negotiation with them. The fact that he had not been given this authority throughout the day was a bad sign in his mind. Hussaini's key concern since being deployed had been that Ben and Jerry would panic and kill Choy and Finkelman before opening the door. That would mean Hussaini would have to take them into custody alive, hardly the heroic ending that could be, and many months of heavily edited paperwork required to assure due justice.

Thus when Hussaini saw the Director's name on his phone ID shortly before 6:00 p.m., he thought he would be given control. The rest would be textbook. Instead the Director informed him that Ben and Jerry had extended the 6:00 p.m. deadline indefinitely while they continued their negotiation with members of the EnvisionInk corporate team. Hussaini had attempted to debate this approach with the Director, to allow him the element of surprise and blow through the door now that Ben and Jerry would be least expecting it. It would not be a ten second operation, it might now take half a minute, but Hussaini was still convinced that speed meant everything if they wanted this to end the right way. The Director had let Hussaini say his piece, and then reaffirmed the answer: no. The Director had given Steyer his word that if Ben and Jerry would voluntarily stand down, he would direct his strike team to wait patiently for a deal to be cut before he would risk any further impact to Choy or Finkelman. The entire operation was about rescuing Choy and Finkelman, not capturing Ben and Jerry, which the Director saw as two separate incidents even though Hussaini saw them as the same. Unwilling to put his career at risk and with complete respect for the chain of command, Hussaini had acquiesced as any loyal underling would. He found himself a nearby motel room to get a decent night's sleep, albeit a cheap one with scruffy white curtains almost translucent in nature.

When Hussaini had returned to the hospital site early that morning, he had not been sure what to expect. There had been no further dialogue with the Director since the order to freeze all action, so at this point Hussaini could only speculate what discussion might be going on between Ben and Jerry and En-visionInk. When Hussaini's phone rang, he had little reason to expect the voice of former Senator Henderson, since the two of them had no previous relationship, and the basic protocol of a former US Senator with ongoing ties to the Justice Department calling a field agent on assignment was essentially nonexistent. Hussaini knew that meant nothing to Henderson, who was pre-disposed to call anyone he wanted whenever he wanted, obvi-ously motivated by an inside bet on the two prize horses in this race. Hussaini could tell this was not business as usual when the Senator announced himself without excuse or qualification.

"Senator, I am not sure it is appropriate for you to be calling me," said Hussaini after Henderson bypassed pleasantries.

"Special Agent in Charge Hussaini, was there any part of my greeting that led you to believe I had a desire to know what you think is appropriate? From what I hear, you wanted to go in last night guns blazing, even after we got those two losers to give us more time. A few dozen stretchers is your idea of appropriate?"

"It would have been a pair, and it would be helpful if you let me do my job, Senator. I am sure you offered useful, impartial advice to the Director, whose instructions I continue to follow without question, but your insertion of yourself in this matter is not good for anyone. It's all about time. Time is everything. Now we're watching the clock instead of owning it."

"You're not a very good listener, are you, Hussaini?"

"I had a full array of clean shots lined up. All I needed was for that door to open or be opened. They changed their minds, I didn't. You changed the plan."

"I know, the element of surprise. Ben and Jerry think they extend the deadline and let down their guard, boom boom, out go the lights. You're the expert, acknowledged, but that's not what the EnvisionInk board wanted, and the links between the private and public sector are critical to the well-being of our nation. Let's get that behind us."

"Why are you calling me, Senator? I don't suspect you called to praise my expert working ability and apologize for having to intervene."

Hussaini was not just irritated by the limitless Washington practice of non-experts sticking their nose in work like his — he was becoming uncomfortable to the point of concern. Too often the orderly work of the bureau was compromised by politicians and lobbyists, by individuals with influence and non-objective agendas injecting opinions in potentially dangerous arenas that needed to be made less dangerous, not more so. Hussaini was a family man, his wife was an elementary school teacher and they had a son and a daughter in fourth and sixth grade. It was not unusual for a field agent to have a family, but Hussaini had sought internet intelligence work not just because of its vital importance and intellectual challenge, but because for the most part it was office work, a place where he constantly observed challenges to public safety but seldom to his own. Problem was, prior to being married, Hussaini proved himself an exceptional criminal negotiator, diffusing small but difficult situations time and again, so occasionally in high tech related matters his name would come up for higher profile assignments like this one, involving corporations with extensive networks and influence in the federal government. None of that bothered Hussaini as long as they let him do his job, because given his own street smarts he would never be much at risk. It was uncontrolled intervention that bothered him. With tinkering came uninformed decisions that were almost impossible to offset. Hussaini never wanted to be on the phone with someone like Henderson, whose tirelessly demanding norms could become destabilizing. Getting home was all that mattered to Hussaini. Henderson was not helping.

"You're not as independent as you are sure of yourself, Hussaini, so I feel a little better," continued Henderson. "I'm actually calling to make an introduction. Sylvia Normandy is the company's general counsel and corporate secretary. She's going to talk with you."

"Is it any more appropriate for me to take her call than yours?" replied Hussaini.

"You seem to think you have choices, Hussaini. If you want to keep moving up the ladder, you better give up that notion and come to terms with how decisions are made. No, she's not going to call you. By the time I hang up the phone she will probably be standing in front of you. She's there in Salinas. I'm calling as a courtesy so you understand what to do when she gets there and you don't waste any of her time."

"What are Counselor Normandy and I to discuss?" asked Hussaini.

"Candidly, I don't know. The conversation is privileged. She is there on behalf of her bosses, Choy and Finkelman. To be clear, the conversation she has with you will de facto not be privileged, but better meet her litmus test of confidentiality to determine whether you stay Agent in Charge there or not. Am I being clear?"

"Respectfully, Senator, if I'm ever subpoenaed on this, I will look to my own counsel for direction on disclosure. Please tell me why is it you who called to make the introduction on her behalf?"

"Guess I drew the short straw," answered Henderson. "This could be a game changer for you, Hussaini. Get it right."

Henderson ended the call. Hussaini clicked off his phone and looked around for Sylvia. Sure enough, an attractive women in her late forties wearing a grey business suit and fashionable heels was being led directly to his post by one of the more junior special agents assigned to the case. Henderson must have been on the phone with her not five minutes before, when she arrived on the hospital site and was allowed to bypass the barricade. Nothing was going to give Hussaini the opportunity to evade a conversation with Normandy. The timing of the power puppet masters was as good or better than his.

"Let me guess, Sylvia Normandy?" said Hussaini as she arrived at the post.

"Just got off with the Senator, did you?" replied Normandy as her escorting agent politely departed. "I asked him to bridge the formalities. I hope you understand."

"He said he didn't know what you were going to tell me," conveyed Hussaini. "I'm not sure I believe him. You must be in touch with Choy and Finkelman. What happens now?"

"As I'm sure the Senator told you, I've had a privileged conversation with Choy and Finkelman. The contents of that conversation have not been shared with any other member of the EnvisionInk board, at the direction of our co-CEOs. I'm here to tell you what they want to do, without judgment or comment. What they want to do involves your team, and you will have to take that up with the Director in deciding what you do next."

"And you drove here to talk to me in person rather than call so that there could be no possible recording of the contents of that conversation?"

"Something like that," answered Normandy. "Here's the deal, there now exists a Chinese Wall between what the company wants to do and will do, and what Choy and Finkelman as private citizens want to do and will do. You can have the Justice Department review this at your leisure. I would expect no less of the Director before you commit to action."

"What do the private citizens want to do?" asked Hussaini.

"They want to use their own money to buy their way out, and they want to use their own jet to fly their way out." Normandy was direct, matter of fact, without judgment or comment, just as she had promised.

"How does that work?" asked Hussaini. "We have a kidnapping and a murder. We can't just let them walk."

"Calvin Choy is prepared to take responsibility for the McFrank shooting incident," explained Normandy. "He asserts that his hand was on the gun in the back of the SUV and there was a struggle. He said it was an accident, but he believes he pulled the trigger."

"This is wrong," argued Hussaini.

"You can also take up that with the Director," said

Normandy. "What we'd like you to do is move all of them — Choy, Finkelman, Ben, Jerry, and a doctor of their choosing. Get them out of here first thing tomorrow morning. Escort them to Choy and Finkelman's plane, which will be on the tarmac at Moffett Field."

"Moffett is federal, tied in with NASA," said Hussaini. "How does a private jet get on a government field?"

"They rent space there, they're a good tenant," answered Normandy. "They have a hangar next to the Google guys, which really irks the Google guys because they thought they got something no one else could have, but all they did was set a precedent. Take them there."

"Then what?" posed Hussaini.

"As of this morning, I have transferred $200 million into a trust account in Shanghai. You offer them a lift to their new home."

"You're giving them exactly what they want, a hundred million more than what they asked for," growled Hussaini. "And you want me to chaperone the ride? It doesn't matter what I think, the Director will never authorize this. That's not bending the rules. That's no rules of any kind."

"I said 'offer,' that was the word I used, I selected it with precision," replied Normandy. "Listen carefully because it would be extraordinarily inappropriate for me to editorialize on the wishes of my clients, who have been quite clear in their offer to back Ben and Jerry in their new overseas venture and facilitate their transportation needs. Given a choice between taking action at a public hospital surrounded by reporters and moving this mess to Moffett Airfield, which is adjacent to a National Guard station and an Army Reserve post, it is my sense the Director may want to exercise some discretion. I believe you should let him make that call."

Hussaini was catching on. Normandy had conveyed exactly what her clients were willing to do, which was within their legal right as individuals. The company was off the hook, no one on the board even knew there was such an offer, but someone with legal authority still had to let that plane fly out of the country—or at least make it look like they intended to do so. Normandy had brought the FBI a gift by bringing them home court advantage, and in the same move she had done exactly as she was instructed. Hussaini could still end this the way it was meant to be ended, only under much safer and less visible circumstances. No, he was not going to make it home for the weekend, and he most certainly was going to need some more clean clothes, probably FedEx'd. He was also going to need to recruit an entirely different back up team. The good news was that would not be a problem at Moffett Field. Hussaini smiled for the first time since arriving in California. He and Normandy had an understanding. He had some selling to do with the Director. The trick would be to keep Senator Henderson out of it, and he could probably count on her for that. They both seemed to acknowledge this could be a turn for the good, and they were only mildly distracted by the heavy set man with stringy long hair driving an Infinity M who was being led into the parking lot by the Salinas police to yet another nondescript canvass overhang. They had never seen him before, and had no idea why he was being offered VIP handling, but unlike Normandy, he did not need an introduction.

$ $

It was twenty seconds before noon. Balthazer was sitting behind an expanded fold-up table, comfortably reclining in a natural fabric lawn chair, a molded inflatable cushion supporting his lower back. His laptop was open, his headphones and microphone were humming Bluetooth, and he had plenty of Wi-Fi on a dedicated channel. Ready to go live, Balthazer looked down to check his home page. Moments before airtime, the visitor ticker counted 221,558. Balthazer opened a thirty-two-ounce full-sugar soda from the nearby ice chest, took a half bottle gulp, mouse-clicked the mic icon, and the afternoon tirade known as his show commenced.

KIMO: Friends, we are back, together again on internet radio.

What a difference a day makes. Before we begin, a grateful shout out to the accommodating mums and kiddos and all the management staff at McDonald's of Stockton for their warmth and hospitality yesterday—it wouldn't have been the same show without you. But today, goodness, do I have something dandy. I am coming to you live from the plaza of Salinas Valley Memorial Medical Center, where in residence we note the presence of one Calvin Choy and one Stephen J. Finkelman, the captured co-CEOs of EnvisionInk Systems—whose stock is up an astonishing thirty percent already this week. If that's not exciting enough in the 'let's share' department, here's an add-on. My invited guests on the show today are the two soon-to-be notorious fanboys who have Choy and Finkelman in their possession. In a few moments you will come to know these fellows the same way I do, by the ascribed names Ben and Jerry. That's right, I have Ben and Jerry ready on the line with me. If you want to talk with them, all you have to do is log onto ThisIsRage.com. By the way, there's a bright yellow "forward to a friend" button on my website, now would be a great time to put it to the test. I paid my hosting bill in full this morning, so when we hit a half million listeners this hour, and we will, we won't crash the site or have the plug pulled. But enough of that, I am delaying the important conversation. Let's say hello to Ben and Jerry. Ben, Jerry, Welcome, *This Is Rage*!

BEN: Uh, thank you, Kimo. We appreciate being invited on the show today. This is internet radio, right?

KIMO: Just like I told you when I called this morning. You think you could get on the air any other way? You have broken a few laws.

BEN: Yes, we know that. We are really sorry. None of this has gone the way we intended. All Jerry and I wanted to do was start a company in Silicon Valley, so we could hire as many people as possible with the economy being so bad, you know. But things didn't go as we planned, so here we are.

KIMO: Let me get this straight for the more than 325,000

listeners you now have as your own dedicated audience. I'll re-cap our conversation from this morning, when you graciously agreed to come on my show. You kidnapped two of the most important rising star technology executives in the world, but you never meant to, it just kind of happened. You accidentally shot one in the leg, that would be Stephen J. Finkelman—and by the way, listening audience, that is breaking news—which is how you ended up at this hospital in Salinas, California, which was accurately reported by one of my callers on yesterday's show. Now you're surrounded by FBI agents, backed up by police from five area counties, and you think somehow this ends okay for you.

BEN: Not just for us, Kimo, for everyone. We always wanted it to be okay for everyone, and that's the way we hope it ends. I can't tell you much more, but I can tell you we are working on a deal. Choy and Finkelman are helping with that, and if all goes the way we think it will, we should have some more news for your listeners tomorrow.

KIMO: Well, that's something. That gives me at least one more day on the air to keep working up these numbers. Sooner or later we're bound to hit a million internet listeners. We're making history, you know? But let's go back to what you just said, Choy and Finkelman are helping you with your deal. How does that work?

JERRY: Hey, Kimo, this is Jerry. Can I talk?

KIMO: Jerry, if I understand it right, you're the brainy one, the chief technology officer of the partnership. I don't know, will Ben let you talk?

JERRY: Sure, of course. And thanks, you flatter me with that CTO title, not sure I've earned it yet. Here's the thing, and the reason we came on your show. We're really not bad guys. I think Calvin and Stephen know that. We've gotten to know them a little, and we have some stuff in common with them.

KIMO: I've heard of that, the captives identifying with the captors. Deeply disturbing, don't you think? So you came on my show, which I do appreciate, to let my listeners know you are not bad guys. Shall we find out what they think?

BEN: Sure, Kimo. What do we have to lose? Bring 'em on.

KIMO: Outstanding. Emma Sue Yu, from Rockport, Illinois, Welcome, *This Is Rage*. You're on with Ben and Jerry!

CALLER EMMA SUE YU: Ben, Jerry, I just want to say, on behalf of my Thursday night bowling league, which I barely can still afford, you guys rock. What you did takes guts. People like me, we appreciate that.

BEN: Thanks, Emma, you roll a two hundred for us tonight.

CALLER EMMA SUE YU: That's my base game. Tonight I try for something perfect.

KIMO: Emma, I want to get this straight. You are sending a virtual high five to two guys who have locked themselves behind a windowless door in a semirural hospital with two CEOs and a gun. Are we all on the same show?

CALLER EMMA SUE YU: Damn straight, Kimo. They got pissed off, they took the company's co-CEOs, now maybe a few other CEOs will think twice before they treat the rest of us like garbage. I wish it didn't have to come to this, but it does. You guys hang in there. You're teaching all of them a lesson.

KIMO: Thank you, Emma Sue Yu. That was some opening act. Let's see if she is alone in her opinion. Stan1234, from Billings, Montana, Welcome, *This Is Rage*.

CALLER STAN1234: Ben, Jerry, how you have kept yourselves from the pulling the trigger is beyond me. The restraint you have shown is remarkable. You're probably not going to get out of there alive, which is probably how it should be, but you will be remembered by folks like me, that I can promise you.

BEN: Well, I'm hoping we get out of here alive. Don't count us out yet. We think there's still a deal to be made.

CALLER STAN1234: No, really, there isn't. I work security part time, I'm pretty sure they got you. But the longer you hold out, the longer Kimo can get your message heard. These CEO types are bad news. I haven't worked forty hours in over three years. I had a great factory job with benefits, then my company merged with another one in Brazil and all the jobs went away, poof. Then the merger didn't work out so well, and the CEO got canned too. Only he retired with a net worth of $400 million to a beachfront compound in Rio. For what? Ruining my company, taking away my job? Like that Emma woman said, I wish I had your guts. I hope it doesn't hurt much when they shoot you. You really don't deserve to die in pain. Stay brave.

KIMO: There's an idealist if I ever I heard one. I don't know, Ben—Stan seemed to know his stuff. What do you say? I'm guessing you don't really want it all to end that way. Is there anything I can say to get you to throw it in right now?

BEN: I don't think that's our best move, Kimo. Like I said, we're working on something, and I think Choy and Finkelman are onboard.

KIMO: How about you let us talk to Mr. Choy and Mr. Finkelman? I'm sure there's nothing more my listeners would like to hear than the sound of their voices.

JERRY: Not what we talked about this morning, Kimo. Calvin and Stephen are safe. They're in the room next to us, but they aren't coming on the show.

BEN: Yeah, don't ask again or this call is over. We're not coming out and you're only talking to us.

KIMO: Fair enough, but you can't fault a host for asking. It's my job, you know, push that envelope, you should respect that. I just hate to see anyone get hurt, and if I can help as well as set an internet record, hey, call me a multitasker. Let's take another caller. Ms B Spears, San Fernando, California, Welcome, *This Is Rage*.

CALLER MS B SPEARS: You know what I think, Kimo? I think there's a reason these two guys haven't been popped. This thing is too smooth. It's too well planned.

KIMO: You think there's some offstage conspiracy keeping Ben and Jerry alive? Do share.

CALLER MS B SPEARS: Sorry, Ben and Jerry, but I think you're bought. I think you're both guns for hire. That doesn't mean you're not cool, but let's be real.

BEN: You don't know what you're talking about, Ms. Spears.

CALLER MS B SPEARS: No, really? You think it's normal you and your brother . . .

BEN: He's not my brother. He's my cousin.

CALLER MS B SPEARS: Cousin, brother, buddy, boyfriend, I don't really care. And like the others, if you really did kidnap a couple of asshole executives, good for you. But I think you were hired. And I think you were hired by the company.

KIMO: The company?

CALLER MS B SPEARS: Their own company, Kimo. EnvisionInk.

KIMO: Oooh, this really is a conspiracy theory. Tell us more, Ms B Spears.

CALLER MS B SPEARS: Hey, I'm no genius. I'm actually a professional attendant, a corporate date. I'm not a hooker, I don't do that, but I get hired as an escort for a lot of these CEO types when they're in town, for trade shows, dinners, when their wives won't come to an event or they're separated. I go along and listen. The shit I hear, it's mind boggling. These kinds of guys will do anything, I mean anything, to close a deal.

KIMO: I'm not trying to rush you, ma'am, but we do have over six hundred thousand people on the Internet awaiting your point, as well as the details of your biography.

CALLER MS B SPEARS: My point is this, read the press release. That Atom Heart deal stinks all the way from the Hollywood sign to the San Mateo Bridge, a pile up of bodies to push profits. They can smell the rancid fish heads in Zuccotti Park on their way to Wall Street. I'm guessing some power players really want this deal to happen, and those two CEOs you got there aren't the guys, or you wouldn't have them. How does that work, the company just oops leaks an uku-billion dollar deal while their co-CEOs are being held at gunpoint? Am I the only one with a nose for stank?

KIMO: You make a good point, Ms. Spears. I wish you could have made it more quickly. What do you say, fellows? Our caller thinks perhaps you were hired to get the real CEOs out of the way, because they would have blocked the Atom Heart deal. I'm not saying there's a rational basis for her argument, but we left rationale behind about a week ago. Are you on someone's payroll, maybe Steyer's?

BEN: That's absurd. That's just utterly absurd.

JERRY: We didn't know anything about Atom Heart when we took Choy and Finkelman. We didn't even want to take Choy and Finkelman.

CALLER MS B SPEARS: Uh-huh, sure. You pulled all this off on your own: the kidnapping, the hospital, the fact that your hearts are still beating. I don't buy it. Nice head fake, bonking Steyer on the noggin, but the act needs some work.

BEN: There's no way we are working for Steyer, lady. Or anyone. This is our situation, and we're going to get out of it.

CALLER MS B SPEARS: Like I said, any of these pompous assholes you get off the street is fine with me. I can always go back to reading tarot cards for lottery addicts, it's not much of a pay cut. Choy and Finkelman are weak, they tried so hard to be nice, they led their lambs to the slaughter. You managed to get them out of the limelight for a quick interlude and they lost control of their company. What kind of leadership is that?

JERRY: That's not what happened.

CALLER MS B SPEARS: Okay, then you stepped in front of a rolling freight train with a pistol and accidentally stopped it. It was all Choy and Finkelman's idea, they planned all along to flip the company they created, but didn't want to take the heat so they had themselves kidnapped. No, they didn't, they're pawns, same as you. And it's the employees who always get hosed. The Investor guys are scary, but nothing kills off employees faster than Operators who can't make the hard calls. The bull market eats them alive, the bear starves them. Either way, they lose, the employees get creamed.

BEN: That's quite a bit of insight from a professional dinner companion. You must listen closely to the conversation around you.

CALLER MS B SPEARS: I make my real money in stock tips. Some people call it insider trading. I call it justice. Maybe someday they'll arrest me. But here's the good news, as long as you hang onto Choy and Finkelman, no merger or acquisition is going to happen. They may have needed Choy and Finkelman gone to make the deal, but they'll need them back to vote their shares if they want to close. And if they wait too long and the EnvisionInk stock price goes high enough, Atom Heart will back away. As far as I can tell, the employees at EnvisionInk are like the callers on this show, we're all rooting for Ben and Jerry, they're the real heroes. They took out a pair of overpaid, arrogant executives, and as long as they hang onto them, they're the only thing standing between the employees and their jobs. I'd say Ben and Jerry did a hell of a job. Screw Choy and Finkelman.

BEN: Damn it, Kimo, you need to keep your listeners under control or we're going to cut this short.

KIMO: This is the Internet, fellows. I can't control the Internet, it legislates itself. Welcome to the twenty-first century, where chaos is regulation. Anyway, she's gone, said what she had to say and off to dinner she went for more tips. I wouldn't worry about it. These listeners love you. You make disruption fun—and we've got the rest of the afternoon for them to tell you. Stick around, we're all going to make a good bit more digital history.

This Is Rage was once again firing up the crowd, costing businesses across the nation untold sums in productivity, magnet of choice for bored and angry cubicle inhabitants. Balthazer's callers were not letting him down. This show was indeed going to be his ticket back. The afternoon was young, Balthazer was just getting started with his exclusive guests, and by the end of the show he would undoubtedly surpass a million listeners, a feat worthy of front page coverage in the industry rag *Talkers*. Where his callers would lead him was anyone's guess, but the biggest challenge he would face that day was clearing his head of the conspiracy notion raised by that escort lady. She seemed to be snapping the pieces into place a little cleaner than he was, and the idea that Steyer did not seem to be trying all that hard to rescue Choy and Finkelman was hard to resist, personally or professionally. If Steyer wanted Choy and Finkelman free, there had to be better ways to do it than feed him Ben and Jerry's phone number. Maybe she was wrong, maybe Steyer did not need them back to close, he was the big money. Maybe he was just working the meltdown of confusion and uncertainty, running up the price and running down the clock. Steyer seemed to be behind everything, and at some point Balthazer was going to want to get to know him a lot better. He might even make a decent guest on the show.

$ $ $ $

<u>1.9</u>
Show Me Your Bulls

Of the more than one million internet listeners tuning into the *This Is Rage* live remote from Salinas Valley Memorial Medical Center, several thousand IP addresses pointed directly to a sprawling business campus in Santa Clara, global headquarters of EnvisionInk Systems. It was too hard for employees of the great tech giant not to watch the bodies being pummeled and drowned in the pond scum by civilian workers across the nation who knew nothing about virtuoso software engineering, nothing about the launch vision of their co-CEOs, nothing about genuine Silicon Valley culture.

Any observer of business norms would almost have to expect a defensive posture from EnvisionInk's tens of thousands of generously paid programmers, network architects, database administrators, sales and marketing types, even administrative and support staff, the majority of whom had benefitted immensely in gains attributed to their stock options from the magnificent growth of the mother ship, the genesis of which would never have occurred without the leadership of Calvin Choy and Stephen J. Finkelman. If Choy and Finkelman were being trashed for the sake of lowbrow entertainment, then the company was being trashed, and by implication they were being trashed. Loyalty would have to rule the day. How could it be otherwise in a place where so much democratic wealth had been created legally for so many lucky participants, for the sole effort of proving themselves intellectually worthy of an EnvisionInk logo on their business card and a colorful lanyard dangling a combination front door security pass / electronic garage parking permit.

Yet that was not how it was going down. Something eerily more powerful had gripped the grey cubicles and cryptically named conference rooms of the Santa Clara office park. For anyone who ever worked in Silicon Valley for any time at all, there were two clear speeds for the rapid capacity engine: high octane creative energy powered by optimism, or apathetic gossip powered by stalled growth. Accompanying these two notches on the gear shift were the two most powerful extremes of morale: twenty-four hour days of nose down work fueled by peer pressure, or lazy complaining about virtually everything fueled by negativity. When the aroma of fear in the hallways became inescapable, any impulse to alter the mood was impossible to come by. Long before layoffs would hit, people knew they were coming. Fear depressed productivity, fear destroyed innovation, fear fed the rumor mill. The one thing all high fliers had in common was the power of the rumor mill, and at EnvisionInk, it was already pumping out warnings even before the webcast. After the webcast, the rumor mill got a colossal dose of Red Bull and pure oxygen that made just about anything anyone said remarkably truthful. Just as it seldom took facts to fire up people and motivate a mission statement, facts were not required to burn a mission statement to fumes. Virtual bonfires were in the making, and leadership was locked in a Salinas hospital room. The secret recipe for malaise salad had been released from the well-traveled commissary.

What was curious about the mass lashing out of employees was the timing and circumstances. Usually the rumor mill announcing layoffs followed a steep drop in a company's share price, and some carefully worded public statement from management that the company's performance had been acknowledged in the boardroom as unacceptable, suggesting matters were being taken seriously. That meant cost cutting was coming, so if employees were not already dismayed by the their stock options dropping under water—a condition where the strike price was above market price, making them for the moment, or perhaps eternally, worthless—they would soon be more fully walloped by the ready tactic of management to reverse that situation, which involved dumping employees by the boatload.

In fact EnvisionInk stock, having been almost mystically flat for well over a year, had only dipped for a day after the abduction of its co-CEOs, then ran straight up almost 40% over the past week, taking it to a new all-time high. That put the company's market cap at over $50 billion, reflecting the metrics of a big growth tech play, trading at over eight times sales and more than thirty-three times net income, now a painful reach for Seidelmeyer. Atom Heart would barely constitute a majority at that deal size, requiring Seidelmeyer to take on significantly more leverage than he ever intended if he wanted to stay at the table, certainly not what he had in mind when he approached Steyer. It also meant almost every EnvisionInk employee was in the money, with paper gains ready to become liquidity just as soon as vesting — enough time spent on the job — allowed them to sell their shares on the open market and take the cash home in barrels, large and medium. Low morale and fear of layoffs seldom followed run-ups in valuation, unless a merger was in the works that anticipated major cost cuts by both the target company and the acquirer to improve earnings, and that rumor was now everywhere. Unvested stock options, regardless of their spreads, were worthless, and vesting required continuity of employment. Start-ups used stock options as golden handcuffs to bolster the achievements of talent on controlled timetables, but releasing the value of this currency was seldom in one's own control. Companies called it sharing the risk; employees called it a crap shoot.

Likewise in the same way the public perception of Choy and Finkelman had been carefully orchestrated through crafting of their image and general likeability to make them poster boys for day traders on retail desks and discount brokerage sites, callers on *This Is Rage* were now equating them with every other scumbag executive known to the headlines. Perhaps it was a self-selecting set of callers sharing their passionate views with Kimo Balthazer, but at a million and counting it was hard to consider them inconsequential. *This Is Rage* had always been successful because it reflected undercurrents in popular opinion among ordinary folks, and that was with a syndicated national broadcast audience. If a million people had found Kimo Balthazer on the Internet just a few days after he took an interest in Choy and Finkelman, the potential extrapolation to the number of public voices they represented could be immeasurable. That the online naysayers were being validated by hoards of EnvisionInk employees made no sense at all. Choy and Finkelman were their co-CEOs, the reason they had jobs, yet employees were joining in the thrashing, not refuting it. Beyond the inability to stay focused on doing the work for which they were being paid, they were not just listening to the rumble, they were part of it. Emails across the company were sent openly from employee to employee offering sympathy for the callers on *This Is Rage*, not for Choy and Finkelman. Ben and Jerry, identified wholeheartedly as criminals, were more often described as frustrated and emerging entrepreneurs, foils to Choy and Finkelman more than foes. Nothing could be stranger, employee tensions were rising faster than the stock price, and employee anger was increasing in lock step with Balthazer's audience. The rumor mill had been set free, ennui was the order of the day, workflow had come to a near stop, and there was hardly a word of expressed worry for the kidnapped executives.

Attempting to digest this with a lukewarm Starbucks d'jour in hand, Steyer was sitting in the tidy office of his fellow board member, Professor George Yamanaka, at Stanford's Graduate School of Business. The two of them were combing through long lists of employee emails that Steyer had asked the IT department at EnvisionInk to pull off the servers for board review in light of security. The fact that there was as much deep-rooted dissatisfaction in the IT department as in the rest of the company only added more wood to the fire pit—the rumor mill was basted and cooking. Employees never took their non-disclosure promises seriously when they felt their jobs were at risk. Now the board was reading their emails in reaction to the Balthazer show, with their real names attached in clear type. Not only didn't the emails stop, employees wrote more emails about the

rumor that their emails were being read, which pissed off everyone even more.

"Explain this to me, George," said Steyer, scanning an employee email on a tablet while deftly balancing his coffee cup.
"Here's what one of the senior engineers on the Advanced Solutions team wrote:"

> I guess we should feel sorry for Choy and
> Finkelman, but I don't. They used to be like us,
> but now they rake in the cash and take all the
> credit. How is that good for the rest of us who
> are trying to do something new? Management
> says they want us to do something new, but
> every time we propose a new idea, they say, no,
> that's not the company's core mission. So we
> keep doing the same thing, because they know
> it works, but of course we're not growing. We
> already corned the ad optimization market and
> decimated the competition. I'm not saying I
> want any harm to come to the bosses, but may-
> be we have to get them out of here to unblock
> the funnel and get this company moving again.

Steyer tapped the tablet to close the window and looked at
Yamanaka in disbelief, then continued. "I don't know, George.
This borders on insubordination, don't you think? Should I can
the guy?"

"Are you planning to fire everyone who wrote an email of
a similar nature?" asked Yamanaka. "Or the roughly 4500 employees who logged onto Balthazer's webcast from their desks?
If you want to fire a few thousand employees immediately for
cause, you better get some temp help in human resources."

"I guess you are saying no," followed Steyer, scrolling the
tablet with his index finger and tapping it heatedly. "Here's another gem:"

> So the stock is up but we're going to have
> a layoff, because no one has any good ideas

how to make more money here. The only way
to make more money is to get rid of us, since
we're all worthless anyway. And they wonder
why we aren't upset that Choy and Finkelman are gone? Why would we be upset? This
is how they run the company. And since our
stock options are finally valuable, why not fire
us before we can cash them in? They just get
rid of us and then cash them in for themselves,
makes perfect sense.

Steyer kept shaking his head, unable to internalize a logical
response. "George, how do they come up with this drivel?"

"Are you asking me as an observer of the enterprise or as a
board member?" replied Yamanaka.

"It was largely a rhetorical question, George. They invent
this stuff in their minds. All they think about is themselves.
For the love of god, Choy and Finkelman are being held at gun
point. Don't our payroll recipients have the basic human decency to care?"

"Is that rhetorical, too?" answered Yamanaka, a bit snider
this time. "I am sure a few of them do, the ones who know them,
the ones who remember when we were smaller. To most of these
employees, Choy and Finkelman are no more accessible than
they are to the people calling Balthazer's show. That happens
after companies go public, you know that. They become more
icons than individuals. And rich icons, with their own jumbo
jet, so when fear sets in, they become easy targets. That was
the same way Ben and Jerry saw them, right after they saw the
same in you."

"Where are they getting the layoff stuff?" asked Steyer.
"They have no basis for that. It's conjecture and it's not healthy.
It's not good for anyone."

"Are you suggesting the company would not be considering
layoffs?" asked Yamanaka. "Our employees may not be as smart
as you or able to remember the discount rate of every deal that
ever happened in small cap history, but most of them have been

through more than one start-up. They know the game."

"But we've never had a layoff at this company, and our share price is up," said Steyer. "They have no reason to be feeding on each other's anxiety."

"Perhaps, until we leaked the Atom Heart deal," said Yamanaka. "As I said, their eyes are open. Why else would our share price be up when our co-CEOs might be dead at any moment?"

"So they think the only reason we leaked Atom Heart was to deflect from the bad news around Choy and Finkelman, to hold the share price," said Steyer. "The truth is we had no choice. If we hadn't confirmed the rumor, Seidelmeyer would have used it on the inside to work our price down, manipulating what happened to Choy and Finkelman to create a scare."

"We did the only sensible thing given the chain of events," said Yamanaka. "The problem is, anyone can read what the analysts are writing, and they like the deal even more than we thought they would. They see efficiencies Choy and Finkelman could never imagine."

"But Seidelmeyer could. They're giving him a lot of credit."

"They have to if the price keeps rising and he still wants the keys," said Yamanaka. "With our current run up, the expected earnings improvement of the combination is now fully baked into our share price. The revenue is additive, but the expected synergies are all on the cost side, not in revenue growth. To hold the inflated share price post transaction, management would have to cut a quarter of the combined staff, and that only gets the NewCo to a P/E of around twenty. That would make it a mature company, practically a value play with $2 billion in savings and about thirty-five percent improvement in earnings. To sell the upside and finance the debt, Seidelmeyer either has to have a new growth story or be willing to cut deeper."

"You can't sell this deal on fundamentals, it's not that kind of deal," said Steyer.

"We've had two market meltdowns in the last ten years, there has to be more to this than ego," conveyed Yamanaka. "I know Seidelmeyer's unparalleled as a storyteller, but until he's honed the growth pitch, all the Street sees are enormous cost reductions. Imagine what the employees at Atom Heart must be writing in their emails."

"You think our employees have it all figured out?" asked Steyer. "They can see with Atom Heart's content and our technology platform that we can unlock a lot of sidelined value without more investment. We can all get along with a lot less R&D, and that's how we justify the improved share price. What if the deal falls apart?"

"You're asking me, O Master of The Valley?" exclaimed Yamanaka. "At this point, you know, and I know, and the Street knows—the deal can't fall apart."

"If it does, we're going to crash big time. Then they'll get their wish, only the layoffs will be worse."

"The only layoff that matters is the one that comes in an envelope to the person who opens it. Right now, a lot of them are coming either way. You want to make the Street happy they bid up the deal, there will be layoffs. You want to tell them there's no deal and our price is due for a correction, there will be layoffs. You can't make everyone happy. I suggest you let it roll off your back and move onto more important things."

"The strategy we tried from Seidelmeyer didn't help. The crowd was against Choy and Finkelman, not for them. That didn't get us anywhere with their release."

"You think Seidelmeyer is going to say something that helps you before he buys us and enshrines himself?" asked Yamanaka. "Your biggest problem now is to get the Atom Heart deal done while the share price is still high enough not to resist, but not so high Atom Heart walks. Whatever common wisdom is out there, you have to close before Choy and Finkelman come back to kill it—we don't need their vote if we have the board, the institutionals will vote with SugarSpring and Throckmore's people. That's the trick you have to pull off, it's all about timing. It's why you are who you are. The impossible has to happen for the real money to flow."

"There's no way we can do this deal with Choy and Finkel-man off the job. The board has no executive authority. We're an instrument of governance. They're on TV with a death threat looming over them and we're supposed to do a merger?"

"I never knew you to be so concerned about conflicts," said Yamanaka. "You know what's right, appearances shouldn't be a factor. An Atom Heart deal will prove visionary. No one cares that Seidelmeyer is your wine buddy."

"He isn't my wine buddy," snapped Steyer. "We know each other through business and shared interests."

"You're the one who kept the hotline open when Choy and Finkelman said no to the proposal," returned Yamanaka. "That's not what I would call governance. It's what I would call the right thing to do. Those two young fellows are still naïve. I know, I saw their genius in the classroom, but they need you to get this done. Down the road they will appreciate you for it."

"No way, the SEC will have our ass," countered Steyer. "Be-sides, you know that no deal this size gets done that quickly, not definitively. We have to hope Sylvia is successful working di-rectly with Choy and Finkelman and the FBI, then hope we can sell them on the concept when they get back, before Seidelmey-er holds us hostage and low balls us publicly."

"You're dreaming," said Yamanaka. "In my humble opin-ion, we have one move left. Getting a deal done can be a matter of perception. You must reach agreement in principle with Se-idelmeyer and have the deal announced before Choy and Fin-kelman get back. Then once it's public you'll convince them the only way not to have their beloved company crushed by an SEC investigation is to affirm the board's position that they bravely authorized it while they were in captivity. If you don't pull that off, our share price is going to tumble, and it's likely to take down the whole market with it. It's in your hands, not theirs."

"These are your students we're talking about," exclaimed Steyer. "You're telling me our only move is to play them, to leave them with Ben and Jerry and hope no one pulls the trigger?"

"The greatest good, which is value creation, will be realized in this outcome," said Yamanaka. "No one is going to pull the trigger. The shootings are over. This is how we all get out and continue to lead the bull market. It's the only way. And it's right."

"You sound like Seidelmeyer," said Steyer. "And you're conflicted. You can't be objective. You have liquidity risk."

"A good deal less than you," replied Yamanaka. "Certainly we have a vested interest. We are aligned with all constituencies, as we should be. We authorize the merger, we protect our shareholders, we protect our board, and we protect the company in case something does happen to Choy and Finkelman—which it won't because they are smart, they will get themselves out. That just can't happen sooner than we want them back. Have you run any of this by your wife?"

"Riley is still in shock over what happened at the house. She never expected guerilla warfare anywhere near our zip code, let alone in our backyard. We hardly ever fight, but now she can't understand why I have to stay on this, why I can't take some time off and let the FBI do its job. She still doesn't understand I can't make business stop."

"Maybe after this deal she'll get what she wants," suggested Yamanaka. "She doesn't need to understand if this one goes in the record books. We get this deal done the way it should happen, you put it all behind you. You put everything behind you."

"Not if the next ten years are in depositions," said Steyer, segueing from the sticky personal turf and kicking back into gear. "Look, there's only one way this happens and we don't do time. Seidelmeyer has to force the deal. He has to put a gun to our head. The public may be against Choy and Finkelman now because they look self-absorbed and weak, but they won't like Seidelmeyer any better. He can force the close by making the deal so far above market it's too good to refuse. That we can sell to Choy and Finkelman, that we had no choice, Seidelmeyer demanded a deal and if we didn't agree, we would all implode in the aftermath."

"His board won't let him overpay by a nonsensical amount, just to get the deal."

"He won't, it just has to look that way," said Steyer. "He has to draw a line in the sky that looks stupid generous and hope that market greed doesn't rocket us above the pull of gravity. He has to sell it, it's all in the positioning. For good faith he has to leave Choy and Finkelman as co-CEOs, he becomes executive chairman and they're all free of me. We just have to hope they don't get released before all that gets done."

"You have that correct," said Yamanaka. "If Choy and Finkelman return before we close and they kill the deal, we crash. No more bulls, the whole thing comes down."

Yamanaka reached for his briefcase, he was late for a class on corporate strategy and alignment. He looked to Steyer for concurrence, but also for reassurance. Steyer grabbed his tablet from Yamanaka's desk and scrolled through another list of employee emails, then another. The EnvisionInk employees did not seem to like their jobs or their company much anymore. Perhaps they preferred something else to complain about. Soon enough, they would have their pick of any number of annoyances, including outplacement services.

$ $

Balthazer was aglow. Yesterday's show had reminded him that he was really good at what he did, something he had forgotten of late, even the last few years on the air where, if truth be told, he knew in his heart he was dialing it in. Sure, he could always get a rise out of people, especially wage earners who were already prone to irritation, that was no harder than having a dog love you because you fed it meat. It had been a long time since Balthazer thought he was worthy of respect, that his show was something other than a repetitive way to spend a few hours each day getting paid to make station owners wealthier, or in the case of internet radio, simply practicing his craft and remaining relevant. The show yesterday did something he had not experienced in some time—it produced unexpected results. He had thought listeners would admire Choy and Finkelman for their track record, but instead they admired Ben and Jerry for standing up to the Entrenched. That might not have been fair,

it probably was not moral, but it was honest and very good radio. It also told him something quite clearly—this anger thread
he had been pulling at oh so gently for oh so many years was
longer and thicker than he anticipated, and tied to something
at its end that if pulled hard enough might surface emotion he
could not predict. It was not a thread but a heavy rope, and the
contest of tug-of-war could result in an unprecedented prize of
staggering change. This was the heart of the new social media,
the real voice of the unedited, and it was a rope that needed to
be unraveled. No one alive was more willing or better motivated
to unravel that rope than Kimo Balthazer.

As pleased as he was with himself prancing around the plaza
of the hospital complex, preparing for another show in just a few
hours, the change in mood from yesterday among the support
staff around him was striking. There was no beach chair for him
today, no back pillow and no ice chest. Where yesterday he had
been escorted to his field position, today he had to remind everyone he was an invited guest. He was not as yet specifically
being blocked, it was more like he was being ignored. No one
would talk with him, and the broadband channel he had logged
onto yesterday was now a dead signal. Balthazer asked around
for some assistance to reestablish his Wi-Fi connection, but no
help was to be found. It did not take long for him to figure out
that the authorities present were not nearly as pleased with his
show as he was. The hope from Steyer's point of view had been
that the show would have put pressure on Ben and Jerry to give
up their folly, but Balthazer's listeners had instead emboldened
them and trash talked the great Choy and Finkelman as if they
were the criminals. As he meandered about, trying desperately
to break the state of being disregarded, a familiar voice caught
his attention, breaking the silence with a happy surprise.

"Yo, Bat Out Of Hell, that was one hell of a show!" It was
the voice of his old producer, Lee Creighton, whom he had not
seen in over a month, but who had tipped him off about a week
ago before the Choy and Finkelman finding that he needed to
get out of his apartment.

"Producer Lee Creighton, who let you on site? This is a crime scene. What is this, professional courtesy, because you work for those broadcast criminals in LA?"

"Not anymore," replied Creighton. "It didn't work out. I called in a favor and stashed myself in one of the local news trucks with a borrowed credential, probably all the political capital I have left. Besides, I'm too old for the overnight. You appear to have survived nicely."

"Internet radio is a step down from the overnight, my friend. I hope you don't think I can hire you back. I'm not in a position to pay a salary."

"Maybe I am," said Creighton. "Like I said, I checked out your show yesterday. You turned audience reaction to this fiasco into a completely different story. All the stations dumped the filtered version and picked up your lead."

"Weird breakthrough, huh?" responded Balthazer. "*This Is Rage* putting up numbers on internet radio. No studio, no tower, just a laptop. Who'd have called that?"

"The only thing missing was a producer," said Creighton. "Minor critique, but you let too many whiners on the air, too downbeat for my taste. Psychos make the show, but only in moderation. Maybe I can help."

"I'm a one man army now," said Balthazer. "How are you going to pay your way? We don't sell ads in Salinas."

"Don't get me wrong, your show was damn good, the callers just need a little fine tuning. Without a wrangler the hogs can ramble. I took the liberty of making a few calls on your behalf. I hope you don't mind. An hour later after sending a few old timers your link, I got a deal memo from satellite radio. They want to uplink the feed. It's not a lot of money, but it will help at meal time . . . and with child support."

"The reunion didn't work out so well either?" inquired Balthazer. "I could have guessed. So you're telling me you cut a deal to syndicate the show from the Internet to satellite? It's supposed to go the other way."

"Until you, the Internet content was crap. You're changing

the paradigm, Kimo. I also have interest from the station groups. Give me a little time, we can get you back on the air at the same reach you had before. No production investment required, you've proven that. All you need is that laptop. They'll pay for the pick-up. Work for you?"

"It's the only offer I've heard since being fired," chuckled Balthazer. "How could I say no? Problem is, no one here is being very helpful today, just when a paycheck is back in draft form. It's like a time warp, yesterday never happened. The great minds in charge aren't too happy my listeners think the good guys are the bad guys."

"We have an important story to follow here, Kimo. This is not just about being back on the air and making a living again. It's about finding out why your listeners think the bad guys are good guys. We do that, we make the hall of fame."

"What about the FCC?" asked Balthazer. "They're also not real happy with me, for a few words that didn't get bleeped."

"Sure, they'll get you eventually, someone will pay the fine," noted Producer Lee Creighton. "But you're originating from the Internet now, where they have no jurisdiction. License not required, we're going to feed the unregulated back to the mainstream. We just have to be careful what we put through, which is why you need someone running the dials."

Balthazer felt sorry for Producer Lee Creighton. He knew his old friend was sincere in trying to make his marriage work and hold down a corporate job. He also knew that Creighton was like him, real radio was in his blood, and real radio was dead. He gave Creighton a lot of credit for putting this deal together, and knew that with his partnership and a national audience something big had to be on the horizon. Somewhere waited Pandora, wanting to let herself out of the box, all they had to do was find the box. With *This Is Rage* in full distribution again and a direct line to Ben and Jerry, it seemed they would have all they needed to get to the next level. There was the immediate issue on the horizon of how to get the show on the air today with no bandwidth, and the approaching even more immediate concern of Special Agent in Charge Hussaini, who as of yet had not given him the time of day, but now was approaching without any hint of endorsement.

"You're going to have to move along," announced Hussaini, a dab or two of sweat breaking through the Oxford cloth. "We are clearing the site of all media, and I'm not even sure you're that."

"My name is Kimo Balthazer," said Balthazer, extending his handshake and for the first time introducing himself to the agent, more to aggravate Hussaini than to extend any sense of formality. "And you would be . . . ?"

"Special Agent in Charge Kaamil Hussaini. You know who I am. Sorry, this isn't yesterday. You didn't exactly impress whoever arranged for you to be here. My instructions are to clear the site, primarily of you. You and your buddy need to leave. We've got the hospital doors opening in a few minutes and confidentiality has been mandated."

Balthazer and Producer Lee Creighton looked across the parking lot and noticed an approaching stretch limousine, the polished executive model that hauls celebrities to banal award shows and corporate egos from drunken banquets. Creighton was right, there was a breaking story here. There was not going to be a strike force attack or there would have been more FBI trucks instead of a limo. Balthazer knew he had to get more information before he left, but he had no idea how to get sweat pits Hussaini to share. Perhaps a trade might interest the overpriced crossing guard, a little gossip exchange. It had to be worth a try.

"Is Steyer changing his mind?" said Balthazer. "He hasn't exactly been Speed Racer bringing home Choy and Finkelman. I'm thinking he may not want them back. Got the idea from a listener. Pretty outrageous."

"Give me a reason and I will arrest you," parried Hussaini, no opening to give and take.

"I hear you, you've been clear," replied Balthazer. "Let me go get my laptop and we'll be on our way."

"You have 120 seconds to be off the grounds," said Hussaini.

"If those secure doors open and you are here, you will be in my custody and I am sure there are others who will find interest in that."

Hussaini directed a junior agent to accompany Balthazer and Producer Lee Creighton as they turned and went back to get Balthazer's laptop. Across the plaza activity was vibrant. True enough, all media were being removed. News trucks were being directed to the exits and satellite links were being pulled down. Hussaini was obviously good at his job, he was fully in control. Preparation was his style and had been complete. When the time came and he gave the order to clear the site, his orders were followed instantly and expertly. Ben and Jerry were at last about to emerge. Where the limo would take them with Choy and Finkelman was anyone's guess.

"We get a picture, we got a scoop," muttered Balthazer to Producer Lee Creighton, just out of the junior agent's hearing range."

"I'm on it," quietly replied Creighton. "Keep it in slow motion, need that door to open."

Balthazer stepped onto yesterday's observation platform, grabbed his laptop, fiddled with the shutdown mode and closed the lid as unhurriedly as he could, attempting to buy as much time as possible to see who was coming out of that hospital door. Appearing to be responsive but letting as many seconds as he could tick off the clock, he packed up his headphones and mic and all the cords, one peripheral at a time, gradually stuffing them into his computer bag.

"Limo, the new federal M.O. for unconditional surrender?" sniped Balthazer, trying to get any hint of the group's destination from the emotionless junior agent. "Or maybe they're taking an exercise break. Golf outing? Team building at a spa?"

The junior agent was not amused and instructed Balthazer that he was at the high end of his 120 seconds, that if the Infiniti was not out of park and following his government plates down the driveway toward the main road at clock expiration, he had been given the authority by Hussaini to make the arrest.

Balthazer knew this was no bluff. He climbed into the Infiniti and was joined in the passenger seat by Producer Lee Creighton, whose eyes remained fixed on the hospital door, about fifty yards away. All the media had been cleared and Balthazer was at the end of the exit parade.

Perhaps Hussaini was distracted, perhaps he was overconfident in executing his plan, or perhaps he was working on someone else's timeline in the nature of a government agent following the orders he was given, but just as Balthazer's Infiniti was leaving the parking lot, the hospital door opened. Hussaini must have given the order, thought Balthazer, noting that Producer Lee Creighton's sightline from the passenger seat remained dutifully transfixed on the hospital door. Balthazer looked in the rear view mirror and got the tiniest glimpse of what had to be Calvin Choy walking out the door, followed by Stephen J. Finkelman in a rolling hospital bed, with what appeared to be a doctor on one side and a nurse on the other. He had seen the co-CEOs headshots online via the EnvisionInk corporate profile, and though they were at distance, he was sure it was them. Balthazer knew Creighton had the same glimpse, probably a little clearer, when Creighton nudged Balthazer to keep the car moving slowly, as slowly as possible without buying them a jail cell. Balthazer eyed Creighton, as Creighton watched Choy get in the limo, followed by Finkelman, the doctor, and the nurse. Still looking in the car mirror, Balthazer saw the perspiring Hussaini standing by the limo door, assisting Finkelman from the hospital bed, talking occasionally into his shoulder mic, eyes maintaining intense contact on the hospital entrance. With the Infiniti now building distance from the plaza, Balthazer at last caught a far off image of his two most important show guests ever, the shadow of what had to be Ben and Jerry. Balthazer came off the gas one more instant, giving Producer Lee Creighton the cue. In a single reaching move through the glass of the rear window, hand kept low and hidden from the junior agent in the car ahead, Producer Lee Creighton raised his smart phone and clicked one camera frame. The suppressed grin formed by

Creighton's lips told Balthazer all he needed to know. They would be tiny and in poor scale, but Creighton got them, Ben and Jerry in a digital image that could be enhanced. Together they laughed aloud. They had what no one else had, and that rendering belonged to *This Is Rage*.

Balthazer was still in good form with the junior agent leading the Infiniti when he looked back over his shoulder and saw Hussaini getting in the limo as well. That made it a party of seven: Choy, Finkelman, Ben, Jerry, Doctor, Nurse, and Special Agent in Charge. It was a party all right—all they had to do next was find out the future venue and keep wrenching the story from secrecy.

The junior agent escorted Balthazer and Creighton back to the motel, where Balthazer now intended to do today's show, especially since he had a producer for the first time in a long while. Unfortunately the junior agent proceeded to check out for them and gave Balthazer five minutes to pack and be on his way, with clear instructions not to be within one hundred miles of the area in the next two hours or his license plates would be picked up by the Highway Patrol. With only minutes to be on his way or enjoy an evening's cuisine in custody, Balthazer rapidly managed to upload an informative bit of copy to ThisIsRage.com:

> Bad News: No Show Today, Technical Difficulties, Will Explain Tomorrow
> Good News: Producer Lee Creighton is Back, I Forgive Him
> Bad News: Don't Know Where Ben & Jerry Have Taken Choy & Finkelman
> Good News: Tomorrow We're on Satellite, Soon Back on AM/FM
> Bad News: EnvisionInk Does Not Seem to Want Choy & Finkelman Back
> Good News: Here is a Picture of Ben & Jerry, Zoom & Spread Viral

Balthazer uploaded the snapshot via Bluetooth that

Creighton had taken while they were departing, bridging his friend's smart phone. Then he tagged the photo with a closing bit of text:

> Daniel Steyer: If You Would Like to Comment, Please Join Me as a Guest.

Balthazer saved and published the web page, saying nothing to the junior agent, instead grabbing the balance of his belongings and returning to his car. He waved goodbye to the junior agent, nodded success to Producer Lee Creighton, and together they headed south on Highway 101. The hundred-mile demand was no doubt a clue. Balthazer knew if he had to be outside that radius then the Hussaini escorted party necessarily had to be within that range. With a million followers and growing, a published photo of Ben and Jerry on his home page, and a hard dare of courage to the chairman of EnvisionInk, he knew it would not be long until he located Choy and Finkelman. How his wacky listeners would digest all this remained the wild card, but the social anarchy he knew he could arouse was much more than entertainment, it was media and technology history. Balthazer truly could not remember his job ever being this much fun. There was only one thing that would make it more fun: Steyer.

$ $ $ $

2.0
IN THE COMPANY OF KINGS AND GOATS

"Picture yourself on a hike with a group of friends and getting
lost. Some worrywart in the group will be the first one to ask
the leader, 'Are you sure you know where we're going? Aren't
we lost?' The leader will waive him away and march on. But
then the uneasiness over lack of trail markers or other familiar
signs will grow and at some point the leader will reluctantly
stop in his tracks, scratch his head and admit not too happily,
'Hey, guys, I think we *are* lost.' The business equivalent of that
moment is the strategic inflection point."
– Andrew S. Grove, *Only the Paranoid Survive* (1996)

"Power tends to corrupt, and absolute power corrupts absolutely. Great men are almost always bad men."
– Lord Acton , Circa 1887

2.1
Format Disk

NASDAQ: ENVN (Day 9)
SHARE PRICE @ MARKET OPEN: $189.05
COMPANY MARKET CAP: $50.4B
VALUATION DELTA SINCE ABDUCTION: +40%

NASDAQ SINCE ABDUCTION: +16%

Congresswoman Sally Payne was not an intellectual giant. By all measures of normal reason, a leadership role in national government was about as good a fit for her as tenured university physics professor or cardiac specialist. The difference was the latter occupations had professional requirements, core knowledge, and some form of recognized expertise. To be a fully privileged member of the US House of Representatives, all one had to do was get elected. Sally Payne liked that a lot. She really, really liked her job. She liked her formal offices, both the one in Washington and the one in her home state of Montana. She liked having a staff to attend to the minutia of her day. She liked the hometown attention for the luminary fashion she selected in her public appearances. She liked hearing her full name spoken clearly whenever she was introduced on the House floor. She liked the generous retirement benefits she would one day collect. She did not much like all the reading of bills in the works that required so much of her attention, but she did like coming up with pithy titles for proposed legislation like the "Let Children Live Act" or the "Teachers without Excuses Contract." She truly liked almost everything there was to like about the package that came with high profile elected office, even voting on legislation she barely understood, but most of all, she liked going on TV and saying things that made her more popular with her devoted followers.

As hard as it was to believe Representative Payne had been elected to Congress not as a fluke once, not a lucky twice, but in consistent and decisive victories across seven consecutive terms, it was even harder to believe that her seniority had landed her as Chair of the House Committee on Education and the Work-force, as well as a leading voice on the massively powerful Judi-ciary Committee. Payne certainly liked to talk about education in front of the cameras, despite constant criticism that the details of her own academic career were sketchy. Payne could not deny it had taken her six semesters of community college and another nine at the University of Montana to get her bachelor's degree in business administration, but she attributed this to the time need-ed to raise her family. Discrepancies in the calendar that did not precisely support this claim had been raised by more than one of her opponents, but for Payne's taste, that was just politics. Payne had never been shy about pointing out her senior thesis had argued that factory workers were historically overpaid, and if they wanted better wages they should have gone to college like she did. Her logic worked for her, which is all she believed it needed to do, providing a comfort zone of firm conviction and independence.

Upon graduation after almost eight years of on and off col-lege studies, the Honorable Ms. Payne was indeed a mom, and a reasonably good one. She had married a star athlete from high school who later became a small town dentist. She had twin daughters whom she home schooled through fifth grade, then enrolled in the local public junior high school, where she joined the PTA and was elected president three years in a row. When a seat opened on the school board, she ran for that and won hands down, approaching the election as a test for her allure on the de-bate podium, where she discovered notable hair style and purse selection were as critical success factors as any issue discussed in the cafeteria. That success led her to a city council election in Billings, which she also won, this time uncontested as her public

speaking skills developed strength not so much in logical argument, but in emotional impact around issues of family values.
She had never actually held a paid private sector job per se, but
she found herself a natural at making presentations, especially
on the touchy issues of tax abuse and government overreach —
or as like thinkers in the circles she traveled referred to such
topics, natural liberties. When the incumbent Congressman in
her district — a moderate Republican of six terms and former
assistant district attorney who had been slipping in the polls —
died of a heart attack at his desk and a special election was held,
she ran for that office on a platform of "Let Business Be Business" and won that as well. Her track record was charmed. She
never lost an election, over twenty years in motion now. It never really bothered Payne that her only measurable experience
was in building campaign visibility. She found it unnecessary to
distinguish the tasks of running for office and being a lawmak-
er — in her mind, if she won reelection, she had to be doing a fine
job. Attempting to separate camera ready campaigning from the
details of governance was bothersome, even unproductive. How
she allocated time in her day-planner was an easy choice — she
would always be running for office, and the day to day business
of being in office was largely left to her staff. This conscious
delegation of responsibility suited her well. With two year cycles
of grandstanding, the US House of Representatives was ideal
for her.

Aside from being on television as often as possible, Congresswoman Payne also relished the unending platform to tell
the people who made television what was wrong with it, and
how they as stewards of our culture were perpetually unwinding the fabric of our nation. She was not sure she even believed
this, but it got her invited on a lot of talk shows and for private meetings with studio executives. She really, really liked the
meetings with studio executives. She would receive great gifts,
fantastic inscribed souvenirs that were priceless in nature, but
safely within the legal limits of monetary value for acceptance.
She would encounter celebrities up close in the commissaries

and she could tell media bosses what she thought of their creativity. Nothing could be more fun. She even discovered that
she could make or break new shows in their premiering episodes
by getting the lobbies that supported her to subtlety comment in
just the right blogs on just the right topics at just the right moments. It was tremendously gratifying work. Power to influence
opinion and trade it for more visibility was pure joy.

Thus, when her staff had been contacted by the Atom Heart
Entertainment government relations people to arrange a personal meeting for her with Solomon Edward Seidelmeyer, she
was elated. There she sat, a middle class mom from Montana
donned in Versace silk, courtesy of an online flash sale, comfortably planted in Seidelmeyer's private screening room. Seidelmeyer and she were sitting together doing what so many
studio executives often shared with government friends. They
were watching garbage.

The reality show on deck was called *What's Yours is Mine*,
where divorcing spouses who had spent over six figures in legal
fees agreed to bypass the courts and make their case directly to
a studio audience to resolve in earnest who should get what in a
settlement. A rented judge would make it so. The contest would
become complicated when the designated plaintiff had to decide whether to go for the prize—the requested settlement—or
the lovely parting gifts where the production company agreed
to pay off existing legal fees. Depending on the couple and the
level of truth, no one knew for sure if the spoils of community
property were worth more than the legal fees accruing interest
on revolving credit, hence the hidden tension extended to the
end of each half hour when the judge's gavel came down and
the tallies appeared on the ticker screen. The show had run as a
midseason replacement and done acceptably in the ratings, but
pressure groups found the show to be anti-marriage and wanted
it gone. Payne suspected that Seidelmeyer had already decided
to kill it—even with decent ratings the ad categories for this one
were a tough sell—but he had not told her that directly, not yet.
She supposed he was going to let her save America and make

the call for him. He might need a favor from her and this was a clever way to make a cheap down payment.

"Pretty awful, don't you think?" acknowledged Seidelmeyer. "Poorly structured, despicable contestants, impossible to redeem and distinguish. Utterly miserable."

"I guess you have to kill projects like this all the time," commented Payne.

"Absolutely," replied Seidelmeyer. "Best part of my job—to insure excellence on the broadcast airways and in the theaters near you. But this one is so awful, it defies imagination. The only good thing you can say about it is we kept the unions out."

"Anything that keeps the unions in their place has my support," said Payne. "And their place is the dustbin of business history, wouldn't you agree?"

"Are we on or off the record?" chuckled Seidelmeyer. "I run a movie studio, too, and I need amicable relations with the guilds. Truth be told, I don't watch much television anymore. I just look at numbers and this one's on the fence. I was hoping you might help me push it one way or the other. You seem to have the pulse of the nation's conscience."

"I don't understand why you don't bring back shows like *Touched by an Angel*," suggested Payne. "Have you seen the numbers on how many people believe there are angels all around us? Those are some numbers. There has to be a Michael Landon for the new millennium waiting to be discovered."

"I played on a softball team with Michael Landon when we were on the way up," said Seidelmeyer. "I miss him terribly. If he were alive today, I might try a remake. But there's only one like him. Absent that, there's a reason Charlie Sheen always has a job. We need to believe there's someone more putrid than ourselves. Wish it were otherwise, believe me, these detox celebrities cost us more than you can imagine. Insurance premiums are from another galaxy."

"You've had a distinguished career, Mr. Seidelmeyer," continued Payne. "An amazing career, like no other of which I'm aware. You've built a legacy corporation, employed so many creative people, and you maintain clear thinking on critical concerns like collective bargaining. I wonder, where does an accomplished impresario like yourself go from here?"

"I've been wondering that myself lately," answered Seidelmeyer. "And please, there are no Misters on a studio lot. Just me, Sol. As for my third act, we both understand there are financial laws that preclude me from discussing unfinished business, but when the time comes, I am hopeful I can count on support from everyone in Congress who cherishes free enterprise."

"You'll get no pushback from me, Sol. If you support the campaigns of those who appreciate the stature of business interests, there is no reason to believe your faith is misplaced. More importantly, I am finding I can count on you to Think Family—that's my campaign slogan, you know. A few more family TV shows, motion pictures without drugs or excessive drinking, Broadway musicals that celebrate the generations, all that makes this a better nation. Think Family is profitable, too. We both understand numbers and we know how quickly they can move in either direction. As I suggested, angels are in vogue. I have polling to support that."

$ $

Seidelmeyer smiled politely, delighted the meeting was going in the right direction, even more delighted it would soon be over and he could get back to dealing with anything less slimy than politics. Agents and producers were practically wholesome compared to this creature. As Congresswoman Payne's gaze was briefly absorbed in the celebrity signed headshots and historic one sheets decorating the perimeter of the screening room, Seidelmeyer glanced at his iPhone and saw EnvisionInk's stock price still climbing steadily, while that of Atom Heart sat fixed in time like an Oscar statuette. It had been a long weekend without inside news. The last Seidelmeyer had heard was from his own broadcast news division that Choy, Finkelman, and their posse had been moved via limo from the hospital to an unknown location. There had been no further word from Steyer in forty-eight hours, so when Seidelmeyer's executive assistant, Ellen Ardor, quietly slipped into the screening room and handed him a small piece of folded paper he was equal parts anxious and relieved that it might be an update of any kind. Seidelmeyer graciously smiled at Payne, then opened the message to find the note:

You probably want to step out. He's on the Story Line.

The Story Line was their inside shorthand, a touch of office humor under tension as Seidelmeyer would always have it. Ardor, a rising star efficiency machine still under thirty with few enough tattoos to front the office of a studio head, had set up a dedicated cell connection between Steyer and Seidelmeyer. Although technically she was a borderline millennial, Ardor was old school at heart and knew what it meant to come up the ranks in entertainment, not much different today than when Seidelmeyer had started his climb, although she had the MBA he never did. Ardor knew the Story Line number could be given to no one, that this Android handset was meant solely for direct titan exchange in times of critical communication that was as off the record as possible. Seidelmeyer excused himself politely and stepped out of the screening room to the empty lobby area adjacent.

"Hope this is important, Steyer," said Seidelmeyer into the phone, quietly but with annoyance. "I'm with my friend, the congresswoman, a beautiful mind. We may need her support to get antitrust clearance, if we ever have a deal. Unfortunately, your price is out of my range now and getting worse."

"Yes, I know, it's a real problem," confided Steyer. "You're not hearing this from me, but you need to bring us back down to earth. Squeeze us a little."

"What does squeeze mean to you?" asked Seidelmeyer.

"It means if this deal does not get done before Choy and Finkelman are back on the job, there won't be a deal. You have to force our hand. Get us to move before we price to the Milky Way, no matter what happens with Choy and Finkelman."

"What's the story with them?" inquired Seidelmeyer. "I saw reports all weekend from our national desk that they left the hospital with the FBI and some medical support in a red carpet limo. You got this moving forward?"

"We don't want it moving forward right now, Sol. That's what I called to tell you. We have a small window to move, and you need to open the window."

"Where were they going in the stretch, in case the congress-woman is curious?"

"To be honest, I have no idea. The only person who knows other than the FBI is our general counsel, Sylvia Normandy, and she's bound by attorney-client privilege."

"You lost me," said Seidelmeyer. "You're the chairman of the board, the largest single shareholder in the company, and you're being frozen out by attorney-client privilege? How in geekland does that work? Who's running this company, Ben and Jerry?"

"Choy and Finkelman seem to be cutting their own deal. That's all I know. They had a privileged conversation with Nor-mandy. She visited with the FBI on site, then they started mov-ing. We have no idea what happens next, so you have to move. We need you to create urgency."

"Urgency, as in we have our eye on another seismic gulp?" exclaimed Seidelmeyer. "Something at a price with digits we can count, but that counts you out? That's a hell of a bluff, even for me."

"If you don't look like you're going to walk away, Sol, we can't make it a crisis vote. If we don't do that, you lose the deal."

"We both lose the deal, let's be clear on that," asserted Se-idelmeyer. "You need me in your chair as much as I want it or you are stuck holding paper instead of cash. Just so we under-stand each other."

"We understand. Can you pull it off?"

"I'm an executive, not an actor. I'll have to carve out time for drama class. Do I get my price?"

"Sol, that's the wrong kind of squeezing. You have to pay a fair premium. I can't control the market. We have to price with the Street or it's lawsuit hell."

"I'm calling bullshit, Steyer. You want me to take a big risk inventing a competitive deal that isn't there, some fantasy company I'm supposed to want to buy instead of yours, then I want my price. If I bring your stock down with a few unkind words, you can't work me back up when the timing is more palatable, when you control the clock. That's the deal. We hit the target, you say yes. Do we have an understanding?"

"We have an understanding," expressed Steyer with a heavy breath. "Just make sure you graduate from drama class. Win yourself an Oscar. This has to be convincing or we'll never get it past Choy and Finkelman when they come back, and that means we'll never get it past the SEC. Choy and Finkelman are going to be working for you, so trust matters. Everyone has to believe."

"I need to get back to the legislative branch," said Seidelmeyer. "She has a thing for Michael Landon. I need to find a substitute to keep her in charm school. By the way, how come you haven't mentioned the photo?"

"The Ben and Jerry image on Balthazer's website?" asked Steyer. "What does that matter at this point?"

"Just saw an expanded version on my iPhone, chart topper on Twitter," replied Seidelmeyer. "My newsroom says someone will certainly ID it before the end of the day."

"Then get some downward pressure on us," affirmed Steyer. "I have no idea how much time we have."

"Don't even think about leaving me naked on this," said Seidelmeyer. "I'm an old man, naked won't go down well, that I can promise you. Now if you'll excuse me, I need to kill a show, reincarnate Michael Landon to lay some pipe in Congress, then figure out how to make you look stupidly overpriced without sounding insulting. I do love my job. Not so sure yet about yours."

Steyer was already gone. Seidelmeyer clicked off the call, reentered the screening room, and handed the Story Line back to Ardor, who was laughing up a storm with Congresswoman Payne. To Seidelmeyer's surprise, he discovered that his assistant was an Idaho native who had taken summer courses in media arts at the University of Montana and was well aware of Sally Payne's long shadow there. Sally Payne obviously had broader constituent support than Seidelmeyer had imagined. Seidelmeyer marveled at how she played to her own strengths, working small openings with abundant charisma, wielding the family values agenda not as sword and shield, but as cane and hat. Her campaign was perpetual.

Seidelmeyer was sure that at some point the Honorable Ms. Payne would prove helpful. He was also certain she was thinking the same about him. Payne may not have been an obvious candidate for high government office, nor would she ever be a feared contender in a National History Bee, but she had mastered the political realm by learning to unwrap people's needs and maintaining awareness in whatever room she entered. He could not help but notice that her eye was also on his mobile, catching a glimpse of the ever rising shares of EnvisionInk, which he had set as a screensaver. ENVN was looking to close the day up another astounding 20%.

$ $

Balthazer had almost forgotten how liberating it was to have a producer. Between the downtime of his dismissal in Fresno and the launch of his internet radio show as a one man hack, Balthazer had been reminded he knew how to get by, but getting by was not nearly as fun as conspiring with a partner. What he had also almost forgotten was how creative a fellow Producer Lee Creighton could be, which is how they had arrived at a wine shed in Paso Robles for their first show together in a long time.

"It's a little dark in here, but I like the smell of oak," said Balthazer. "What possessed you to walk into a tasting room and randomly ask if there was room at the inn for a DJ?"

"Why wouldn't they?" answered Producer Lee Creighton. "You've got more reach than any sponsorship they could afford. All you have to do is mention the winery once an hour and not only can we work in air-conditioned splendor, we can knock back as many bottles of vino as we can crack open on the shift."

Producer Lee Creighton reached for an aged cabernet from the wall rack to make his point. In seconds, the cork was out and two full glasses were poured, the bottle completely drained. It was coming up on noon, their self-appointed air time, and Creighton had gotten an early start synchronizing their laptop output signal with the satellite relay. Balthazer knew he could count on Creighton to pull off the satellite deal, despite their lack of professional amenities. If anyone could make this first day patch work without a studio set-up, it was Producer Lee Creighton, master of innovative improv. They had arrived in town over the weekend, knocked on a few doors where wine tasting was open to the public, and the first time Balthazer was identified by a winemaker, Creighton struck decisively without prelude. Silver Crest Vineyards was hardly a mainstream brand, but Creighton had suggested a few kind words from the great and famous Kimo Balthazer could change all that. They were welcomed into the barrel room, where it was as noise proof as they could hope during the day, with AC power and a long in-door picnic table with plenty of room for their facing laptops, cables, peripherals, and a half case of empties—everything they needed to take *This Is Rage* and Silver Crest to the next level. Once the satellite feed was proven, terrestrial deals would follow without fail, delivering the income that would settle all their problems while letting them originate on the Internet without rules. It was low-tech perfect, a cheapo remote like no other, a restarting of their partnership and a powering of their noble vision to crush a gargantuan corporation because, hey, why not?

The only thing they did not yet have to make this show legendary was the actual location of Choy and Finkelman, which despite their best efforts, they were unable to surface from the million-listener network. Where they had succeeded was in bringing in endless leads attempting to identify the image they had posted of Ben and Jerry, ranging from the outrageously nutty (more abandoned love children of celebrities from Schwarzenegger to Edwards) to the wholly unsubstantiated (proud hackers who had taken down every network from Sony to Citibank) to the absolute ludicrous (secret third-tier followers of the Manson clan formed in a civics study group at

Berkeley). Balthazer had wanted to open the show with the real names and backgrounds of the soon to be accused, but wading through the endless muck of anonymous submissions was daunting. There were plausible names, made-up names, ethnic names, ciphers—no lack of conjecture, but nothing substantiated. Producer Lee Creighton had stayed patient through the weekend, reminding Balthazer how powerful the Internet could be, how explosive this story really was, and how the combination of viral messaging and social networking would get the job done, if not on their timetable then sooner than any other source they could pursue. Balthazer was unsatisfied with the unpredictability, and was looking for another angle to follow when Creighton's attention was snagged by the video window on the landing page of YouTube.

"We've got some action," said Producer Lee Creighton. "Check out this video clip, breaking news upload. One of the TV networks just went live with it."

"Ben and Jerry?" asked Balthazer.

"Try Swerlow and Kisinski," declared Creighton. "To be precise, Dennis Swerlow and Sam Kisinski. Apparently they're from Oregon."

"How do you know it's legit?" asked Balthazer. "How can you be sure? Just because a TV anchor went with it doesn't make it real."

"The other TV networks just picked it up," said Producer Lee Creighton, pounding on his keyboard, window switching tabs as fast as his fingers could move. "They're all leading with Swerlow and Kisinski, every channel, every stream. Hulu has it aggregated."

"We have to be sure," reiterated Balthazer. "We introduced them to the world. We have the most at stake. We have to be undeniably sure."

"Now *Wall Street Journal* has it, *New York Times* has it, *USA Today* has it," itemized Creighton, scrolling from screen to screen, from link to link. "*LA Times, San Jose Mercury News, Washington Post, Deadline, Daily Beast, TMZ*, they all have it. It's moving like rocket exhaust. This is as positive an ID as we're going to get."

"Who ID'd them?" asked Balthazer.

"Their moms."

"Not possible, no way!" said Balthazer. "Quick, we have to get them on the line. We have to open the show with them. How do we get in touch, on the front burner?"

"Right there with you," chimed Producer Lee Creighton, flying across his keyboard like a master concert pianist. "We've got their last names: Swerlow and Kisinski. Got the state: Oregon. Got my $12.95 per month 100% legal public records stalker database account . . . Logging in . . . Typing in data . . . Retrieving search returns . . . Here we go, two phone numbers in the area code, one for Dennis's mommy and one for Sam's. Need to get lucky now, Kimo. You pick, I dial. Get those headphones on. I'm uplinking."

"Go with Sam's mom," chose Balthazer. "He's younger. She's probably more worried than the other woman. Dude, we've got one and half million followers today, all logged in and registered on ThisIsRage.com for our webcast. We're going to scoop every journalist in the nation."

"I've got Ms. Kisinski on the phone," relayed Creighton, sharp as ever. "Stand by while I give her the legal spiel, so we can take her live and have some prayer of not getting sued."

"This is too good to be happening," said Balthazer. "Our picture lands the ID of Ben and Jerry, their moms serve up the ID, and we get the moms."

"Just one mom now," said Creighton. "She's ready to go live. By the way, Swerlow and Kisinski are cousins. The other mom is her sister. She's trying to get her."

"How do you know that?" asked Balthazer.

"She just told me, Kimo," blurted Creighton, bringing up the heat on Balthazer's microphone and pushing the signal live. "She's texting her sister now with my contact info. Her name is Eleanor, Eleanor Kisinski. Go, you're on the air!"

KIMO: Welcome, my 1.5 million online devotees, and also

welcome to those of you joining us on satellite today. Welcome, welcome, welcome–*This Is Rage*! Well, it's Monday, it's noon, it's been over a week since the great Calvin Choy and Stephen J. Finkelman were kidnapped from a Silicon Valley cocktail party. For the past week, your host, that would be me, Kimo Balthazer, has been following this story carefully. If you'll recall, in our last scheduled episode, which I had to cancel, we lost track of the Choy and Finkelman party at Salinas Valley Memorial Medical Center, when they and their abductors, Ben and Jerry, were escorted from the hospital in a stretch limousine by the warm graces of your taxpayer funded Federal Bureau of Investigation. In our departing move from that location, we managed to capture and upload a distant photo of Ben and Jerry, in the hope that one of you listeners might identify them. Well, if you've been watching any news source in the last several minutes, you probably know that the real names of Ben and Jerry are Dennis Swerlow and Sam Kisinski. You also know that the two of them are cousins, and that they hail from the great state of Oregon. What you don't know is that my personal reunion last week with the best board runner in the business, Producer Lee Creighton, has resulted in us working today on our first internet radio remote from the barrel room at Silver Crest Vineyards in Paso Robles, California–you can order from them directly at SilverCrestVineyards.com. Producer Lee Creighton has blown my mind and served up an exclusive phone interview with none other than the mother of the younger of the two kidnappers. Eleanor Kisinski–Welcome, *This Is Rage*.

CALLER ELEANOR: Hi, this is Eleanor.

KIMO: Hello, Eleanor. I am guessing you are not a regular listener to this program. To remind you, my name is Kimo Balthazer.

CALLER ELEANOR: I know who you are. Your partner told me, plus we've been on your website, my sister and I. That's how we found the photo. Well, we didn't find it, it found us. So many people sent it to us and sure enough there, when we saw it, were

Dennis and Sam. I can't believe they did this. It is so not like them.

KIMO: Tell us about the boys, Eleanor. What do they do?

CALLER ELEANOR: Until this, they were programmers, but it seems they took that in a wrong direction. I don't know how it happened. Oh, my sister is here now, I texted her. This is Dennis's mom. Her name is Candace, Candace Swerlow.

KIMO: Candace Swerlow, Welcome to the show, This Is Rage.

CALLER CANDACE: Kimo, we are going to have to cut this short. We have no idea what's going on, and I'm pretty sure we shouldn't be on the radio with you.

KIMO: What makes you say that, Candace? It's just an internet radio show. There is quite a fascination out there for the gentlemen formerly known as Ben and Jerry. As I'm sure you know, I had them on my show last week and my audience was entirely supportive. That's a pretty rare set of circumstances, for sympathy to be with the kidnappers and not the kidnappees.

CALLER CANDACE: I don't know anything about kidnapping. All I know is that people started sending us this photo a few days ago, and when we blew it up, it was pretty clear who was in the picture. We talked about it, we told the police, and they promised us confidentiality. A half hour ago the whole thing is on national television, then my sister texts me, now we're on the Internet with you. The whole thing is not very comforting.

KIMO: It's the media, Candace. You can't trust them. You told your local police, they told the FBI, some paid insider snuck it to the Associated Press and now I'm the best friend you have. I'm someone you can trust.

CALLER ELEANOR: Kimo, aren't you the media, too?

KIMO: I'm a renegade, Eleanor. I play by honest rules. Producer Lee Creighton and I are outside the system. We broadcast from fast food joints, motels, parking lots, from Silver Crest Vineyards, wherever we can snag a digital hook-up. We despise corporations as much as anyone—more than anyone—we've been fired by all of them. People across this nation are getting screwed, and it's companies like EnvisionInk that are screwing them. We're here to help.

Producer Lee Creighton was all smiles at the keyboard. Balthazer knew he was back in the swing, and his wing man was firing him up hot. Creighton opened a bottle of Syrah, tossed the cork on the floor, took a gulp, handed the rest to Balthazer, then opened another for himself. Balthazer could tell Creighton was not sure where this interview with the sisters was going to take them, with stacks of callers virtually assaulting him on the line to get on the air with Eleanor and Candace. With the satellite feed going strong, their listenership had easily passed two million. Balthazer could see it was all Creighton could do to delete the hordes, mouse click by mouse click, as fast as they came in, until one call in a holding pattern appeared to make his heart stop.

"Kimo, you aren't going to believe this," whispered Creighton.

Balthazer covered the mic, poured the open Syrah in his glass and whispered back in mock annoyance. "I'm working, Creighton. You forget how that goes? When I'm on the air, you let me be on the air."

"I've got Ben and Jerry," said Producer Lee Creighton, gleeful but wary. "I mean, Dennis and Sam. They are not happy you are on the air with their moms."

"Take 'em live," plowed Balthazer. "It's a family affair."

Producer Lee Creighton made the click and merrily put their fate in Balthazer's gab.

KIMO: Well, this is really shaping up to be some Monday, that I can assure you. We began the show with the identities of Ben and Jerry, then we welcomed to the air their moms, Candace and Eleanor from Oregon. Now who should we have on the show but the very men of the hour. Dennis and Sam—Welcome, *This Is Rage*.

CALLER DENNIS: Kimo, are you insane? We trusted you! This is how you pay us back?

CALLER CANDACE: Dennis, is that you? Where on earth are you?

CALLER DENNIS: I can't tell you that, Mom. I wish I could but I can't.

CALLER ELEANOR: Sam, are you there with Dennis?

CALLER SAM: Yes, Mother. Dennis and I are in this together.

CALLER ELEANOR: What are you doing? You're not a kidnapper. You're a software engineer. Did you let Dennis talk you into this? Is this another one of his investment schemes? You can still go to work at Microsoft, you know. It's not too late.

KIMO: Actually, ma'am, I think it is too late.

CALLER CANDACE: Shut up, you moron. You are taking advantage of this situation, of this family, of all of us. You're making this all about you, about your stupid show, *This Is Rage*. We are getting off this call. All of us are getting off this call.

CALLER DENNIS: Mom, let me just tell you, this is going to work out. Trust me, we have this all figured out and it's going to be fine.

CALLER ELEANOR: It's not going to be fine, Dennis. You need to listen to Sam. Whatever you are doing, you need to stop it immediately. Let those CEO guys, Choy and Finkelman, go. Maybe no one else will get hurt.

CALLER CANDACE: Eleanor, we are off this call. Now, we are dropping the line. Dennis, I wish you a lot of luck. You and Sam are going to need it. Whatever you do, don't come home. There is no place for you here anymore. This is the best you could do with your talent, you live with that.

There were two clicks on the monitor followed by silence. Producer Lee Creighton checked the signal, took another swig of Syrah and checked the satellite output for continuity.

"We lost Oregon," said Creighton, tipping his bottle toward Balthazer with no loss of enthusiasm. "You still have the boys. Work them for a location and we take the brass ring."

KIMO: Dennis, Sam, your moms are not too happy with your choices. You have the floor. What can you tell our two million listeners other than your names?

CALLER DENNIS: We're done with you, Balthazer. You betrayed us. You brought our families into this. You humiliated us. You made this personal.

KIMO: Come on, be a big boy. Of course this is personal. You have the entire nation on the hunt for you. Just like we ID'd the photo, it's only a matter of time before we find you. Let me come to you. We'll keep your message flowing, let everyone know what you want, maybe you'll get it.

CALLER DENNIS: We'll get it, Balthazer. We already have it. What we don't need is you, just leave us alone. Stop talking to us. Stop talking about us.

CALLER SAM: Sorry, Kimo, but you're really not helping our cause. We know your listeners like us. We appreciate that, we want everyone to know that. We also want you to know that Calvin Choy and Stephen J. Finkelman are here with us, or we're with them, whatever, and everyone is fine. Pretty soon this will be resolved, and hopefully we'll be out of the headlines.

KIMO: That's good to hear. Any kind words for the employees

at EnvisionInk, to let them know when their co-CEOs can be expected back at their desks?

Another click on the line, another stream of silence. Swerlow and Kisinski had no more to say, at least for now. Producer Lee Creighton finished off the Syrah and reached for a merlot.

"They're gone," said Creighton. "They dropped the line. It's just you now, solo shot unless you want some callers. Do what you're good at, Kimo. Bring it home."

KIMO: Well, I guess it's going to be a bit short and sweet with the principals today. Not exactly what I hoped, but I have to tell you, my adrenaline is pumping. How about yours? I did have a thought though, as Producer Lee Creighton and I open a nice bottle of reserve something here at Silver Crest Vineyards. I was thinking all through that dialogue with Candace, and Eleanor, and Dennis, and Sam, that there is one voice still missing on *This Is Rage*, and we really do need to get him on the show. You know who that would be? I think that would be the chairman of the board of EnvisionInk Systems, the visionary Investor with whom all this began, Mr. Daniel Steyer. Steyer, I asked you nicely on the website and you did not reply. I know you are busy negotiating your purchase price with the megacorp, Atom Heart Entertainment, but what I think you should do is come on my show this week and explain to my listeners, as well as your own employees, why you aren't doing anything at all to help poor Calvin Choy and Stephen J. Finkelman. We all need to know why your latest deal is more important than their lives, and what's going to happen to your employees when that deal is closed. Are there going to be layoffs? Is everyone going to get fired? How rich are you going to get off this deal, you sick, conniving, wretched corporate criminal? That's what I want to know, and I want you to come on this show from anywhere that's convenient and tell us any truth you want. Because if you don't, I'm going to kindly suggest that every single one of your employees walks off the job until you do, and then we'll see if they're sitting quietly in their depressing gray cubicles listening to you or to me. Think about it, Steyer. You are the only guest I want at the moment, and if I don't get you, your company might just come to a standstill. Want to see how that impacts your stock price? I sure do. Right now I'm going to take a break for a glass of wine and let Producer Lee Creighton tell you about the many fine varietals at Silver Crest Vineyards. This is Kimo Balthazer, and *This Is Rage*.

$ $ $ $

2.2
Functional Spec

NASDAQ: ENVN (Day 10)
SHARE PRICE @ MARKET OPEN: $226.80
COMPANY MARKET CAP: $60.5B
VALUATION DELTA SINCE ABDUCTION: +68%

NASDAQ SINCE ABDUCTION: +23%

Trading in Atom Heart Entertainment was at fever pitch after Sol Seidelmeyer's Tuesday morning "rare and unscheduled" appearance on CNBC. Prior to that, Atom Heart shares had traded unwaveringly flat alongside EnvisionInk's freakish run up, with the Street hoping for a new player to emerge and a ludicrous bidding war for EnvisionInk ending in the stratosphere. There seemed to be little fear that Atom Heart could pull off the expense reductions in the imaginary analysts' forecasts if it got the deal, but all that accomplished was keeping the sellers out of play on Atom Heart. If Atom Heart got crushed on a lack of belief that EnvisionInk synergies could lead to sustained earnings improvement, there would be no bidding war, so Atom Heart had to be kept in the game despite the fear of leverage it would have to assume. There was no reason to bid up Atom Heart until the dust settled, making it increasingly less likely that Atom Heart would prevail in an auction the more EnvisionInk climbed.

This indelicate game of cat and rat had not sat well with Seidelmeyer or his board. At air time there was no other player for EnvisionInk at the current unfathomable price, the presumed competition was all street conjecture, artificially inflating the value of EnvisionInk in its time of co-CEO crisis. Only

Seidelmeyer knew the buying opportunity was time restricted, with affordability as much an issue as opportunism. Coming into the interview, Atom Heart and EnvisionInk were essentially equally valued, an impossible place for Seidelmeyer to negotiate given his value had legs and EnvisionInk was a street ploy. If Seidelmeyer was the only player and he was going to have to pay a reasonable premium for EnvisionInk, his stock was going to have to go up and EnvisionInk's was going to have to come down, both as the result of a single interview. If he pulled this off, he would be worthy of an above-the-line deal from his own studio.

The very appearance of the finance press-shy Seidelmeyer on CNBC to "address the state of negotiations and wild rumors in the marketplace" signaled to traders that something big was up, and if they wanted to get in on it, they had but moments to do so. Seidelmeyer was charming and calm, in the hot seat a total of less than seven minutes, talking generally about the bright outlook for his summer film schedule, reinvigoration in the network TV upfront expected in the new season, peace with Netflix and Amazon that would indeed replace a lot of home video revenue, and boundless optimism about mobile, social, and every other new horizon of digital distribution. There was no mention for six of the seven minutes about anything concerning mergers and acquisitions leaving the generic CNBC morning host almost lost in the dialogue, unable to decipher why the chief executive officer of a $35 billion glamour machine was on the midday filler show cheerleading absent an earnings report, warning, or giving updated guidance to avoid a shareholder lawsuit. It was not until the host tried to close the newsless interview with an open-ended question about Atom Heart's future strategic outlook—with or without EnvisionInk—that Seidelmeyer responded with carefully worded comments that there were now "several enticing options for Atom Heart in light of convergence." When the host pressed for detail, Seidelmeyer baited that given obvious circumstances, "current discussion with EnvisionInk was mutually non-exclusive" and extended industry dialogue had yielded "broad interest in a number of attractive M&A candidates with surprisingly unrealized value" that he believed would result in "a vastly improved outlook in almost any path of choice, of which there were many." Seidelmeyer added that he thought "EnvisionInk was a terrific company," but that he and his board would be prudent in preserving shareholder value, and that it was likely only financially feasible for him to close "a single project of the scope in consideration." With that, Seidelmeyer abruptly thanked the host for allowing him to be a guest, smiled courteously, then took off his microphone and stepped out of the shot with the camera light still red.

That was all it took for Atom Heart shares to experience record volume in the next forty-five seconds, all on the buy side, running up Atom Heart a solid 15% and knocking down EnvisionInk an equal amount and then some. Atom Heart reached past a new historical high with a market cap of $70 billion, with EnvisionInk slipping back to $51 billion, still not too shabby for a company that less than two weeks ago was worth roughly two-thirds of that. This was still a tough deal to get done, but once again it was at least approachable without anything materially substantiated or improperly shared inside.

$ $

Choy and Finkelman had been watching Seidelmeyer's broadcast on the high-def monitor fixed to the wall of the comfortably appointed living room of their Boeing Business Jet, a custom refitted 737, fueled for half the outbound itinerary and parked motionless on the tarmac at Moffett Field, not far from the storybook 747 owned by their rivals at Google. Choy and Finkelman were not shy about saying they had wanted their own tricked-out 747 to further vex their cross town competitors, but at twice the price they deemed that an aspiration for the future, leaving them humbly satisfied in sharing the exclusive runway rights available to so few. The BBJ was always stocked with abundant provisions, plenty to eat, all the supplies an oversized executive aircraft could offer. Sitting with them, in equal parts disbelief and anxiety, were Swerlow and Kisinski.

Finkelman had stabilized considerably since leaving Salinas Valley Memorial; he had been detached from the IV and was now in a supported leg cast, allowing the doctor and nurse who had been transported with them in the limo to be released the prior day after a considerable appeal from the co-CEOs. At first Swerlow had wanted the additional hostage value, but Choy had managed to argue successfully that holding onto unnecessary innocents only made their new partners less sympathetic. Finkelman made the additional point that getting clearance for two more passengers who did not want to go to China was not going to speed things up. Swerlow and Kisinski had stepped into the BBJ's private cedar-paneled business office to discuss it, and in the end it was Kisinski who convinced his cousin that keeping things as simple as they could was in their best interest, so they let them go. Swerlow sensed that Kisinski might be further pulling back, losing confidence in their chances, and in the event of a bloodbath, he wanted there to be less blood. For the moment, the fifth member of their party, Special Agent Hussaini, was outside the plane, ostensibly trying to negotiate release clearance after four days of failed attempts that were not sitting well with Swerlow and Kisinski, especially Swerlow.

"How is it that the two of you are managing to negotiate a multibillion dollar sale of your company sequestered in your own plane?" asked Swerlow. "Do you have some telepathic abilities, of which we are unaware, in addition to being able to write wizard potion algorithms?"

"It's not our deal," explained Finkelman. "We said no to that deal weeks before we ended up with you."

"Seidelmeyer is bluffing with a crappy hand," added Choy. "He knows there's no deal with EnvisionInk, but pretending to nix it helps him go shopping for stealth deals with a boost in his price. Good luck to him on that. It's pathetic, a global CEO on CNBC with a sandwich board howling, "Let's Make A Deal!"

"Then what's the story with your board putting out the announcement last week, acknowledging discussions between EnvisionInk and Atom Heart?" asked Swerlow, becoming more irritated. "You sure you're not playing us, you're in contact with Steyer somehow, getting coded messages to him?"

"We told you before, it's a bullshit deal," said Choy. "Sure, it's driving up the price of Atom Heart short term, but all that does is create an ugly liquidity opportunity for insiders in the next open window. There are no synergies, there's no long term vision. Once the costs are cut, that's it. They have our price bid up too high anyway, it's all hype. They expect a deal that isn't going to happen. When the Street figures that out, our price will correct to where it was, maybe lower. It's already happening."

"That's why we told Steyer no deal when he originally brought it to us," added Finkelman. "We told him we didn't see value, just a story. This convergence crud makes old timers do nutty things to hang onto power. We're a different kind of company. We don't take advantage of short term trends. Why this discussion is alive is beyond me."

"Maybe your board is using it to get you back," chimed in Kisinski. "Maybe they think somehow a deal in the works that you don't like puts pressure on us to let you go home. Hard to believe there could be more pressure on us though."

"Our deal is with you," said Choy. "You let us go, you get your $200 million cash infusion and a ride to Shanghai. Steyer knows nothing about our deal with you, just our general counsel, and you've already verified that Sylvia moved the money into escrow."

"The only reason Steyer could have leaked the concept of an Atom Heart deal was to keep our share price from crashing while we were at risk," added Finkelman. "As soon as we're out, that deal goes away. Seidelmeyer knows that, so he's got to be fishing for another deal before that happens. Everyone is playing it for their own gain."

"Unless Steyer is selling you out," said Kisinski. "Maybe there really is a deal he wants with Atom Heart that he's planning to jam down your throats when we let you go."

"Enough noise," barked Swerlow. "We don't need to talk about letting anyone go because it doesn't appear we're ever going to get this plane in the air. We've been stuck here at Moffett for four days. I smell a different kind of bullshit, the kind where it's getting rubbed in our eyes. What do we have to do to fly?" "I'm not sure we can help you there," returned Finkelman. "We did our part. We got you the money and the plane. Unfortunately we're parked on a government strip, that's a deal Calvin and I made for convenience. It's up to the tower to let us fly, and I'm sure someone in a high place somewhere has to approve that."

"That, unfortunately, remains between you and Special Agent Hussaini," added Choy. "If he can't get the authorization to fly, we don't fly. I don't know what else to tell you."

"Well, maybe I should just blow one of you away and toss your carcass on the runway," shouted Swerlow. "That would get Hussaini's attention. Something has to give or we have no deal."

"Respectfully, Dennis, I don't think you should be threatening them just now," said Kisinski. "We are in this private plane at their invitation. Without both of them, I'm guessing we have no money and no ride."

"Don't lecture me in front of them," countered Swerlow. "We may as well have neither. If we don't get airborne, what does it matter what deal we made with them? For all we know, we're surrounded by massively armed ground forces. How do we know they didn't set this up, that they didn't know we would never get out of here?"

Swerlow felt himself beginning to buckle under the pressure. He had known that coming to Moffett was a risk, but he believed Choy and Finkelman were valuable enough and powerful enough to deliver what they had offered. While he maintained only lingering doubts that Choy and Finkelman were prepared to meet their promise, he was coming to realize how little control any one individual could have on events and circumstances. They could not control the airbase, the National Guard, the FAA, the FTA, the FBI, or any other wing of the federal government. At the same time, it appeared on television that business as usual was continuing at EnvisionInk Systems, including activity around the company's most important deal ever, co-CEOs or no co-CEOs at the helm. Swerlow realized how many moving parts had been created by his random decision tree, and as unlikely as it had been that he could take it this far, taking it home would require another set of tricks he had yet to design. It all seemed to hinge on Special Agent Hussaini, whom he knew he could not trust, maybe not even pressure, but if he did not find a way to cause him to act in his interests, the plane soon could be overtaken by trained military personnel with almost no impact to civilians other than Choy and Finkelman. Swerlow had given up the leverage of civilian casualties by leaving the hospital and its surroundings, gambling the potential of a real escape against total isolation and siege. Either he was being played by Hussaini and everyone around him at Moffett Field, or he had to get Hussaini to deliver against the deal that had been cut with Choy and Finkelman.

As Hussaini boarded the plane again, Swerlow looked out the door to see how many guns surrounded him. A barrage of ready M-16s formed an inner layer that encircled the fuselage, backed by a second line of secured tripods he could barely separate into individual muzzles. Swerlow knew he was going to have to try something different. He closed the door to the living room and walked to the front of the plane to meet Hussaini, the two of them alone in the entryway.

"Damn these bureaucrats," muttered Hussaini, closing the door behind him, unapologetic for the duo of armed guards posted on the ramp a few steps beyond the portal. "I argued with them for two hours, but no one seems to be in charge. I still can't get flight clearance."

"You're lying," vented Swerlow. "We would have been in the air days ago if this was going to happen. You brought us here as a set up."

"Slow down, Swerlow," eased Hussaini. "This was your idea. I came along on orders, to keep you from getting shot roadside. I am one individual among a lot of agencies and departments involved in these decisions. I am doing everything I can to get us in the air, but what you are asking is unprecedented. It's like hijacking a plane from the ground, and the United States of America has strict policies about hijacking."

"There's no hijacking," yelled Swerlow. "This plane is on loan to us. You want video of Choy and Finkelman making the offer, we'll record it and put it on YouTube."

"Excellent, wear burlap hoods, then you'll look like terrorists, with the gun only slightly out of frame. At the moment, you have public opinion on your side. You want to lose that?"

"I want to fly to Shanghai and I want to go there now," insisted Swerlow. "Either you can deliver on that or you can't. If you can't, then we may as well get a half dozen body bags right now so it will be easy for your strike force to mop us all up."

"We don't need body bags," said Hussaini. "And you're right, this is not a hijacking, which is why I think we can get it to happen. We just have to get the powers that be to see it our way. When they lift the lockdown, we fly."

"Be clear, Hussaini. If they do mop up, you'll be in the mess right along with us. You're in it now. The only way for you to get out is to get us to Shanghai, then come back with Choy and Finkelman. Anything less is a no exit slaughter."

"You're taking a more ominous tone than you have before," said Hussaini. "I know you're feeling the heat, but that's the path you've chosen. You keep your head on straight, maybe I get you out. You lose your cool, you're right, there are dozens of guys with automatic weapons all around this plane who would love to take out you and your cousin. They are good at what they do, and they will do it if you give them a reason. I'm trying to make it otherwise."

"I don't trust you, Hussaini. I just don't have a choice other than to deal with you. Who are the powers that be? Who the hell is the decision maker?"

"I thought it was the FBI Director, and so did he, but apparently given the Homeland Security Act . . . well, as I said, there's no precedent for what you're asking, to be flown to a another nation that may or may not want you, in a borrowed jet with a huge international commercial bank account waiting, all of which is being interpreted as an act of coercion."

"It's a friggin' business deal," shouted Swerlow. "Choy and Finkelman are investing in us. We are setting up shop in China with their blessing and complimentary transportation. It's private property, it's a private investment. How hard is this?"

"It's hard," said Hussaini. "But so far it's not hopeless, maybe not impossible. We are at a roadblock, not an impasse. I am negotiating on your behalf that the best outcome is to let us all fly to China. You need to stay patient. I'm not there yet."

"Who makes the call?" repeated Swerlow.

"All I know is that Homeland Security has taken it from the FBI. They'll have to get a judge who is willing to rule, federal court at the least. Maybe it goes to the Cabinet. Like I said, there is no rule book for what you've done here."

"The President of the United States has to green light our flight plan? I should start shooting now."

"There is another way," said Hussaini. "You could change your mind."

"We're not going to prison," asserted Swerlow. "Sam and I have discussed this. You get us a flight clearance or you have Waco the Sequel. I can live with either outcome."

"No, you can't," said Hussaini.

"I know what I meant," replied Swerlow.

Swerlow opened the door to the living room and saw Kisinski, Choy, and Finkelman's eyes still glued on CNBC. Talking head analysts from around the world were trying to make sense of Seidelmeyer's appearance, Atom Heart's price pop, and who else, if anyone, was really a player for EnvisionInk at the moderate decline just realized. Swerlow saw Hussaini cautiously watching them from the hall. He believed he now had Hussaini on the ropes, that Hussaini was worried he might come unglued. Swerlow had regained his cool in the gambit. The cabin was as it had been, impossibly tense, but without incident. Hussaini tried to step into the living room, but was stopped cold when Swerlow slammed the door in his face. Swerlow had made it clear the next move belonged to Hussaini. He wondered if Hussaini had any idea what that might be.

$ $

Silver Crest Vineyards was nearly sold out. The one-day sales record had cleaned out the tasting room, the storage room, the library, and now the owners were selling futures for the next bottling as well as taking deposits for drinking rights to vines that were not yet planted. Inviting Balthazer onto their property had been such a good marketing move, the winemaker woke up the next day and called all his peers in Paso Robles, asking them to unload unsold inventory to him on consignment. He would either broker it on the website at a courtesy discount or re-label it Silver Crest with an autograph from Balthazer and a 50% mark-up. This internet thing was definitely catching on, he was sure of it.

Balthazer had elevated himself so far into the bully pulpit following his conversation with the Swerlow and Kisinski families the previous day that he had not even noticed he had achieved a new milestone, the crashing of his own website. Traffic to ThisIsRage.com following the identification of the Ben and Jerry photo and the guest appearances by their moms had been so extreme, the site had essentially gone dark and crushed the hosting company, which no longer wanted Balthazer's business, good credit card or bad. Balthazer had won the badge of honor usually reserved for Victoria's Secret online runway shows, and word of the crash created more buzz and spread KimoMania deeper into the workplace heartland. Producer Lee Creighton, half way through a case of oaky chardonnay but nonetheless on the ball, had kept the stream flowing through the satellite signal he had ad hoc licensed, until something strange happened — hackers across the nation grabbed the satellite feed and began redistributing it through peer to peer networks without ever being asked for their help. Creighton had discovered that when the hacking community loved you, all was well with the Internet. The hacking community, which globally shared widespread disdain for corporate cruelty, unvaryingly had come to love Balthazer. Within a half hour of the site going down, ThisIsRage.com was enjoying virtually unlimited bandwidth, as office workers across the nation listening from their cubicles borrowed un-used capacity from corporate networks and seamlessly relayed the packets from Paso Robles across every identifiable pirate hub they could access. The unofficial network had become so vast so quickly that the only way it could have been stopped by company CIOs in every city in the nation would have been to shut down and then reroute their internal server infrastructure, and interrupting business continuity at that scale was not an option. The Internet itself had taken ownership of *This Is Rage*, not only an emotional reflection of its opinions, but validated by the strength of its back office support.

With countless Central Coast varietals now being delivered from every seller in the region to the Silver Crest wine shed for resale, Balthazer had gone on the air Tuesday at noon rant-ing about the obvious market manipulation being caused by Seidelmeyer's appearance on CNBC. His warning to workers across the nation declared it was time for them to put up or shut up—they could no longer let the titans of industry manip-ulate their livelihoods through endless mergers that did nothing more than make Investors, Bankers, and Operators zillionaires, while cutting payrolls and health plan costs as fast as high-paid lawyers could draft the separation agreements. Balthazer's com-ments were naïve, as usual he was not completely sure what he was saying or its broader implications, but caller after caller fed on his energy, and that energy radiated. The outpour of office apathy was unprecedented, a river of sorrow that set as common ground the confusion, complexity, helplessness, and dashed hopes of a working class of listeners that desperately wanted to fight back, but had no idea what Wall Street actually did every day, how it worked, how it affected and impacted them, and what they could ever do to protect themselves. For now they were finding community in their shared sentiments of anger, and Balthazer was doing what he always did—transforming their unfiltered calls into amazing radio.

News of the site crash, however temporary, had provided

Producer Lee Creighton with more ammunition to get Balthazer's signal spread farther and faster, with analog syndicators now assaulting him in real time for access to the feed. If BitTorrent and all its imitators, legal and illegal, were going to have the signal, if satellite radio and all its dishes and relays were going to have the signal, then AM and FM needed the signal to stay relevant, bringing Kimo Balthazer and *This Is Rage* back to the platform from which he had been banned. There was so much joy, so much irony, so much dark humor in seeing how the fickle entertainment world played with taste, but when it came to must-haves, all rules went out the window and the story was the thing. Balthazer's voice was everywhere, more widespread than at any time in his career, with looming danger in every word that passed from his mouth to the microphone, and audience anticipation awaiting each next word of the rant, each next exasperated caller, each next conjecture of what might, should, and would happen to Swerlow and Kisinski.

The fate of Choy and Finkelman became ancillary to the discussion. Sure they were victims of a criminal kidnapping, but as the signal spread, listeners seemed to care increasingly less. There were no good guys and bad guys — they were all bad guys. The only thing the listeners wanted to know was what it meant to them, and how they could use this opportunity to regain control of their lives. It was a content circus, a feast of verbal dumping, a fiend's pageant that comes once in a host's career, only if he is very lucky. Balthazer had all but won the lottery. Producer Lee Creighton spread it, Balthazer fed it, and within this context, in the midst of an endless string of random afternoon calls repeating the sad themes, Balthazer would get his wish.

"Ready for me to make your day, boss?" asked Producer Lee Creighton, looking up with wide eyes from his laptop monitor.

"What, you sign another syndication deal, getting us on the air in all of English speaking India?" replied Balthazer, muting the mic in front of him while a caller continued to ramble.

"Nope, better," proclaimed Creighton.

"Find a rare '97 estate cabernet nestled in one of the crates you're going to keep for our slovenly consumption rather than sell at auction?" joked Balthazer.

"That was an hour ago, I poured it in your green tea. What do you really want today, Kimo? What would put us over the top?" Creighton's grin said it all.

"Are you telling me you have Steyer?" conjured Balthazer.

"I have Steyer," confirmed Creighton. "He called us. Said you have your head up your ass about Seidelmeyer and he wants to go on the record helping you understand the fundamentals of business enterprise."

"He's willing to go on the air with me, at this moment?" played back Balthazer.

"All yours," offered Creighton. "Make it good. Remember, we're making history."

Balthazer abruptly truncated the rambler, took a deep breath, stared past the empty shelves in the warehouse, and unmuted the mic. He looked at the clock, well past 1:00 p.m. PST, the equity markets were closed. EnvisionInk was down for the first time in days, Atom Heart Entertainment landed a healthy record close, and the NASDAQ itself was bloating into bubble land, up more than 20% in less than two weeks since the EnvisionInk and Atom Heart extravaganza made its debut. Steyer was not stupid. Seidelmeyer had commented that day while the stock market was open with purpose. Anything similar from Steyer could be seen as collusion. Balthazer knew he was calling for a reason, it was not just his baiting. If Steyer wanted to talk in a public forum, he was looking for an outcome. Balthazer would have to figure that out live and cut him off before he got what he wanted, whatever it was. The on-air game was always one of control, a contest that Balthazer had long ago mastered. This was the lottery.

KIMO: Friends, there comes a time in every talk show host's career when he finally gets the guest he always wanted. For some that is a fallen political leader, for some a naked movie star, for me as you know, it has been the chairman of EnvisionInk

Systems, Daniel Steyer. I am pleased to report that Mr. Steyer has decided to join us today, entirely of his own choice. For those of you who have been following the show of late, Daniel Steyer does not need an introduction, so let's just get to it. Daniel Steyer—Welcome, *This Is Rage*.

CALLER STEYER: Thank you, Kimo. I appreciate the opportunity to say what I have to say. But let me say first, this will be brief, and given SEC regulations and the need to protect all of our employees, I will not be able to take questions other than from you, nor talk on the air directly with your listeners. Are you good with that?

KIMO: I am wonderful with that, Chairman Steyer.

CALLER STEYER: Daniel is fine.

KIMO: We shall see. So Daniel, let me ask you a question . . .

CALLER STEYER: I would prefer to begin with a few things that need to be cleared up.

KIMO: So you're the host and I'm the guest?

CALLER STEYER: I don't know what that means, Kimo. Let's try this. First off, I think you and your listeners need to understand and appreciate the difference between two companies exploring or discussing a deal and actually doing a deal. We talk to other companies all the time. Most companies do. However, comparatively few deals are pursued to completion. That's how business is done. The difference is not trivial.

KIMO: No argument from me. That's how business is done. I think my listeners understand and appreciate that. Here's what I don't understand and appreciate. If your co-CEOs are being held at gunpoint, why are you having any discussions at all, other than to secure their safe release?

CALLER STEYER: Not a fair question, Kimo. You know that. I won't be baited.

KIMO: I'm missing the part where you're being baited. Why is it an unfair question? Because you don't want to answer it?

CALLER STEYER: Because, number one, we as a law-abiding company cannot negotiate with criminals, there are professional government authorities whose job it is to do that. And second, because I would be violating corporate protocol and non-disclosure provisions to share with you any reasoning, real or hypothetical, that might or might not result in an unfairly narrow release of information that could impact current, historical, or potential shareholders.

KIMO: Do you have writers for this material, Steyer, or do you just wing it?

CALLER STEYER: Not productive, Kimo, but let me make another point regardless. We do care deeply about our founders and co-CEOs, Calvin Choy and Stephen J. Finkelman. To the extent that I can say anything at all, let me assure you and everyone listening that we are doing everything we can to bring them home safely, and that we are making progress working through proper channels.

KIMO: Damn, you use lot of words to say almost nothing. Tell us this, where the hell are they? Last we saw them they were leaving Salinas Valley Memorial Medical Center in a limo with the former Ben and Jerry, now identified by a picture posted on my website as Dennis Swerlow and Sam Kisinski. I had them as guests on my show yesterday, did you know that? Their moms, too!

CALLER STEYER: Yes, that was mentioned to me. I also heard you riled them up a bit. I am not sure that was particularly helpful to our guys.

KIMO: You ducked my question. Do you know where they are?

CALLER STEYER: The truth is, Kimo, I do not, and if I did, there is no way I would tell you, especially on an internet broadcast.

KIMO: Internet, satellite, and terrestrial radio, to be clear. Why wouldn't you tell us if you knew, which I'm sure you do?

CALLER STEYER: Do you really think you helped the situation when you originally revealed the Salinas location? You created a frenzy. You put crowds at risk along with those who were already at risk. I don't see any reason to replicate that kind of dangerous situation. All I know is that I have been assured Calvin and Stephen are in a safe place. They are making good progress and we will get this resolved.

KIMO: Well, I'm no sleuth, but it doesn't seem to me you're doing everything you can to get them released. And I'm sure you have your own reason for calling me, some secret agenda you're attempting to accomplish right now, but are unwilling to share.

CALLER STEYER: I don't answer to you, Balthazer. You are a B-list talk show host, without a respected brand standing behind you, without any noticeable self-discipline. I am the Board Chair of a multinational growth enterprise, with absolute responsibility to all related stakeholders. I am meeting my fiduciary duty, which is how Calvin and Stephen would want it. As I said, I am not going to let this discussion go on forever. My only goal is to assure my stakeholders—owners, partners, customers, employees—that EnvisionInk is a rock solid entity, that the company acts with decency and integrity, and that we are keeping all interests fairly balanced in making the best decisions we can in a challenging time, no matter what exploitation you concoct. You demanded I make myself available for transparency. I have done so and said what I can say. Are we done?

KIMO: Nice volley, but no spike yet. I want to float a concept by you, and I want an honest answer. Can we try that? Mostly simple words, if possible, sans corporate speak, one to two syllables at a time. Then I'll let you go. Game?

CALLER STEYER: We can try, as long as your question is sensible and answering it does not violate any laws.

KIMO: Got it, decency and integrity. My take is, I think the reason you don't work harder to bring back Choy and Finkelman is because your stock has been trending mountain bound ever since they were taken away, and you're afraid if you bring them back it might tank.

CALLER STEYER: Utterly absurd, Balthazar. That's not how business is done. Not at EnvisionInk, not anywhere of consequence and substance.

KIMO: Maybe exclusively at EnvisionInk. Maybe Choy and Finkelman don't like the Atom Heart deal as much as you do. Maybe if they show up, the deal dies, bringing your stock price back to sea level. You saw a little of that today. Am I getting closer?

CALLER STEYER: You are getting crazier, Balthazar. That's nonsensical. Calvin and Stephen are visionaries, as well as great guys. Everyone at the company wants them back, no one more than me.

KIMO: Then why don't you table your Atom Heart deal until they come back? Show a little faith in your co-CEOs. Show a little faith in humanity. Put their lives above the almighty dollar. How could that not be the only sensible thing a man of moral courage would do?

CALLER STEYER: We are done now, Balthazar. You are making stuff up, and I told you, I have no comment on an Atom Heart deal beyond the information that is publicly available. We are on the record to the extent we can be.

KIMO: What happens if Seidelmeyer buys someone else, a big someone else who is cheaper than you, like he hinted on CNBC this morning? He can't afford to do more than one deal that size, that's obvious. What happens if you get left at the altar with your

A-list retirement party planned? Up until this story your stock price was flat for a year and a half, because your growth was flat for a year and a half. Now suddenly you talk mega merger and it rockets to Olympus, only you got a little reality check today from Seidelmeyer, didn't you? Can you live without growth like you have been, or does that make your company yesterday's leftovers? Are you the new Microsoft, a monster ATM that's going nowhere?

CALLER STEYER: We've had issues with organic growth, I'll give you that. Our ability to generate new concepts beyond our core media revenue optimization has been lacking, I'll give you that as well. If we have to live with no organic growth, we'll live with it. I won't be happy about it, but we'll live with it until we have a way past it.

KIMO: So you are admitting, confessing actually, that you have a lack of faith in your own staff. You do not believe the thousands of brilliant people you have hired can help you innovate your way out of stagnation, so now you are focused on liquidating your way out of stagnation. Is that the case?

CALLER STEYER: Those are your words, Balthazer, not mine. If there are no deals to be made on terms that make sense, then there are no deals to be made. What we have ahead of us may not be explosive, but it is sustainable. I am completely prepared to live with the earnings that we have.

KIMO: How truly mediocre. So do you have an organic growth plan?

CALLER STEYER: No comment.

KIMO: Do you have the creativity among your workforce to bring forward a new idea that can advance your company beyond what Choy and Finkelman thought up ten years ago?

CALLER STEYER: Again, no comment.

KIMO: Are you willing to bet any fraction of the money you would receive from Atom Heart Entertainment on your own team and tell the world right now that you know you have the talent in your company to get to where you need to go? Or do you simply plan to fire as many of these disposable bodies as you can, as quickly as you can, to drive up your profits by cutting as many costs as you can?

CALLER STEYER: Balthazer, this is absurd. You're absurd. We're done.

Steyer was gone. He had hung up mid-rebuttal, as Balthazer expected he would, giving Balthazer the rare behavioral win in a battle of bad manners. Producer Lee Creighton looked at all the activity on their home page and did not know where to turn. Thank the hacker gods for all the bandwidth! Among the multiple venues of distribution he had secured, there was no way to tell how many listeners had just heard New World Master of the Universe Daniel Steyer insult his employees, throw his own company under the bus, bow his head to Sol Seidelmeyer, spontaneously melt down and probably lie outright, all in a matter of moments. Quite satisfied with the muck draining performance he had coached from Steyer, Balthazer continued.

KIMO: Thank you, Mr. Chairman. You have been an open, engaging, and enlightening guest. I know our listeners across the nation are much better for experiencing your profound thinking. I wish you well at the office, and I know you will do all you can to bring the boys back home. I'm going to take a quick break and breathe for a moment. Here's a few recorded words of thanks from the owners of Silver Crest Vineyards, who have been gracious hosts to us this week, and whose winery you, our listeners, have forever put on the map.

Balthazer signaled Producer Lee Creighton to roll the homespun commercial they had recorded earlier in the day for Silver Crest, grinning like a jackal, as pleased with himself as he had ever been. Balthazer knew Steyer thought he could beat him at his own game—an absurd, arrogant error Steyer now would swallow. Balthazer had won the round, hands down, and Steyer had left the call in much worse shape than before he had made it. Taking the victory forward, Balthazer began pounding on his keyboard, putting Google to a new set of tests, smiling again with the search returns displayed on his monitor.

"Ready to take another caller?" asked Producer Lee Creighton. "High rise window washer denied disability, dominatrix CPA seeking discrimination damages, receptionist suffering extreme carpal tunnel—you have your pick. We can stay on all night if you like."

"I know where they are," blurted Balthazer, eyes locked on his computer screen.

"Swerlow and Kisinski?" confirmed Creighton, suddenly releasing his mouse.

"Swerlow, Kisinski, Choy, Finkelman, Special Agent Asshole. I figured it out. They're on Choy and Finkelman's private plane."

"You're not going live with that, are you?" asked Creighton, his grip hugely uneasy.

"Not yet," said Balthazer. "We've got some groundwork to do, so no one gets hurt. How soon do you think we can make Moffett Field?"

"Back in Silicon Valley?" said Creighton. "We can be there in a few hours, as long as one of us is sober enough to drive. But that's within one hundred miles of Salinas. The FBI was clear, if they see us anywhere near there, they will arrest us."

"Then they better not see us," said Balthazer.

"How did you figure it out?" asked Creighton.

"They left a trail," said Balthazer. "I'll tell you in the car."

$ $ $ $

2.3
Source Code

NASDAQ: ENVN (Day 11)
SHARE PRICE @ MARKET OPEN: $186.30
COMPANY MARKET CAP: $49.75B
VALUATION DELTA SINCE ABDUCTION: +38%
** ENVN DELTA FROM PEAK: < 18% > **

NASDAQ SINCE ABDUCTION: +31%

About a hundred employees were already camped out in the parking lot by the time the board members had arrived for their regularly scheduled meeting early on Wednesday morning. It was a weird scene with blue plastic tarps tied to aluminum poles supported by sandbags to form tent structures, a few kerosene stoves producing aromatic coffee, and boxed Krispy Kremes all around. If this were not Santa Clara it might have looked like the beginnings of a strike, but picket lines at high-tech office parks were as out of place as Investment Bankers at Salvation Army outlets. A few handmade signs caught the eye, particularly:
Glad You'll Live With What You Have,
We Don't Need You Either
And another:
Sorry For Taking Up Cubicle Space,
You Can Have It Back
And yet another:
Why Invest in Employees When Your Buyer
Can Pay The Severance?
It would have been hard to call this a movement, but it was *something* — a little more REI than UAW, but no less lacking in invitation. It was also coming on a strange day, the day after EnvisionInk stock had begun to slip from its recent record high,

a trend that was continuing and now mirrored by the major indices, all of which had been running positive until this morning. Yesterday the trends were in line with Atom Heart, not EnvisionInk. But that was yesterday. Since the first trade at market open, EnvisionInk was already off another 10%, while the NASDAQ had sunk half that.

Steyer had driven to the EnvisionInk complex feeling more upbeat than the night before, the unexpected gift of half a night's sleep. Today the board was to see him without the hulking plaster cast that had engulfed his head at their last gathering. Now it was mostly patchwork bandages, darkening bruises, and placeholder front teeth for the pair that had been shattered in his yard. It occurred to Steyer that going on the air the previous day with Balthazer in hopes of showing management's commitment and sensitivity may not have been his smartest decision ever. If the employees in the parking lot and the traders on Wall Street both took objection to his commentary, it was possible he had not said all the right things. Ever the optimist, Steyer thought perhaps he did not deserve the blame, perhaps the market was reacting to Seidelmeyer and the employee concerns were limited and short term. Then again, maybe all this was a coincidence that had nothing to do with either of them. A survivor like Steyer bolstered himself with such self-assurance, but he was also a realist. He knew he had a backlog of simmering problems, and the board was more than likely to add to his troubles rather than resolve them if his game was not perfect. Speculators played poker. Steyer played chess.

Although the board meeting was one of eight regularly scheduled slots for the year, there was nothing ordinary about this get-together—particularly with the location of Choy and Finkelman known only to General Counsel Normandy, the stock having peaked after a much enjoyed steep ramp, and the mini-protest forming outside the building. The board had to decide what next to do about Choy and Finkelman, and what now to do about Atom Heart Entertainment.

Several hours had gone by, containing perhaps the most

authentic and spirited discussion the board had ever experienced. Silicon Valley board meetings were in most cases predictably rote. As long as a company was producing cash and growing, there was little about which the board could complain. Without question, management was always better versed on the topics of the day than any board member could be, never any second guessing there. A meeting would be called to order, attendance noted for the record, then minutes would be passed with only minor comment or correction as carefully drafted by counsel. Financials would be reviewed in a few perfunctory charts by the CFO. A presentation or two from the CEO's top VPs would provide entertainment value and kill time. Any strategic activity including M&A would be floated and rubber stamped, and various routine and consent resolutions would be passed unanimously. Unanimous was the working order of a board. Tension was for management and staff, not for the board. Unless a CEO was about to be dismissed for cause or lack of confidence, a shareholder lawsuit was filed and had to be defended, or the company was tanking in the face of debt and going on the block, board meetings were meant to be requirements of law, not deliberations. Criticism was kept to a minimum and guarded. Compliments were frequent. It was an honor and financial windfall to serve on a board. To upset one's own status and assert a minority voice held little upside, either for the present appointment or to stay in the club as future seats emerged around town.

Attendance at this meeting was reminiscent of their last meeting, conducted orderly in crisis mode, with a full house excluding Choy and Finkelman, and former Senator Henderson on the polycom. Venture capitalist Barton Throckmore and Stanford Professor George Yamanaka had expressed sympathy for many of the points made by Steyer, with Melissa Stanton-Landers, Rebecca Gutierrez, and Dr. Philippe Francois less yielding than Steyer had observed them. Henderson, the sub-woofer sage on the phone from the East Coast, was the hardest to call — he could be the day's swing vote if it came to that. No doubt Steyer had expected some rebuke for his performance on Balthazer's show, but the actual concern he was hearing was why he had called in at all, and what on earth had Seidelmeyer been thinking going on CNBC tossing rumor grenades into their bunker. Steyer had done his best to assure his colleagues that it had been a carefully calculated move on his part to be responsive to Balthazer's threats and bring order where emotion was prevailing, but the words he kept hearing were "bad judgment call" and the need for "damage control" with their already testy employees whose loyalty and patience were withering. Steyer attempted to defend Seidelmeyer as a good salesman trying to close, but again, he was getting pushback, prickly defensiveness where he normally would hear support, with certain more temperamental members of the board struggling to see coherence and finally breaking ranks.

"What were you thinking going on that show, Daniel?" asked Dr. Francois. "You must have had an objective in mind."

"I was thinking if I could just appear less demonic than Balthazer was painting me, I might be able to take some heat off. I was thinking that Swerlow and Kisinski might be listening, that they might call in and be desperate enough to dig a way out. I wanted one more chance to open that door, to bring Calvin and Stephen back safely."

"You mean you weren't thinking how hard it would be to get the Atom Heart deal done with our employees walking out on us?" grumbled Stanton-Landers, violating traditional meeting protocol. "Curiously, that's what we have in spite of your acquiescence to Balthazer's demand."

"I'm confused," said Gutierrez to Steyer. "Swerlow and Kisinski, were you trying to shake them up, or put them at ease? And what made you think you could do either?"

"I was trying to get them to engage," explained Steyer. "That's all. It didn't work. Then Balthazer spun me down. I played into his trap. I could only say what I could say. I was on the record and who knew how the SEC would play it back."

"Yep, you bombed, especially with our employees,"

continued Stanton-Landers. "Between you and Seidelmeyer, we can consider the talk show circuit a bust."

"I don't think words of disrespect are going to be helpful, Melissa," said Yamanaka. "We're all disappointed, but we are on the same team. Daniel took a risk as he has so many times before. This particular one didn't pay off. We advance."

"I'm with the Professor," affirmed Throckmore, the individual in the room with the most to lose after Steyer if the wheels came off the wagon. "We can talk all day about what Dan shoulda' or coulda' done, but Dan's been running point for us since Choy and Finkelman were grabbed, and he's done the best he can to keep things on track. Better than that, the stock is still way up since the incident, so we have nothing to complain about if we don't drag our feet. We need the Atom Heart deal now for stability. Before it was an elective, now it's core curriculum."

"I appreciate the metaphor," remarked Yamanaka with a grin. "And I agree, for stability, a deal with Atom Heart looks to be our best course of action. Seidelmeyer is a smart fellow. He can read the tea leaves. He is doing what anyone with leverage would do, he's squeezing a little. Let's not fault him for delivering value to his shareholders, that's his job."

"I know all about squeezing," boomed the voice of Henderson from the speakerphone. "I can't disagree with George. I probably would do the same if I were Seidelmeyer. But I'm not him, and I don't like it. It's Hollywood. It's lowbrow."

"I'm having a hard time with this whole discussion," said Gutierrez. "We are still facing a situation where our co-CEOs are in harm's way, and we are spending most of the meeting discussing a transaction. That doesn't seem right."

"I agree," added Stanton-Landers. "I've run a tech company, granted nowhere near the scale of EnvisionInk. I can't believe if either Calvin or Stephen were in the room, selling the company would be on the table."

"That's a nonstarter," shot back Steyer. "You can't try to imagine how executives would think about matters of their own capture and release in light of a timely opportunity. The logic is circular, it's impossible."

"We'll have to agree to disagree on that, Daniel," argued Stanton-Landers. "You may have institutional knowledge encoded in memory, but I see the world from their vantage point. They didn't like the deal when we first discussed it. There is no reason for them to like it now, especially given their absence. I wouldn't want to come back and give a hundred percent to a company that was sold out from under me, with the acquisition approved by the board in my absence. Not a chance."

"You have a well vetted opinion, Melissa, no question about that," reflected Dr. Francois. "The heart of your issue is whether this buyout will be understood by Calvin and Stephen as necessary in their absence, and that remains an item of conjecture, because we do not read minds. My deeper concern has to do with what we saw in the parking lot when we arrived today. Prior to this, my assessment of EnvisionInk was that it has been a relatively harmonious workplace. If those few employees declaring some sort of work stoppage remain isolated, we can deal with it appropriately. The real question is, how deep is the ennui? Is this likely to spread? Are we going to see more employees walk out on the campus? And if they do, will that spiral if we announce a combination with a . . . how did you refer to it, Senator—a Hollywood lowbrow concern?"

"Like you said, good doctor, we can't read minds, we can only do what we think is right," returned Henderson. "Personally, I don't care if they all walk out. They're a bunch of spoiled babies out there in San Francisco. Private chefs, on site massages, no exhaust bus rides to and from work, metal scooters tearing up the carpets in our hallways, Zumba classes and Pilates marathons around the clock, free day care for babies and toddlers, free exploration time for personal projects—if they want to walk out on all that, let them. See if they can replace all that and stock options at a real company . . . any company that isn't in Silicon Valley catering to whiners. They got it good. They want out? Let 'em out. I don't think the Atom Heart grunts get served daily afternoon high tea, let's see if they complain."

Henderson had said his piece, finishing abruptly, switching

his receiver to mute to accent his end note. Sylvia Normandy and CFO Sanjay Basru had been sitting quietly, taking a few notes, barely participating in the discussion of their company's future. They were the most senior executives present, but without their bosses in the room, no one seemed interested in their opinions. Steyer knew Normandy would document any actions approved, but expected the minutes she kept for this meeting would be brief, the permanent record subject to subpoena if things did go south. Beyond reporting requirements, Steyer was never much interested in Normandy's opinions. Like most of the lawyers he dealt with over the years, she was too protective, too prone to obstruction. He found her to be isolated by choice, needlessly lonely, much too attached to her job responsibilities given her tiny ownership stake and straightforward chores. He didn't care that their relationship was awkward. Of course she was there for objective reasons, but when he needed a yes, the logic of no was not helpful. Steyer found Basru of equally little value in decisionmaking, a trickling fountain of anxiety obsessed with minutia. There sat the company's CFO, staring at his smart phone, watching EnvisionInk stock plummet in real time. Steyer knew Normandy and Basru were hungry for any clarity the board might bring, but none seemed apparent. They had been trying to keep their heads down, but suddenly became less invisible as the discussion refocused on the pragmatic.

"Let's go back to the most important issue at hand, if we possibly can—how we secure the release of Calvin and Stephen," suggested Gutierrez. "Sylvia, I understand attorney-client privilege, but aren't you taking this to an absurd extreme?"

"I agree with Rebecca," said Stanton-Landers, words that had never before crossed her lips. "We are fiduciaries. The attorney-client privilege should be transitive. Whatever you know as a matter of company business, we should know, starting with where the hell are Choy and Finkelman being held? We have a right to know that. We are all subject to the same confidentiality requirements. No one here will misuse the information. How else can we act if we don't have all the facts that can be known?"

"As usual, you make excellent points from an Operating perspective," responded Normandy. "Believe me, there is nothing more I would like to do than spill the beans. There are two things that prevent me from doing that. One, Calvin and Stephen told me not to. For the strangest of reasons, they don't trust one or more of you, and certainly don't want their location to be publicly leaked. And two, the only way I could defy their wishes would be if I believed it would make a material difference to the betterment of the company, which I represent as an entity, beyond anyone's personal interests. I don't see how all of you knowing where they are helps them return. The FBI knows and is working on it. That's good enough for me."

"What about Balthazer?" asked Throckmore. "I'll bet he knows, or he finds out before we do. Then he'll just tell everyone on his show and we'll find out when our employees do. We can get a radio and put it on the surround sound system in the parking lot with the hippies—if anyone can find a radio."

"Our stock is down nineteen percent for the day now, in case anyone is interested," blurted out Basru. It was another glorious non-sequitur, but it did serve to capture everyone's attention.

"The rest of the market is down about half that," said Throckmore. "That's a single day correction following an unnecessarily interrupted bull market run. The more we sit here talking, the more we let our company take down the market. We need to act."

"This is not good," continued Basru. "The only stock gaining is Atom Heart Entertainment, hockey-sticking like us last week. Seidelmeyer is stockpiling currency."

"We need to come out with a definitive point of view," stated Yamanaka. "We have never seen anything like a 19% decline in our stock in one day."

"After almost seventy percent improvement in a fortnight, I don't think we can easily toss about superlatives," noted Dr. Francois. "We have many unprecedented variables in play. We need to approach this methodically."

"Right, like the collection of pissed off employees in our

parking lot, holding up signs that say they know how much they're unloved," commented Stanton-Landers. "That's unprecedented, too. Hell, that's unprecedented in the Valley. We're the victims, but we're succeeding in making a mess on all fronts."

Steyer was beyond frustration. The dialogue was going in circles. He needed to move it forward. It was time to push.

"Folks, I appreciate your passion," eased Steyer. "Each of you comes to this crisis with wisdom. Each of you is showing a good deal of heart. What we need to do is park our emotions and proceed with objectivity. It is very much my sense that an agreement to merge with Atom Heart Entertainment with a reasonable premium to our current trading value will stabilize our situation, while we ascribe the balance of our efforts toward resolving the release of Calvin and Stephen. Besides, a vote from our board at this stage is largely ceremonial, a deal would require shareholder approval as well as board approval. This buys us time to get back employee confidence and let things settle down."

"I agree," said Throckmore. "Let's put this to a board vote and get it behind us. Then the shareholders can decide."

"We're not preschoolers and we're not idiots," proclaimed Stanton-Landers. "A board vote to have the company acquired is anything but a dip in the suggestion box. If Steyer's fund and Throckmore's fund vote for liquidity—and I don't see how they don't given this meeting—the institutionals will take that as guidance and follow in lockstep. The board vote makes it a done deal pending a rubber stamp."

"It also locks in a premium we haven't seen in a good long time before we squander it," countered Throckmore, his ire unleashed. "Plus it provides real liquidity for those who have remained patient—very, very patient."

"The stock has only been stagnant a year," offered Dr. Francois, trying to bring calm. "I listened carefully to what Daniel said on the radio yesterday, but how do we know we are completely out of ideas for growth? If we stay the course, perhaps in a year or so we are worth twice what we are now, maybe three times."

"Or we could be worth half," interjected Yamanaka, carefully taking the floor. "That is a real possibility in these circumstances. Perhaps less. We have seen that outcome before on this peninsula. My sense is that a standalone posture means we must go on our own acquisition spree, with highly aggressive cost elimination, and that has not proven to be a natural skill set for Calvin and Stephen. With Atom Heart Entertainment as their sandbox, Calvin and Stephen might get back to the kind of innovation for which they are renowned. That to me seems like a win for all."

The room fell silent with the Professor's summation. In too little time, with too much pressure, Steyer saw that sides had been drawn. There were any number of ways to see the future, any number of risks, too many unlimited variables controlled by market forces and whim. No one was more aware than Steyer that boards never liked to prognosticate, no one could ever clearly see the future. This was precisely where fiduciary duty had to be enacted and process maintained, the insider's carefully played wild card.

"I hereby motion the authorization of our chairman to seek a tender offer from Atom Heart Entertainment," declared Throckmore, "to purchase all shares of EnvisionInk Systems at our closing price today plus ten percent, subject to the formalities of a motion to be drafted by counsel with requisite due diligence and shareholder approval, blah blah blah."

"Thank you, Barton," nodded Steyer. "There is a motion before the board that I be empowered to negotiate with Atom Heart Entertainment within the stated parameters. Is there a second?"

"Second," added Yamanaka.

"Any further discussion before we vote?" asked Steyer.

Silence prevailed again, the most profound of which continued from the polycom. The assembled wondered if perhaps Henderson, following his own soliloquy on company culture, had stepped away, dosed off, or lost interest in disgust.

"Counsel, please note that a quorum is present," said Steyer.

"With seven of nine directors, a quorum is present, though the record will reflect that neither of our chief executive officers is present, highly unusual for a vote of this nature."

"So noted," snapped Steyer. "To reflect the significance of the motion under consideration, it would be appropriate for counsel to individually poll the board."

"As I call your name, please vote Aye or Nay," said Normandy, recording the vote on her notepad and laptop in synch as she rounded the circuit. "Choy, absent. Finkelman, absent. Steyer?"

"Aye," said Steyer

"Ayes One, Nays Zero," said Normandy, keeping the tally. "Throckmore?"

"Aye," said Throckmore.

"Ayes Two, Nays Zero. Yamanaka?"

"Aye," said Yamanaka.

"Ayes Three, Nays Zero. Gutierrez?"

"Nay," said Gutierrez. No surprise there.

"Ayes Three, Nays One. Stanton-Landers?"

"No freaking way," said Stanton-Landers, raising a few eyebrows.

"Ayes Three, Nays Two. Dr. Francois?"

"I believe I must say no," said Dr. Francois after a pause, gently nodding his head with kindness toward Steyer. "My apologies, Daniel. I do not mean to insult. It is just what I believe is right."

"We are even, three votes to negotiate being acquired, three to abandon, one vote remaining," summarized Normandy. "Tie breaker will be cast via polycom. Senator Henderson, you have the floor."

There was another long pause from the phone box. Again, no one was sure if the Senator had taken another call or implicitly resigned. Normandy was about to dial him directly on his mobile when his voice again permeated the room.

"Sorry, been chewing on this all through the meeting. We can't do this deal now. It won't fly. I checked, no chance at the

SEC. I have to say Nay."

"The motion is defeated, 4 to 3," said Normandy, matter of fact, looking to Steyer for direction. "Shall we move onto other business?"

Steyer was speechless. He had never been defeated in a boardroom of his own design. The discussion was complete. With no alternatives backing his bravado and a manufactured run up in his price, Seidelmeyer was going to be hung out to dry.

"Daniel, perhaps we should discuss potential actions with regard to Calvin and Stephen," suggested Basru. "We can put our heads together and brainstorm potential locations where they might be. I have one in mind."

"Let's do a revote so the official record is unanimous," said Steyer.

"Is that appropriate?" asked Stanton-Landers, caught off guard by the chairman's suggestion.

"It's necessary," emphasized Steyer. "Whatever this board does now, it must act with a single voice. I am not sure where we are all headed, as a company or an industry, but I have suspicion it is going to be a terrifying ride down."

"Did you say terrifying?" asked Dr. Francois, eyes wide open. "Daniel, I don't believe I have heard you use that descriptor before."

"Can we poll again?" Steyer repeated to Normandy.

"We can do that," said Normandy, tearing up her notes and deleting the text on her laptop. She polled again and this time the Atom Heart motion was unanimously defeated. The official minutes of the meeting would reflect only that. Discussion would now turn to Choy and Finkelman, as soon as someone broke the next awkward silence.

"If anyone would care to be interested, I believe I know where our co-CEOs are currently being held," said Basru. "The company mistakenly received a substantial bill yesterday from the fueling station at Moffett Field. The account statement was meant for the personal attention of Choy and Finkelman."

Normandy swallowed hard. Basru had done his job, but this

was not going to make anyone's life less complicated. There was a long afternoon of discussion still ahead, and not a lot of camaraderie left in the room. Before the markets would close at 1:00 p.m. PST while the board was still in session, EnvisionInk stock would fall another 4%, more than a full 23% for the day at close.

By the end of the board meeting late that afternoon, when the board members returned to their cars, the number of employees in the parking lot had tripled. There would also be one more surprise waiting for them outside when they adjourned.

$ $

Three data crumbs had tipped off Balthazer to Moffett Field. First, there was the hundred-mile rule; he knew from the FBI warning that the limo had to be headed within one hundred miles of Salinas, although that did not narrow it much. Second, when Swerlow and Kisinski had called the show with their mothers on the air, Kisinski had fumbled on the words, "they are with us, or we are with them," which led him to believe Choy and Finkelman might have taken the upper hand in their negotiation, so their location was likely to be within their control. Third, when Steyer was on the air with him, he said Choy and Finkelman were in a safe place and all would be resolved soon enough. Balthazer was not even sure that Steyer knew what he was saying, but he did know the only place that Swerlow and Kisinski would accept and where the FBI would allow them to go had to be neutral ground, and the only neutral ground he could imagine was Choy and Finkelman's beloved flying mini-fortress. A little internet research by Balthazer revealed that when EnvisionInk had gone public, Choy and Finkelman tried to stay low key, but in the big ego landscape of bell ringing, they also wanted to make a statement. Being the only twenty-something private owners of a 737 was about as memorable a statement as they could imagine. They claimed it had not been about bragging rights, it was a public relations move to cement their reputation as the next Google, but everyone knew it was about bragging rights. The PR had not been bad either.

Balthazer and Producer Lee Creighton had driven up the

prior day from Paso Robles and spent the night at another non-descript motel, this time in Fremont, in the East Bay. That set them up to cross the Dumbarton Bridge in the morning and make their way back into the heart of Silicon Valley. With laptops and wireless relays in tow, they were mobile again in the Infiniti, headed late morning back into the belly of the techno-beast, making their way across the water to connect with Highway 101, then bypassing the exits to Stanford in Palo Alto and heading south, with Moffett Field not far ahead.

As they drove south past Moffett Field on Highway 101, they marveled in sight of NASA's renowned Ames Research Center and sometime home of the Space Shuttle, a Silicon Valley temple of innovation. It was not uncommon to see the neon painted jumbo jet owned by Choy and Finkelman out on the runway near the gargantuan landmark Hangar One, but not today, it was not at all visible. That did not surprise Balthazer. He would have bet his website there was no way that plane was going to fly anytime soon. Keeping it entirely indoors in a custom hangar had been another part of the bragging rights, a garage only for billionaires, but in this case it would conveniently allow the government to surround it with ready weaponry out of public sight. The puzzle pieces fit together nicely, for everyone except Swerlow and Kisinski.

"Their stock is tanking," said Producer Lee Creighton in the passenger seat, scrolling through multiple financial screens on his smart phone. "The whole market is down big time, except Atom Heart."

"Only the beginning," said Balthazer behind the steering wheel. "The hotter the rocket goes up, the more Gs it pulls on the way back down. Think of us as inertia assisting gravity."

"You really want to squash these bastards, don't you, Kimo?"

"I want them to experience humility," said Balthazer. "I want them to understand what my listeners are saying. If I can cost them several billion dollars in the process, that's just sport."

"What makes you so sure you're right about Moffett, that they're here?" asked Creighton. "There is a bit of speculation in your logic."

"I listen to people for a living," said Balthazer. "I hear what they say. I make pie out of fruit. Then I make it fun. You've seen enough to know that."

Balthazer continued along the highway, seemingly absorbed in his thoughts, missing the first and last exits for the base.

"I also know that we're zipping past Moffett Field now," said Creighton. "Were you thinking of exiting anytime soon?"

"They aren't ready for us yet," said Balthazer. "We were warned, remember?"

"Yeah, Kimo, I told you that before we left Paso Robles, where it was going so well for us. It didn't seem to faze you."

"We have to wait to be invited onto the tarmac," explained Balthazer. "So we need to be in striking distance when opportunity calls."

"Got it, then what is our plan? We have a show to do today, right?"

"The show will go on, what we do best, remote," replied Balthazer.

"I feel like a guest on the show, I'm being led somewhere I may not like," said Creighton.

"I got a tip, right after the Steyer call, from one of the EnvisionInk rank and file. Google 'EnvisionInk parking lot' on your phone. See what comes up in news feeds."

Producer Lee Creighton did as he was told, entered the keywords in the mobile search box and saw a list of unexpected returns. He clicked on one, then another to verify, then another.

"Employee Walkout at EnvisionInk?" read Creighton. "They're playing picket line games in the parking lot? That's brave. No one calls a strike in a non-union town."

"It's not union organizing," said Balthazer. "It's a protest. The employees have had enough. They're making a statement, an old fashioned work outage."

"And we're going to broadcast from the EnvisionInk parking lot?"

"Abundant wireless bandwidth our peer to peer network

can tap, a welcoming committee of tattooed friendlies, all the angry guests a host could want," said Balthazer. "It's paradise."

"And Santa Clara is a nice short drive from Moffett," tagged Creighton, trying to follow along.

"Striking distance as we await our invitation," said Balthazer.

"Just a few loose ends," replied Producer Lee Creighton, snapping in some puzzle pieces his companion might have missed. "You do remember that Swerlow and Kisinski aren't talking to you since you embarrassed them on air with their mommies, correct? That's beside the point. Given the easy striking distance, EnvisionInk is also within the hundred-mile radius. We'll be arrested."

"On private property, in the middle of Cal-Woodstock?" laughed Balthazer. "Not a chance EnvisionInk will let that happen. They think they have a PR problem now, with a parking lot full of demoralized Walkouts, the last thing they are going to let happen is have us hauled off. The war zone is the safety zone, my friend. That cement campground is our DMZ."

"Because you know people, right?" said Producer Lee Creighton. "Why do I know it's not going to be that easy?"

"If it were that easy, we wouldn't be getting paid the big bucks you got licensing us to every audio channel in America," said Balthazer.

Balthazer exited 101 and made his way to the world headquarters of EnvisionInk Systems in Santa Clara, with uncanny glee that the giant was bringing itself down. He and Creighton had no idea the board was in session, but on approach they saw what they liked, the Walkout was real. Almost two hundred scruffy employees wandered the parking lot, dressed as they would be for work in the uniform of coders—threadbare jeans, rumpled cargo shorts, faded logo t-shirts, jagged piercings, no sign of influence from Brooks Brothers, not even Men's Wearhouse. Some had tablets, a few net books, the only way they could tell these team members were off the job was by the stenciled protest banners, and they said it all against a backdrop of stucco and steel. Like all low-rise compounds on the peninsula, there was no security in the outdoor parking lots. Cars came and went without interference. Security clearance was only required to get into one of the many adjacent buildings, none of which held interest for Balthazer. He just wanted to join the fray, which is what he was about to do when the Bluetooth phone ringer in his car sang out.

"Why would Swerlow be calling me now?" asked Balthazer. "He's way ahead of plan."

"What makes you think it's Swerlow?" countered Creighton. "The screen says Out of Area."

"The only two people who have this number are you and Swerlow," answered Balthazer. "Unless one of you gave it out."

Producer Lee Creighton shook his head no, prompting Balthazer to pull the Infiniti to the curb outside the entry to EnvisionInk Systems. Balthazer left the engine running and kept the windows up, attracting modest attention from a few members of the dissent group beyond the shrubs, more curiosity than suspicion. Waving a friendly hello to those who saw him stopped in the driveway, Balthazer put the call on the Infiniti's integrated audio system.

"Yes?" Balthazer answered the call on speakerphone, offering no warmth or lure.

"Kimo Bawl-thuh-czar," came a rumbling male voice from the speaker, horribly mispronouncing Balthazer's name as only a non-devotee could.

"Who is this?" inquired Balthazer.

"Please hold for Congresswoman Payne," said the male voice.

Balthazer turned to Creighton, utterly clueless who Congresswoman Payne might be. Creighton had no idea either. A female voice subsequently permeated the space.

"Mr. Bawl-thuh-czar?" greeted Congresswoman Payne, properly but incorrectly.

"Kimo Balthazer," he replied, correcting her pronunciation.

"Mr. Balthazer, do you know who I am?" continued Congresswoman Payne, purposefully shrill.

"I do not," said Balthazer. "Deductive reasoning tells me you're a member of Congress, unless you're phone phishing."

"I do not fish, Mr. Balthazer. I am a ranking Republican in the US House of Representatives, from the state of Montana. I chair the Committee on Education and the Workforce. Are my credentials clear to you?"

"How did you get this phone number?" asked Balthazer, excessively irritated.

"I work for the government, Mr. Balthazer. We have many resources. We also have expertise in GPS technology. I was listening to recorded bits of your live discussion yesterday with Daniel Steyer. I found your tone to be discourteous."

"It's the act," said Balthazer. "It's what I do."

"Let me tell you what I think you need to cease to do, Mr. Balthazer. You are not an expert on business. You are sticking your nose into the affairs of two very important companies, EnvisionInk Systems and Atom Heart Entertainment. Clearly your expressed views are having an impact on equity trading today, useless negative energy. I believe you need to let free markets be free."

"Does the First Amendment mean anything to you, Madam Congresswoman?"

"It means everything to me, which is why when a foul mouthed, anti-family annoyance like you inserts himself into the dialogue of great entrepreneurial leaders, intervention can be appropriate," avowed Payne. "I want you to apologize to Mr. Steyer on your show today, and withdraw any judgment you previously stated about corporate iniquity in his arrangements with Mr. Seidelmeyer. May I have your word that you will do what is right for America?"

"Blow me," said Balthazer. "You don't need GPS. I'll send a sedan chair for you."

"Mr. Balthazer, you need to understand that I do know who you are, and that you have a past, and that many agencies of government are displeased with that past. That can be your problem, or it can go away with bureaucratic shuffle. I advise you to think through your actions carefully and promptly, or your revitalized career could be brief. Urgency matters. The correction must come today."

"Blow me, too," added Producer Lee Creighton, hearing it all on speakerphone.

She never heard him, the line had gone dead. Balthazer and Creighton were equally stunned. This was new ground for them. They had defied plenty of authority in their time, but thus far they had escaped national politics. Given the scope of their new adventure, that was no longer to be the case.

"Was that real?" Balthazer asked Producer Lee Creighton.

"Is any of this?" responded Creighton. "Let's get unpacked. We have a show to do. You can decide anytime this afternoon if you want to kiss some Steyer butt."

"That's not Steyer talking, not his style to call Mama of The Hill," said Balthazer. "It's Seidelmeyer. He needs the deal more than anyone. He called in a marker, but this casino is closed. This jock eats no crow."

Shaking off the attempted shakedown, Balthazer rolled the Infiniti forward and parked it near one of the makeshift tents, then proceeded with Producer Lee Creighton to unload the minimal gear needed to do the EnvisionInk remote. Being a radio guy, he could easily slip into crowds unnoticed, but his voice was always distinct, especially to a loyal few who could place him on audio cue. As Balthazer expected, there were more than a loyal few in this crowd. These were the hard core opinion makers who made viral happen and had been listening to him online since McDonald's.

"Anyone up for a little internet radio today?" Balthazer asked no one in particular. The response was instant recognition, Moses among the Liberated, the familiar vocal chords of *Rage* come to the flatland wilderness. He and Producer Lee Creighton were offered bountiful food and drink, plus access to AC power and decrypted wireless routers. They immediately started a sign-up sheet for the many volunteers who would go on the air with him that afternoon, all with something to say.

"Do we have a special theme for today?" asked Producer Lee Creighton. "Something new and different in honor of the Walkout?"

"We do," confirmed Balthazer. "I have a concept I've been cooking up for a while that I want to float on the show."

"Something that might tweak the Honorable Ms. Payne?" asked Creighton.

"This will tweak way more than Payne," taunted Balthazer. "It's called a Merger Bill of Rights."

$ $ $ $

2.4
Test Compile

NASDAQ: ENVN (Day 12)
SHARE PRICE @ MARKET OPEN: $143.10
COMPANY MARKET CAP: $38.25B
VALUATION DELTA SINCE ABDUCTION: +6%
** ENVN DELTA FROM PEAK: < 37% > **

NASDAQ SINCE ABDUCTION: +17%

> FOR IMMEDIATE RELEASE
> SANTA CLARA, CA
> ENVISIONINK SUSPENDS M&A
> DISCUSSIONS
>
> (6:30 a.m. EST) EnvisionInk Systems (NAS-
> DAQ: ENVN), a global leader in digital adver-
> tising platforms, announced today that it has
> terminated all strategic discussion with Atom
> Heart Entertainment.
>
> The company's board of directors confirmed
> that its focus must remain fully on the safe re-
> turn of co-CEOs Calvin Choy and Stephen J.
> Finkelman. Other than maintaining continuity
> in the day to day business, which is operating
> normally, significant corporate decisions will
> remain on hold until the current situation is
> resolved.
>
> "All of our efforts must center on the release
> of Calvin and Stephen," said Chairman Dan-
> iel Steyer. "With the deepest of respect for all
> our stakeholders, our Board has unanimously

resolved that pursuit of any other matter at this time would be a distraction. We are hopeful that we will be back to business as usual soon, but until then, our fiduciary duty directs us to table major actions that might otherwise be considered."

The company confirmed that negotiation for the safe release continues with appropriate government oversight, but that the known location of Choy and Finkelman cannot be revealed for their own safety as well as that of the public. Confidentiality remains a key factor in expediting a timely and positive outcome. Commentary in this notice may contain forward-looking statements within the meaning of Section 27A of the Securities Act of 1933, as amended, and Section 21E of the Securities Exchange Act of 1934, as amended . . .

$ $

Sol Seidelmeyer had established a personal routine of waking with the market open and immediately checking overnight headlines on the three handheld electronic devices he kept bedside. He would then proceed downstairs to his home gym where he read the *Wall Street Journal* on his recumbent bike, the *New York Times* on his treadmill, and the *LA Times* over a post workout cup of mild Ethiopian coffee with his wife of thirty-six years, Amanda, a talented landscape architect who had become so used to the routine she could practically clock it on a stopwatch. Seidelmeyer would then shower, dress, and be driven in a Town Car to the studio lot, logging East Coast phone calls en route, and arrive at his office in West Los Angeles before 9:00 a.m. for his first meeting of the day.

Awaking Thursday morning, his first glance at the EnvisionInk press release on his iPad told him there would be no routine today. Within seconds of seeing the headline, he dialed his assistant on her mobile line and told her to be in the office in twenty minutes, no excuses. He did not even know where she lived or if this was possible. It was seldom expected that studio chiefs consider real world details like geography when they barked orders.

Within minutes, Seidelmeyer had his tie knotted and was driving himself to work. As he reran the press release in his head, he could not understand how he had allowed himself to be played, and for what reason. The press release had been unexplainably dropped by EnvisionInk precisely at market open, and after yesterday's 23% haircut, ENVN was down another 8% on the first few trades, institutions dumping speculative run-up positions and taking the DOW and NASDAQ down in tandem. A few hundred words released over the wire had wiped out billions in market value not only for EnvisionInk shareholders, but for everyone with a pension or 401K invested in the broad market. On the surface this could not have been good for Steyer, so why had he done it? What had Steyer been thinking? Where was the upside in lying about how to get this deal done? Seidelmeyer was good at this, a negotiator like no other, a lifetime of making deals, knowing when to trust. Steyer had led him by the nose to his own slaughter.

Or had he? Something about the metrics on the ticker told a different story. EnvisionInk was in free fall over a two-day arc, and most indices were rounding the bases past a correction, on the way to a bear market. The only stock holding its price was Atom Heart. Not only was it unaffected by the EnvisionInk announcement, it was hanging onto the gains it made after Seidelmeyer appeared on CNBC. Seidelmeyer knew that meant the Street bought his story, that there were many cheaper targets for Atom Heart, and the reason EnvisionInk must have walked away was because it could not allow itself to be sold at super discount so soon after the grandeur of exuberance. The EnvisionInk board was just as greedy as the Street, the Choy and Finkelman rescue angle was an excuse. The Street had believed if it knocked down EnvisionInk, it might still be taken out by Atom Heart, but unaccepting of those economics, EnvisionInk simply withdrew itself from play. That withdrawal put the entire market in the toilet, leaving Atom Heart as a hedge against broad declines, to let it gobble up what no one else could. With little measurable volume in a volatile week of trading, every healthy share of Atom Heart that was sold to raise cash—by institutions with no other alternative to covering soft positions—was bought instantly by competitors, with demand still outstripping supply. Atom Heart's price climbed another 3% and would remain fixed until there was more news, at which point it would be expected to climb again. All that was fine, except Seidelmeyer knew the truth. He had no miracle buy in his sights to announce anytime soon. He had not dodged a bullet. He had simply delayed the firing squad.

As Seidelmeyer entered his office suite slightly before 7:30 a.m., already there at her desk on command performance was Ellen Ardor. The personal switchboard she ran for him was lit like the curtain call for a rock concert. As Seidelmeyer grabbed a pile of old-fashioned pink message slips from her on his way through her workspace to his interior haven, he knew he was in triage mode. The call list was overwhelming, even for a studio head. Everyone wanted to talk to him—his head of Corporate Communications, his head of Investor Relations, more than half of his board members, the financial press, the trade papers, the unions. He could start returning calls now and at a minute each he would be on the phone through the weekend, but there was only one person Seidelmeyer wanted on the phone.

"CNBC wants to know if you'll do a follow up," shouted Ardor through the interior door. "They'll come to us with a camera crew. Name the time."

"Negative interest, whatever comes after negative interest, black hole interest," bellowed Seidelmeyer as he dropped into the deep, padded chair behind his desk and peered into the assembly of live monitors around him. "How are we doing getting Congresswoman Payne?"

"I heard you loud and clear from the car, I have calls into all of Representative Payne's lines," responded Ardor. "I left urgent messages with each of her key aides. I think she's on the House floor. There's a vote."

"Get her off the House floor," commanded Seidelmeyer. "I need her on the phone."

"I'm working on it," asserted Ardor. "In the meantime, WSJ wants a comment. Variety wants an email interview. *Entertainment Tonight* wants an updated head shot."

"No to all," answered Seidelmeyer. "Get Payne. You bonded with her while she was here. Try the BFF angle."

"I'm doing everything I can," said Ardor. "You have calls from our Government Relations office in DC, general counsel wants to get on your sheet this morning. Fidelity wants lunch. Goldman Sachs wants to know when you'll be in New York."

"Payne," compelled Seidelmeyer. "I want Payne."

"I understand, Mr. Seidelmeyer. If I had a cell number for the Speaker of the House, I'd use it and interrupt. Silicon Valley Bank, Morgan Stanley, Jim Cramer, any of these sound interesting while we wait?"

"Not interesting," pronounced Seidelmeyer. "Beg, pay someone, get her."

Seidelmeyer's eyes wandered from screen to screen. Trading volume was extraordinary in every sector, in every category, and almost universally the trend was downward—except Atom Heart, still holding steadily. Seidelmeyer looked out the office door at his assistant, saw how many lines and chat sessions she was working, then noticed a small smile as she appeared to connect. Ellen Ardor was good, an executive in the making who never gave up on a task, no matter how ridiculous it seemed. She was about to score again, the unattainable delivered.

"Hang on, I think I've got her through a page, we're going to need an autograph from Justin Timberlake," conveyed Ardor, tapping her wireless headset and pointing to Seidelmeyer that she was about to transfer the call. "Yep, score, she's stepping off the House floor. Stand by, here's Congresswoman Payne."

Seidelmeyer waved a brief thank you, pushed a button under his desk to activate the automatic door close spring that was his privilege, took a deep breath and picked up the receiver.

"Thank you for taking my call, Congresswoman," welcomed Seidelmeyer, no fret in his phone manner. "I understand you're in the middle of something and I appreciate the special attention."

"You do understand the legislative process and my role in it?" came the voice of Payne, foregoing pleasantries. "It's not my favorite part of the job, but when I'm doing it, I don't step out for social calls."

"I'm not calling with theater tickets," replied Seidelmeyer, hastily shifting tone. "You didn't get the retraction from Balthazer. Now I need a bag over my head. We can use the gallows on the back lot."

"I tried, he's a tough fellow to motivate" said the congresswoman. "I realize the damage he did to public opinion was considerable. I don't think Steyer was able to navigate through that."

"What am I supposed to do now?" asked Seidelmeyer. "That bastard Steyer has me in an impossible situation."

"Buy something else," advised Payne. "That's what I would do. Impress the hell out of us with your moxie. It's a good thing you have options."

"What rung of The Inferno could he have descended to?" continued Seidelmeyer. "This can't be good for him. But he wouldn't do it if it wasn't good for him. I can't read Sanskrit, I see no meaning in his strategy."

"Is there something more you would like me to do, Sol?" asked Payne. "I need to get back on the floor and show my colleagues I do, at times, care about the law. I don't see why you're so upset. It's a free market, prices are soft. Buy something cheap, then cash in your chips and book a Grand Duplex on the Queen Mary 2."

"It's not that simple," said Seidelmeyer. "This was the deal that needed to happen. I need you to call Steyer for me."

"I am a member of Congress," said Payne. "The only thing I can do is evaluate the deal when it comes before the judiciary. I can't be your broker, or your advocate."

"You have to call Steyer and convince him it's essential that he reopens our dialogue. Look at the market drop. Trust me, it doesn't stop here. You're in government; you have to protect the economy."

"Sol, you're out of line, I can't go anywhere near that," shot back Payne. "Pick up the phone and call him. Use that special Fairy-Tale Phone of yours."

Payne was smarter than he thought, she had not missed a detail of her visit to his office. Now her knowledge was ammunition, and he was unable to deflect it.

"He can't pick up the phone if it's me," said Seidelmeyer. "He's on the record. His board has taken a position, they don't want any more interaction with me. Unless there are unique circumstances he is bound to oblige their governance."

"I'm already out on a limb for our friendship with Balthazer," said Payne. "I need to put some distance between us. I'm sure you'll do fine with one of your other acquisition options. Let go of your anger with Steyer. He did what he had to do. You go do what you have to do. Remember that it's only business. I'm sure it's not personal."

"It's most assuredly personal," snarled Seidelmeyer. "Like that other bastard Balthazer, his name calling and finger pointing destroyed us. He erased Steyer's credibility after I played the perfect talking head on CNBC . . . unless Steyer set it all up and got me to sink myself just to crush me out of spite."

"But your price is holding, Sol," argued Payne. "You aren't making any sense. You're rambling. How about this, you worry about your deals, I'll worry about Balthazer. On that we concur, that is personal. That door is just opening. Now if you'll excuse me, one of my aides just informed me I have to go on Fox News and explain why Atom Heart Entertainment not buying EnvisionInk is not apocalyptic, regardless of the market turmoil. But first I need to have my hair and make-up done. I guess I won't be making it back to the floor for this vote."

Payne ended the call. Seidelmeyer slammed down the phone, then looked at all the blinking lights awaiting attention, the hundreds of emails on his screen, the nonstop texts from his assistant trying to direct incoming traffic. For the first time in his career, he had no idea how to tackle any of it. The damage was done and could not be contained, only delayed. He picked up his mobile and placed a call to his personal lawyer.

$ $

Balthazer's initial remote the prior day, from the Envision-Ink parking lot, exceeded expectations. Within minutes of going live at noon, Security descended and asked him to leave the premises, private property and all that. When Balthazer refused, the entirety of the leading edge Walkout crew surrounded him, part blocking shield, part human moat. Live on the air, he dared Security to drag him away, which would have involved climbing over several hundred already demoralized EnvisionInk employees who were providing him protection. One of the early-stage malcontents shared that the company's board happened to be in session, suggesting that Balthazer hang tough given the company's culture, which avoided visible conflict. It was not much of a reach for Balthazer to surmise that the board had enough problems at the moment and did not need any more news trucks on site than were already there. The show was allowed to go on, likely in hope that it would putter out as attendees grew weary of Balthazer's tirade. To the chagrin of anyone naïve enough to believe that, each hour gone by had added another hundred unhappy workers to the Walkout.

There was no shortage of volunteers speaking up for themselves and the crowd. Producer Lee Creighton formed lines of the assembled and alternated them with live callers, sometimes putting callers right on the air with the Walkouts in mini-dialogues. Themes banged about were consistent, regardless of geographic location or industry—management was in it for themselves, job security was as ancient a myth as the protective rule of the Roman Empire, C-level executives bought weekend ranches while employees lost their leveraged homes, and job engagement was limited to a tiny guild of decision-makers invited with invisible whispers to join the inner circle. It may well have been a self-selecting set of participants crying foul, but the malaise was inescapable. Employees were afraid. They felt help-less. They were angry.

Balthazer asked what had happened at EnvisionInk, with its legendary private chefs, lavish free meals and massages. To be fair, many of the Walkouts said initially it had been Camelot, that there was an initial rush of adrenalin fueling the company with a mission statement they believed would change the world—and that had lasted right up until the day of the IPO. Once that Wall Street bell rang, their mission, as they came to understand it, became about driving the stock price. At first they had been focused on developing new products and services, excellence in technology and speed to market. That had worked for a while, followed by a mass hiring in sales and business development to position the company for taking market share through healthy competition. When the healthy competition was behind them, it was replaced by more aggressive competition, clever market-ing constructs and blind pricing schemes that brought segment domination as competitors moved too slowly. When competitor apathy no longer drove the share price, it came time for a string of small acquisitions that utilized the company's immense cash reserves to buy up would-be challengers and functionality add-ons that secured barriers to entry. Almost no one was ever laid off in these "partner mergers" presumably out of guilt, the com-pany just bloated with margins still strong enough to support the fat, but each step of the way, people went from being more important to less important. Innovation moved from being the lifeblood of all activity to organic initiatives that could not move the needle. The many perks at EnvisionInk were enjoyable, but it was clear they did not replace life purpose, and underlying it all was that too real suspicion it all could be taken away at any time. When it suited management to cut costs and that was all that could be done to drive earnings, employees believed they were no more than costs, and gone they would be.

Balthazer had been surprised how unswerving the themes had been, and where other companies may not have offered any of the perks of EnvisionInk, the stories of detachment

were equivalent. Employees wanted purpose, employees wanted security, employees wanted to be appreciated. They wanted
to make a living too, and some aspired to wealth, but mostly
what they wanted was for the tug-of-war of "us and them" to
stop pulling everyone apart, and for the divide between them
and the Investors, Bankers, and Operators to reflect some form
of fairness, if not kindness. Layers and levels were more than
anachronisms in the flats of twenty-first century org charts —
they were archaic restraints, unbearably insulting, as stupid as
performance reviews.

When Balthazer first mentioned that he wanted to crowd
source a Merger Bill of Rights, no one was sure what to make
of his proposal. Most were aware of the US Constitution and its
Bill of Rights, but a messy war had been fought to allow that to
happen. While many people were happy to walk out on their jobs
and make a point on a temporary basis, no one wanted an outright war. Some had heard of a once proposed Airline Passenger
Bill of Rights following a string of travelers getting trapped in
planes stuck on runways in the sun without food or water, but
that had been largely dismissed as a public relations stunt, not a
set of policies with teeth. Balthazer was more confident, and as
always, more provocative. He told the crowd and his audience
that if they wanted a Merger Bill of Rights and could agree on
what it was, it was within their power to stand behind it and see
it adopted and enforced. People were skeptical, but that did not
stop them from firing in suggestions, however weird and outrageous, to a mobile text code and anonymous email box that
Producer Lee Creighton was making well-known. Some of the
more impractical suggestions included:

· Anyone doing a good job who is fired in a
merger for cost savings should get a big pile of
money, same as those at the top. A gargantuan
pile, plus benefits.

· Any employees not fired must not be expected

to do the work of the departed, thus doubling
their workload, unless they get a pay increase
of 100%.

· Every executive who survives a merger must
be able to explain to a jury of their subordi-
nates why they were worth what they got paid,
and if unconvincing, they could be voted off
the island.

· Any federal official rendering a judgment on
antitrust approval must be able to explain in
twenty-five words or less what the merging
companies do. The assignment will be graded
by a sixth grade teacher.

· If the combined share price of two merged
companies has not met the pretend forecast
which helped sell the deal, the prior two CEOs
have to give back all the money they took home
for themselves. And wash everyone's laundry.

Snarky office humor percolated through the commentary,
but the underlying substance was authentic. All this emotion
had poured out with endless candor from those in the parking
lot as well as those calling in, and the momentum continued today, with word of other Walkouts spreading across Silicon Valley. There were now rumors of people assembling in the parking
lots of Yahoo, Google, Oracle, eBay, Facebook, Apple, and Microsoft—not huge crowds, but pockets of sympathizers who had
listened to Balthazer's show and been touched. Silicon Valley
life, for the most innovative engineers and creative designers,
had traditionally been about being a part of something, and this
something seemed like it had more substance than sitting in a
cubicle trying to create shareholder value, whatever that was,
especially on a day like today when the stock market was sliding
by the minute and no one seemed sure if there was a floor.

"Did we make our point and stop the Atom Heart merger

dead in its tracks?" shouted Balthazer, waving a copy of the press release above his head, the new pirate flag of rebellion. The parking lot crowd, now over a thousand strong, cheered in support, but it was clear this was not enough. They wanted more, and at the same time they were worried that somehow they had been responsible for the stock market slide. They were walking out on management whose vision they questioned, but they wanted to be able to return on their own terms and for their own sustenance. If the market continued to implode, that might not be the case, and the least loyal among them would undoubtedly be the first asked to exit for good. It was with that backdrop that Kimo Balthazer took to the air, attempting to make sense of the muddle.

KIMO: We are live here on the campus—the parking lot actually—of EnvisionInk Systems in Santa Clara, California, surrounded by what looks to be over a thousand EnvisionInk employees who have walked off the job in protest of the pending Atom Heart Entertainment merger. We have all seen the press release issued today with a statement by company chairman Daniel Steyer declaring the merger is off, at least until the company's co-CEOs Calvin Choy and Stephen J. Finkelman are released from secret captivity by Silicon Valley's own Butch and Sundance, Dennis Swerlow and Sam Kisinski. Producer Lee Creighton is with me again on location and says we are reaching millions now via internet radio, satellite radio, old fashioned radio, pretty much any way you can get a signal, we are getting it to you. So if the Atom Heart deal has been defeated by this peaceful employee uprising, why are employees still filtering into the parking lot by the hour? And why are we getting rumors of similar employee Walkouts all over Silicon Valley, not just at EnvisionInk? To kick things off today, and for no particular reason beyond that, standing here with me I have a gentleman who is a Systems Architect for EnvisionInk, who goes by the handle of Hacker Deep Six. On the phone from another parking lot in San Mateo at a start-up no has ever heard of called GrindX is their lead graphic designer, Antigone1. Hacker Deep Six, Antigone1—Welcome, *This Is Rage*!

HACKER DEEP SIX: Thanks, Kimo.

CALLER ANTIGONE1: Yeah. Thanks, Kimo.

HACKER DEEP SIX: Dude, this is so cool. We're really pissing people off, aren't we?

KIMO: I hope so, that's the point. Let me ask you something, you're both relatively young, and from what I can tell, smart and employable. What possible reason could you have for walking out on your companies, especially when you've already succeeded in defeating the Atom Heart deal?

HACKER DEEP SIX: We have no delusions that it's over, Kimo. It's just over until the next one comes, or until this one comes back. That's what companies do, gobble each other up and spit out employees.

CALLER ANTIGONE1: I agree, Kimo. I'm twenty-nine, and I've been laid off three times. This start-up pays half what my last job paid, and sure, if we get bought by IBM or Cisco someday my stock options might be worth something. More likely, I'll get canned again and have to look for another gig. It's no fun. I can do it because I'm young, but my resume is already a train wreck, and what happens when I'm old, like thirty-five, is anyone going to hire me or do I join the permanently unemployed without enough cash to retire?

HACKER DEEP SIX: It's hard to hear the way someone like Steyer talks about us. "He's willing to live with no organic growth." He's a deal junkie. What he really wants is to unload all his shares for cash, but if he can't, we're the consolation prize. They make a big deal at company rallies that it's all about the employees, but we know they see us as costs. They don't think the big ideas come from us, not even the little ideas, just the grunt work. They can live with us, they can live without us. They're ambivalent, so we're ambivalent. Everything is short term, that's why we're not more grateful, because in truth, no one cares if we come or go, as long as the stock price goes up. When it doesn't, we're gone. Hard to give your heart to that.

KIMO: You two seem awfully pessimistic for frolicking in the meadows of legal wealth creation. What do you say to all the mini-millionaires that have already spun off, your brethren? They're not here in the parking lot. They must think the system is okay.

HACKER DEEP SIX: Actually, some of them are here, Kimo. You can't tell from someone's looks how much money they have. I'm happy for everyone who wins, really I am. I used to like working at EnvisionInk, when we were smaller and it was about something. But right now the guys who started this place are being held at gunpoint, and all everyone is worried about is what it's doing to the stock price. That's weird.

KIMO: If the guys who have Calvin and Stephen are listening, what would you like to tell them?

CALLER ANTIGONE1: Can I answer that, Kimo? What I would tell them is that they've actually done us a favor. I know that sounds spooky, they killed some rich guy in another rich guy's backyard, and I don't want them to hurt Calvin or Stephen. But if they hadn't done what they've done, you wouldn't be doing this show now. We wouldn't be talking about this. People from every department and salary level wouldn't be walking off their jobs to make a point.

KIMO: And what point is that?

CALLER ANTIGONE1: That our jobs are supposed to be about something, and when they are only about filling wheelbarrows full of money for others to roll away no matter who gets hurt, then it's not worth it. It's just not worth it.

HACKER DEEP SIX: She nailed it, Kimo. Those two guys who have our co-CEOs, they may not be good guys, but good can come from evil, and they definitely have us focused on the right thing. We have you to thank for that too, you coming out here and standing with us is so amazing, and the fact that this Walkout is spreading without anyone leading it, that's even more amazing. It's kind of like Arab Spring, only no one gets killed. I mean hopefully no one gets killed. We just need to get on that Merger Bill of Rights you talked about yesterday, and if we get that done and Calvin and Stephen come back, the whole thing will have meant something. Then things can be different.

KIMO: Well, that's certainly a nice call to action. Hacker Deep Six, live here at EnvisionInk, Antigone1 over at GrindX, I thank you both for sharing your Rage and hope you'll get your friends to join us on the program. Meanwhile, for all you listening out there in parking lots and cubicles and office dungeons, we want to hear from you. What do you think you should get in a Merger Bill of Rights? Yesterday we set up short codes and email addresses and lots of other ways for you to get your thoughts to us. As long as you keep sending them in, Producer Lee Creighton will keep posting them unedited on ThisIsRage.com. Sound a little wacky? Maybe, but most ideas for change start out sounding wacky. Producer Lee Creighton and I call it "wacky doable." Remember, we didn't all start out with the same wacky right to vote—that life and liberty and pursuit of happiness thing gets redefined from time to time. Let's redefine it with the right to keep your job, so a few people can't get richer pocketing your salary. Send us your demands, the longer the list on our site gets, the more fun it will be when you send the link to your boss—and don't worry, we have a button on the site that keeps the sender of those links secret. Like Hacker Deep Six said, we don't want anyone to get hurt, no career limiting moves. Keep telling us what you think, who knows how far we can take this together. Call me, I'll be in the parking lot. This is Kimo Balthazer, and *This Is Rage*.

"Killer set, Kimo, never better," lauded Producer Lee Creighton, watching his screen light up with avatars in every quadrant. "This crowd is all yours, they'll follow you anywhere, like a Bat Out of Hell."

$ $

Steyer, Normandy, and Basru had been careful to make
their way to Moffett Field without drawing any attention. Special Agent Hussaini had been patched into their surprise call the
previous evening immediately following their board meeting,
and while they wanted to come then, it had taken him almost the
full day to clear the meeting through Washington. They arrived
at night in a rented Oldsmobile, cleared security as arranged in
advance under assumed identities, and parked just out of range
of the BBJ so they could quietly enter the private terminal un-
seen. Hussaini had arranged the meeting cautiously, with no potential tip off to Swerlow and Kisinski, mission critical that not
even a rumor creep out. They would use Choy and Finkelman's
private conference room in the hangar, windowless and invisible
to anyone onboard the BBJ. Hussaini established a precedent
for getting on and off the jet in his alleged negotiations with base
staff, so there would be no reason for anyone to suspect whom
he might be seeing. He was less surprised that the EnvisionInk
team had figured out their location than how long it had taken
them, and Normandy's ability to keep her silence as promised
to Choy and Finkelman. Normandy would have made a decent
FBI agent, he thought, which gave him modest comfort there
was someone on the other side of the desk with the good sense
to remain low key.

Steyer's performance on Balthazer's show had baffled Hussaini, and had further antagonized Swerlow as a stall tactic.
Everyone on the plane had been listening to all of Balthazer's
broadcasts, and while Swerlow had pondered aloud the inclina-
tion to get on the line with Balthazer and Steyer, it was clear to
Hussaini that Swerlow had become too paranoid to pursue any
further contact with company. Likewise, when EnvisionInk earlier that day announced an end to its dialogue with Atom Heart
and recommitted to freeing Choy and Finkelman, Hussaini had
to assume Swerlow knew he was being worked—he had to have
figured out the no-fly status they were enduring was not an accident, and without more pressure applied soon, he and his cousin

were never going to get out of California.

"Swerlow could go over the edge any time," said Hussaini to Steyer and his two C-level executives. "I've seen a lot of guys like him in this state, and it usually doesn't end well. He's not a professional, and the stress is getting to him. I'm not sure how much more time we have before he loses it."

"He seemed wound pretty tight when he was on the show with Balthazer and his mom," noted Steyer. "That was days ago. How are you holding it together?"

"Kisinski is more level-headed than Swerlow," conveyed Hussaini. "Maybe because he's younger, maybe because he's talented. I think he sees a scenario where they get out alive, do some time, and still have some kind of life, however many years down the road. Swerlow has moved past that, it's all or nothing for him. The only way out is his way and that's slipping away. Kisinski has been keeping the balance. Balance buys me time."

"What are you doing with that time?" asked Normandy. "You can't believe you're actually going to get a flight clearance. That plane isn't going to Shanghai. You know that. Do they?"

"I think until your press release this morning—that said Choy and Finkelman were your sole focus—Swerlow was allowing himself to be deluded that I could get this done. But just before I left them to come see you, I saw a different picture of him, much worse. The desperation is kicking in. I half expected him to shoot me, but he still has enough of his wits about him to know the sound of a gunshot brings everything to an end. I'm going to need a way to convince him that I haven't been dragging my feet just waiting to wear him down. He has to believe there's hope, or we're likely to lose someone."

"So you have just been making up delay after delay, and he has been buying it?" asked Basru. "He does not see that he is surrounded and it is only a matter of time before you give the signal to end it."

"Like I said, he's an amateur," replied Hussaini. "He has no idea what he's doing, and I do. It's all about the exhaustion factor—whoever becomes exhausted first loses. This is the opposite of Salinas, where we missed our window by not moving fast. All I need is a moment for him to look away. Then I have the gun, then we're done. I have all the time in the world, as long as he does."

"What's the current working version of the story?" asked Steyer.

"That your pilots won't do it, they have no interest in getting involved in anything like this, which actually isn't a lie. I just don't think Swerlow will buy it's the last hurdle we have to clear. There really is no way this plane is going to Shanghai."

"Suppose our pilots would do it," said Steyer. "What's your preference, to take them in the air or on the ground?"

"I'm agnostic, I just want to get home to my family," said Hussaini. "This has turned into a long assignment. What did you have in mind?"

"The plane doesn't have to go to Shanghai, it just needs to take off," proposed Steyer. "That could get you enough of a window of trust for him to lose focus. He closes his eyes to rest, looks out the window in relief, any second he lets down his guard, you take him and the pilots land the plane. You're in the air less than an hour, maybe half that."

"It's risky," said Hussaini. "We'd be disarming a man with a loaded gun in the air."

"An amateur with a gun," said Basru. "Is it really that hard?"

"I'd have to get approval from the Director," said Hussaini, dismissing Basru's comment. "But it sounds like something we could sell. We may need your friend Henderson to help. Can I take the gun from him if he thinks he's already won? I don't know, but given the potential for a clean outcome, I'd be willing to try."

"What happens if you botch it," said Normandy. "Who gets sucked out the window, all of them? You included?"

"I don't think we have a pressurization problem on takeoff. I just have to move very quickly before we do. We tell the pilots if they hear a gunshot to land, at that point we're all in, nothing to debate."

"I don't like it," said Normandy. "These are cowboy moves. We have too much at stake."

"Boarding the plane and taking Swerlow by force is its own kind of cowboy move," said Hussaini. "It gives him the most time to react, which is why we haven't done it. Besides, with his mood now, I need something to tell him when I go back on that plane. If I don't have a story, it could be over. I really am out of material."

"What if I came onboard with you?" asked Steyer. "I'm the one they wanted in the first place. If I go on the plane and tell him I'm going with you, it shows him we have more skin in the game, that we're serious."

"It's a sign of good faith," said Hussaini. "At least it's a new story for him to chew on. You'd be an additional trading card, he might like that. Do you really think you can get your pilots to do it?"

"Do you really think you can take his gun right after take-off?" asked Steyer.

"I do," affirmed Hussaini. "And I think I can get the Director to bless this plan. The hard part is going to be explaining to Swerlow that you want to come onboard. His trust levels are expectedly low."

"Let's see how far each of us can get and meet back here in the morning," said Steyer.

"Don't forget to tip off Choy and Finkelman that our chairman might be coming aboard," said Normandy. "You can credit Sanjay for his detective work if they ask."

"One last thing," said Hussaini. "We haven't discussed the wild card, Balthazer. If he shows up and we get a crowd, that quickly narrows our options."

"Balthazer is in our parking lot creating a revolution," said Steyer. "He's found heaven. He obviously doesn't know you're here or you'd have the insurgency instead of us."

"We're pretty sure Balthazer does know we're here," said Hussaini. "We put a tracking device on his car before he left Salinas. We know exactly where he is. He made a run by Moffett looping around the Bay on his way to your shop. He was casing us, clever fellow. Then he threw down his soap box in your backyard. That's why we left him alone there, to keep him busy and away from here."

"Then I guess we'll have to keep him on our home front," said Steyer. "I don't see that being our biggest challenge. We'll send down a care package from of our chefs. Maybe Sylvia or Sanjay can offer him an interview. I'm sure they'll do better than I did."

Normandy did not appear amused by Steyer's closing remark, another rotten volley. Basru did not acknowledge it, maybe he did not even hear it. Hussaini had seen information that Basru had already updated his resume on LinkedIn, it was obvious he wanted out. Steyer and Hussaini shook hands, then Hussaini headed back toward the plane. As the EnvisionInk team departed in the rental car, Hussaini knew he had more than one hard sell ahead of him. His time in California had not at all been what he expected. The conflicted negotiation, the obsession with stock prices, the escalating employee Walkouts, the sudden geek stardom of Balthazer—so much intervention, none of it was letting him do his job well. All he wanted to do was go home.

$ $ $ $

2.5
Debug Mode

NASDAQ: ENVN (Day 13)
SHARE PRICE @ MARKET OPEN: $127.85
COMPANY MARKET CAP: $34.15B
VALUATION DELTA SINCE ABDUCTION: < 5% >
** ENVN DELTA FROM PEAK: < 44% > **

NASDAQ SINCE ABDUCTION: +6%

"I will be making a brief statement and then taking a few questions," announced Congresswoman Payne at her hastily arranged Friday morning press conference. "I have some thoughts I wish to share on the subject of Kimo Balthazer, and then I will be convening the Education and Workforce committee to discuss the impact of his irresponsible commentary on the equity markets."

Although usually lacking in substance, a Payne press conference was always a top ticket. The entertainment value alone could draw an amphitheater of reporters on short notice. What she said might not mean much, but it would almost always make the evening news and the media brand's home page, which all journalists liked. Besides, for Friday afternoon drinking with buddies going into the weekend, nothing beat crapping on a Payne press conference off the record, and you had to be there to get the full ambiance. Her DC office was well attended.

"Although there is no reason for the likes of a distinguished gathering of fine journalists like yourselves to care, until recently Kimo Balthazer was a third-tier radio talk show host. Having been dismissed from his employment in New York and then Los Angeles, Mr. Balthazer was working at an AM station in

Fresno, California, which for those of you who are unaware is a suburb of Yosemite National Park. Mr. Balthazer had a modest syndication agreement for his radio show called *This Is Rage*, an inane forum for the unemployed. Not long ago, he was fired from his Fresno job for using profanity on the public airwaves, and on his way out the door committed acts of violence that were never revealed to the public. Kimo Balthazer clearly was at the end of his career, a loser's loser, unemployable, intoxicated daily, aimless—until he decided to insert himself in the business of EnvisionInk Systems upon the kidnapping of their co-CEOs, Calvin Choy and Stephen J. Finkelman, who as you know remain today in captivity in a yet to be revealed location. I am sure we can count on Mr. Balthazer to let that cat out of the bag as soon as he has bagged it, and further endanger the public. I recently appealed to Mr. Balthazer to please extract himself from the EnvisionInk dialogue, specifically so that our hard working officers of the FBI could work in secrecy. His response to me was, well, unrepeatable at a gathering of this nature or any other family function. Because Mr. Balthazer is now using the Internet for the origination of his broadcast, federal law does not give us jurisdiction to end his profanity, even though technicalities I do not fully understand allow his transmissions to be carried broadly to a global audience. We do and will respect the First Amendment—that is our government responsibility—thus it is up to the public to decide how far we will allow a renegade like Kimo Balthazer to spread this hysteria. In reaction to misinformation that Mr. Balthazer has shared regarding EnvisionInk Systems, Atom Heart Entertainment, and who knows what other great American corporations, employees are now walking off their jobs for no apparent reason all along the US West Coast, from San Diego to Seattle. Again, with respect to individual rights, I would certainly never suggest what people who enjoy receiving generous paychecks from their gracious employers might or might not do with their time, but let me suggest two points and then conclude my prepared remarks. First, a bag of wind like Kimo Balthazer can only continue to broadcast and have impact if people continue to listen, so I ask you to exercise good judgment and vote with your taste. All you have to do is change the channel. If no one is listening he will go away, or it simply won't matter that his jaws are moving. Second, the West Coast Walkout is not helping the stock market recover, and I would ask that everyone throw in the towel on this antic and return to work Monday morning so that equities trading can stabilize and we can return to the kind of productivity our nation counts on to lead the world in greatness. Thank you."

The applause that followed was as unexpected as it was earned for pure spectacle. The reporters and analysts present were not so much applauding the content of her speech, but that she had done it in a single breath and left no clause of common sense untouched. It was as if Lucky's monologue in *Waiting for Godot* had been loosely adapted by a reelection committee chair, then translated into every language but English before being translated back into English. This nonsensical stream of consciousness was meant to get the congresswoman's name in the headlines, it had no other purpose, pure buzzword bingo. It was magnificent. It would probably lead on *Entertainment Tonight*. Payne was one of one.

"As I suggested, I will take a few questions," continued Payne.

"What did Balthazer say specifically when you called him?" came the first question from the bull pen, a buttoned-down television correspondent from one of the still standing broadcast networks.

"Because I am a lady as well as a public official, it would be inappropriate for me to be more specific," replied Payne. "Suffice it to say that my gender played a role in the framing of his remarks."

Payne was on her game. She could say it without saying it, draw the big laugh, hurl the dart on a perfect arc, all with the same sentence fragment.

"Do you hold Balthazer accountable for the fact that Choy and Finkelman have yet to be released?" asked the next reporter, a grizzled columnist from one of the major market newspapers.

"I do," answered Payne without hesitation, only to receive a muttering from the crowd, wherein she clarified. "Let me say that differently. Of course Mr. Balthazer had nothing to do with the abduction of Mr. Choy or Mr. Finkelman, nor can we consider him an accomplice or criminal in that regard. However Mr. Balthazer did reveal the initial location of the crime scene which put them and the public at risk. He poured high octane gasoline on an already flaming bonfire when he had the mothers of the perpetrators on his show. In broadcasting from the parking lot of EnvisionInk and calling for this national employee Walkout in a time of financial turmoil, I would say that his actions can only be described as lacking in patriotism. At its extreme this seems to me a form of economic terrorism, and if you walk out, the terrorist wins. I would say anti-American, but that has historical associations of its own that aren't worth returning to discussion, but if he really wanted to help, I think he could do a lot better."

"I don't have reference to Balthazer calling for a National Employee Walkout," said a third reporter. "Is that something he mentioned to you as a line item during the gender specific phone call you shared?"

Another laugh drifted through the crowd, which Payne handled with typical flair. "No, we never talked about his hidden agenda. I guess I just presumed what he thought was good for Silicon Valley and California would spread to the rest of the nation. I may have gotten that wrong per se, but I don't put the intention past him. Next?"

"What do you think of Balthazer's Merger Bill of Rights?" shouted a voice from the back.

"Spectacular, if you're running on a Socialist ticket," slammed Payne. "Seriously, we live in a post-union economy, it has taken us a great deal of learning and negotiation to achieve this milestone. If Kimo Balthazer wants to live the European lifestyle, with two-month family vacations and subsidized health care for all, I will gladly buy him a one way ticket across the Atlantic. Last question, please."

The final question came from the *Wall Street Journal*: "Congresswoman Payne, there are rumors you have had direct dialogue with Solomon Edward Seidelmeyer, CEO and chairman of Atom Heart Entertainment, whose company has been the subject of several communications from EnvisionInk Systems since the abduction of Choy and Finkelman, and is said to be the catalyst in the current twenty-five percent drop in the broad market. Can you comment on your relationship and/or interaction with Mr. Seidelmeyer?"

"Sol Seidelmeyer is a first class visionary and vastly respected leader of American business and popular culture. In the course of my concern about the quality of home entertainment and the portrayal of family values in the media, I have been privileged to share an intellectual dialogue with Mr. Seidelmeyer, who needs little input from me to run the national jewel that is his studio. I can also tell you as an aside that we both share a deep appreciation for the incomparable Michael Landon, and with any luck, we both hope to see the return of his angel or another to our nation's consciousness. Thank you all for coming today on short notice. We have press packets for all of you on your departure, and remember to tell those who follow you on Twitter: Turn off Balthazer, Turn on America."

Payne stepped off the podium with dozens of reporters' hands still in the air. The questions could have gone on all morning if she let them. Like the media she so enjoyed shaping, Payne knew enough to leave the crowd wanting more. This crowd definitely wanted more, and in not getting it from her, they would seek it elsewhere. Payne knew that, her intention had only been to be the spark that set Balthazer ablaze. Her work was far from done, in fact her task list for the day had much more damaging paths to pursue. So little time, so many sound bites to issue. Soon she would be en route again to California, which left her just enough time to pick up a new outfit or two that would play well in the sun and still make a quick appointment with her hairdresser before wheels up.

$ $

"I am so sorry to hear of your loss," spoke Seidelmeyer into the phone. He was on the line with Ogden Feretti, Managing Director of Dardley Scott Silverman. Feretti's associate, Charles McFrank, had been gunned downed at the Steyer party, where Choy and Finkelman had been captured when the attempted abduction of Steyer failed.

Seidelmeyer's sentiments were coming a bit late, but he would argue that was no fault of his own. Until recent events, Seidelmeyer had never heard of Dardley Scott Silverman, a boutique investment bank that specialized in small to midsize technology acquisitions and secondary positions in IPOs, never anything close to the size of EnvisionInk. When Seidelmeyer learned through his network that one of Darley Scott's own had been pitching for the EnvisionInk business ever since an Atom Heart deal was a vague rumor, he decided to see how much of that interest remained. Not surprisingly, given the ample transaction fee involved, the interest was considerable. Although to the world the deal was dead, to a Banker there was no such thing as a dead deal — a deal was either completed or looking for a way to be completed, simple bifurcation. A Banker knew the world was filled with noise — maniacal press releases, threatened nuisance infringements, mail-ready shareholder lawsuits, body slam Investor conferences, cryptogram analyst reports — the only thing that mattered was a tombstone, the little acyclic success statues stacked on the mantle to signify a deal was done and the remains were buried. Until a tombstone was minted a deal was up for grabs, no matter the context, and an EnvisionInk - Atom Heart tombstone would be a game changer for Dardley Scott Silverman, a stretch deal that would put them on the map forever with the biggest of big dogs. McFrank had known that, he had been willing to risk his life to get that deal when the chance emerged to look good with Steyer. That risk had not paid off for him, but his partners might be back in the game with Seidelmeyer's phone call and a kind downstream referral from Seidelmeyer to Steyer if the deal ever reignited. McFrank had given his all for the team. Feretti would have to make his great sacrifice somehow worth it.

"Charles was a fine man," waxed Feretti. "He was an excellent Banker, too. We miss him already. He will be a Silicon Valley legend. Dan Steyer let us know what he did at that party, and when all this is over, Steyer will set up an MBA scholarship at Stanford in honor of Charles. The McFrank name will not be forgotten on the peninsula."

"You can count on Atom Heart to contribute generously to that scholarship fund," offered Seidelmeyer. "If we do succeed in putting these companies together, it could be a united memorial, which I think would be the strongest testament to Charles' vision."

"He did see this deal coming, maybe even before you and Steyer," said Feretti. "It really is a shame all this had to transpire. That could have been a hell of a combination, you and EnvisionInk. People talk about convergence so much you fall asleep in your drink listening. You would have made it happen, take some of the stink off AOL."

"I'd hate to think it's all behind us," said Seidelmeyer. "The signals I'm getting say the FBI is making good progress with Choy and Finkelman. We should have those two putzes who snagged them soon enough. Little chance this ends badly. It would be a shame for this deal to die when we know we have a good outcome ahead."

"It's all about the timing," said Feretti. "When that timing is good, I do hope you'll keep Dardley Scott Silverman at the top of your list. We are a smaller firm, but I think you've seen we have heart. If anyone can get this deal done without friction, it's Dardley Scott Silverman. That's awkward, I shouldn't be talking in the third person. It's me. I'll get the deal done. You have my commitment. When Steyer or the boys are ready, we'll be awaiting their call."

"Ogden, I'm calling you now," emphasized Seidelmeyer. "I need a low profile firm to move the ball downfield. The timing is precisely on our side."

"Help me understand that better, Sol," replied Feretti, his

inquisitive tone adjusting to Seidelmeyer's lead. "You've seen the definitive statement from the EnvisionInk board. How does that make the timing a win for us?"

"Let's think of it as a different kind of deal now, why don't we," explained Seidelmeyer, realizing that Feretti was catching on, that he was not teeing up a payback referral. "If you happen to have noticed, EnvisionInk stock has lost all its run up as of this morning, plus a little more. It's just below where it was before the kidnapping incident. If it continues to track the market on the current trajectory, by next week it will be even cheaper. The only ticker symbol on the board that's holding is mine."

"That's because the market expects you to buy something and wants to make it easy for you," translated Feretti. "That's pretty much what you told the cosmos when you went on CNBC. Your implication was that it was either EnvisionInk or someone else, but something was getting done one way or another. You'll need to deliver on that promise pronto or you'll join the market slide soon enough, that my experience can assure you. Are you looking for us to represent you on the buy side? I was guessing you'd have retained one of the Wall Street firms that specialize in media to do that."

"I didn't promise the market anything," contended Seidelmeyer. "I helped everyone see what makes sense. Atom Heart with EnvisionInk makes sense. We don't need representation. We need iron resolve to threaten to go around the board and take a tender offer directly to the shareholders. With their current price collapse, I can make what appears to be a very generous offer."

Seidelmeyer reveled in the bomb drop and pictured Feretti choking on his tongue. If Feretti had heard him correctly, Seidelmeyer believed Feretti would think he was in comic book country, a rejected storyline from one of Atom Heart's mercifully unproduced tier-B screenplays.

"You want to end run Steyer and go straight to the shareholders, with all the crap that's flying though the jet stream?" belted Feretti. "Sol, you really are something. You're either a madman or my hero, but there's no way you can pull that off."

"Bullshit, real talent can pull off anything. Big challenge needs a big champion. I have six times the revenue of Envision-Ink, three times their earnings and five times their cash. My balance sheet is so clean you can eat off it. So they trade at a better multiple than we do even after their pounding, that's what debt is for, to make the whole stronger."

"You're thinking a hostile takeover of EnvisionInk, while their price is collapsed, their CEOs are in captivity, and their board already said no? I'll say this, Sol, you have balls of titanium. Very old school. Nice commission for the Banker, too."

"Put you right on the map," goaded Seidelmeyer. "You'll be taking over penthouse leases at a discount from those Ivy League Wall Street schmucks and throwing them down the elevator shaft without a severance package. And EnvisionInk won't be at anything times anything if they don't lock in their price now. They have to be motivated with the market in free fall. This is a lay-up once you see your way to the paint."

"There is zero chance you're even going to get a response from Steyer given where we're at."

"I know I can't get a response from Steyer," said Seidelmeyer. "That's why I'm calling you. You think I like paying monster commissions on deals I create? This one is going to require an assist. Someone other than me who can sell has to open their eyes."

"You want me to run it by him, is that it?" asked Feretti. "Any chance you're doing this to see what else you can shake out of the woodwork at a discount? Companies will throw themselves at you if you give the signal."

"I don't want other companies, I want this one," insisted Seidelmeyer. "I want all of their revenue and none of their people."

"None of their people?" echoed Feretti. "That's good margin."

"Well, maybe half their people to look after the genius technology, including the two founder geniuses who can think up something new that makes even more money. And I don't want it hostile. I just want to send along a little motivation. Steyer doesn't work for EnvisionInk, he works for SugarSpring Ventures, for all the limited partners who pump money into his piggy bank waiting for it to fatten so he can crack it open. Steyer has to want this deal, he must have run into some resistance from his gutless Luddite board. Maybe this will help him make the point that I am a serious man."

"They say old media is dead, but I don't think so, Sol. You've got the same evil edge they play with on Sand Hill Road. You threaten a messy hostile and the press fiasco that goes with it, maybe you pull it off, maybe you don't. Maybe Choy and Finkelman get released midstream, maybe they don't. You either help Steyer do the right thing or you don't, but if they don't cave and you don't take it the finish line, you're going to wish you had their share price, the vipers will feast on your carcass. Sure, I'll take it to him as an intermediary, if that's what you want. Can't argue with the choice fee for a couple of phone calls and some stenography. I just need your assurance of one thing so I don't end up losing my company in the process."

"Speak," beckoned Seidelmeyer.

"If you have another target on deck and you're only playing mind games to get that done at a better price—if that deal is in first place and gets done because this deal is in second place—that deal will never, never happen, I promise you that, and neither will this one. I don't know you, Sol, and I'll trust you if you say so, but if you screw me on this the way Steyer just screwed you, it's a nuclear meltdown, mutually assured destruction. None of us will be left standing."

"You have my word," said Seidelmeyer. "Off the record and I'll deny it in court, there's no other deal. We need this one, and we need it next week."

"Hence the call today," said Feretti. "Of course, in addition to the condolences for Charles, which I appreciate. You do walk on a wire, Solomon. Let's see if your buddy Steyer wants to come out across the canyon on a tricycle and meet you half way. Have a nice weekend."

They both hung up. Seidelmeyer assumed Feretti had seen a lot of scary ways to close over his thirty chaotic years as a Banker, but none remotely like this. Seidelmeyer was all in now, he was a seller, sort of, unless Feretti could get him back to being a buyer.

$ $

Daniel Steyer's personal convictions and self-assurance had remained steadfast until this moment in his career, beginning with the vicious assault in his backyard, now his willing return to Moffett Field. This was a new test for his management style, events with a random rule set, and he was fighting without balance. He had failed to secure the release of the two most important prodigies he had mentored, facing instead the mistrust of his executive staff and defeat in the boardroom. The reality that more than a million employees had walked off their jobs over the past few days for no apparent reason made no sense to him, with more walking every hour despite the lack of understandable value in their actions, especially for themselves.

The self-injection of Congresswoman Payne into Steyer's battleground was even more baffling. She could add no value of any kind, yet she could not be ignored. Steyer did not think of Payne in a judgmental manner. It was not that he was authentic and she was a façade, but she was different. He presumed career politicians like Payne believed in themselves the same way he believed in himself. She simply did not have the perspective to see how her approach lacked efficiency, and how many poor decisions she would make to serve the media that followed her, largely to strengthen her fundraising agenda. He was convinced that Payne thought she was helping, just as he thought he was helping, but why she had reached out to the former Senator Henderson on his board and advised him she wanted an inside look at the EnvisionInk matter before she could get out of the way—that was beyond Steyer. It was real, he had to deal with it, she was coming on Monday, but he needed his distance. More importantly, he did not want to let her slow down his plan, which was in seeing distance of resolution, if only he could allow

Hussaini the breathing room to resolve it.

Steyer's comfort zone was evaporating. Human will was driving chance outcomes. There seemed to be few behavioral responses he could still accurately predict. Hussaini had assured him earlier that day he would be received by Swerlow and Kisinski as an acceptable addition to the Shanghai manifest, albeit with skepticism. His pilots would be the selling point to close the deal, but they were not with him, and that was going to make things hard. He had told Hussaini of the intervention as he was driving over, that Payne had created another layer they would have to navigate. Balthazer hung in the balance.

Steyer quietly walked the ramp to Choy and Finkelman's plane and took a hard breath at the door. One of the posted guards checked his identification and opened the jet way near the cockpit, through which Steyer could hear an argument within the fuselage between Swerlow and Hussaini. Steyer stepped through the portal hesitantly and listened for a few moments to get his ground before making his way down the aisle. Swerlow was sitting with Hussaini, Kisinski, Choy, and Finkelman in the main central living room of the custom aircraft positioned between the aft sleeping cabin and the private office behind the pilot's door. Apparently Swerlow did not hear Steyer enter and continued lambasting Hussaini, who had just shared the partial update.

"This is absolute zero-respect bullshit," yelled Swerlow.

"I thought you saw it as a show of good faith that Steyer is coming with us," responded Hussaini, cautiously taking notice of Steyer's arrival. "You seemed fine with it this morning. That's what I told him, after I got word my boss was good with it."

"That's when I thought we were leaving tonight. The deal was that we bring on Steyer, he brings on the pilots, and we're wheels up at sunset. Now you're telling me we have another delay. You're playing us. Every time we have an agreement the rules change. Either we go or we die. I don't care anymore."

"You do care, Dennis," compelled Kisinski. "And I care. And even though they aren't talking to us right now, our moms care. There is a big difference between what we've done and what you're talking about. Let's just roll with it. We don't have a choice."

"That's what they think," blasted Swerlow. "That's why they keep playing games. Any minute they could come through that door and gun us down. We need to be in control."

"The only person coming through that door is Daniel Steyer," continued Hussaini. "I'll let him explain. He's been on this all day and we almost had it. We just hit another snag."

Steyer tapped on the wall, as if knocking on a door to make sure everyone knew he was there, then stepped into the main living room. He had been waiting for the right moment, listening to the discord a few feet away.

"Permission to come aboard," said Steyer, attempting to lighten the mood as he advanced front and center. "I thought I heard my name. I guess you didn't hear me close the door."

"I heard you," muffled Swerlow. "I don't miss anything. Not you, anyway."

"Hi Daniel," greeted Finkelman, seeing the chairman for the first time since arriving at Steyer's party where he initially encountered Swerlow and Kisinski.

"How's the leg?" asked Steyer.

"Healing," answered Finkelman. "I received good care, both at Salinas and here. Thanks for seeing to that."

"We did the best we could," said Steyer, turning to Choy. "Calvin, they taking good care of you, too?"

"Any day on our plane is a good day," said Choy without conviction. "We appreciate that you're here. Any more offers from Hollywood while we were gone?"

"I think we're on the record there," replied Steyer.

"Looks like you got your teeth back," said Choy. "You're a tough fellow. You repair nicely."

"They're temps, the final molds are in the works," said Steyer. "They do make eating a little easier. It's good to see you, both of you."

"Loving the family reunion, guys," blurted Swerlow. "Where

are the pilots?"

"You must be Dennis," said Steyer, extending a handshake, refused by Swerlow. Steyer turned to Kisinski. "And you're Sam, correct?"

Sam returned the handshake. "Yes, Sam Kisinski. It's an honor to meet you, Mr. Steyer. It's been great to spend time with your guys. Despite the circumstances, I want you to know what awesome respect we have for EnvisionInk, for what you've created."

"I understand you're quite a coder," said Steyer. "That's what Stephen and Calvin are betting on, that when all this is behind us, your talent will be a very sound investment."

"I'll do my best," said Kisinski. "That's my promise, and my apology. I will do my very best. Learning Mandarin — that could take some time."

"I'm sure you're a quick study," praised Steyer.

"It's Shanghainese," offered Hussaini. "It's a local dialect, not Mandarin per se. You'll pick it up quickly enough, especially if you're hungry and want to order at a restaurant."

Swerlow was not up for chit chat. "Right, if we get there, which is going to be hard to achieve without the pilots you promised coming onboard with Steyer. Where the hell are they?"

"Well, I have the proverbial good and bad news for you," said Steyer.

"I told you this was bullshit," said Swerlow to Hussaini. "If we're all going to die I might as well get the ball rolling now and shoot this suit."

"We're not all going to die, Dennis," interjected Kisinski. "Hear the man out. Mr. Steyer, Special Agent Hussaini suggested you encountered a complication."

"Right, this is all very real-time," said Steyer. "Here's the good news, I have the pilots ready and agreeing to fly, that's a done deal. They are cool with the circumstances. We just have one more hurdle to clear, so I thought it was a better idea to keep them rested and off the clock until that hurdle is cleared. They're completely ready to make the long journey as soon as we get through this last checksum."

"What checksum?" hollered Swerlow. "It's one excuse after another. What's the delay now, the President's cell phone has a dead battery?"

"Something like that," said Steyer. "No, this hasn't gone to the President, but it has come on the radar of a very high-profile member of the US House of Representatives named Sally Payne."

"That nutcase," said Kisinski. "How did she get involved in this?"

"You know her?" asked Hussaini.

"Not personally, but Montana is not that far from Oregon," said Kisinski. "She likes to visit from time to time, hunting trips usually, looking for nutcase sympathizers."

"What's with this congresswoman?" asked Swerlow. "What does she want?"

"Well, as you probably know, there are a bunch of electrons orbiting the nucleus here," said Steyer. "Entertainment companies, radio talk show hosts, employee Walkouts, the impact has kicked off quite a string of events—and where there are events, there are politicians looking to be helpful. She wants to make a site visit to understand what's going on before she releases her hold."

"You got us the pilots, you got the FBI to support us, you put yourself on the plane with us, and a whack job congresswoman from Montana has us grounded? I'm supposed to believe that?"

"You have my word, it's true," said Steyer. "I just got off the phone with one of my board members, former US Senator Henderson. Payne called him earlier today and said she was going to shut the whole thing down because it extends to Balthazer, where she has a blood feud on. Henderson convinced her these were separate issues, that he had been in touch with the Director of the FBI, and everyone was convinced the best thing to do was let you fly. She wants to check that out for herself. She'll arrive over the weekend and we should be out of here early next week."

"Astounding bullshit," exclaimed Swerlow. "I'm ready to call it done."

"Dennis, think about how far you've come," implored Hussaini. "This is not the time to throw in the towel. This is a checkmark on a form, a talking point for a politician. Leave it alone, we will be out of here soon. You have Steyer, you have the pilots. We're almost there."

"I agree, Cousin," said Kisinski. "Steyer's story makes sense. This woman is clueless. I heard her press conference this morning. She has the laser on Balthazer's back. She wants him, not us. She'll get distracted and let us go."

"Fine, then let's set up a call with Balthazer," declared Swerlow.

"Uh, we're not talking to him anymore, I thought," said Kisinski. "Is this an on-air live call you want?"

"Yes, an insurance policy," said Swerlow. "We're going to use his show to let people know where we are now."

"That's not a great idea," asserted Hussaini. "We don't want to bring the public into this."

"We absolutely want to bring the public into this," said Swerlow. "We want a crowd, a big crowd, just like she wants. Only if she doesn't let us fly, that crowd is going to see each one of your bodies when I throw them on the tarmac with a bullet in them."

"You don't want to put the public in danger," said Steyer. "Let's keep them out of this, and maintain the goodwill we've established. We don't want Balthazer anywhere near here."

"He knows where we are," said Hussaini. "He's been uncharacteristically cool not giving away the location so we don't have a repeat of Salinas. Please don't give him a reason to go renegade. He's the Pied Piper now, the Walkout crowds will follow him here. Then we have a fiasco."

"Not if she lets us fly," argued Swerlow. "I'm out of patience. Sam, I have to keep the gun on these people. Get Balthazer on the line and tell him we're ready to do his next show."

Kisinski shrugged, he seemed game. Steyer fully exhaled for

the first time since boarding the jet. Swerlow's show request was far from ideal, but at least he and Hussaini had succeeded in the immediate task at hand, putting a few more hours on the clock. Those hours would be tense, no question about that, and with the dangerous brew of Payne and Balthazer in the mix, no one could be sure when Swerlow might snap—least of all, Swerlow.

$ $ $ $

2.6
Run Time

NASDAQ: ENVN (Day 16)
SHARE PRICE @ MARKET OPEN: $112.05
COMPANY MARKET CAP: $29.9B
VALUATION DELTA SINCE ADDUCTION:
< 17% >
** ENVN DELTA FROM PEAK: < 50.5% > **

NASDAQ SINCE ABDUCTION: < 2% >
** NASDAQ DELTA SINCE RECENT PEAK:
< 25% > **

The email Steyer had sent to Seidelmeyer on Sunday night was meant to be considerate, definitive, and confidential. After numerous attempts he had endeavored to deflect, Steyer had succumbed to the persistent Ogden Feretti and taken his call via mobile on Saturday afternoon, slipping into one of the two well-appointed bathrooms on the still grounded BBJ, talking as quietly as he could. At the time, Swerlow had not seemed to either notice or care that Steyer's muffled voice was echoing in the bathroom chamber. It was sort of expected that Steyer would be on his mobile throughout the weekend to keep their exodus plan moving forward, yet it had been all Steyer could do to contain his reaction given the substance of Feretti's communiqué.

Having allowed the matter to settle peaceably in his mind, Steyer composed his email with great thought. He let the first rough draft sit for almost twelve hours overnight, then edited it again three times before hitting send with what he hoped would be a message that would park the escalation, at least for now, and serve as reference material upon discovery if a deposition became necessary downstream. It was, in his mind, a very well-written email:

Sol,

I have been in touch over the weekend with
your representatives who reached out via
phone, and I thought it only cordial that you
hear back directly from me. While you may
think it an option to attempt to buy Envision-
Ink by going directly to our shareholders, you
and I both know that is not going to happen.
A hostile takeover of our company, given the
temporary dip in price we are experiencing and
the attendant market turmoil, would never be
acceptable to our shareholders, and we do not
see your "generous offer" of Friday close plus
12% as a solution to locking in a fair price for
our holdings regardless of the potential risk of
further market declines. My sense is that you
know this and you are only testing the waters
to reinvigorate other discussion, but just so
that we are clear, any such action on your part
will be met with the fiercest defense and cause
us both a distraction from more fruitful matters
while our legal firms benefit from the folly.

Likewise, if as mentioned your underlying
intention is to cause our board to reconsider
its unanimous rejection of your prior acquisition approach through direct negotiation, that
remains off the table at this time—it is even
less possible given more recent events, which
I am not able to share. While I do appreciate
your passion, tenacity, and creativity, my most
heartfelt suggestion is that you let go and move
on. Should there be some appropriate time in
the future for us to talk again with the support
of our board and management, that of course
remains possible, provided you are wise and do
not poison the well. Given the more immediate
matters with which I am dealing I would ask

that you not respond to this email or pursue the
matter any further at this time; I believe that
would be in the best interests of all involved.

Regards,
Daniel

Although Steyer had sent the note via wireless while on the
737 from his secure SugarSpring Ventures email account specifically so that it could not be seen by anyone in the Envision-
Ink IT department, he had underestimated the number of displeased individuals he had stirred within the company. At first
he thought maybe he had made a rookie mistake when he hit
send, one of those "reply-all" fiascos every executive fears and
only some survive. No, he checked his outbox log, he had been
appropriately careful, there had to be malice on the back end.
The combination of clever technical talent, institutional imma-
turity, and passive-aggressive churning in a software company
freely flowed through the air ducts, so much that Steyer should
have assumed his laptop was bugged by his own people, which
it was, numerous times over. That Steyer had been hacked nonetheless came as a surprise to him, even more so given the sensitive nature of the email, despite his careful wording. Choy and
Finkelman were much less surprised when they learned of the
hack, the generational divide a market force of its own, yet even
they were stunned that the anonymous infrastructure assailant
not only forwarded Steyer's email to the All Company Distribution List, but hastened its viral travels by cc'ing the *Wall Street
Journal*, the *New York Times*, the *Los Angeles Times*, the *San Jose
Mercury News*, the *Washington Post*, *AP*, *Reuters*, CNBC, *Fox Business*, *Bloomberg Businessweek*, *Techcrunch*, *CNET*, and just about
every major or minor financial blogger with an active domain.
    It was a Managing Editor's field day. Because Steyer had
conveniently sent it Sunday night and the intervention was in-
stantaneous, the EnvisionInk hacker syndicate had succeeded
in making press deadlines, so Monday morning analog editions

were able to reprint the email in full as front page news with such imaginative headlines as "EnvisionInk Won't Drink Atom Heart Poison" and "Steyer to Seidelmeyer: Don't Buy, Don't Call." Bad timing for a material disclosure made drama possible for the often boring financial beat, and this much-welcomed brush stroke created enviable theatrics to paint the page. News of EnvisionInk's definitive rejection, despite Atom Heart's secret threat, was a buzz machine on all the morning television news shows, all the drive time radio talk shows, and the home pages of every global media brand still grasping the resources to publish, poseurs along with Wall Street pros. All this frantic attention served to take the aggregate market, upon open, down another 7% and EnvisionInk down another 12%, below the critical support level $30 billion market cap. With the clear weakness in its posture exposed, Atom Heart dropped an astonishing 18%, allowing it to catch up with some of the previous market declines and entirely erasing any implied premium since Seidelmeyer went on CNBC. Unless Seidelmeyer hurriedly made good on his threat to go hostile with EnvisionInk or announce a better surprise acquisition, Atom Heart would become another beaten mutt in the kennel. The Street was daring Seidelmeyer to act, yet the instant collapse in his price presumed he had no board support for a fallback position.

Steyer had been skewered without the slimmest chance of undoing the damage, served up on his own monogrammed billboard by a nameless underling and left exposed to the thrashing of public opinion. There was nothing he could deny without setting the table for perjury. His only move was to become unreachable. Steyer texted his office and instructed the remaining loyals to put out the word that despite his email, all of his attention had to be directed to Choy and Finkelman. While the press inquiries poured into both his venture office in Palo Alto and the EnvisionInk communications department in Santa Clara, he would stay focused on the best possible outcome and seek forgiveness later if circumstances might allow. Steyer knew Seidelmeyer would not be so lucky. This would be the

worst day of Seidelmeyer's career, an iron mallet to the forehead he never could have seen coming. Steyer thought about
faxing Seidelmeyer a brief apology—no room for intrusion in
that old world mechanism—but given the increased scrutiny he
was under, Steyer knew there could be no more communication
between them.

Steyer sat anxiously with Choy and Finkelman in the living room of their plane, the tension no less than when Swerlow
and Kisinski were with them. Following the early morning rev-
elations when they saw the first reprints online and about as
many expletives as a half dozen Type-A males could utter over
each other's sentences, Swerlow and Kisinski were, for the moment, out of conversation range in the fore office, near the main
jet way where they always posted guard through the night and
could monitor anyone coming or going. They had taken a time
out to reassess their odds, leaving Steyer alone with Choy and
Finkelman for the first time since he boarded. Special Agent
Hussaini had disembarked a half hour prior with Swerlow's approval, to touch base with the Payne road show and make sure
nothing more would interfere with their departure once Payne
landed and got herself comfortable with whatever it was she
hoped to glean from her visit to the EnvisionInk parking lot,
only hours away. Steyer tried to keep his voice low, expecting
to be joined by Swerlow and Kisinski at any moment, but Choy
was pushing him hard.

"You're incredible," attacked Choy. "You come here to help,
and you're still negotiating with La-La-Land. Is there no limit
to your hubris?"

"I was trying to dispose of the matter," said Steyer. "Was
that not clear from my email?"

"Why were you even sending him an email?" asked Choy.
"Why are you communicating with him at all? Given all the people you've pissed off, you should have presumed all your contact
was being monitored. You know how the Internet works. You
know there's no privacy with email, you may as well be skywrit-
ing. You've spent your whole life in hacker culture."

"You're right, I never suspected I'd be hacked by one of ours," returned Steyer.

"What do you think you're accomplishing by continuing a dialogue with Mr. Beverly Hills and his movie minions?" continued Choy, more ardently. "Somewhere along the way you forgot that you don't run this company. Stephen and I do."

"I never forgot that," replied Steyer. "But you've been off the job a while, sort of indisposed, and business continues. I was doing my best to maintain continuity."

"Well, you've maintained something," inserted Finkelman, looking up from his tablet. "Your email is everywhere. There is nowhere it isn't. You may get in the Guinness Book of World Records for most distributed email ever, without even a sex photo attached. That's internet history."

"Funny," said Steyer. "An honor every VC relishes, coverage."

"It couldn't have come at a worse time," added Finkelman. "The market is getting pummeled again. Atom Heart is getting annihilated. The Walkout is getting worse, too. This morning, employees started walking off their jobs on the East Coast."

"I know, the timing couldn't be worse," continued Steyer. "We're starting to see a spiral effect. The stock market is in sell off mode, the number of employees walking off the job has crossed a million, and the analysts are now factoring the productivity losses into future earnings declines. It's the opposite of a virtuous cycle."

"The quicker we get back to work and get our employees back at their desks, the quicker this will start to settle down," commented Choy. "We have to get this pair to Shanghai or this is going to keep getting worse."

"You think the minute the two of you are back on the job, everyone goes back to work?" said Steyer, taking the defensive. "Just like that, you hold a pep rally, our employees fall in line, and the whole country gets back to normal? You don't see this as a little bigger than that?"

"At least they'll know we aren't trying to sell the company

out from under them, or doing dopey deals with fossilized film studios," pronounced Choy. "Yeah, we'll give them a shot of stability. That's what they need."

"It was an unsolicited offer, a stupid one that needed to be rejected," said Steyer. "Seidelmeyer called a Banker, the Banker called me. I tried to duck the call, but the twenty-seventh time his name came up on the screen, I thought he might have something I should hear."

"So you listened to the offer and didn't bother to tell us?" said Choy. "The whole issue of trust — the whole issue of chain of command — none of that popped into your head? It's time we take a hard look at how we're operating."

"We haven't exactly been in normal times," said Steyer, attempting to hint that Choy consider their surroundings. "Nor are we in a secure conference room. Transparency has limits, especially in shared spaces like an onboard lounge."

"I am abundantly aware of how sounds fill this plane," said Choy. "Stephen and I designed the interior. We know how voices move through the corridors. We like openness. You should try it sometime."

"There was nothing to be open about," said Steyer. "The Banker told me Atom Heart was considering going hostile. I said that was a joke. Then he said we could make it go away by reintroducing formal negotiation. I said that was off the table. I said no to everything. There was nothing to talk about. Seidelmeyer will not take this to the shareholders. If you believe nothing else I say, take my word on that. He's screwed, the same way I'm screwed."

"I feel badly for you," commented Choy.

"I'm sure you only feel numb," said Steyer. "It's been a hell of a few weeks. I did what I thought made sense. The market is crashing, we have a nationwide employee revolt, and technically you're still kidnapped. Stephen almost lost his leg and I have a broken jaw. I guess on top of all that I didn't want to read about an attempted hostile takeover of our company in the Monday paper, so I tried to shut it down."

"Do you like these headlines better?" asked Finkelman, holding up his tablet with the reproduced images of Steyer's email. "Instead of a rumor, you're tied to the discussion. We're probably going to have to fire someone for this, don't you think, Calvin? But that won't make the headlines evaporate, or Daniel's email."

"Yes, someone will have to leave the company when we get out of here," answered Choy. "Hopefully we'll get the opportunity to sort that out."

Choy's point was not lost on Steyer. He would have responded, but their discussion was interrupted by the arrival of Swerlow and Kisinski, appearing as if on cue. Swerlow still had the gun in his hand, as if it had been cemented to his palm, impossible to remove. They had come down the aisle from the office and seemed as thrown for a response to the hack as everyone else.

"This is really a mess," began Kisinski. "Do you realize this Walkout is now in more than twenty states? New York, Massachusetts, Connecticut, they're all joining in. Pretty soon it could be the whole country. No one wants to go to work. They don't trust their employers — this movement started all because Kimo Balthazer made you a villain."

"Victim is more like it," said Steyer. "All I wanted was to get Calvin and Stephen back. I can't win."

"You can't win because people are seeing how you play," said Swerlow. "Maybe when we're gone you'll get another chance. I think that's going to be tough, but I really don't care. All I care about is getting that Payne woman to let us fly."

"We all want the same thing," said Steyer.

"We have a lot more at stake," said Swerlow. "That's why Sam and I are going on Balthazer's show today. It's all arranged. We're going to bring the crowd to us."

"Balthazer comes with a lot of baggage," noted Steyer. "Payne comes with even more."

"Right, like you're a master at taking the world's temperature," said Swerlow. "This is the last move we have. If this doesn't work, it won't matter to any of us."

"I'm telling you, leave the crowd out of this," maintained Steyer. "If someone gets hurt, they'll storm the plane. That's not what you want."

"I want to bring this to an end," said Swerlow, tapping the gun against his leg, pacing aimlessly from side to side. "One way or another, it has to end."

Heads turned to the front of the plane as the jet way portal creaked open and Hussaini boarded. He had a large stack of newspapers carrying the day's headlines, hard copies for all.

"Your email is everywhere," said Hussaini to Steyer. "No one in Silicon Valley has ever seen anything like this."

"So I'm told," said Steyer. "What's the update on Congresswoman Payne?"

"She just landed at SFO," said Hussaini. "She should be at EnvisionInk in a few hours. I've been in touch with her staff. She's baffled, same as everyone, why you and Seidelmeyer are collaborating on a new definition of masochism for Wikipedia, but she's more fixated on Balthazer. He's the one who can get her the votes she needs to move up the food chain. I'm still hopeful when she figures out the landscape, she'll give us the green light to fly."

"Sam and I are going on Balthazer's show," said Swerlow, bringing Hussaini up to date. "That should move her along."

"How so?" asked Hussaini, looking directly at Swerlow and then Steyer for a clue.

"You better call for crowd control," said Steyer. "Best case scenario, we're going to have a send-off crowd. They're going for a mob and they'll probably get one."

"Call the pilots and tell them to be ready," said Swerlow to Steyer. "We either fly tomorrow or we don't."

"Let's hope for a good show," added Kisinski, not drawing a chuckle. He took the stack of newspapers from Hussaini and began distributing them around the cabin. Steyer was on the cover of every one.

$ $

By the time Producer Lee Creighton spotted the curious

high profile caravan approaching the EnvisionInk parking lot, more than five thousand of the company's employees had joined Balthazer in the Walkout, almost half the employees based at the company's Santa Clara headquarters and more than a fifth of the company's global population. They felt empty, they felt their company had lost its way, and they were in shock that their chairman was still corresponding directly with Atom Heart's CEO. The capture of Steyer's email to Seidelmeyer was a brief moment of empowerment—the crowd knew it was one of their own who had intercepted it, and the chances of anyone revealing who that was were nonexistent. The employees believed they had stopped the deal dead in its tracks and they were taking back control of their company, in the event they actually might decide to go back to work. The Walkout was spreading, and they were leading the way.

Indeed the national employee Walkout championed by Balthazer was becoming more than an annoyance for a lot of corporations. Producer Lee Creighton estimated that in California over a half million people had walked from their jobs. In Washington and Oregon, internet data told him another two hundred thousand were in their company's parking lots. Along the Eastern Seaboard he identified another several hundred thousand who had powered down their desktops and pitched camping gear. Pundits predicted that by the end of the week over two million, mostly professional, employees would be part of the Walkout, with no real catalyst to get them back to work since there was no real catalyst that had driven them from work. Unlike a union strike, this Walkout came with no specific set of demands. These were not union employees and there was no collective bargaining being suggested. Balthazer's Merger Bill of Rights remained amorphous, a conceptual manifesto that people were struggling to put into words because there was no real precedent. The list of crowdsourced demands posted on ThisIsRage.com had grown into the thousands, but it was almost all tongue-in-cheek office humor, no one could structure a credible straw man to rally around. Employees had walked out to make a statement that their jobs needed to be more secure in the face of endless consolidation. Management had to be worthy of trust, and the workplace needed to make sense as a place to spend more than half their waking hours. Until they got a sign that they were being heard, it was more satisfying not to work than to work. Producer Lee Creighton could see that Balthazer would be key in breaking the stalemate, and that was not likely to happen soon. Balthazer was having way too much fun.

Until the moment of the Creighton sighting, Balthazer was still digesting the direct attack from Congresswoman Payne's press conference, which he had effectively spun to his advantage by letting his listeners defend him while he prodded their distaste for Payne's detachment. Balthazer was in the middle of just such a broadcast when the convoy arrived. He was especially taken by the vast number of news trucks and portable satellite dishes bearing their stenciled call letters, gleaming logos adorning a parade of media vehicles end to end.

"What's with the pageant?" asked Producer Lee Creighton from his trusty laptop, looking beyond their tent station at the arriving line of town cars escorted by a pair of police motorcycles.

"This could be the arrest we're looking for," observed Balthazer.

"We're not that lucky," said Creighton. "They won't let us off nearly that easily. But those cars have federal plates. It's someone important. Escort could be FBI or Secret Service."

"Google the local celeb blogs for arrivals at SFO in the past few hours," said Balthazer. "See if the paparazzi report any big name sightings headed our way."

Producer Lee Creighton performed the search and looked up with a grin. "I should have known. Rhymes with stain."

"You're kidding," said Balthazer. "Ms. Claus came directly to our chimney? We surely haven't been very good boys."

"That's why she's here," said Creighton. "Your favorite congresswoman and hers, making herself available, real time in the flesh."

"That's disgusting," said Balthazer. "But her timing is

impeccable. Let's open up the mic and see if we can get her to interrupt us."

Producer Lee Creighton uplinked to the satellite and synchronized the syndicated feeds, while Balthazer put on the headphones and waved to the crowd that he was about to resume. The government motorcade slowly pulled to a stop directly in front of them, in the same parking lot adjacent to their makeshift stage. This was not a coincidence. Security had followed the GPS tracking tail closely, with Balthazer in their cross hairs right up to the moment he stepped forward to applause. Precisely as the motorcade unloaded, Balthazer went live.

KIMO: Gang, we've got a very big day ahead of us, and at least one big surprise I'm about to share with you. Producer Lee Creighton, is this a very big day?

CREIGHTON: This is a very big day, Kimo. A very, very big day.

KIMO: Am I overpromising if I say we're going to have a very important guest with us oh so soon?

CREIGHTON: You, overpromise? You're Kimo Balthazer. Not your style. Bat Out of Hell.

KIMO: I'll tell you what is my style—let's get this show kicked off with one of our favorite new segments, a bit of group shout-out I like to call Ten Things We Hate About Payne.

CREIGHTON: Callers standing by, Kimo. Ten newbies ready to share on your signal.

KIMO: Let's get this party started. Callers, Gimme a Big Ten!

CALLER 1: She's a fascist.

CALLER 2: She gives fascism a bad name.

CALLER 3: She doesn't have a Twitter account. And her Facebook page is managed by PR slime.

CALLER 4: She spends more money on her hair in a day than everyone in this parking lot does in a year. And you can hardly tell.

CALLER 5: She's from Montana, and I like Montana, so that ruins it for me.

CALLER 6: If she weren't in Congress, she'd be on unemployment. We pay her bills no matter what.

CALLER 7: No one on her staff can write code. Or use a debugger. Or color in between the lines.

CALLER 8: She thinks exercise is talking.

CALLER 9: She doesn't read e-books because they are books.

CALLER 10: The stick up her ass is industrial grade steel, which really slows up the TSA lines at the airport.

KIMO: Not bad at all. Not our finest round, but there's always next hour. Can't get enough of a good thing, which is why we keep doing it. But this hour it helps provide a warm welcome for today's extra special guest.

Congresswoman Payne stepped from the back seat of her town car, a security guard on either side of her, and without hesitation approached Balthazer. A few in the crowd recognized her and began to boo, but Balthazer waved her forward to join him. Producer Lee Creighton handed her a wireless microphone and pair of headphones, and as if it had all been rehearsed, smoothing the grand entrance. As word spread rapidly through the parking lot about who had joined them, the growing crowd surrounded Balthazer and Payne as she stepped onto the raised platform and joined Balthazer on the air.

KIMO: Yes, Producer Lee Creighton and I promised you a surprise, and this is a surprise if ever there was one. Please welcome from the US House of Representatives, the Honorable Sally Payne. Congresswoman Payne, Welcome—*This Is Rage*.

PAYNE: I see that my message has failed to get through, Mr. Balthazer. You have no respect for anything or anyone.

KIMO: Not true at all, Madam Congresswoman. I have great respect for all these employees gathered around us, and the millions of others listening from parking lots around the nation where they've walked off their jobs as well. Care to share any deep thoughts with them?

PAYNE: If you like your jobs, go back while you have them. What you are doing is not good for the economy and it's not good for any of you.

KIMO: That's an insightful bit of sharing. Do you have any idea why all these people walked off their jobs?

PAYNE: Because you told them to, Mr. Balthazer. No other reason.

KIMO: I told them nothing of the kind. I suggested that everyone express themselves as they thought best, and this is their reaction. These aren't the unemployed, Congresswoman. These are people with good jobs who have lost trust. They don't know when the next merger is coming, when their jobs might be whisked out from underneath them. All they know is they can't count on people like you to help.

PAYNE: That's not our job. Our job is to protect free enterprise, so they can have their jobs. If they don't want them, what are we supposed to do?

KIMO: For starters, as an elected official you can help them understand if their voice is being heard. Do you think it's time for a

Merger Bill of Rights?

PAYNE: I think there are plenty of laws on the books and there is plenty of employee friendly legislation. We don't need any more micromanagement than we have.

KIMO: You mean regulation. No more business regulation?

PAYNE: Not more than we already have.

KIMO: Fascinating. Then what do you think of Daniel Steyer's email to Sol Seidelmeyer, the one that's printed on the front page of every newspaper in the nation today? Is that just healthy free speech?

PAYNE: It's a private communication from one business leader to another. It has no business being on the front of anything. However it got there is plainly wrong.

KIMO: Nothing about it bothers you other than that? Is that your position?

PAYNE: I have no position, other than to try to get it through your head that if you want to do all these people a favor, please ask them to go back to work. That's why I came here today, to ask you in person to be helpful.

KIMO: Really? That's why you're here, to use your powers of persuasion to convince me to convince them to go back to jobs they bailed on? I don't think so, Congresswoman. I think you have another agenda.

PAYNE: And what would that be?

KIMO: I don't know, maybe it has something to do with all the TV crews that followed you here. You get your picture taken putting me in my place, you convince a few people to go back on the job, maybe the stock market stops falling. Maybe you get the credit. Next election rolls around, maybe you become Senator Payne. Maybe something even bigger.

PAYNE: You live in a fantasy world, Balthazer. People need to work. The stock market needs to function. Choy and Finkelman need to get back to their company. If I can help make any of that happen, that's my job. I have no agenda beyond that. I just want to help, and I just want you to help.

As Balthazer and Payne continued to exchange barbs, Producer Lee Creighton became focused on a call in he had not expected. Clicking on his screen a few times, he managed to verify the authenticity and waved his hands to get Balthazer's attention.

"You need to pick up," mouthed Creighton. "Swerlow and Kisinski."

"They're early," mouthed Balthazer, volumeless. Congresswoman Payne was standing inches away, her eyes widening with the message.

"Now or never," mouthed Creighton, shaking his head.

Balthazer shrugged, then nodded. Creighton whispered into his mic to confirm to Swerlow and Kisinski they were going live and switched the call to Balthazer. Payne stood in place next to him, almost motionless, impossible to read.

KIMO: Gang, we have yet another treat for you today, if not inspired by our visit from Congresswoman Payne then certainly in her honor. On the line I have a pair of fellows who I was pretty convinced would never talk to me again, which gets them into a pretty big club. Please welcome Oregon's favorite sons, Dennis Swerlow and Sam Kisinski—the kidnapper dudes formerly known as Ben and Jerry. Dennis, Sam, Welcome—*This Is Rage*.

CALLER SWERLOW: Kimo, good of you to take our call.

KIMO: Did you think maybe I wouldn't?

CALLER SWERLOW: No, all you care about is public attention.

You're smart enough to know there's no one who can bring you more of that than us.

KIMO: Guess we're stuck with each other, Dennis. Ain't that something?

CALLER KISINSKI: Yeah, it's something. Hey there, Kimo. It's Sam.

KIMO: Good to hear your voice, Sam. You too, Dennis. We haven't talked in some time, certainly not since the great employee Walkout. Do you have anything to say to the million plus people who have walked off their jobs in the last week to let their employers know what corrupt mutant swine they truly are?

CALLER SWERLOW: Yeah, go back to work, everyone. Work is good, it's important. If you remember it's where we started. Sam and I just wanted to work, and with any luck, when all of this is behind us, that's what we'll go back to doing.

KIMO: I can't tell them anything, Dennis. You know that. I'm trying to get a few people onboard for this Merger Bill of Rights. Any thoughts on that?

CALLER SWERLOW: No, that's not really our thing. I'll leave that to you and the congresswoman to hash out.

KIMO: So you have been listening to the show! That makes me feel good, Dennis. I hope some of this is making sense to you, because none of it would be happening without you. Now we need to find out what's going to happen to you. Is that why you're calling today, to give us an update?

CALLER KISINSKI: Sort of. Not exactly. I guess.

KIMO: Which one is it, Sam?

CALLER KISINSKI: Here's the thing, we've been trying to get out of everyone's way since this whole thing started. We didn't want to cause an employee Walkout. We didn't want to crash the stock market.

CALLER SWERLOW: We just wanted to raise some money to start our own company. Now we have the chance to do that. We've reached an agreement with Choy and Finkelman, but no matter how hard we try, we can't break free.

KIMO: You made a deal with Choy and Finkelman? But you kidnapped them. How does that work?

CALLER SWERLOW: It just does, okay. It's our business. It has nothing to do with EnvisionInk, even though we have Steyer with us now. It's between us.

KIMO: My good friend Dan Steyer is with you as well? You really do seem to have things under control. Do you want to tell us where you are so we can come help?

CALLER SWERLOW: Actually, Kimo, that's exactly what I want to do. That's why we called today. Because if you can bring the crowd over here, I think that might be enough motivation for Madam Payne or whoever else is calling the shots to let us go.

KIMO: Think carefully about what you are going to say now, Dennis. Are you sure you want to tell all our listeners and all the employees who have walked off their jobs where you are? Because undoubtedly some of them are not going to be too pleased about what you've done, and they could get in your way.

CALLER SWERLOW: We're not worried about that, Kimo. They can't get to us. We're on Choy and Finkelman's personal jet parked at Moffett Field, about fifteen minutes from where you are at EnvisionInk. With any luck we won't be here long. We need a few folks to come wish us bon voyage, then we'll be out of your hair forever. Pretty soon you'll have Choy and Finkelman back. You can have Steyer too, if you want him. Then everything goes back to normal.

KIMO: Moffett Field, on the Choy and Finkelman party plane. Well, gang, you didn't hear that from me, make a note of it, in case these nice officers haul me away in handcuffs. That was Dennis Swerlow, who, with his cousin Sam Kisinski, took Calvin Choy and Stephen J. Finkelman hostage, and now seems to be going into business with them.

CALLER SWERLOW: That's all we have to say, Kimo. The rest is up to your listeners. I hope you get your Merger Bill of Rights passed by whoever it is you think is going to pass it, but right now, we want to get on with our lives and go somewhere we can be successful

KIMO: I thank you for that, Dennis. I appreciate your candor and I do wish you and Sam luck. Congresswoman Payne, anything to say to the infamous Ben and Jerry?

An awful patch of dead air followed as Payne looked into Balthazer's eyes with unspeakable contempt. She tore off her mic and headphones, stepped down from the podium, and motioned for one her aides to join her near the town car.

"I need to send a text to Special Agent Hussaini on that aircraft," said Payne. She grabbed her mobile and without a care that Producer Lee Creighton was looking over shoulder pounded out the typed words in under 140 characters: *You have the go ahead to fly. Crowd on its way to Moffett. Get out of here before someone gets hurt. Make sure it's a very short trip.*

$ $ $ $

2.7
Event Loop

NASDAQ: ENVN (Day 17)
SHARE PRICE @ MARKET OPEN: $99.90
COMPANY MARKET CAP: $26.5B
VALUATION DELTA SINCE ABDUCTION: < 26% >
** ENVN DELTA FROM PEAK: <56%> **

NASDAQ SINCE ABDUCTION: < 11% >
** NASDAQ DELTA SINCE RECENT PEAK:
< 32% > **

Tuesday morning brought breaking news from Los Angeles that Atom Heart Entertainment's chairman and chief executive officer, Solomon Edward Seidelmeyer, had resigned, with an interim office of the president established by the Atom Heart board of directors while a search for a new CEO was conducted. The terse statement on the wire at market open said little more, and Seidelmeyer was neither quoted nor available for comment. The prior day's hammering of Atom Heart shares had now stabilized in line with broader market declines, no better or worse, putting the company at about 85% of its value prior to the run up—a total loss from peak of almost 30% —with no mention of change in revenue or earnings, making it an attractive takeover candidate like so many similar companies that had been beaten down by the recent market panic rather than fundamentals. Luckily pretty much everyone had been trampled by herd hysteria, so very few wolves were on the prowl.

Painting the market plunge as a temporary flash crash, the sea of institutional Investors holding substantial positions in Fortune 1000 companies maintained a profound commitment to hope, at least with their public game face. With history on their side, fund managers declared that the sell-off would be short term, and that cash raised in liquidation would ignite a market rebound following an end to the EnvisionInk crisis and a return to work of the now estimated two million Walkouts. Losses incurred on the fast slide down would be recovered by cheap buys on the way up, so the story went, with commissions paid in both directions, further conflicting the story. Retail was a lot more skeptical, with consumer confidence on a straight decline, the near term memory of several similar wipeouts in the past decade too much for the non-pros to stomach again. Sharp witted talking heads on CNBC provided little solace to the inestimable counts of individuals who had seen their 401k's decrease by a third or more in a matter of days, many of them Walkouts, and the words "buying opportunity" rang empty. Surely the market had survived the Dotcom bomb of the Millennium and not ten years later The Great Recession triggered by the housing bubble, but no matter how many times a rebound came, no one could be sure another would follow. Pundits who had proclaimed the end of the American economy celebrated the realization of their doomsday prediction, if only to carve out a little media time in front of the endless video cameras and microphones at one of the many parking lot protests around the nation.

If Congresswoman Payne had succeeded at anything on Balthazer's show, it was instigating exponential growth in the Walkout, which had doubled since her appearance at EnvisionInk. Walkouts now reached to Atlanta, where Coca-Cola employees set up shop in their parking lot, to Cincinnati where Proctor and Gamble staff joined in the demonstration, to the headquarters of Wal-Mart in Bentonville, Arkansas, an unlikely outpost for camping that was not actually camping. The Walkout was nationwide, in every state, and while not every major corporation had yet been impacted, the descriptor "epidemic" had already been assigned by most correspondents covering the story.

The stock market had been falling for a week and half, every major index well past bear territory with no sign of a safe haven or protected sector. Each day that went by, as clusters of employees left their decks and moved into their parking lots to join the Walkout, more shares were dumped, with economists losing hope in near term corporate earnings as productivity ground to a halt across the country. Only the most opportunistic hedge funds would snap up such terribly thrashed equities, cheap trades by bottom feeders, soon to see their positions decline again as analysts could not predict an end to the work stoppage. The irony of the Walkout was not lost on market makers—where employee reductions resulting from mergers usually meant reduced costs and improved earnings, employees walking out on their own meant companies could not produce expected earnings. It was a strange kind of revenge for employees—they were protesting the loss of their own jobs by temporarily giving them up, and in so doing making the point that they were valuable. Employers wanted them back at work, but more of them were leaving, and that was taking down the stock market all on its own, with the catalyst of EnvisionInk's run up and run down all but an artifact at this point, just days after it had been the shot heard round the valley.

Television, newspaper, and digital source headlines were as constant as they were consistent:

> "Employees Want Respect"
> "Mergers Take Toll, Employees Say Enough"
> "Shareholders Worried, Employees Furious"
> "Workers Ask Whose Wealth Is It Anyway?"
> "Job Security Nowhere, Same with Workers"

Corporate parking lots across the nation became a cross between outdoor festivals and civil rights marches, equal parts celebration and demonstration. Journalists fed on the storm of energy, and their coverage turned the Walkout into spectacle. Somehow all these employees had to be convinced to go back to work, but there was no semblance of organization to their action and no way to negotiate since they had no common leadership. Walkouts across company lines had no common business attachment. They were organized without being organized. Balthazer's Merger Bill of Rights was too thin a starting place to allow any sensible common ground for reparation, more rhetoric than reality, yet Walkouts wanted precisely that, some basic ground of assurances. Walkouts wanted to know if they did return to work, that there would be no retribution, and some form of common understanding going forward that would protect them from newer and bigger deals, deeper cost cutting, and more serious reductions in work force. Their cause was clear, but there was no model for addressing it—legal, practical, or conceptual—and that made it all the more difficult for any solution to emerge. Getting employees out of their cubes was never very difficult, all they needed was an excuse. Getting them out of the parking lots called for a rule book that had not yet been written.

One parking lot that had yet to open, despite the growing line outside its gate, was the visitor's area at Moffett Field. As the sun came up Tuesday morning, US Highway 101 from Palo Alto to San Jose was frozen solid, with all exits to Sunnyvale jammed without relief. An early crowd of several thousand led by Balthazer had assembled on one side of the gate demanding entry, while inside the gate Congresswoman Payne had been provided an office and added security despite her culpability for turning up the volume with her failing attack on Balthazer. Special Agent Hussaini had advised Payne that the only way to get rid of the crowd at Moffett was to get Choy and Finkelman's jet into the air, but far too much media attention had arrived as a result of her exchange with Balthazer, and the FBI Director had withdrawn his permission to fly pending assurances that could convince him public safety would not be compromised. Payne had inserted herself into the equation too late and now was responsible for the hold up. If she did not source a relief valve, she would undoubtedly take the blame for any ensuing casualties, and that was not going to do her a lot of good in the next election cycle.

Inside the private aircraft tensions had peaked. The pilots employed by Choy and Finkelman and coaxed by Steyer with a juicy kicker had boarded shortly after Payne's text to Hussaini the previous day. They had planned to take off that evening, precisely at the moment Hussaini was informed they were back in a holding pattern. Few in Congress had been paying attention to the old news — the Choy and Finkelman story — given the more pressing stock market crisis and national employee Walkout. When Payne appeared on Balthazer's show, followed by the call from Swerlow and Kisinski, political opportunity ruled anew. It seemed everyone in Washington wanted a piece of the widening wreckage that had become Congresswoman Payne's trajectory. The stock market could not be fixed real time, the Walkout could not be fixed real time, but if the delete button could be applied to Payne by saddling her with the Envision-Ink stalemate, everyone with a government paycheck wanted in on that — same party as well as opposite party rivals, there was a bounty of upside if her rising star could be snuffed. That let Washington do what it always did best, maintain the status quo so that no action could be taken until a consensus emerged around how credit could be sorted out and blame properly allocated. It was also keeping Hussaini from bringing this episode to a close and testing the limits of Swerlow's ability to manage stress. The gang at Moffett had been sitting idle more than a little too long and the only relief valve had been tightened.

$ $

Hussaini could see that Swerlow was crossing into delirium. Swerlow had been systemically underpowered and randomly improvising from the outset, but even a pro would have folded by now and cut a deal for leniency. Swerlow had not slept a full night since taking Choy and Finkelman. His sentences were forever unfinished, and no matter the temperature inside the plane, his shirt was a glob of sweat. Hussaini had to play to his fatigue. He knew Swerlow had to be wary of the gassed and loaded private jet not going anywhere. It would not be much longer before Swerlow would have to make good on his threat. Hussaini had

begged Swerlow to give him until that evening. Swerlow had eerily agreed, provided the door stayed shut. Hussaini could phone,
text, email, or Skype, but he was sealed in now with Steyer and the
others. He did not have much time to concoct a convincing next
move. That's when he decided to call Balthazer, albeit not on the
show, instead using a video phone app.

"Why are you calling me?" asked Balthazer, only half looking at Hussaini in the tiny high-resolution screen. "We're busy
trying to mount a webcast, you know?"

Hussaini could see Balthazer juggling his mobile, obviously
readying for another remote. Beyond Balthazer, Hussaini could
see the scaled image of Producer Lee Creighton banging on
his keyboard. Hussaini knew Creighton had to be trying to tap
wireless bandwidth from the air traffic control tower, unable to
crack the encrypted security codes at Moffett. His security team
had shut down every commercial node in the vicinity.

"You want to get on the air?" queried Hussaini. "I need you
to put that crowd to work."

"What does 'put them to work' mean?" asked Balthazer, staring incredulously into the micro camera. "I could have
sworn you didn't want us here."

"We didn't, but you're here," replied Hussaini. "The Director wants assurances the public safety is not compromised.
There's no way my team can deliver that in a day's time, but we
can show it might get worse if we don't get out of here. I want
you to fire up that crowd."

"You think the people here with me are safer with the
plane in the air than on the ground?" asked Balthazer. "That's a
stretch, even for me."

"Not if we lose control of them," said Hussaini. "We need
to get evidence to Payne that they are going to storm the gate.
She has no credibility after that stellar performance on your
show yesterday. If she has evidence that crowd is going to come
through the gate and can make the point that someone is likely
to get hurt, she might be able to convince enough of the right
people to let us get out of here. I can get the Director to support

that given our broader agenda."

"You want me to commit a felony for your broader agenda?" replied Balthazer. "You want me to incite a crowd to violence, to storm a military base, after you said you'd arrest me if I came within one hundred miles of here? This is a tough bit of trust to take on."

"You have my word," said Hussaini. "If I don't get this plane in the air, Swerlow is going to blow and who knows where that puts us. First shot, first body on the runway, maybe they storm it anyway. Then we have innocents in the crossfire, or no crossfire and we lose control. There's no good outcome if anything like that happens."

"So I'm supposed to get them fired up enough that it looks like they're going to riot, but not enough that they actually do," proposed Balthazer. Hussaini could tell he was catching on, understanding he categorically had to get the plane in the air immediately for his own reasons and needed any excuse, Balthazer was just his bridge. In the long shot, Hussaini could see Producer Lee Creighton looking at Balthazer like he had lost his mind.

"We have video cameras on you from all angles," assured Hussaini. "Payne knows what I'm doing. As soon as we have the footage she can build the support we need to let us fly. The TV crews are already out there so public opinion will be on our side, to do what it takes to disperse the crowd before someone gets hurt."

"And I have your word that, win or lose, I walk away clean?" said Balthazer. "You can see why I am having trouble with this. I don't come out looking so good."

"You come out the hero," affirmed Hussaini. "First chance you get, you calm them down, tell them to go back to the parking lots, you did your civil duty."

"This is nutty," said Balthazer.

"Tell me something I don't know," said Hussaini. "Look at it this way, if you don't help, I will have to make good on that hundred-mile promise. It's not like you can get very far with the onramps all stacked."

"You're a prince of righteousness," said Balthazer. "Is your buddy Swerlow nearby, inside that luxury tub?"

"Not two body lengths away," answered Hussaini, only half believing Balthazer was going ahead with it.

"Tell him to come on the show with me in five minutes, he knows how to tap in," said Balthazer. "Tell him it will be ugly, but let him know you'll get the outcome you want."

"You watch your every word," said Swerlow, leaning into the shot next to Hussaini.

"You asked for the help, I do the show my way," said Balthazer, making brief eye contact with Swerlow. "We're play acting, Dennis. You play the role of you, I'll be me, and we'll get this done."

"And release all the wireless you can give me," chimed in Produce Lee Creighton, popping his face into extreme close-up.

"Got it, Swerlow on the show and pull the passwords from the wireless routers," said Hussaini. "You sure you can be convincing enough?"

"Just make sure you don't change your mind and decide you want the genie back in the bottle," said Balthazer.

Hussaini could not be sure what Balthazer meant by that, but he was not thinking much about genies. He was thinking about his home, his wife and children, and how little they knew that dad the desk jockey had put up his hand one too many times out of loyalty to a job that was unlikely to appreciate the extent of his creativity.

$ $

Balthazer clicked off his mobile and looked at Producer Lee Creighton for a status update on bandwidth. Just that quickly, the password boxes on his screen had been deleted and he was wireless to the Internet with all the bandwidth they needed. Producer Lee Creighton gave Balthazer the thumbs up. Balthazer looked up to the clouds, as if in some strange prayer, snapped on his headgear, and the show commenced.

KIMO: Walkouts across America, Welcome—*This Is Rage!* We are webcasting coast to coast, where I'm told more than two million of you have told your employers to go to hell until we get our Merger Bill of Rights. This morning, the CEO of Atom Heart Entertainment voluntarily stepped down, and the author of that infamous backroom email to him is on the private jumbo jet directly in front of me sharing captivity with the co-CEOs he put into power and then set out to betray. A lot of people think public opinion doesn't lead to justice. I think it does.

A cheer rose up from the crowd in front of Balthazer, echoing into the microphone for all to hear, Pepsi to Cisco. Producer Lee Creighton scribbled on a piece of paper and held it up for Balthazer to see — their starring guest was on the line and ready to go live. Balthazer knew he was climbing out further on the edge. This interview would be a different kind of test.

KIMO: As you know, yesterday while we were chatting with the highly esteemed and genuinely gifted Representative Sally Payne, we received a call from Dennis Swerlow and his cousin Sam Kisinski, letting us all know where the gang who couldn't do squat was holed up. Now here we are, just a few football fields away from them, although cowards that they are, they have locked themselves inside a custom pimped 737 belonging to Choy and Finkelman, and we're locked outside the gate of the airfield that was once home to some of NASA's proudest achievements. On the phone with me now for an encore performance, I have our very favorite flunkout criminal. Dennis Swerlow, Welcome—*This Is Rage*.

CALLER SWERLOW: Thanks for coming to our sendoff, Balthazer. Sam and I appreciate you and the crowd showing up. Now if we could only get a real decision maker to let us go.

KIMO: And where would you be going, Dennis?

CALLER SWERLOW: You know I can't tell you that.

KIMO: Uh-huh. Let me get this straight. You've held Calvin Choy and Stephen J. Finkelman at gunpoint for almost two weeks. You've taken control of their private plane. You have their chairman of the board with you. You have the FBI's Special Agent in Charge with you. You have a couple of private citizens who have graciously agreed to pilot the plane for you. And you don't want to tell this crowd where you're going?

CALLER SWERLOW: I'm not going to stay on the line if you're out to bash me, Balthazer. I'm not that idiot congresswoman you had on the show yesterday.

KIMO: No, not at all. She's a law-abiding elected official, Dennis. You may agree or disagree with her scrappy world view, but she has pursued a respectable career, with vested retirement benefits. You, on the other hand, aren't much more than a pig-headed, no-strategy street thug. I can't see how you think you're worthy of this crowd's support.

CALLER SWERLOW: That crowd loves us, Balthazer. We've heard the calls. We've been on the air with them. They understand us. They believe in us. They know what we've been through, which is why they're walking off their jobs.

KIMO: Really, you think that's the case? You think you have the broad support of this crowd? Should I ask them what they want to see happen here?

CALLER SWERLOW: Yes, absolutely yes. Ask them.

KIMO: Well, friends, we have before us a pair of post-juvenile truants who've stashed themselves in someone else's big ol' jetliner. They've kidnapped two of Silicon Valley's finest, now they want to hijack their plane. Do you think they should be allowed to zoom-zoom fly away?

The crowd rumbled angrily with apprehension, then responded with a resounding NO. Producer Lee Creighton gave Balthazer the double thumbs up, he was pumping the volume and pushing the base notes to redline.

KIMO: Doesn't sound like you have much support, Cousin Dennis. You are what you are—a lowlife, a derelict, and a murderer. And from all I can tell, you're also a really lousy coder.

CALLER SWERLOW: Why are you turning on us, Balthazer? I thought you hated these corporate pukes as much as we do.

KIMO: Just because we have a common enemy doesn't mean we're all good guys, Dennis. Regular folks don't like the idea of what you're doing once they understand it.

CALLER SWERLOW: Right, but do they understand that as soon as we get to where we're going, the plane turns around and brings back Choy and Finkelman? They can have Steyer back too, if they want him. Everyone goes on with their lives.

KIMO: Friends, what do you say? If Dennis and Sam pinkie promise with the triple secret boo-boo handshake to let everyone go when they get what they want, is it okay with you if they go bye-bye?

Balthazer had notched it up and was at his best, shaping opinion to his whim. The crowd had been poked with a stolen jetliner, made irritable by sloppy logic, then serenaded by Balthazer with what he needed them to deplore enough to want to stop it, even at their own expense. Fury was spreading with the revelation that no matter the circumstances, Swerlow and Kisinski were nothing more than criminals seeking their own reward. No one could be good with that.

"Don't let them fly!" came an unprompted voice from the audience.

"No way they fly!" harmonized another.

Within seconds the chant was in unison: "Don't let them fly! No way they fly!" Swerlow heard it over the phone line. Millions listening in parking lots across the nation heard the echo across the Internet. Those still at their desks heard the reverb through headphones in their cubicles. Texts began replaying the refrain on the ThisIsRage.com home page.

The crowd's response was crystalline and inarguable: "Don't let them fly! No way they fly!" If Balthazer didn't back them down soon, they were prepared to storm the gate. Every bit of it was caught on video. Balthazer imagined Payne watching the monitors frame by frame with deep concern from her protected enclave, wherever she might be, relaying the signal back to her staff in Washington to spread as quickly as possible, hoping the crowd would not come unglued. Before reporters had it on the midday news, Balthazer knew everyone with decision making authority had to know that plane would either be dispatched immediately or crowd control was going to migrate to the runway where armed guards already stood their posts around the aircraft.

Balthazer muted the mic and whispered directly to Swerlow, still on the phone: "Sorry to have to throw you under the wheels, so to speak. Bon voyage." Balthazer terminated the call. He had masterfully pulled it off, and Swerlow was finally going to get what he wanted. The crowd most assuredly would not get what they wanted, but by the time they came across the fence, the 737 would be airborne.

$ $

Choy and Finkelman often expressed mixed feelings about owning a jet this size. It did give them immense pride and a unique set of bragging rights, a tech trophy worthy of their accomplishments. It was also comically ostentatious and antithetical to their widely evangelized beliefs. Perhaps now it would prove its value, an exit hatch from this crisis that would let them move forward and make sure no one outside their circle was harmed. Although they had been kept in the dark by Steyer and Hussaini, and had no reason to suspect they were not going all the way to Shanghai on wheels up, they were not naïve. The weeklong delay on the tarmac held its own meaning. With all of Hussaini's coming and going, they had a pretty good idea some scheme had been cooked up, although they had not discussed it with each other or anyone else given the close quarters. There really was no upside in knowing more than they did, and soon enough anything that was going to happen would reveal itself to them. If they were to have a role in what happened next, it was largely unknown, which for the moment worked just fine.

As the plane soared down the runway, there was little sign that Swerlow was any more at ease. He stood in the hallway at the front of the plane between the private office and the main lounge area, next to the exterior jet way door and in front of the bolted cockpit where the pilots would remain. Kisinski sat nearby in the office, with a sightline to Swerlow, nervously keeping watch on his cousin. The gun remained in Swerlow's hand, as it had throughout the ordeal, only finding separation from his palm in the brief moments when he slept and Kisinski was posted on armed duty. Swerlow had been sleeping increasingly less, not fully trusting his cousin to hold the line when he had the watch, although Kisinski had been a good enough relief man and held his own when expected. The lack of sleep combined with ceaseless stress, delays, and lack of experience all weakened Swerlow's thinking, revealing him unsteady, yet there was never any question his threat was serious. He had demonstrated that he was willing to take a life without remorse if that had to be done, not because he was inhuman, but because he could be backed into unintended consequence by losing control. Swerlow was not nearly as smart as he wanted to be, he was coming to understand that, but control was everything to him. Where Swerlow seemed most certain he still had control, there was little question among those around him that his grasp was tenuous. That unnerving unpredictability made him a bigger threat than ever. Any test of his authority would have to be swift and exact.

In the main lounge of the cabin sat Steyer, Choy, Finkelman, and Hussaini. The takeoff had been a long time coming, but once Payne had relayed transmission of the near rioting crowd outside Moffett back to Langley, it had taken the Director just minutes to assume responsibility for the decision and tell Hussaini to go before someone overrode him or he changed his mind. The last thing the Director wanted was mayhem on the runway and the public complicating a controlled action by inserting themselves between armed forces and the plane. On that green light, the pilots had confirmed approval with the control tower, rolled the plane from the opened hangar to the runway, and gone airborne in almost no time. Choy and Finkelman used the ascent to take a few breaths, relieved that progress was being made, but in no way deluded into thinking this was the last bit of anxiety they would endure pending a quick roundtrip halfway around the world.

Steyer wondered when Hussaini would make his move, and what he would do once that happened, particularly if he was unsuccessful. He was trying to second guess Swerlow—would he really fire the pistol with the plane in flight, or would he know better than to risk everyone's life including his own? He might have wondered who Swerlow would shoot first, but of course he knew it would be him. Choy and Finkelman were the meal ticket, they could not be harmed if any recovery was possible and the itinerary was to be met. Hussaini was a federal agent, taking him down would end the excursion—were the pilots to wire that information back to the tower it would be an instant relay to Washington, undoubtedly calling for the order to return to California. Only Hussaini could give the order to continue flying after a direct confrontation, and only Choy and Finkelman could make good on their promise to fund their enterprise. Clearly if Hussaini did not succeed, Swerlow's target would be Steyer. In some senses, if it all did unwind, Steyer welcomed it, there would be no way out for him in that scenario. The last thing he wanted to do was spend the remaining years of his career in court, reciting rehearsed depositions, and reading his own sad interviews in trade papers trying to make sense of the senseless.

Hussaini was consumed by an entirely different set of thoughts. Although he had once been a field operative, that was an awfully long time ago. He was back-office smart, nothing about that had changed, but he was soft on the beat, and he knew that. He was an expert at negotiation, he had proven that

again playing out this assignment, an intelligence professional of the finest order, but for most of the past dozen years he
had stared at computer screens. Taking a loaded gun from an
armed nutcase was tough to practice while interpreting a wire-
tap or role-playing on VOIP. No one in Langley could assemble
or restructure a collection of random images or ciphers better
than he could, but almost anyone at his level was better at target
practice and floor wresting. Hussaini had maintained his regi-
men at the firing range, stayed fit, trained at the company gym,
and took refresher courses in hand to hand when required, but
he had never been tasked with taking a live weapon from another man without being backed backed by a team of sharpshooter
reserves already surrounding an assailant, the last time over fifteen years ago. He had come to embrace the notion of domestici-
ty. He liked having a wife and children, and he liked going home
to them every night, perhaps too much for his line of work. He
had been assigned this project in California because it was unlikely to require physical interaction on his part, just wise vision
and effective planning. For the job he had accepted there could
be no one better, but this was no longer that job. Had he been
left alone, with the earnest discretion to direct the operation to
neutralize Swerlow and Kisinski at the hospital in Salinas as he
designed it, the episode would have been over in a few hours.
He kept playing that back in his head, how he had pushed for
fast action because he knew it was the only way to get this done
without complication, but corporations, and board members,
and talk show hosts, and politicians kept inserting themselves
in his decision tree. Now he was alone, unarmed, on a Boeing
Business Jet with a handful of people depending on him to pull
off the disarm. One way or another, an array of gaggling reporters on the ground covering the Walkout would soon be writing
about him. He tried to clear his mind, but the fog was inescapable. He needed to move now, before they hit cruising altitude
and the cabin was fully pressurized, when Swerlow and Kisinski
would discover the plane was not going to continue across the
Pacific.

"Now that we're airborne, I'd feel a lot safer if you put the gun away," said Hussaini, opening the critical exchange. He rose from the sofa in the main lounge area, but did not yet approach Swerlow.

"I don't care what you think," replied Swerlow, the sweat on his forehead still forming, an equal amount of perspiration seeping past his neckline.

"I can see why you'd feel that way, but generally speaking, guns and planes taking on altitude are a bad idea," awkwardly continued Hussaini. "Can you agree with me on that?"

"My ride, my rules," said Swerlow. "I don't want to talk. Sit down and shut up. Watch a movie or play a videogame. We have about six hours to kill before we refuel in Hawaii. The conversation is old."

Hussaini was keeping the average climb rate in mind and not liking his progress. A private jet tracking its own independent course over the Pacific would gain about two thousand feet per minute once it gained reasonable inertia after takeoff. Just over five minutes in the air, they had to be crossing ten thousand feet. Hussaini had not seen a safe window to act and pressurization was becoming a concern.

"I kind of agree with Special Agent Hussaini," said Finkelman, joining the dialogue without prompting. "You got what you wanted, we're on our way. You were patient, we appreciate that, but that's behind us. Guns and planes don't mix. Maybe you could respect that and put it away."

"Not going to happen," said Swerlow. "Let go of the concept. You sit over there, I'll stand over here. The gun stays with me."

"Are you going to stand there the entire flight?" asked Choy. "That's a bit impractical, not to mention unnecessary. The pilots are locked in, and there's no one planning to open that door for at least fourteen hours."

"Stop talking to me," said Swerlow, the edge in his voice cracking. "I don't have anything to say to you. Go about your business and leave me alone."

"How about we ask your cousin?" suggested Hussaini as he slowly began to walk toward Swerlow, tiny steps, slowly forward. "Is it okay if I talk to Sam for a minute?"

"Why is that necessary?" asked Swerlow. "He doesn't need to talk to you. He has nothing to say to you, same as me."

"I have no problem talking to Special Agent Hussaini," came the voice of Kisinski from inside the office. "Easy, Dennis, we're past the hard part."

"There's no reason to trust any of these guys, Sam," said Swerlow through the open office door. "Look how long it took them to deliver. They don't have a lot to offer us. Leave it alone."

"To be honest, I don't like the gun either, Dennis," said Kisinski. "You're tired, beyond tired. If you slip and blow a hole in the fuselage, we go down with the wreckage."

"Sam, I've had this gun in my hand for two damn weeks and it has not accidentally gone off. What are you thinking? I told you not to contradict me in front of these guys. You need to clam up."

"Let me hang onto the gun, Dennis," said Kisinski, obviously as worried as the others about a loaded gun in midflight given Swerlow's condition. "I'll hold it right here. No one goes anywhere. You go to the back and get some sleep. An hour would be great. Two hours would be even better. Then you can have it back."

Hussaini could not have asked for anything better. Kisinski shared their trepidation of Swerlow's state, but was acting on his own to ensure safety in the cabin. Hussaini took the message of Kisinski's welcoming words as an opening to continue to inch forward. Altitude had to be more than twenty thousand feet and options were narrowing.

"I don't need to rest," insisted Swerlow, his wavering tone an argument against him. "I want everyone to shut up and leave me alone."

Kisinski walked to the doorway of the office near Swerlow, seeing the exhaustion in his cousin's drooping red eyes. It had been an insufferable journey to this milestone. Swerlow was not just on edge, he was about to pass out, a delayed reaction to the takeoff. Kisinski could see that. So could Hussaini.

"Dennis, get some sleep," said Kisinski. "I can take the watch. I'll sit in the office with the gun and everyone will be a lot less nervous."

"You're lucky to have a cousin who cares about you like he does," said Hussaini to Swerlow. "Get the rest while you can. We'll all be better off."

Swerlow was breaking down. He felt the heaviness of his eyelids, the strain of all that had brought him here. They were right. He needed to rest, and he knew he could trust Kisinski, there was never any indication otherwise.

"Take the bedroom in the back," said Steyer to Swerlow. "No one will bother you. Kisinski is the boss."

"Yeah, we're cool with Sam," added Finkelman. "Sam is the boss."

Hussaini saw his opening was close. They had gotten through to Swerlow, he was ready to take a break. Swerlow reached to hand the gun to his cousin through the office door, about eight feet from Hussaini, the three of them forming a triangle. The plane had been airborne about fifteen minutes and they were easily at cruising altitude above thirty thousand feet. Hussaini would have to take Swerlow without a gunshot or all bets were off. He was only going to have one chance.

"Okay, I'll get some rest," said Swerlow, turning to his cousin, his side only briefly facing Hussaini as he made the exchange. "Maybe an hour."

As the gun moved from Swerlow's hand to Kisinski's, Hussaini lunged forward with full body weight, an iron square hit on the two of them.

"You asshole liar," screamed Swerlow at Hussaini. "I knew you were full of shit."

All three of them had two hands on the gun in an instant, no one in control. Steyer launched forward and threw his hands into the mix as well, but could not get his fingers on the gun handle or barrel. Choy came flying off his chair and leapt onto

Swerlow from behind, attempting to pull Swerlow out of the mix. Finkelman was still in his leg cast and could not get up, but opened a speaking line to the pilots from the panel in his armchair.

"We have a struggle in the cabin," said Finkelman into the console microphone. "Stand by for further instructions." The pilots had to know they were not getting combat pay for a milk run, they had been on notice from the outset that they would need to be nimble. Steyer had told them as much when he first called and painted a true picture. It would come as no surprise to them that an extremely quick turnaround might be the flight's corrected routing.

"None of you has any honor," shouted Swerlow, wrestling to shake Choy off his back and Steyer's arms from his own, all the while never taking his hands off the gun. "Do not land this plane, that isn't our deal."

"Let go of the gun," demanded Hussaini. "This is over. One way or another, this is over."

"Pull harder, Sam," yelled Swerlow, attempting to pry Hussaini's fingers from the gun, grinding the metal encasement with all the weight he could apply into Hussaini's thumb.

Choy was beating on Swerlow's back with his fists and elbows, weeks' worth of anger and frustration pouring out. Finkelman picked up the ENVN monogrammed ceramic dinner plates from the fixed table in front of him and tossed them to Choy. Choy began breaking the plates on the back of Swerlow's neck and upper shoulders. When the third plate shattered and blood began to run down Swerlow's neck, he released his hands from the gun as his body collapsed in the aisle.

That left Kisinski in a wrestling match with Hussaini for the gun, on either side of the office door. Kisinski tried to pull the gun into the office and close the door on Hussaini's arm. Hussaini felt the lashing pain but was not letting go of the gun. Swerlow saw the motion of the door working against Hussaini's arm and sprung forward to help his cousin, pulling the door forward as Kisinski pushed it. Steyer and Choy tried to pry Swerlow's arms from the door but he was unnaturally determined, adrenaline had kicked in and the combination of his strength pulling and Kisinski's leverage pushing pounded on Hussaini's arm, over and over, slamming his arm in the doorjamb until finally on reflex his fingers released and he pulled back his arm in agony.

The office door slammed shut, Kisinski inside with the gun in his possession and everyone else outside in the hallway adjacent to the main lounge. Hussaini did not let the pain impact his thinking, he turned immediately to Swerlow who was ambling to his feet and put a fist into his face, sending Swerlow straight back to the floor. Hussaini reached down and picked Swerlow up from the carpet by his hair, hit him again, then threw him into the living room area where he hit the wall near Finkelman, knocking most of the drinking glasses from the table and shattering them in the process.

"We're leveling off, any update?" came the voice of one of the pilots on the intercom. Finkelman looked at the microphone in his armchair, stunned by the turn of events, not sure what to say.

"Sam, get out here now," bellowed Swerlow, beaten and bloody but not giving up.

The door to the office opened and there stood Sam Kisinski, holding the gun, drawn on Hussaini. He was as serious as he had ever been, but remarkably restrained.

"Shoot him," said Swerlow. "Shoot all of them."

"I don't want to do that seven miles above the ocean unless I have to," said Kisinski, somehow at peace. "You need to back off."

"Sam, don't do this," said Finkelman, beckoning any remaining goodwill he had established with Kisinski. "You're not a criminal. You're an engineer."

"Don't be stupid, Kisinski," lobbied Steyer. "You can come out of this a good guy if you do what's right. Show us you can do what's right."

"There's nothing right," said Kisinski. "Back away from my cousin. Tell the pilots that all is well, to forge ahead."

"There's no flight plan for this plane to continue across the ocean," said Hussaini. "The pilots have to hear otherwise from me or they'll land."

"If we're going down now, we're not going to land on a runway," said Swerlow, getting up from the floor under cover of his cousin."

"You lied to us from the start," said Kisinski, holding onto the gun firmly with both hands, almost expressionless.

"You can't believe the FBI was going to let you hijack a jet with a bunch of kidnapped hostages and go free halfway across the world," said Steyer.

"We made a deal," said Swerlow, wiping the blood from his forehead as he joined his cousin at the front of the plane, then turning to address Hussaini. "You make good on that deal, or I take the gun back and shoot out a window. We'll all get sucked out and evaporate, that's fine with me. You choose. Tell the pilots what you've chosen. I'll listen."

The 737 was well out over the blue water divide, the jagged shoreline of the Bay Area disappearing in the distance. It was clear from the darkening horizon easing through the starboard windows that the plane had commenced a slight banking turn, as if it intended to circle. Kisinski continued to hold the gun steadily drawn, now pointed directly at Steyer. The standoff was silent, the interlude impossibly long, if in its entirety a minute. All eyes drifted to Hussaini as he reached for the microphone button in the armchair console near Finkelman.

$ $ $ $

2.8
Upgrade Path

NASDAQ: ENVN (Day 18 - Morning)
SHARE PRICE @ MARKET OPEN: 82.35
COMPANY MARKET CAP: $22B
VALUATION DELTA SINCE ABDUCTION: < 39% >
** ENVN DELTA SINCE PEAK: < 63% > **

NASDAQ SINCE ABDUCTION: < 19% >
** NASDAQ DELTA SINCE RECENT PEAK:
< 38% > **

The Military Police escort that greeted Balthazer outside the front gate of Moffett Field early Wednesday morning before his show was not on par with what he expected after his heroic assistance to Hussaini. Choy and Finkelman's jet had left the tarmac four hours prior, without any news since its departure. Wild rumors swirled the web about the plane vanishing into the void. Crowdsourced conspiracy theories of all flavors forwarded across texts, tweets, blogs, and podcasts speculated on where the plane had been dispatched and who was calling the shots. Involvement of the FBI further fueled internet lunacy—if the FBI was involved, then so was the CIA, and for all anyone knew Swerlow and Kisinski were undercover agents meant to take down a great Silicon Valley company because SEC bureaucrats feared the power it wielded. That Swerlow and Kisinski had gotten this far and taken a private 737 to an undisclosed location after a high-profile kidnapping could not be explained any other way, how else could they get away with it? Nothing, not even the federal government, could be so screwed up that it would let this all happen as a random series of events, not a chance. Internet junkies could always be counted on for fabulous storytelling, escalating the improbable to the unruly, no matter how wrong.

When the MPs arrived at Balthazer's broadcast outpost, he was more than a little surprised, especially with the media circus encamped alongside him. Credentialed journalists, as well as citizen reporters from every imaginable media outlet, had arrived soon after the plane departed, and having missed the most important part of the story, they had stayed in place overnight in hopes of getting any story at all. They wanted Payne, but she was not to be found. They had their fill of Balthazer, but he had little news, none whatsoever with regard to the plane's destination, expected arrival time, or possible return. The MPs gave Balthazer new reason to worry about his own exit strategy, and provided the hordes of reporters a colorful photo opportunity as they diplomatically walked Balthazer and Creighton aside for a chat. The four sharp-dressed men who pushed their way past Balthazer's followers added plenty of window dressing for the press corps to exploit: pressed uniforms, white helmets, nonceremonial batons, high-gloss regalia, no hint of any sense of humor. They had come prepared for crowd control, riot gear by their side if the crowd decided to come to the aid of their loud-mouthed leader. Balthazer would never let it come to that. He was a showman, not a warrior. The only point he really wanted to make was whether he remained relevant. Were it to come to blows, he would never let his listeners take a beating on his behalf, and the last thing in the world he wanted was a beating on their behalf. Spiritual beatings were the stuff of ratings. Physical beatings could impact your speech patterns.

Hussaini had all but promised Balthazer diplomatic immunity for his support, not to mention grand acclaim and maybe even a few kind words in the mainstream press. Balthazer had done precisely what he was asked to do: fire up the crowd, freak out the feds, and get the plane airborne before his followers posed a threat to themselves. He had then succeeded in calming them, so much so that without further incident they were expected, out of sheer boredom, to soon fall back to EnvisionInk and the other various parking lots from which they had migrated.

Producer Lee Creighton was afraid the very appearance of the MPs could undo all the goodwill Balthazer had secured and set off a spark, though the crowd allowed the MPs through as much out of confusion as fear. Balthazer was further taken aback by the formality of their approach. This was much more direct than the attention he had received from the FBI at Salinas, where he had started out as an arranged hero, only to depart as a sad sack goat. Balthazer wondered if anyone in government bothered to talk to each other, or if they did, were listening skills required in the tool belt of their abilities. If Hussaini had not relayed his conversation and handshake deal with Balthazer to the other powers that be, then *This Is Rage* was going to have a hard time getting on the air that day, with Balthazer locked in the brig for whatever crime he had or had not committed, inadvertently or in the act of entertaining. Surely the First Amendment had application, deal or no deal with Hussaini, but Hussaini had left the ground late the prior day and was not available for a testimonial.

Balthazer sagely put up no fight and followed the MPs with Producer Lee Creighton through the gates at Moffett Field, their first time on the government side of the divide. Balthazer had already formulated his argument that he had not trespassed, not broken the law in any way, was a true American exercising his rights of free speech and assembly, and in fact was in cahoots with the FBI, if only they could please go looking for the possibility of a recorded conversation with Special Agent Hussaini that might have been archived for posterity. As he was rehearsing his opening statement for whatever authority figure he would soon be facing under austere conditions of arraignment, it occurred to Balthazer that he had not been handcuffed nor read his Miranda rights. Actually, it had not occurred to Balthazer, Producer Lee Creighton asked him whether he found their arrest curious in that they were actually being treated quite politely for a pair of disruptive thugs staging a hippie fest outside a government airfield from which they had been banned. Balthazer was delighted on both counts. He knew well the discomfort of handcuffs and did not have any desire to experience them again. At the same time he found the Miranda failure to be a marker he could play should his argument fail on its own merit and an attorney be necessary to secure release. Creighton commended Balthazer for his optimism but reminded him they appeared to be under military rather than civilian law, and regardless of how many episodes of crappy legal television they had internalized, they had no idea what they were facing. For all they knew they could disappear for a while, forever, and the loss of *This Is Rage* would be explained by their own resistance to arrest and a proper hand of authority. Were they to disappear, who would know the truth? Absent the two million Walkouts and his email list, no one would much care, and there were any number of talk show hosts who would gladly step in and carry the torch for Balthazer. The hard part was over and the ratings boon would be up for grabs. Fear and cynicism around military fatigues were hard to bat away.

Following a long walk-the-plank style trek through a procession of pictureless, windowless, beige hallways, Balthazer and Creighton were deposited in a pictureless, windowless, beige conference room, about the size of a doctor's examining room. Décor took direction from a 1950s film set in a prison where one would expect to see visiting hours kept with minimum security prisoners. There were only two items of note in the room that contained a nondescript table, three unpadded folding chairs, and bare fluorescent lighting: a state of the art polycom on the table, and beside it, the Honorable Sally Payne.

"Congresswoman Payne, I never would have guessed this was your invitation," opened Balthazer. "Why I never would have guessed is beyond me. Maybe it was my last vestiges of belief in the American democracy."

"It's good to see you again, Mr. Balthazer," replied Payne, her tone suspiciously friendly.

"And me, too?" asked Producer Lee Creighton.

"Yes, you too," said Payne. "What did you say your name was again?"

"It doesn't matter," said Producer Lee Creighton. "You'll see it soon enough once they take our mug shots."

"You're not under arrest," offered Payne. "Were you concerned about that?"

"I don't know, you tell me," said Balthazer. "You have four shiny tin soldiers intercept us outside the gate, lead us down a maze of confined passages and then dump us in an interrogation room. The thought had entered my brain. I'm guessing Producer Lee Creighton thought the same."

"What would be the charges?" asked Payne, much too compassionate for the person they had met earlier in the week on the show.

"That's what we were wondering," replied Producer Lee Creighton. "Forgive us, we're neither students nor fans of the law. We don't get many politicians on the air."

"You did take some big time hits on my show though, don't you think" said Balthazer.

"Not my finest public appearance, I'll give you that," replied Payne. "It's mostly mopped up. I went on the *Today Show* this morning. We talked about you. I think the important sympathy is back where it needs to be."

"I'm guessing I didn't get any credit for helping," said Balthazer.

"That wasn't how the interview went, but who knows, there's always next week. I'm doing *Good Morning America* and a half dozen local shows in the top markets. Their audience doesn't much overlap with yours."

The room was suddenly permeated by the sound of a deep male voice coming from the polycom: "Are you going to introduce me, Sally, or do I need to do it myself?"

"Forgive me, Senator," continued Payne. "Gentlemen, on the squawk box is my distinguished colleague, the gentleman from Florida, former Senator Mitchell Henderson. Senator, please meet Kimo Balthazer, with whom I know you are familiar by reputation, and his Producer, the other fellow."

"Why would I be known to a former US Senator outside my market?" asked Balthazer. "He doesn't exactly fit my demographic."

"Come on, don't give us the humble act, Balthazer," boomed Henderson. "Lots of people know you for all kinds of reasons. I happen to be on the board of EnvisionInk, so I know you better and for a different set of reasons. I've been your guardian angel. Who do you think got you VIP treatment in Salinas?"

"I thought Special Agent Hussaini and I enjoyed a preferred relationship," said Balthazer. "I'll take it on good faith you're the power behind the trench coat. You all seem to be enamored with angels. Must be a retro thing."

"I'm guessing there's a reason we're here," inserted Producer Lee Creighton, attempting to navigate past the small talk.

"Yes, each of us has an agenda," said Payne. "We would like to ask you for some help with ours."

"We already did what Hussaini asked to help get that plane out of here," said Balthazer. "He said you were in the loop, Congresswoman. That was supposed to be our get out of jail free card."

"Special Agent Hussaini was doing what we asked him," interjected Henderson. "Sally sent the video to me, and I went to bat with the Director."

"Well done, Senator," applauded Balthazer. "I'm guessing your interest in EnvisionInk had no bearing on your willingness to help. So when do we see the plane again with Choy and Finkelman back on the job?"

"With any luck, fairly soon," said Henderson. "Unfortunately we hit another snag, which is in the process of being corrected. But that's not what we want to talk to you about. We want to talk to you about getting these two million people back to work."

"I have to go back to the plane," said Balthazer. "Any chance you can tell us where they were going? No one's heard a word since they left last night."

Payne stood silently before them. Balthazer could see in her eyes she knew the answer, but she stayed silent, as if she did not have the authority to speak. She looked off to the beige side walls, avoiding eye contact, waiting for Henderson to continue.

"As I hinted, things didn't go the way we planned," explained Henderson. "Imagine that, after the precision clockwork of the last few weeks. The plane was supposed to go up and come down, but our man onboard didn't get the gun. Now it's going to Hawaii, ostensibly for refueling on its way to Shanghai."

"Hussaini muffed it?" chortled Producer Lee Creighton. "After a week of prep?"

"Hand to hand isn't his area of expertise," replied Henderson. "And thank you for showing so much concern. Yes, everyone onboard is okay. I know you meant to ask."

"That plane has no clearance to go onto Shanghai," added Payne. "It was all we could do to get approval to let it take off on the expectation it would be a quick return. Now we have to fix it."

"Tell me you're not going to shoot it down," gasped Balthazer, hardly believing the words coming from his mouth.

"No, we aren't going to shoot it down," blasted Henderson. "That would be insanely stupid. We're just normal stupid. We have a runway secured at Hickam Air Force Base in Honolulu. We're going to take the plane there, quietly pump it full of knockout gas during refueling and then unload—all wrapped up in a bow like the professionals we pretend to be."

"Nitrous oxide?" asked Balthazer.

"Something a little more industrial strength," said Henderson. "It's classified, what does it matter to you?"

"No matter to me, as long as I keep my distance," said Balthazer. "I have a deadly allergy to that stuff. It's how I got my military discharge, right before basic training for the Gulf."

"I remember that, you were drunk beyond belief," said Producer Lee Creighton. "So trashed you took a dare to poke your head in a recruiting station."

"Wasted, cynical, and unemployed, a bad combination," said Balthazer. "They promised me Voice of America, my own Good Morning Kuwait City. I signed the papers, but when I woke up, surprise, no microphone. Luckily, they discovered I needed a root canal before I could hit basic. Army dentist hit me with nitrous and almost killed me. I was discharged before I ever suited up. Couldn't even look at a gas mask."

"Damn, you dodged a bullet," said Producer Lee Creighton. "You in the desert with a backpack and a rifle—yeah, sure. Talk about a soft recruiting environment."

"Could the two of you please shut up," belted Henderson. "We don't need your help with the unload. We need your help bringing this spontaneous revolution to an end. The stock market is not going to stabilize until people go back to work. We think you can be of true service to your country. Just go on the air and nicely suggest to people that they stop celebrating anarchy and get their asses back to their desks."

"This game really does have to end, fellows," said Payne. "It starts with you going on the air and telling the two million people who have walked off their jobs to go back to work."

"Could be more like three million by the weekend, according to our latest polls," bragged Producer Lee Creighton. "It's hard to keep an accurate count when the numbers get that big."

"I've got a fast shuttle to Hawaii leaving in twenty minutes," continued Payne. "The nice people at EnvisionInk have graciously offered use of their Gulfstream-V."

"I thought Swerlow and Kisinski had their plane," said Produce Lee Creighton.

"No, that's Choy and Finkelman's personal jet," said Balthazer. "This is their official company jet. Try to follow along."

"That's right," said Payne. "We're going to put Choy and Finkelman's plane into a circling pattern until we're ready to take it on the ground, wear them out as much as we can. Then I am going to be there to congratulate Hussaini on the capture."

"It's not Hussaini's capture," said Balthazer. "You guys just make up whatever you want the headlines to be? And aren't you worried about spooking them, circling the plane for hours?"

"We do what we need to do to make things right," replied Payne. "We want you to come along and be part of the celebration, to tell people on the air it's time to go back to work."

"I can't do that," said Balthazer. "Not until we get our

Merger Bill of Rights."

"Please, you can't be serious about that," asserted Payne. "That's comic book rubbish."

"My listeners love comic books," countered Balthazer. "Usually the good guys defeat the bad guys. We need something to give the Walkouts. If you can't get me a Merger Bill of Rights, what can you get me?"

"All the charges against you dropped, how's that for a start?" proposed Payne.

"What, Hussaini's deal is no good?" asked Balthazer.

"There was no Hussaini deal," said Henderson, resuming his commentary. "He told you if you didn't help he'd have you arrested for being inside the hundred-mile radius. We have FCC, abandoned alimony payments, assault and battery, Homeland Security escalation, and that's before we invite the IRS to take a walk on your wild side. You break up that crowd or you sign off."

"So you're threatening a conditional arrest," said Balthazer, looking at Producer Lee Creighton, who was nodding in agreement. "I want to make sure we understand our options."

"Look, Balthazer, I'm not explaining this well, let me try it another way" voiced Henderson. "I like you. You're a bona fide celebrity now. You could be the next Rush. Heck, you could be the next Oprah. Someone could build a company around you — radio, TV, books, plush toys. I'd invest in it myself. Maybe we'll hire Sol Seidelmeyer to help you run it, he's available. But first you need your broadcast license back, and for that to happen, we need all those people you motivated to walk off their jobs to go back to work. We're asking for a little help. It's not like it doesn't cut both ways."

"So it's a job offer or jail time," replied Balthazer, more snidely then he intended. "We take the trip to Hawaii or the locked cell behind door number two?"

"I suppose that's an adequate executive summary," affirmed Henderson.

Balthazer looked at Producer Lee Creighton, who shrugged.

There really was no choice. They could either stay in play and look for their next move, or they could be benched and broomed aside while the US government hosed down its mess and boxed them in mothballs. Flying with Payne to Hawaii to help her win accolades was not their idea of a holiday, but vaporizing into obscurity was equally unlikely to advance their cause. Leaving the door open was their only sane option, and that meant being team players, or at least appearing to be.

"We're supposed to be on the air at noon," noted Balthazer. "Do we have time to put a message on our website that says no show today for reasons beyond our control?"

"You do, as long as you also mention the special follow-up show that is coming soon," agreed Payne. "Tell your listeners that you are going On Assignment. Build a little anticipation, like a teaser. We have clothes and toothbrushes for both of you on the plane. The MPs will show you to the ramp. Wheels up in ten minutes."

"Thank you, Gentlemen, you're far more reasonable than I was led to believe," concluded Henderson. "I had a feeling that in your hearts you were patriots. Your nation thanks you for your service."

Henderson terminated the polycom line, leaving Payne alone with the much bewildered and overwhelmed pair of radio guys. She gathered her belongings, readying herself for the catch-up flight on which they would now be her accomplices.

"What about the crowd at the front gate?" asked Producer Lee Creighton.

"We'll get word to them that you had to attend to more critical matters," said Payne, in rapid departure mode. "I'm sure they can find their way back to the EnvisionInk parking lot until you tell them it's time to completely disperse."

Payne smiled courteously, a rehearsed mannerism it was clear she could deliver at will. She extended a handshake to each of them, then walked the few steps ahead of them to the narrow doorway, nodding graciously to the four MPs, still on post. Payne disappeared down one of the hallways, leaving

Balthazer and Creighton to quickly post their "coming soon" message online before being escorted behind her to the tarmac for their journey.

$ $

The 737 was about 2400 miles from San Francisco, circling over the Island of Oahu, barely visible from the windows unless you were looking closely for the few tiny concentrations of urban radiance through the dark of night. Swerlow and Kisinski had known the plane did not have trans-Pacific range and would have to refuel in Hawaii, but since the failed assault by Hussaini their trust levels were nonexistent. They had been told by the pilots that a runway was now being secured for landing, which had not been the case previously since the plane was not supposed to get this far, leaving Swerlow with no sense of what he could believe. Swerlow was already impatient, irate, disturbed by the lies, it was all he could do to contain his anger, which was being managed by his cousin Sam with an eye on the outcome, not on revenge.

For most of the flight, Hussaini sat near the back of the plane. Swerlow had to believe Hussaini was playing back in his head where things had gone wrong, anticipating some way to make them right. No doubt Hussaini's spirit had been crushed. It would have been painful for him to admit, but he just did not have the physical acumen to finish this job. Swerlow the amateur had humiliated Hussaini the pro—that was some coup! Hussaini had also been way off the mark misreading his cousin, convinced that Sam wanted a way out, to abandon the crime if only he could let someone else make the decision. Swerlow knew his cousin would never betray him, that poor calculation cost Hussaini the arrest. So why had Hussaini kept the plane in flight after the takeoff encounter failed? Swerlow presumed he was again buying more time, the alternatives not much of a choice, hopeful he would get another run at them in any moment of weakness, ready to accept the consequences of fully crapping out later rather than on the spot. Hussaini had told them the plane could never land in Shanghai, that would have taken a heavily negotiated act of the State Department, an order of magnitude longer in the making than their planned flight time. Swerlow refused to buy that. He still had faith in Hussaini's bargaining ability, especially when the chips were down, a learned response Hussaini had reinforced.

Swerlow and Kisinski were in the front of the plane in the office quarters with the door ajar, their muffled conversation private. Everyone else was in the main lounge area. Swerlow had the gun again, but it was on the table in front of him, in easy reach. Swerlow still had not slept, but the adrenalin rush from the fight had revived his momentum and he was operating with a clearer head. As Swerlow gazed out and saw the few distant lights below, it was more time clock than geography lesson. He had no idea what would happen on the ground, only an instinct that Hussaini's FBI buddies would use the landing to try something, and that Hussaini would try to redeem himself when they struck. Hussaini's intentions had been revealed, and Swerlow could not rule out another clash. He remained guarded, but there was increased confidence in his outlook. He could take Hussaini and his pals if that was what they wanted. Like any promising entrepreneur, Swerlow was rebounding, focused on the future, only the least bit tentative.

"You did a good job, cousin," said Swerlow. "I was never really sure where your head was at, but you showed me what you're made of."

"We're in this together," said Kisinski. "I hope we make it to the finish line."

"No question in my mind, we're going to the finish line," replied Swerlow. "Tomorrow we send these guys back home and we start a new adventure. We're even going to learn to speak Shanghainese."

"You're not mad at those guys for lying to us?" asked Kisinski.

"Of course I am," said Swerlow with marked indignation. "They're poison sewage, cheesy corporate criminals. But we have a deal, and we're going to honor our side, as long as there are no more surprises."

"Can I make an unlikely suggestion?" asked Kisinski.

"Sam, what are you thinking?"

"I'm thinking our chances of getting off the ground once we land in Hawaii are not very good," said Kisinski, reinforcing what Swerlow was already thinking, but in the negative, rather than the positive. "They've had us circling for no good reason, probably to disorient us more. They tried to take us down when we took off, they'll try again when we land. This time they might get it right."

"We have to beat them on their playing field," whispered Swerlow. "They only think they control the game. That's our advantage. Take the underdog for granted, you get bit, just liked we showed them."

"What if we offered them on olive branch?" said Kisinski. "We could tell them that as soon as we land we're willing to let Choy and Finkelman go."

"That's not a branch, that's an orchard," replied Swerlow. "You want to give away more than half our leverage? Just give those guys back?"

"It's a suggestion, a deal point, as you would say," reasoned Kisinski. "We get a little ahead of their game, so whatever they're thinking, they let us land, we give them Choy and Finkelman, we break their rhythm, maybe they let us continue. It seems fair. And they don't expect it, so we get some good will, at least from Choy and Finkelman."

"That's a pretty big cave," said Swerlow, loosely considering the idea. "We'd be trading something for nothing."

"They're good guys, they've proven that by letting us get this far. I even wish we could keep them around. We could learn so much from them. But that wouldn't be fair. They have to get back to running their company."

"Their company is going to shit," declared Swerlow. "Look what happened when they left Steyer in charge. Not only did their employees quit, millions followed them out the door. That's hard to do."

"Things need to get back to normal," said Kisinski, his tone ever hopeful.

"Yeah, right, normal," chuckled Swerlow, the first time he had revealed any form of a grin in over a week. Cousin Sam seemed a lot less naïve than he had at his sign on date

"When we started, all we wanted was Steyer. We have him. We could even kick Hussaini, but I doubt the feds will go for that. I say we keep Steyer and Hussaini, give them back Choy and Finkelman, and hope they don't blow up the plane when we land."

Their sidebar was interrupted with a polite tap on the open door, as Choy gingerly popped his head in the office doorway. Swerlow and Kisinski barely acknowledged him, though Swerlow's eyes ricocheted off a quick angle check with the gun in front of him.

"Hey, guys, we just got word from the pilots," said Choy. "We have clearance to land in Honolulu. They have a runway for us at Hickam Air Force Base. We should be on the ground in forty minutes and they'll start refueling."

"Doesn't it make you a little uncomfortable owning a plane like this for yourselves?" asked Kisinski, seemingly out of nowhere.

"Two weeks together and you're just asking me now?" jeered Choy.

"I guess it just hit me," replied Kisinski.

"We like the plane a lot, but we don't let it define us," said Choy.

"How do we know they're going to let us refuel and get back in the air?" asked Swerlow, putting it directly to Choy.

"You're asking me?" said Choy. "You're holding us, aren't you? We've come this far. I don't think with two million people out of work and a dead stock market they can risk another fumble. But I can't guarantee it. This is all first time for me, too."

"Sam thinks we should let you and your partner go when we land," shared Swerlow. "He thinks it would be a show of good faith on our part. We'd still have Steyer to finish the trip, then we'd send him back. What do you think?"

"I don't think I want to be the guy who says let me go and

keep the other guy," said Choy. "But if that's the choice you make, I can promise you Stephen and I will make sure they know what you're thinking and why you're thinking it."

"They've had us circling a long time," said Kisinski. "That doesn't feel like a good sign. If letting you go keeps us moving forward, it seems like a fair trade."

"I don't know much more than you," said Choy. "But I can run it by the others."

"I don't much care what Steyer or Hussaini have to say, they're worthless scum," exclaimed Swerlow. "You're the one who is into Burning Man, aren't you?"

"I'm not sure how that's relevant," answered Choy. "Yeah, I go to Burning Man. It's not an event that Stephen and I share, but it helps me stay focused."

"Just trying to get inside your head," replied Swerlow. "You seem smarter than that. Why don't you go get your partner and we'll talk a little more."

"You got it," said Choy, more baffled by Swerlow's thinking. "I'll get Stephen and then if you want we can get in touch with someone on the ground before we land."

Choy waited for them to acknowledge his suggestion. Swerlow looked guardedly at his cousin, who also seemed perplexed with his musings, then ran a quick glimpse by the gun before turning back to Choy and nodding. Swerlow was willing to take a chance, to attempt the uncharted. Choy returned the nod, then slipped back out of the office and momentarily revisited the main cabin to silently retrieve his partner.

$ $

Balthazer and Producer Lee Creighton were seated inelegantly in the aft lounge chairs of EnvisionInk's corporate G-V, making its way to Honolulu at about six hundred miles per hour in attempts to get there as near it could to meet the landing of Choy and Finkelman's slower but long leading plane. Congresswoman Payne was in the front of the cabin with her entourage of five impeccably dressed assistants, apparently working together to craft some congratulatory remarks for the presumed

resolution later that evening. Her optimism for a successful release seemed palpable if not warranted, rooted in expectation
more than reconnaissance. She expressed no interest in talking
further with Balthazer or Creighton, her comments as muffled
as theirs, everyone's voice kept low.

Also on the flight, planted in the mid cabin even before
Balthazer and Creighton had boarded, were EnvisionInk's general counsel, Sylvia Normandy, and the company's CFO, Sanjay Basru. Sitting with them was an attractive woman in her
fifties who would be introduced as Daniel Steyer's wife, Riley.
Balthazer had seen Normandy once before, at the Salinas hospital site, but other than that this was a first encounter for all.
Following the brief introductions before takeoff, it was made
clear that Normandy and Basru had come to meet Choy and
Finkelman, and Steyer as expected by her husband. Their ascribed level of confidence that the feds now had everything under control had to be high, with a well-sold belief that Swerlow
and Kisinski soon would be artifacts of crime history, otherwise
there would be little reason for them to tag along on such short
notice. Like Payne, post the initial pleasantries they had nothing
much to say to Balthazer or Creighton during the flight. They
hardly had anything to say to each other. With so much unsaid,
it seemed obvious the three of them were anything but on the
same page, bound working associates more than colleagues, certainly not friends.

As the G-V made its way westbound, Balthazer was unusually preoccupied in thought. For the longest time he stared out
the window into the darkness, occasionally looking over at Producer Lee Creighton, but no words came to him. Somewhere in
the boxing match, maybe round eight or nine, he had taken one
blow too many. Creighton tried to boost his partner's spirit with
kind words, conveying he saw the opposite in the pugilist—that
he marveled at how adroitly Balthazer was operating in the
sludge. Balthazer was having a hard time seeing it that way,
he doubted the drama of psychological politics and corporate
warfare wasn't affecting his output. Balthazer was encouraged

that their next, and potentially best, remote had been arranged with the bad guys in the rear view mirror, yet there was more on his mind than the next webcast. None of the government's intervention in the kidnapping to date had gone well. They were meddlers, not solvers. Something had to go wrong, swallowing their chance to do anything that could matter.

"Do you think our Merger Bill of Rights is a crock?" asked Balthazer of Producer Lee Creighton, interrupting the quiet. He did not think Payne could hear him, but at such close range, he could not be sure.

"That's a bit out of left field," said Producer Lee Creighton, the pun not his intention.

"We might be out of our league," continued Balthazer. "No one is taking us seriously. Do you think I crossed a line?"

"I have no idea, Kimo, way above my pay grade," answered Creighton. "You do the content. I just make sure folks have access to it and the calls flow."

"Yeah, but you have opinions," said Balthazer. "Was this the stupidest idea I ever had, injecting myself where I have no idea what I'm talking about?"

"The stupidest?" echoed Creighton. "No, not the stupidest. We've been together a very long time and you always find new paths to the edge. I think your heart is in it; that counts for a lot. Remember, we never asked for the Walkout. It happened by itself. We just tossed dry palm fronds on the embers."

"Same as we always do," said Balthazer. "A few thatched leaves to send up smoke signals, maybe get a laugh or two."

"It's been a hell of a few weeks, Kimo," replied Creighton. "We made radio history. They can never take that away from us."

"It doesn't bother you, the cost?" asked Balthazer.

"More from left field," said Creighton. "You're awfully philosophical today. Did you eat?"

"I didn't mean to screw up your life," said Balthazer, wandering to a new topic, but not really. "Your wife, your family, all that. You came back. I couldn't have done this without you. But you wonder, is it worth it?"

"I screwed up my own life when I decided to do radio," said Producer Lee Creighton. "It's not you, it's the gig. People like us are a wee bit different from the mainstream."

"I didn't mean to screw up my life either," said Balthazer. "It just kind of happens when a door opens. The show has always been everything for me. When they took it away, when I pissed it away, that was not good for me. I walked away from three marriages and I survived, but walking away from the show, not so much. This internet radio thing has been another chance, it's a miracle. I don't want to blow it again."

"Maybe you should help the suits get people back to work," suggested Creighton. "Would that betray everything you believe in?"

"We have to get something for all those Walkouts," said Balthazer. "We have to pay for all the cheap laughs or all we did was roll a gag reel. That's not what I want."

"Canceling the show today will be good for buzz," said Creighton. "I mentioned on the site our attention had been temporarily diverted by a certain member of Congress who suggested anyone who voluntarily left their job should lose it."

"How did you phrase that in the ten seconds you had to post?"

"The good Congresswoman wishes you to Think Reagan, Think Air Traffic Controllers."

"That'll go viral! Nice going, Creighton. That should get us another half million Walkouts, maybe more."

"The more people feel in the dark, the less likely they are to cave," said Creighton. "We've made a real difference, Kimo. However it ends, we did something right."

"I think so, now all I have to do is figure out what to say when we open the mic on the runway."

"I'm not worried, you'll figure it out," offered Creighton. "When the time comes, you'll know what to say. You'll say what has to be said."

Payne had finished an intense phone call in the front of the cabin and was making her way politely down the aisle past the EnvisionInk contingent to Balthazer and Creighton. She stared at them, a cold stare of doubt. It was as though she was insulted to have to share breathing space with them, but had no choice given the time table, it was her concession. Again Balthazer wondered if she had heard him pondering his own conviction, but at this point, it did not matter. Payne took an open seat near them. Balthazer figured if she was sinking so low as to visit with them, she must have been trying to avoid discussion with Normandy or Basru. Balthazer and Creighton waited for her to speak, which for some reason she felt compelled to prolong, as if she wanted them to speak first, even though she had approached them.

"Clever bit of copy on your website," said Payne. "You made it sound like I cancelled your show. You made their jobs my problem, as if I had anything to do with it. Pleased with yourselves?"

"The nuts are good," said Balthazer, noting the small spread on the coffee table between them. "I'll give them that, they do have excellent mixed nuts on this Gulfstream. Do you and your colleagues always get this kind of treatment? Because you work hard, you deserve it."

"Private transportation provided by corporations for government employees is limited to special circumstances," replied Payne. "It's hard to argue this doesn't qualify."

"Hard to argue," echoed Balthazer. "Very hard to argue."

"Swerlow and Kisinski are about to land," continued Payne. "We've had them circle as long as we could. They now require refueling. We're about ninety minutes behind them, but we should get there right about the time the guys on the ground are ready to move. Of course we have a hitch."

"There's a surprise," said Producer Lee Creighton. "Let me guess, Henderson wants a piece of their IPO and won't open the jet way until he gets his option grant."

"They're thinking about releasing Choy and Finkelman," announced Payne.

Balthazer and Creighton had no response. They had no idea what this meant, or what it meant to them.

"They wired the tower and the tower wired us," added Payne, nervously avoiding eye contact with Riley Steyer. "It could be a ploy, we don't know. They say it's about good faith. They're considering if it makes sense, if they give back Choy and Finkelman, we let them fuel up and get moving again."

"They can't be thinking you'd really let the plane go onto Shanghai," said Balthazer. "There's no way the Chinese would let it land, given the circumstances."

"There is an Intelligence meeting taking place right now to decide what to do," relayed Payne. "We're not sure our original plan still makes sense. If they figure out what's happening we might not get back Choy and Finkelman. Swerlow could really lose it."

"I'd hit 'em with the gas after they give up Choy and Finkelman," said Producer Lee Creighton. "It's a hell of a lot less risky."

"That's what I think," said Payne. "But others are involved, as always a good many opinions are being considered. I'm going to give Normandy, Basru, and Ms. Steyer the same update and I'll brief you again when we land."

"She's going to be worried about her husband," said Balthazer. "The trade isn't favorable to him."

"Your ability to read an audience knows no limits," sniped Payne. "There isn't going to be a trade. There's going to be a favorable ending. You're going to need to be flexible. I don't know what happens next, but whatever it is, when you go back on the air, you have one job—tell people to go back to work. We're clear on that, right?"

"Oh yes, we're clear on that," confirmed Balthazer.

"Eat something besides pecans and cashews," said Payne. "We have a long night ahead of us. I am not sure when you'll get a chance to eat again."

Payne got up and approached Normandy, Basru, and Riley Steyer. The congresswoman seemed hesitant to open the dialogue, but Balthazer knew she had no choice. The G-V continued across the Pacific, making fast time in the night sky. Balthazer took some relief knowing that Choy and Finkelman's plane soon would be on the ground, and with any luck they might be safely released. Where it went from there was anyone's guess, Balthazer hadn't the slightest clue, no prophecy possible. He reached in the back pocket of the seat in front of him and found a menu hand drawn in calligraphy. Chef's choice sustainable sushi. Fresh whole wheat pasta salad with organic Roma tomatoes. The meal selections on this private rig were even beyond the quality of the mixed nuts. Too bad he wasn't hungry.

$ $ $ $

2.9
Blue Screen

NASDAQ: ENVN (Day 18 - Evening)
SHARE PRICE @ MARKET CLOSE: $66.15
COMPANY MARKET CAP: $17.5B
VALUATION DELTA SINCE ABDUCTION: < 51% >
** ENVN DELTA FROM PEAK: < 71% > **

NASDAQ SINCE ABDUCTION: < 27% >
** NASDAQ DELTA SINCE RECENT PEAK:
< 44% > **

Producer Lee Creighton was baffled. He and Balthazer were on the Hickam AFB tarmac with their laptops primed, stationed in a small, yellow, roped area under a tented awning about a football field from Choy and Finkelman's jet. They were accompanied by a fresh pair of local MPs, who would be within several body lengths of them for their remaining time in Honolulu. Despite the fact that they had been provided essentially unlimited network bandwidth—wireless or wired—Creighton could not get to the Internet.

Anyone who has every used a personal computer knows to fear the blue screen of death, and Producer Lee Creighton had just faced it, blue as the ocean seen from space. When he attempted to boot Balthazer's laptop in addition to his own and got the same menacing blue, he was pretty sure the computer problems were not routine. Creighton could not rule out hardware abuse, at least initially. The laptops he and Balthazer were using for their webcasts were hardly industrial strength, pure consumer cheap, mail order intended for short life and nextgen upgrade as retail commerce depended on lifecycle replacements to compensate for paper thin margins. This pair of PCs had been carted from one end of California to the other, raced up and down Interstate 5 and Highway 101, dragged in standby mode inland and to the coast, often tossed hastily in the back of the Infiniti sans travel bag without a soft leather landing. On inspection, the hardware proved fine, no hard drive crash, no acrid smoking chip. Creighton had procured a geek store wireless mobile card along the way specifically for daily system and security updates between shows, and so far their systems had avoided any signs of a nuisance virus, malware, craplet, or firewall penetration. The software checked out clean, the system and application layers were uncorrupted. Creighton was well-versed in the world of nasty crashes and this freeze did not appear at all normal—none of the error messages appearing in dialogue boxes were familiar, some were so strange they seemed to be leering at him, daring him to click on the close button for a bombshell Easter egg, masking an erase or format command. Creighton was frustrated and time constrained, but he was much too smart to fall for that old gag.

"This is weird, I can't get to our upload server," grumbled Creighton. "I can't even get to ThisIsRage.com."

"You sure we didn't trash the laptops somewhere along the way," said Balthazer. "It's not like they were ever intended for the workout we've put them through."

"No, I've tried mine and yours, I can boot until I try to go online" said Creighton. "Then we're frozen out, blue meanie swelter. I think it's a DNS attack."

"We've been hacked?" asked Balthazer, surprised but not really.

"It looks that way. If I can't bridge it, I don't know how we can webcast today."

"Pro or amateur?" probed Balthazer.

"They have our website and our connection to the hub. I can't even jump a link to the satellite feed. Whoever it is knows what they're doing."

"I thought the hackers were on our side," said Balthazer. "They have been from the beginning."

"Not all of them," said Producer Lee Creighton. "There's a guy on that plane who's not too bad with a keyboard."

"You think it's Kisinski?"

"Hard to explain otherwise," said Creighton. "At least we know they know we're here."

"Can you get our hackers to hack his hacking?" suggested Balthazer.

"Only if I could get a message posted on our site as a shout-out for help, but I can't," said Creighton. "It's kind of an endless loop."

"Use your smart phone, go post on some of the less well-traveled tech blogs, where the real geeks hang out," said Balthazer. "Our followers have probably noticed our site is down. Tell our hacker fans what you suspect and see if they can work around whatever Kisinski is using to block us."

"I can try that, but don't expect we'll be back up by the time they get off that plane," said Creighton. "We can beat it eventually, but I have no idea how long that will take."

Producer Lee Creighton posted the virtual ticket on a half dozen of the more obscure rebel hack blogs, knowing that if it was Kisinski blocking them, he was as likely to see these posts as the hackers who would come to their aid. This was shaping up to be a digital arms race, always fun in cyberspace, the winner never predictable. Creighton did not like surrendering to helplessness, but his technical prowess could only take him so far. After all, he was an old school radio guy, all this internet stuff was self-taught.

$ $

Across from the holding pen where Balthazer was supposed to call the Freedom Sweepstakes play-by-play were the makings of a combat firestorm, of little distraction to the consumed Producer Lee Creighton, but impossible for Balthazer to ignore. The private 737 was surrounded by dozens of heavily armed guards, a military deployment on high alert. Anywhere Balthazer looked, all he saw were guns, guns, guns. Semi-automatic rifles, side mounts, turrets, the formation was clearly intentioned and complete. A garrison of fire trucks and armored vehicles flashing red encircled the plane, and an overhead rig of pivoting spotlights lit the scene as if they were filming a movie. It may as well have been daylight in the target zone, bordered by the shadow backdrop of the ocean disappearing into the horizon. Every relevant resource that Hickam Field had to deploy was locked and loaded, with additional reinforcements on standby at Pearl Harbor should the overkill require a curtain call. Air stairs had been mounted to the jet way door, a line of standing uniforms tracking a path to the terminal. Each and every troop was waiting for that door to open, either for arrest or attack, both seemed viable options for the operation.

The Boeing Business Jet sat motionless on the runway, with no formal or informal communication from Payne or her entourage since they landed an hour ago. It was a waiting game now, no one had been advised what was supposed to happen next. Payne had disappeared into the terminal minutes after they landed, leaving Balthazer and Producer Lee Creighton in the company of base staff to set up their webcast station and await instructions. Now they were just stuck. Waiting. Followed by waiting. Then more waiting. While Producer Lee Creighton continued to struggle with yet another fruitless attempt to salvage the laptops, Balthazer was joined in the roped area by Normandy, Basru, and Riley Steyer, who also had disappeared for the past hour. It was an awkward setting, the roped observation ring not a great milieu for small talk with the unknown bit of remaining time before the jet way door would open.

"Enjoy the flight?" asked Balthazer, directing the comment mostly to Normandy, given their history. "If you have to travel a lot, I can see how you could get used to that."

"Business travel is always stressful, this in particular," answered Normandy. "Ms. Steyer has been under a lot of stress, so the idea of flying commercial was to be avoided."

"It's nice that Ms. Steyer came to meet her husband," said Balthazer. "I'm sure it will be a great relief when everyone is released. Surprised there's no family presence for Choy and

Finkelman."

"Neither of them are married, not seriously involved at the moment to my knowledge either," said Normandy. "They're still pretty young. They work a lot, as you can imagine. Their families couldn't be contacted with much lead time, given all the moving parts, but we've been keeping them updated. They should be waiting at Moffett when we get home tomorrow."

"What do you think changes at EnvisionInk when they go back to work?" asked Balthazer, not quite as innocently as he meant it.

"I can't really say," dodged Normandy. "I think they'll take it a day at a time. They're good at what they do." She seemed uncomfortable to Balthazer, perhaps it was the presence of Steyer's wife.

"Choy and Finkelman are going to be pissed off about the Atom Heart fiasco," blurted Basru. "I expect they are going to be doing some house cleaning, once they get back up to speed and figure out exactly what's been going on."

Normandy shot Basru a stark gaze, a not subtle reminder of caution that reinforced Balthazer's suspicion about her guard-edness in front of Ms. Steyer. Riley may or may not have heard Basru, but displayed no reaction. She did not have to say much to stand her ground, her presence was commanding, likely adopted along the way from an incomparable peer group.

"Let me ask you a question," continued Balthazer, making eye contact with Basru. "What do you think the chances are they'll support this idea we've dreamed up for a Merger Bill of Rights? Is that something you think Choy and Finkelman could get behind? Seems like it might be in their wheelhouse."

"Are you kidding?" proclaimed Basru. "That's preposterous. It's a joke, right? You think anyone in authority in a public or private company is going to put limits on themselves for growth? It's hard enough to comply with government regulations. Why would anyone take a talk show host seriously on M&A policy? If it were funny it would be laughable."

"Got it, you're not a fan," flexed Balthazer. "I wasn't asking for your support. I was asking about theirs."

"A CEO is a CEO," said Riley Steyer, speaking for the first time just behind them. "Ask yourself—what's in it for them?"

"Could be the only way they get their employees back to work," said Producer Lee Creighton. "If EnvisionInk employees don't go back to work, there's little chance any of the other Walkouts are going back anytime soon."

"You make a good point," said Normandy. "Calvin and Stephen are extremely smart fellows. They're not just visionaries, they're pragmatists. I don't know how they'll react, but I'm guessing they'll listen—once they get their sea legs back. They do have a few other critical items to deal with ahead of that, including catching up on a few board meetings they've missed."

"They aren't going to get rid of my husband," interjected Riley, surprising everyone with the comment, fully absorbed by Balthazer. Another uncomfortable pause followed.

"I'm sorry, Riley, did you think I implied that from one of my remarks?" said Normandy.

"Don't take me for a fool, it's obvious how you feel about Daniel," said Riley. "He created this company. He created Choy and Finkelman. If you think you're going to spill him down the sewer, I can tell you that's not going to happen."

"You have a right to be upset, Riley, but I'm not sure this is the right time or place for that discussion," conveyed Normandy.

"No, then perhaps Sanjay can share what's on his mind as it pertains to Daniel," blasted Riley, more in the loop than Balthazer previously imagined.

"I don't have an opinion on your husband's options," countered Basru. "He is a great man, a tremendous man. I'm just the CFO. I don't advocate. I tally the scorecard."

"If only you meant those words," said Riley. "I don't believe you do. I believe you think you can do this without him. You can't. Choy and Finkelman may need time to get back up to speed, but they'll never get back to normal, whatever that is, without Daniel. It will take as much time as it takes, and you can't push it along just because your stock options might be momentarily underwater. That's all you care about."

"Ms. Steyer, I don't understand the point you wish to make, but there isn't a lot of time for anyone to get back up to speed," replied Basru. "If we don't get people back to work soon, we are going to have to restate guidance to the Street. Once the top four hundred or five hundred companies lower their earnings outlook, you can kiss goodbye any stock market recovery. We are at a new low, hopefully we've found the market bottom, but who knows. If a recovery doesn't come quickly, it won't come for who knows how long. Then it won't matter if people Walk-out because we'll be in a recession. We'll all be out."

"You're a cheery fellow," remarked Balthazer. "Remind me to ask you on the show sometime. You can pick up where the congresswoman left off, maybe tag team."

Once again, Balthazer's timing was impeccable — or maybe he just saw her out of the corner of his eye, as they were joined on the tarmac by the Honorable Sally Payne and her handlers, emerging from the nearby terminal door. Payne maintained an antiseptic distance, but her presence was again the center of attention, the self-appointed command center. This was her project. This was her chess board. There were no journalists on the beat, she controlled the story as she intended through Balthazer. The only photographer present was her own, who took a few careful documenting shots at each step of the mission. Payne was on parade, and yet, somehow she was not herself. Maybe Balthazer was the only one who noticed, but there was a sliver of second guessing in her step. She seemed unusually nervous, possibly because she knew the day's outcome would be determined by actions she could not control.

"We have a change in plan," said Payne with crafty determination. "FBI and base security are going to try to take them on the handoff."

"If that rules out the gas, you have no argument from me," said Balthazer. "I don't care how far away we are, I don't want to be near the stuff."

"They've agreed to release Choy and Finkelman, like they

suggested," articulated Payne. "As soon as they do, we're going full press."

"Full press as in assault?" asked Normandy. "You know that's s not what Swerlow and Kisinski had in mind when they offered the release. If they see it coming we may lose the offer."

"There's no quid pro quo and there'll be no tipoff," stated Payne. "All these well-trained people out here, all these uniforms, all this equipment—you don't think they know what they're doing? This is what they do. We're going to let them do it."

"What about my husband?" challenged Riley. "He won't be in the clear. Plus you have that FBI man onboard, and the pilots. This isn't smart. We flew here to bring them home. You told me you had a plan. After all the screw ups, has anyone thought this all the way through?"

"We're adjusting as we go, Ma'am," replied Payne. "Yes, we had a plan. Then they had a plan. Then we adjusted our plan to incorporate their plan. Our people think if we move fast once the door opens, we can board the aircraft and take them without a shot. They're amateurs, they won't know how to react. That's what I'm told."

"Everyone keeps saying they're amateurs," countered Riley. "What are we, six year olds playing soccer, chasing the ball wherever it goes on the field, only the ball is a loaded firearm encased in a private jet? You're lunatics, you wouldn't last forty-eight hours in private business, yet here you are in charge."

"I'm not making the call, Ms. Steyer," said Payne. "This is coming from above me. I think we're doing the right thing, but even if I didn't, I've said what I can."

Balthazar figured Payne would have loved to argue the verbal assault by Riley, but had nothing to win. Any further confrontation with Riley could only get Payne into more trouble, especially if things did not go well. Payne politely excused herself from the pack and took Balthazar aside, summoning him with her index finger, walking several steps along the tarmac until they were out of hearing range.

"That was unpleasant," lavished Balthazer. "I'd say you handled it well, but I don't think anyone could have handled it well. This is seriously dangerous what you're trying."

"It is what it is," said Payne. "As I said, it's not my call. Are you ready for show time?"

"Yeah, that's another problem," related Balthazer, feeling the sting before it bit. "I don't think we can have show time."

"You've decided not to help us, after you flew with us here? Are you really that self-destructive?"

"Candidly, I am, but this one's not my call either," replied Balthazer. "Our computers have been hacked. We have no access to our site, no access to the Internet. We have no way to webcast."

"Very convenient," tossed off Payne.

Balthazer presumed her disbelief in his every word, but tried to reason with her anyway. "I know it sounds bad, but I promise you it's the truth. Ask Producer Lee Creighton. We think the attack is coming from the plane. I'm guessing they don't want me to do the show."

"You're on an Air Force Base," asserted Payne. "Can't they get you on the air?"

"In the next few minutes?" asked Producer Lee Creighton, maneuvering behind them unannounced. "Doubtful. Kisinski seems to have us tied down. He's really good at this."

"We're trying to get some of the hackers we know to break us through, but we're not there yet," said Balthazer. "What can I say? It's a code war. We're not in the club."

"You're just digital damsels in distress, awaiting the code knights," derided Payne.

Convinced she still thought he and Producer Lee Creighton were lying, Balthazer was about to respond, but before he could, he got a text ping on his mobile. He looked down and read the message, then back at Payne, who seemed to be starting to drift. Payne was running out of levers, and if she did not begin caring about a better outcome, the day would not end well.

"Tell your sharpshooters to lock their safeties," urged

Balthazer. "It's Hussaini, he kept my number. He's coming out."

"That's not what's supposed to happen," countered Payne. "They're supposed to release Choy and Finkelman, then our guys are supposed to board. We have to stick to some plan."

"We have to pivot," implored Balthazer. "You do what you want, but he texted me for a reason. I wouldn't send in the cavalry on this cue."

Payne stared out at the 737, at the barrage of readiness, then grabbed Balthazer's mobile and read the video screen. It was Hussaini, and he was coming out. She tossed the phone back at Balthazer, turned and abruptly headed back into the terminal. Once again she had called the scenario wrong. Hubris was becoming much more her adversary than those who would contest her authority. The real enemy was almost incidental.

"She sure wants this photo op," mumbled Balthazer. "Guess that's what it takes to get first chair on *The Today Show*."

"She's not as good at this as I would have thought," replied Producer Lee Creighton. "She has everything perfectly choreographed, but the dropped lines are a real problem for her. She wouldn't last long in radio."

"She even made us part of the dance," said Balthazer. "Too bad we don't know the right steps."

Formal communication flowed across the base rapidly after Payne entered the terminal. Balthazer was aware that a chain of command had been established to transmit breaking information in real time as every critical military action was expected to function. Spotlights on the 737 blazed at full power and the surrounding militia took aim at the jet way door. The portal opened and there Balthazer saw Hussaini alone, standing at the top of the air stairs. Hussaini showed that his hands were empty, waited for safe acknowledgment, then hurriedly walked down the ramp and approached the holding area, bypassing the line of guards connecting the entrenched dots across the runway. By the time Hussaini neared the roped area holding the receiving party, Payne had returned and intercepted him, waving off the others to remain in the adjacent pen. This time Hussaini pointed at Balthazer to join them, leaving Payne no choice. Producer Lee Creighton again invited himself to the sidebar.

"I take it you have some action planned?" said Hussaini, directing the gut check to Payne.

"We've had several plans," said Payne. "They're all on hold. Why'd they send you out? I thought we were getting Choy and Finkelman."

"That was their plan, until they saw Balthazer," shared Hussaini. "They aren't very good criminals, but they are learning about human nature on the job."

"What do I have to do with it?" asked Balthazer, incensed by the implication he was responsible for the unfolding chain of events.

"They figured if you were here to do a show, there had to be a reason," replied Hussaini. "The only reason that made any sense to them was that you thought you were bringing them down, and the congresswoman was going to use Balthazer's show to gloat. So the first thing they did was kill your connection."

"I knew it was a hack," said Producer Lee Creighton. "That Kisinski is a talented coder. I won't have the site back for hours."

"They really hate my show, don't they?" asked Balthazer, less immodest than it sounded.

"More than your show," replied Hussaini. He did not have to say more.

"What do they want to happen now?" inquired Payne. "We're already out on a limb. I don't know that the base command isn't going to give the order to disarm the plane anyway. This is an Air Force Base, these guys are serious about security. I have no authority here."

"You're not going to like what they want," presented Hussaini.

"Try me," said Payne.

"I wasn't talking to you," said Hussaini. "I was talking to Balthazer. They want him."

"They want me on the plane?" asked Balthazer. "That's insane. I'm a talk show host. I don't have anything to do with this."

"You do now," said Hussaini. "They want the show off the air until this is over. Getting you onboard guarantees it. I don't think they'll hurt you, unless they hear any extra footsteps on the ramp."

"Or gunshots," said Producer Lee Creighton, not giving Balthazer reason to feel better.

"Is this a trade?" asked Payne. "Choy and Finkelman for Balthazer? How does that help us get to a resolution?"

"It doesn't," said Hussaini. "But if I'm not back on that plane with Balthazer in the next five minutes with the door closed behind me, instead of having Choy and Finkelman, you're going to have a plane full of dead bodies. I'd call it a time bridge."

Normandy, Basru, and Riley Steyer were still in the yellow roped area, anxiously watching the interchange bouncing around Hussaini without picking up enough words. Out of patience for being excluded from the discussion, they granted themselves permission to leave the holding area and approached the special agent.

"Can we get an update please?" demanded Riley Steyer. "Is my husband okay?"

"I apologize, Ms. Steyer. I'm Special Agent in Charge Kaamil Hussaini. I've been on this case since it started. Your husband is no better or worse than when he joined us."

"I can't believe he's on that plane," continued Riley. "He never told me he was going with them. I didn't find out until he was onboard and called me. Are they still planning to release Choy and Finkelman? Can't all these people with all these weapons bring this to a close?"

"They do want to release Choy and Finkelman, but we don't quite have a safe exit plan for the rest of us," responded Hussaini. "Not yet."

"There's no way we can get them to release Daniel?" asked Riley, attempting to hold back tears she no longer could. "No way at all? We have a lot of money, too. Not as much as Choy and Finkelman, but my husband made that money for them. It's not right. They have to let him go."

"It's not about money at this point," said Hussaini. "He was their original target, you know that. They're negotiating for their own release, to get out of the country. And they do have another request."

"They want me to join the party," said Balthazer, Hussaini's exhausted eyes on him. "I'm not sure who helps the congresswoman get her millions of Walkouts back to work if I do that, but maybe we have bigger problems."

"They're not my Walkouts," corrected Payne. "And I can't tell you to go on that aircraft. Much as I'd like it to be my decision, it's not. It's yours."

There was no argument in Balthazer's mind, Payne had called this one wrong. She, more than anyone, had to know that now. Had she left Balthazer in California, she might be posing for the front page of the *New York Times*. Now she would not even get a half-inch in the Honolulu Star-Advertiser. Hubris was costly, and her next election was getting a lot more expensive.

"What are you thinking, boss?" asked Producer Lee Creighton. "You don't have to do this. You really don't."

"I know that," said Balthazer. "But think of the ratings if I come out alive. We may get ourselves back in a real studio, with padded chairs and a mixing board. Wouldn't that be peachy?"

"Radio history, Kimo," said Producer Lee Creighton. "Bat Out of Hell."

"Let's go, Special Agent Hussaini," conveyed Balthazer. "Let's give the economy back Calvin Choy and Stephen J. Finkelman. Let's see if they can solve the Walkout problem. Maybe Swerlow and Kisinski will let me email my audience when we get onboard. They can screen my posts. I'll only say the nicest things about them."

Handshakes were tentatively exchanged, Balthazer's daring less a surprise to those on the airfield than an unsatisfying continuance, an empty hole without a cover. Congresswoman

Payne went back in the terminal to communicate the revised plan and ensure the armed forces would stand down. As Balthazer turned toward the aircraft, Normandy stepped aside and intercepted him.

"Balthazer, be careful around Steyer," she offered without prompting. "He keeps up appearances, but he'll throw you under the wheels if there's an open hatch."

"Appreciate the warning, but I think I had him pegged," replied Balthazer. "And you're telling me this about your chairman why?"

"I'm an attorney, it's full disclosure. Just want a fair fight, mostly for my conscience."

"He's not the worst liar I ever met, but close," commented Balthazer, testing for an opening. "You ever consider a cup of coffee with an almost-famous radio schmuck?"

"I tend to keep business and personal pretty compartmentalized," replied Normandy. "But if you know one who's not a complete schmuck, have him give me a call."

"I'll see what I can come up with," said Balthazer. "Situations can change."

Normandy extended a business handshake and stepped back with the others. Balthazer rejoined Hussaini, walking across the tarmac and past the posted brigade, heading back to the dreaded 737, everything ahead of them uncertain after boarding—except for the radio history.

"What was that about?" asked Hussaini.

"Briefing, attorney-client privilege," replied Balthazer.

"Are you sure you want to do this?" asked Hussaini. "Last chance."

"Best chance," said Balthazer. "At least Choy and Finkelman get another chance. They won't blow it. I probably would."

Balthazer followed Hussaini up the air stairs. At the top of the ramp, the door opened from within without prompting. They were being monitored closely by all sides. Precisely as Balthazer and Hussaini entered the doorway, Choy and Finkelman squeezed past them onto the exterior ramp — no small trick since Finkelman was still hobbling in a stiff leg cast and maneuvering a crutch, but they made it work as if it had been rehearsed. The passing pairs said nothing to each other, there was no time, nothing intelligent worth saying. There was a glance of hope, they all carried that, and that reinforced the choice as correct. The jet way door was not open for thirty seconds in all, then pulled shut tightly the moment Choy and Finkelman exited. Swerlow and Kisinski were not seen by the assembled, nor was Daniel Steyer.

Balthazer looked out the window portal from inside the plane. The brilliant spotlights framed Choy and Finkelman on top of the ramp, giving them almost movie star presence and casting a colossal shadow against the fuselage behind them as they made their way down the air stairs to the tarmac. The military personnel aligning their path remained on high alert, weapons still drawn on the jet way door, but no order had been given for engagement. Everyone waited for an order to come, but there was none. No gas, no siege, no storming of the plane.

Choy and Finkelman were free. As they crossed the runway, all of the guns around them were lowered. They joined Normandy and Basru in the roped holding area and were welcomed with perfunctory affection. The trade was complete. Balthazer was locked onboard with Hussaini, Steyer, Swerlow, and Kisinski. Not a single shot had been fired, it was simply a prisoner exchange at a 50% favorable discount, with the additional ask of an international travel visa not likely to be issued.

Riley Steyer stood alone.

Producer Lee Creighton stood alone.

Congresswoman Payne stood alone.

There was no photo op, no capture, no celebration, no webcast. One standoff had been substituted for another. Two soft-spoken hostages had been swapped for one very loud one. No one was sure who was in charge, or who would signal the next move. The five million people who had walked off their jobs would be reacting in short order to news that the crisis was not over, but their spokesman was even more at its center.

Not that anyone should have been thinking about it, but the stock market, sunk to bottom, was not going anywhere anytime soon. Balthazer was not the only one who knew a good trade would be hard to find.

$ $ $ $

3.0
THEATRICALITY

"A moral being is one who is capable of reflecting on his past actions and their motives — of approving some and disapproving of others . . . The fact that man is the one being who certainly deserves this designation is the greatest of all distinctions between him and the lower animals."
– Charles Darwin, *The Descent of Man* (1871)

"You'll never work in this town again. Until I need you."
– Louis B. Mayer
– Harry Cohn
– Jack Warner
– Your Boss?

<u>3.1</u>
Oxygen is Underrated

Chief information officer might be the least glamorous executive title in all of business. To be fair, it is a real title, a real C-level title, not one of those ego-catnip made-up C-level titles traded in negotiation for tight cash compensation. CEO, chief executive officer, that has always been real, everyone knows what that is. CFO, chief financial officer, also real, not a lot of argument on job description there. COO, chief operating officer, okay, if combined with president and an actual portfolio, fair enough. CTO, chief technology officer, sure, in a technology company, how could you not have one? Then comes credit creep, inflation masquerading as parity, no one fooling anyone inside the alpha cocoon, the aggrandized deceived by the defeated. Only room for so many big dogs on the high thread count upholstery, just try getting them all on the pads. CMO, chief marketing officer, there's some hand waving. CRO, chief revenue officer, that's a language swap for VP of sales in case anyone missed it, and they still have to carry the bag. CPO, not the chief petty officer of Navy rank, but the chief people officer, a head of human resources who won't bid out benefits. Chief digital officer, chief learning officer, chief customer officer, chief performance officer, chief resources officer, chief transformation officer—all big ticket labels, all inventions of pretension, cluttered rank demolishing clarity in the twenty-first century.

The CIO was born not of ego but necessity, a reflection of the shift in corporations from pure dependence on the CEO's vision and the CFO's accounting to the company's reliance on data more than physical inventory as key company assets. In the age of intellectual property—whether the company's source code or customer files, all of which were increasingly bound by poorly drafted and half understood numbskull laws—someone with a mega hunk of stock options had to own the data. The CEO didn't want it, except in dashboard summaries. The CFO didn't want it, except for required reporting and forecasting. The CMO didn't want it, except to cast blame. The CRO and CPO didn't know what to do with it, so they didn't want it all. Thus the CIO was essential, invisible and invincible, usually respected, and in many cases the longest serving C-level executive in a company. Who would put a knife in someone's back for that gig?

Monty Dadashian was the CIO of EnvisionInk Systems. He was also Employee Number Four—the fourth person hired by Choy and Finkelman after the company took actual form, joining immediately after the first draft of the business plan was printed in an alcove at Stanford. Employees one to three had long ago departed to wealth and their own serial start-ups in more tax-friendly havens, making Dadashian the company's longest serving employee, with tenure essentially equal to Choy and Finkelman. EnvisionInk never named a CTO, mostly because the co-CEOs always felt if one of them was not CEO he would be CTO, so they would both be CEO and CTO, but not call themselves co-CTOs. Two enormous titles like that felt over the top to Choy and Finkelman, like CEO & President, and they never figured out why people were compelled to title themselves twice when everyone knew who was boss. That made Dadashian the company's de facto CTO, but he would never say that, at least in a public forum. Political survival in the senior ranks of any company demands quality self-editing.

Dadashian had no desire to be lumped into the taxonomy of suits inside or outside EnvisionInk. His title was unimportant to him as a leveling device, he much preferred the distinction of Wild West class clown. Most Silicon Valley companies have a captain of the goof guard, and at EnvisionInk Systems that was Monty. At six foot four and 175 pounds, his head would often peer above others at company all-hands, but when he turned to the side, you worried if he had nutrition issues. Dadashian refused to sit permanently in an office or a cubicle. His work-place was wherever he set his laptop for the upcoming hour, be it a conference room, a table, the stairwell, the courtyard near the organic vineyard, or Teavana. Dadashian usually kept a Nerf air rifle strapped to his back and was not afraid to wear a Daniel Boone faux coonskin cap, reminding people that he was a hunter and trapper, the guy who could pinpoint the one bit or byte that was holding up the show, and as important as that always seemed, he did not paint himself with any self-importance. At age thirty-three, Dadashian had exactly the same time in the trenches as Choy and Finkelman, his life to date consisting of an undergraduate degree in Computer Science from Berkeley, an MS in engineering from Stanford, four pre-public start-up years with EnvisionInk as the data guy, and five years with the public company as CIO. That was it, his life, a third over and flawless. He was satisfied, he was chipper, he was loyal, he was never bored. When trouble did not find him in one form or other — whether it was endless nagging complaints from the non-techs about desktop support, patching servers as fast as new open source was published or vendor code was pushed live, reconciling tabulations to justify the company's metrics and valuation, or implementing the latest in privacy policies by government decree — Dadashian would go looking for trouble. It was not so much that he liked trouble, he just knew it was always there whether he heard about it or not and he did not like surprises. He wanted to find the hole before he stepped in it — straw cover-up mats never fooled Monty. Filling the holes with code plugs not only helped him sleep the full four hours he got every night with mobile alerts waking him every twenty minutes, it gave him intellectual stimulation equal to that which he had enjoyed as a student, and that was what mattered most to him in a job. The money was okay, but he never spent much of it. The challenge was amazing, and that is what motivated him.

Perhaps the only thing that bothered Dadashian was how inaccessible Choy and Finkelman had become. It was not like he fumed about it, more that he found it puzzling. Choy and

Finkelman had changed so much from the engineer-entrepreneurs he had met in the Stanford Computer Lab. He was not even in the same program with them, but from the day they met he knew they had shared values and were going places. When Choy and Finkelman first showed him the algorithm for removing waste from keyword bidding, he was sold. He had never applied for a job. When Stanford handed him his master's degree, he just started working "more with than for" Choy and Finkelman out of their eight-hundred-square-foot apartment. Then came the funding, then the rented office quarters, then the marketing and biz dev departments, then the expanded tech campus, then the human resources handbook, then the IPO. Somewhere along the way, Choy and Finkelman stopped thinking of themselves as coders backed into being Operators as their role as co-CEOs became a job in itself. They spent less time together as the months passed, and now, even though he was their CIO, they hardly ever spoke. Staff meetings were with the general counsel and CFO, sometimes the head sales honcho, but the CIO was an atoll set free. Dadashian marveled at how inaccessible friends could become when they had too many meetings, and emails, and phone calls, and texts consuming their days, and even when something was important, it could be days before they would return his emails. Absent their input, Dadashian felt free to act anytime he felt something was imperative, and they never called him on it, so that became good enough for him. He wanted more face time because he thought it would be productive and help the company grow beyond its current flattening, but if he did not get it, he was okay with that too.

Had it not been for his longstanding relationship and good-memories with Choy and Finkelman, Dadashian surely would have joined the Walkout. Other than the part where it was a slap in the face to Choy and Finkelman, the Walkout made remarkable sense to him. All those people in the parking lot had a right to worry about their jobs given the kill-or-be-killed mentality of the Valley, but more than that, they seemed to be having fun out there on the concrete. Volleyballs were bouncing around, makeshift bands were jamming, new vegan recipes were making the rounds, yet none of this undermined the seriousness of the message: Don't let management's merger dreams become employees' nightmares. As much as he wanted to be part of the revolt, Dadashian knew in his heart he was management and could not join the antics. He knew he owed Choy and Finkelman that much, especially during their un-planned hiatus. With the office getting quieter all the time, he used the interlude to write a new set of queries to cut through the database, exploring some worrisome anomalies he had been watching for some time.

The basic working premise at EnvisionInk had been that revenue was flattening because they had reached saturation in market share and customer base, and the only real means of growth available was new initiatives. Dadashian was all for in-novation, but he did not buy the flattening theory. The market for keyword ad buying was growing at a predictably healthy clip, so EnvisionInk's revenue should have been growing along the same trajectory. Dadashian had written a dozen lengthy emails to Choy and Finkelman over the past few months ques-tioning their assumptions, but their response was that "it was what it was." That was not the healthy paranoid Choy and Fin-kelman he had known at Stanford, but they were busy with oth-er matters. Now Dadashian had his first compiled report back from the queries and he did not like the implications. For the past four and a half years, their revenue had grown in lockstep with channel shift. The more companies spent on keyword ad-vertising—moving their budgets from newspapers, and maga-zines, and radio, and finally television—the more EnvisionInk could save them, and the more it kept for itself in its widely embraced performance-based fee structure. Then it went flat as advertising kept growing. It was not market share. It was not that the client base was oversaturated. Dadashian did not have the issue pinned, but the trend was unmistakable. The deterio-ration in their performance curve was absolute. Regardless of twice daily proactive updates to the source code, something was wrong with the core algorithm.

Dadashian had been delighted that Choy and Finkelman had been released the prior day and were on a flight home for a board meeting late that afternoon. He had to intercept them, get in front of them and bring this to their attention, at the very least for feedback and direction. This time he would not send an email, he would wait outside their office door, sleep there with his Nerf rifle if necessary. But they never made it to their office, they went straight to the conference room for the emergency board meeting. When Dadashian realized he had been bypassed again, he asked their administrative assistant to interrupt them for thirty seconds. She would not, there was too much going on, too much at stake and they were already overwhelmed. Dadashian texted both of them repeatedly in the board meeting but got no response, there really was too much on their minds. So Monty Dadashian did what he always did, he took matters into his own hands and kept digging—trolling through terabytes of ugly conflicted data, excavating tens of thousands of lines of lean uncommented source code. He knew he would find a way to get in front of Choy and Finkelman soon enough, and eventually he would get his hearing. When he did, he had to be ready to make his case. Choy and Finkelman needed to hear what he had to say, they just didn't know it yet. He would make sure they did.

$ $

The boardroom at EnvisionInk felt a whole lot different with Choy and Finkelman back at the head of the table. It felt even more different with the absence of Steyer, whose one vote could now be outweighed by the co-CEOs, curious in its irony. Perhaps it was the absence of Steyer, but the tension level for a meeting this thorny seemed remarkably low.

Choy, Finkelman, Normandy, and Basru had departed Honolulu with Riley Steyer just hours after the release event, following an abbreviated briefing by the local FBI and a promise of more such meetings when they arrived home in California. Payne had disclosed she was headed directly to a debriefing in DC and would connect with a military transport flight headed there at dawn with enough room for her accompanying team. The company G-V had flown eastbound through the night to arrive back at Moffett Field at Thursday midday, inclusive of the time difference. After six awkward hours of minimal interaction with Riley during travel, they arranged for her to be taken home by town car without any further indication of when she might see her husband again or how they might be able to secure his safe release. Returning to more immediate matters, they had themselves whisked backed to the nearby EnvisionInk offices in Santa Clara, where they quickly showered and prepared for the board meeting that had been confirmed during their plane ride.

Following a brief welcome back to the founders and an even briefer summary of their abduction tale, Counselor Normandy noted there were three key topics that needed to be vetted at this unscheduled special meeting of the board. First, Choy and Finkelman were entitled to a full recap of what had in fact happened with Atom Heart Entertainment while they were away. Second, the board needed an agreed approach on how to get their employees out of the parking lot and back to their desks. Third, the company needed a plan to bring life back to the ENVN stock price, hoping that its rescue from the dumper might help reignite the market at large. The only upfront note of consensus was that any reversal of the national Walkout and ignition of the stock market would have to be led by the catalyst where it started, with all eyes on EnvisionInk. At some point they would also have to deal with the matter of their now sequestered chairman, although for the moment it was decided that would be the province of government authority, leaving the private enterprise to focus on what it did best, restoring profits.

With five million people, across every business type, now camped out in office parking lots, media coverage was a carnival of noise. Endless interviews with Walkouts dominated radio and television broadcasts, filled the swelling streams of YouTube, sent syndicated headline links across portal landing pages, and gave familiar but declining magazine covers gleaming screenshots on electronic tablets. The freeing of Choy and Finkelman and taking of Kimo Balthazer halfway across the Pacific barely registered as a blip on newsfeeds compared to Walkout Madness. For all anyone who had walked off the job cared, the new standoff between Swerlow and Kisinski and the would-be rescuers of Steyer and Balthazer was but a footnote in minuscule font underlying the more timely typeface documenting the work stoppage. The nationwide movement had a life of its own, with the common theme of employees everywhere sick of uncertainty. They wanted to be seen as people, not costs, regardless of their company's segment, size, or scale.

The mood of the Walkouts had momentarily shifted to hope with spreading word that Choy and Finkelman were liberated from captivity and back on the job. Perhaps because the journalist community had threaded the topic, it was expected that the release of Choy and Finkelman would cause the Walkout voice to be heard. That put enormous pressure on the Envision-Ink board to chart a model path, when all they really wanted to do was heal their own company. The media was not going to cut Choy and Finkelman any slack for being captured. If they had learned a lesson in the abduction and wanted to prove that, the chance was available to them, but otherwise there was little sympathy for their ordeal. Any return to normal would follow EnvisionInk. Without a new chapter in Santa Clara, nothing could be expected to change in Denver, Dallas, or Miami.

Inside the boardroom was the quorum absent Steyer, with Henderson as usual on the polycom. Normandy and Basru had already briefed Choy and Finkelman privately in flight on events leading up to Atom Heart's friendly takeover approach, which had been rejected by unanimous board vote even before a formal tender offer had been submitted. Choy and Finkelman were having a hard time understanding how so much time and energy could have been invested in conceptual due diligence in the days they were gone, only to be unanimously rejected, which the record summarized in the briefest of minutes. Dialogue around this topic was terse, with no one brave enough to throw Steyer under the bus in his absence. Choy and Finkelman probed for a

crack in the narrative, but the room held the company line: Sol
Seidelmeyer had used the non-presence of Choy and Finkelman
to make his move, knowing they had resisted his prior over-
ture; the board had acted in its fiduciary capacity to consider
the notion; and given the circumstances micro and macro, the
board felt comfortable passing even before the final numbers
were presented. Choy and Finkelman were not snowed, they
knew they were being avoided for fear of retribution by Steyer,
and if anyone was going to give up the truth it was not likely to
emerge in this forum. After hours of getting nowhere, they reluctantly agreed to move onto the healing agenda, knowing they
would get another run at the treason agenda when somebody's
conscience finally gave way, by accident or intention.

"How do you think Balthazer plays in the Walkout now?"
asked Choy, trying to turn the discussion to toward better purpose. "I get that he's been in the background through all of this,
stoking the fire and coming after Steyer without a lot of love,
but until we have a resolution, he's likely to be closely associated
with Steyer, at least by the media. Is he out of the equation until
he can do a show again?"

"I don't think he's out of the equation," offered Professor
Yamanaka. "He is off the air, not out of the negotiation. An
argument could be made that he is even more important than
when he had the microphone."

"This is lunacy," barked Barton Throckmore, the anointed
proxy for Steyer, acting chairman of the meeting given his investment stake. "I don't give an owl's asshole about radio talk
show hosts or Walkouts. I care about share price and ours
stinks. That's what we need to focus on, recovery of the equity
markets where we drive up demand. Everything else is arts and
crafts. If Dan were here I know he would agree with me."

"Dan is not here, so you don't need to speak for him," replied Rebecca Gutierrez. "Has it not occurred to you that the
Walkout and the stock collapse are linked?"

"I don't see cause linking their resolution," reasoned Throckmore. "The timing might overlap, but there is no economic

principle for them to remedy simultaneously."

"I disagree," countered Finkelman. "The economics are inescapably tied. No one works, productivity drops, earnings fall. Market pricing is an indicator of the future, not the present. Traders think the economy will suck soon, so they price it that way now."

"Fate is made reality, sounds like a paper you'd write for Yamanaka," jeered Throckmore. "Come on, Stephen, get real, you're a CEO. I'm not talking about the past, that's textbook, anyone with a pen can write that paper. I'm talking about resolution."

"You're not making a lot of sense to me, Throckmore," boomed the voice of Henderson from the polycom. "Cause, resolution, you sound like Congress—lots of words to describe nothing, which is mostly what we did the entire time I was in office. Try some kindergarten concepts the rest of us can read on the chalkboard."

"It's not that hard," said Throckmore. "We need the stock price to start moving. One stock price in motion drives another. That's momentum trading, which is emotional, and it works. It begins with someone who is not emotional accepting the risk to acquire the stock at its current discount level, getting a much rewarded jump on the pack. It's a question of embracing value, not a question of temporarily reduced output."

"You're saying we don't need people to go back to work to get the stock price moving again?" asked Melissa Stanton-Landers, sounding perplexed by his argument.

"I don't care a crap if they go back to work, if the cost cuts are permanent we can forecast improved earnings," stated Throckmore. "Moving the stock won't get people back to work. That matters to us, not to the Walkouts. Uncertainty is the problem, what markets hate more than anything is uncertainty. That's what has to be resolved."

"I don't see our strategy making a lot of progress," offered Dr. Francois. "Perhaps we should go back to the root and answer the simplest question: How do we get our own people back to work to set an example for the rest of the nation? Until that happens, I believe we are just having a sociological salon among ourselves."

"All directions point back to Balthazer," said Finkelman. "That's where Calvin teed this up. Balthazer got them to dial out. We need Balthazer to dial them back in."

"I think that is too kindergarten," said Basru, drawing a hard set of looks from the table for the direct critique of his boss. "Excuse me, that did not come out right."

"No, that's fine," replied Finkelman. "This is an open discussion, Sanjay. You're the CFO, you have a point of view and we respect that. What's your thinking?"

"The talk show host did not get people to leave their jobs," continued Basru. "He suggested it as a defense mechanism to stop the takeover of our company, which would have cost some of them their jobs, but never happened. They walked out on their own."

"And you think that was because of what?" asked Normandy.

"Must I say it?" teetered Basru. "Fine, I'll speak the obvious. They walked out because of Steyer."

"That's not far off the mark," added Choy, a refugee of the Steyer fan club. "We watched Steyer on CNBC. He basically declared our employees weren't doing us much good kicking over the growth engine. The insult was powerful. The timing was especially bad and then the market tanked in response to the deal bubble popping. They were punishing us for threatening layoffs, for not believing in their value, and then their actions resonated. The market implosion fed the fear creating the Walkout, and the Walkout added kerosene to the market implosion. All that created a spotlight, and guess who loved the spotlight? Our friend Balthazer. No one could have choreographed this, but if he could have, this was the perfect dance for him. A lot of bad luck and awful timing on the trading floors let him be a star again. He almost didn't need Stephen and I to be kidnapped, that was sort of incidental."

"I wouldn't call it incidental," said Dr. Francois. "I'd call it opportunistic. There may have been others who felt the same, but we've beaten that dog into submission."

"No, I think that dog still needs to be in a kennel," commented Finkelman, the jab not lost. "So where are you going with this, Calvin? What do you think we have to do?"

"No one is going to much like this, but I think we may need to take Balthazer's Merger Bill of Rights a little more seriously than we intended, maybe more seriously than he intended," posited Choy. "We have a trust issue with our employees, and until they trust us, they aren't going back to work, and neither is anyone else."

"I have a better idea," followed Throckmore. "Why don't we just start firing people? That will give them some feedback about our point of view on trust. Once again, I'm sure Dan would agree, as soon as you let him out of the kennel."

"Not that I have a vote in the matter, but I do agree with Barton on this point," said Basru, taken by Throckmore's candor. "This whole thing is ridiculous. Employees walk out fearing a layoff that never happened, angered by a merger that never happened, and now we have millions of people following their lead. We need to make a clear point of management, establish chain of command. I hope I am not out of line saying this."

"You make an interesting point, Sanjay," said Yamanaka. "We all know there are two main motivators in human financial activity: fear and greed. Our employees are acting out of response to our presumed greed. Perhaps they should be on the truer end of fear. A modest announcement of a reduction in our workforce could be a motivator."

"That's ridiculous, George," announced Choy. "They are already acting out of fear. If we make the dreaded real how does that regain us their loyalty?"

"I agree with the Professor and Throckmore," rang the voice of Henderson. "It's not about loyalty. It's about establishing rules and enforcing them. The contract says you work and you get paid. You don't want the job, we'll give it to someone who does."

"There are five million people saying they don't trust their employers," noted Finkelman. "You think every single one of them is replaceable?"

"Yep," said Throckmore. "We're all replaceable—every one of us, every one of them. Why is this so hard?"

"I hate to say it, but as a former CEO, I have to agree," said Stanton-Landers. "I know you had a tough few weeks, guys, but you need to act decisively. You need to lay down the law or this thing will go on indefinitely and we will destroy shareholder value. We have a fiduciary duty to prevent that."

"We'll take it under advisement, but I don't think Calvin and I see it the way the rest of you do," said Finkelman. "I'm thinking some form of a Merger Bill of Rights might be worth trying, it's a nice gesture at the least. Could be great for PR. I don't see how it hurts us since we've never had a layoff anyway."

"Stephen, I'm actually with you and Calvin on this, but whatever you offer will need to have some teeth," added Gutierrez. "If our employees see through it as a PR stunt then we'll really look two-faced. You either give them something or you don't. It depends on how well you think it will work."

"I'm not so sure we can't have it both ways," said Normandy. "May I take the liberty of drafting something that sounds better than it is applied and maybe we can see if there is broader support in the industry? If the tech sector leads with a shared point of view, we might be able to nudge Balthazer to get behind us, at least with an email, which would help a lot. We could find ourselves in a very good place and get a lot of people back to work before new analyst earnings forecast come out."

"I think it's worth a try," agreed Choy. "Stephen, do you support having Sylvia take a run at this?"

"Yeah, let's see what she comes up with, and see if Swerlow and Kisinski will let us stay in contact with Balthazer," said Finkelman. "We can also make a few calls to our network and see if any of the other CEOs we know could stomach something like this."

"This is mind-numbing," roared Throckmore. "I thought

you were smart guys, smart business guys. Yeah, you've had a shock to the system. Maybe you need some time to recover, but don't do this."

"Throckmore is right," agreed the voice of Henderson. "I'm sure there is an idea in some boardroom stupider than this, but it would have to involve rusty oil barrels, kerosene, matches, and every bit of cash we ever earned. If there is an IPO for value destruction, a Merger Bill of Rights comes as close as I can imagine."

"I don't see the harm in trying some outreach," said Choy. "That's the kind of company Stephen and I always envisioned this to be."

"What kind of self-righteous brain infection is that?" blasted Throckmore. "Don't read to me from the About Us section of our website. That's promo copy, not who we are. We are a voracious competitor headed for seventy percent market share in performance based ad optimization. We got there by annihilating our competition and giving Google a good scare. That's the kind of company Steyer and I envisioned this to be—and that's why we backed you. Don't kid yourself that it's something else. That's what it is."

"Maybe in your mind, but Calvin and I have a set of values that matter to us, and we run this company," asserted Finkelman.

"You may run it, but Steyer and I created it," said Throckmore. "How many employees do we have now, ten thousand?"

"Eleven thousand two hundred eighty three," said Basru, running a fast query on his laptop. "Including full time contractors, but not open reqs."

"More than eleven thousand jobs that didn't exist six or seven years ago, you think the two of you created all of those? Investors created those jobs by taking on risk. Investment capital created the employment opportunities you now want us to choke on. Your fiduciary responsibility is not to the employees, it's to the owners, the shareholders, the investors who took a chance on you. You owe us."

"We owe all of you, Barton," said Choy. "We just want some

forward thinking that reflects fairness and gives employees a sense of stability."

"What innovation ever came out of stability?" growled Throckmore. "Read Grove, *Only the Paranoid Survive*. We're not here to make peace on the playground, we're here to push people to invent, to add value or vaporize. Honestly, if this is the direction we're going, maybe we should sell. The rumor of a sale might start our price climbing and supercharge the market."

"I thought the board was unanimously against selling," replied Finkelman. "We've come full circle. Were there some board minutes that we missed? We're not here to sell. We're supposed to be the next Google."

"Right, and like Google, in terms of invention we're a one-trick pony," said Throckmore. "If you're not willing to roll our cash to be an acquirer and weed out synergies, which Steyer and I don't think you have the stomach for, then you leave us few alternatives."

"Barton, you're crossing the line," interrupted Normandy. "Let's slow this down. It's their first day back. They aren't even twenty-four hours away from those nut cases."

Throckmore took a breath and rose to his feet, bumping his knees into the conference table. He seemed to be aware he had gone too far, but he had clearly had enough of the soapbox mush. He closed his netbook with a swift snap and gathered his papers in a bunch. "Calvin, Stephen, I really am sympathetic for what you've been through, and I'm going to attribute today's discussion to mental fatigue or whatever residual ailment you want to call it. I can't do this, it's stupid. My fund still has a gob of hard leverage in this company and no clear window on liquidity, especially with the market in the toilet. Daniel and his partners are more exposed than we are, none of us has any breathing room. I know you think this is your company, but it's not, it belongs to the shareholders. If you want to bumble around with radio talk show hosts and employee rights then step aside and let someone else run the company. You need to think this through. Call me when you have done that."

Throckmore thudded out of the room, leaving an uncomfortable silence. Choy and Finkelman were mind linked with each other, but obviously not the board majority, and that did not include Steyer, who could certainly not be counted as a supporter. Given her knowledge and prescribed code of conduct, Normandy seemed the most uncomfortable in the room, although Basru was not far behind.

"I think Calvin and I need to better understand the unanimous board vote on not selling while we were unavailable for discussion," gingerly resumed Finkelman. "How unanimous was unanimous?"

"We have covered this subject in detail," said Dr. Francois, matter of fact. "The board voted unanimously. There is no better way to put it."

"Then why did Throckmore just suggest selling?" asked Choy, more brazenly than his partner. "If you moved on from that discussion, you moved on."

"Take it from a fellow who has been in government most of his life," said the voice of Henderson. "Everything that's negotiable is fluid. There's no black and white except in Charlie Chaplin movies. Of course we all said no when you were absent, how could it have been otherwise? But now you're back. Any discussion that's been tabled can be revisited if it makes sense to revisit it. That would be your prerogative as co-CEOs. What you must do is enact your fiduciary duty."

"So was the proposal defeated or tabled?" demanded Choy. "We're hearing a lot of multi-purpose adjectives for one decisive board motion. How about you all stop worrying about Steyer and tell us the truth."

Now it was Yamanaka's turn to get up from the table. The look on his face reflected an unusual level of disgust for his normally collegial manner. "Daniel Steyer helped make you very wealthy and trusted you in senior leadership roles when you had little experience," enunciated Yamanaka in an even tone. "Not everyone would have allowed the concept of co-CEOs, but that's what you wanted and he supported that. He also put himself on that airplane with you, and whether he did or didn't affect the outcome, he was willing to do whatever needed to be done to return you to where you are sitting. You might want to think about the past few weeks before you render final judgment."

Yamanaka shook each of their hands, Choy and Finkelman, then turned and exited the room without bidding the other board members farewell.

"Hey guys, I've got a call I have to take," spoke Henderson after a pause. "No surprise, Congresswoman Payne wants an update. She's getting ready for a press conference tomorrow. If you decide anything between now and then, let me know."

The polycom line went dead, all but signaling the de facto end of the meeting with three board members departed in addition to Steyer's absence. Nothing of substance had been decided, but the weight of activity had shifted from shared board responsibility to the shoulders of Choy and Finkelman.

"This might be a good place to end for today," said Normandy, fashioning her way to as cordial a transition as she should concoct. "I'll see what I can work up and get you a draft statement quickly. When you reach out to Swerlow, will one of you try to touch base with Dan Steyer so he knows what you have in mind?"

"Thank you, Sylvia," said Choy quietly. "We'll see what we can do about reaching out to Swerlow. We need to keep Kimo Balthazer in the game. If Swerlow goes for that, we'll make sure Steyer gets an appropriate update ahead of the draft board minutes. We don't keep secrets."

"Yes, thank you, Sylvia," added Finkelman, looking around the half-filled room with hesitation at Stanton-Landers, Gutierrez, Dr. Francois, and Basru. "We'll also test the waters with some of our colleagues at companies around the Valley, to see if there is any shared sympathy for a Merger Bill of Rights." He could not make direct eye contact with anyone other than Choy. This was not what they expected, not a great first day back.

"Any other formal business to discuss today?" asked Normandy.

The boardroom was silent. The meeting was over.

$ $ $ $

3.2
All PR is Evil

To My Loyal Listeners:

Guess where I am! You won't believe it. I
don't believe it. I'm in Hawaii, locked inside
a private business jet, parked on a very hot
runway at an Air Force Base. And guess who
I am with? I am with Dennis Swerlow and
Sam Kisinski, who are my hosts, and who will
be approving these emails to you before I send
them for as long as I send them. I am also
with Daniel Steyer, chairman of Envision-
Ink Systems, and an FBI agent whose name
I cannot release. If you get news headlines on
any of your electronic devices, you probably
know that I took the place of Calvin Choy and
Stephen J. Finkelman, who were released two
nights ago and are back in California. Swerlow and Kisinski are in their own negotiation
in which I have sworn I will not inject myself,
otherwise this will be my last email to you, and
that won't help them anymore than it will help
you.

Now that we are all up to speed on the news,
let's get to the commentary, understanding that
I have very tough editors.

If you are receiving this email, you are among
the two million friends or fans or followers or
whatever you want to call yourselves who have
given me permission over the years to contact
you. Mostly I have abused that privilege and

sent you junk, spam, dopey reminders about
when the show is on and who I might be skew-
ering as my guest. But you stuck with me for
a reason and I am glad you are here. I'm sorry
to report that I won't be doing the show for a
while. Producer Lee Creighton has managed to
get ThisIsRage.com live again, so please visit
and update our list of demands for the Merger
Bill of Rights, which I understand is now over
a thousand pages of your clever suggestions.
That is very helpful. Keep it coming!

As I mentioned, the founders of EnvisionInk
are free and back on the job. I have been in
touch with them, and they are thinking hard
about the Merger Bill of Rights and what they
might be able to do to make it happen. It's
too early to predict where this might go, but I
can tell you they are going to be sharing some
concepts with other CEOs they know this
weekend, and if they make any real progress, I
will be the first to report it to you. I can safely
say we won't get everything you've asked for
in the thousand pages of suggestions you have
submitted. We will more likely have to try for a
broader set of concepts, but if they come back
with anything that makes any sense at all, maybe things can get back to normal. Maybe.

You will probably be hearing more from Representative Sally Payne on how I am solely
responsible for most of the ills of the world,
including this unresolved aircraft situation.
Despite my state of captivity, the Honorable
Ms. Payne still holds me responsible for all
five million of you who have Walked Out. She
would like me to tell you unconditionally that
you need to get out of those parking lots and go
back to work, but I would be a scumbag corrupt loser liar if I told you that. I do know you

are all getting screwed, day after day, month
after month. They are going to keep merging
your companies and firing you to make bigger
and bigger profits. So until you get some kind
of promise to take care of you at the next open
screwing window, you hang tough. Sorry, Sally, I was born this way.

I will write to you as often as my hosts allow,
so you know I'm still cheering for you and I'm
okay. If you don't get an email from me and
a lot of time has passed, check the news feed
on your gadget of choice or visit ThisIsRage.
com to make sure we're still here. You stay out
there, you stay strong. You get something for
this. The Walkout matters. You matter. This is
the beginning. Don't Cave.

This Is Rage!
Kimo

$ $

The email was sent by Balthazer from the locked down jet
in Honolulu to all the email names in his database. It would be
the first of many he hoped to send in the days to come, until his
own situation was resolved, however that might end. Swerlow
and Kisinski were being strangely cooperative, allowing Choy
and Finkelman to contact Balthazer and Balthazer to contact
his audience, in as much as they remained at a standoff on an
Air Force Base with no permission to leave and little negotiation leverage. Balthazer was not sure what impact this or any
subsequent email might have, but he knew that regardless of his
inability to webcast, he needed to stay in touch with his loyals,
the brave souls he had championed through the Walkout, even
if he could not take credit or blame for their actions. Perhaps
Swerlow and Kisinski felt the same, that somehow Balthazer's
messages would rekindle public sympathy for them, relaying
their own implicit support for the Walkouts by their goodwill of
letting Balthazer stay in contact. Perhaps they just didn't know

what else to do.

Balthazer felt good about the email. He believed his listeners needed his support. That was what he had always provided, a voice and a sounding board for office survivors across the nation, who needed him as much as he needed them. Swerlow and Kisinski would not allow Balthazer to do a show—that was beyond their comfort level—yet Balthazer had found a way to work around that. He might not be talking, but he was not disappearing.

Right up until Choy and Finkelman's plane landed at Hickam, Balthazer had been on the fence about whether to take the congresswoman's kind advice and do what he could to get people back to work. Balthazer knew it served few people well to go without a paycheck to make a point, and all along he had been pretty sure that no one of substance would take him seriously about his Merger Bill of Rights. As Producer Lee Creighton had said, they had made history, they had made a difference, and unless Choy and Finkelman were behind him, there was no further polemic to push. Balthazer liked his soapbox, but he was not delusional. A radio talk show host was not going to change the world. No matter how many people walked off their jobs, companies were going to keep firing as they pleased. The five million Walkouts garnering global media coverage ensured this event would be engraved in the continuum of America's unplanned outpourings, following in the footsteps of Woodstock, the national Women's Strike for Equality, the Lennon vigils, Obama's election night gathering in Grant Park, the Occupy Wall Street encampment and its clones—all communal campfires evoked in folklore, symbols of progression, landmarks of populist achievement. Whether the millions stayed in the parking lots another day or month, nothing was likely to change about the legend in creation. If it ended now, it was probably best for those who most needed the money, the Walkouts.

Balthazer was beginning to grasp how much power he currently had, fleeting as it was. He found it invigorating—the notion that he had any power at all must have been pissing off

Payne, Henderson, Steyer, Seidelmeyer, along with every Investor, Banker, and Operator on the war map, all of whom were suffering the plunge of the capital markets. If Balthazer's moment of clout reminded him of anything, it was that in any right functioning capitalist economy, time was money. It probably did not matter a hoot to the significance of the Walkout if it lasted much longer, the historic footprint was ensured and would forever be useful at future bargaining tables—and if not, then at least a Daily Double on *Jeopardy*. Yet for a trader, or backer, or CEO, every day capital was reduced was a day that could not be recovered, the time value of money was perishable inventory. The monster winners in business may have talked a good game about thinking and acting long term, but everyone who participated in the top-tier supply chain and embraced economic consumption models had learned to think only one way—short term. Miss earnings for the quarter for any reason, get punished. Loan money at the wrong interest rate for any period of time, get punished. Buy puts or calls without a sense of market direction, get punished. There was almost no instance when time did not play an essential role for the ownership class, so if circumstances were out of joint, the reaction had to be addressed with urgency. Urgency ruled the trading desk. Urgency ruled the reality of transactions. Urgency stopped a contained loss from becoming a wipe out. The compounding math was staggering, and anyone who stood in the way of those exponents had, by transitive logic, the same power. No one in the nation knew how to end the Walkout at this moment, and while some entity would undoubtedly figure it out sooner or later—if by no other means than awaiting the literal starvation of the Walkouts—ending it now was better, much better. Balthazer was their path to urgency. That made Balthazer the man of the moment, and led him to do the only sensible thing a man of his values could do—stay as visible as he could.

It wasn't like Balthazer hadn't seen this before. He knew the importance of time, he just never knew the real value of controlling the clock having spent his entire life on the other side of control. As a survivor radio personality, Balthazer knew that any show could be his last, all he had to do was say the wrong thing or cross the tastes of the wrong individual, something at which he had proven repeatedly he was immensely good. Balthazer had been fired half a dozen times in his career, and whenever he moved fast to get a new gig, he had inevitably traded up. When he had stirred the pot so thoroughly that he had boiled himself into steam, getting started again was no cheap trick. The longer he was out of work, the longer he would stay out of work, and staying out of work too long was almost certainly a career ender. Bars and bowling alleys across America were littered with fallen talk show hosts, once promising voices that had been canned and not recovered fast enough, then faded into low volt static.

Balthazer had tempted obscurity a few times, but he had always rebounded, never off the air long enough to be forgotten, which was what he most feared. His own father, a trophy life insurance salesman based in Cincinnati with twenty-two years of steady commission income, had lost his job in a terrain re-alignment when Balthazer was nine years old. Always an optimist, his father had decided to take six months off and enjoy the severance package. He was a steady closer, customers loved his ethic, he was sure he could climb back on the hamster wheel anytime he wanted, so why not enjoy an extended vacation, get to know his wife and son, travel the back roads, see the sunrise from somewhere other than a highway driving to or from a sales call. Sadly enough, when his father did try to go back, he had already been forgotten. As good a salesman as he was, in half a year's time he had been forgotten by his industry. The optimism faded, the family savings ran hollow. Then came cliché depression, ritual drinking, and one day, his old man just left. If only his dad had been a little more urgent, if only he had controlled the clock, so much might have been different.

Balthazer started his illustrious career as a part time night janitor at a local radio station while still in high school, handing over his paycheck to his mom to help with the rent. College was not an option, but one night the midnight jock failed to show and Balthazer co-opted his shift. From that first unpaid gig he learned to talk his way up. He had something to say and he learned how to say it so that people would predictably listen and advertisers could not ignore their numbers. The paychecks got better, the media markets bigger, the act more outrageous to improve the predictability. Shortly after Balthazer first got national air time syndicated out of New Jersey, he took a live call from someone who knew his father, an unknown voice from Ohio who told him on the air what a great sales guy his father had been in the day, which Balthazer knew. He told Balthazer that his father had attempted several comebacks, peddling annuities and first/theft/auto, even for a brief stint selling used cars off the lot, but none of them stuck and he never regained his good name and confidence. He took his own life in an unlocked gas station garage somewhere near Cleveland. He pulled into the bay, rolled down the metal door and let the engine run. The caller never gave his name, but wanted to assure Balthazer his father was proud of him. Dad had heard the show, was probably listening in that garage, and was glad his boy was on the right side of things. That was the only endorsement Balthazer ever heard that he considered completely honest, the only attaboy that was not conflicted, a second hand account of his father's praise via a radio stranger. It was not enough. He needed it to be more.

Balthazer's father had not understood the power of time, but Balthazer did. Even locked in that plane with a pair of unstable losers and a gun, Balthazer knew that for this micro-moment, he controlled the clock. If Payne and Henderson and all of them wanted him to end the Walkout, that had to be the wrong thing to do. Had Balthazer not taken the seat they reserved for him to Hawaii, he knew they would have tossed him in the clink and found a way to warrant it, there was zero value in him waiting around to fight it. There was almost nothing in his mind that a member of Congress, an ex-Senator, a couple of CEOs, and the FBI were incapable of doing when told "no" to their faces. Balthazer had bet on his own passion, taken an uninformed risk, and nonetheless made the smart decision. For that instinct, the clock was his, he did not have to leave his fate to chance. Now with Swerlow and Kisinski, he need to work his clock, see what Choy and Finkelman could deliver, then play his card with the Walkouts. It occurred to Balthazer that given his unwillingness to cooperate with Payne, being invisible was a good move for him right now, especially if she attacked again, blood soup being readied on the stovetop, which he could smell stewing across an ocean and a continent.

$ $

Madam Payne was thankful to be back in Washington. One might think, after the events at Hickam AFB in Hawaii, a swing through her home town of Billings might have been in order, giving her a few days to gather her thoughts and touch base with family and friends. That was not her style. She wanted preemptive air time, and there were a lot more cameras, microphones, bright lights, and journalists at any given hour in DC than might emerge in Montana in a lifetime. Seven terms in office had taught this triumphant street fighter one thing — you fight where you can be seen. Montana was where voters sanctified her seat in Congress, but the halls of Congress were where she made voters proud. The good people of Billings knew that they were not the first stop on any reporter's junket, and with few exceptions the citizenry was happy not to have poorly behaved, unnaturally demanding outsiders crowding their airport and soiling their motels. Their marvel gal, Sally Payne, was putting Billings and Montana on the national map just by being from there, and that was more than enough bragging rights for the voters. Whenever she appeared, Billings got equal billing with Payne, and that seemed like a fair enough trade. Payne was happy, her constituents were happy, and the road show could go on, and on, and on.

Payne had set up this press conference on the outdoor plaza of the Smithsonian Air and Space Museum for visual effect, to keep focus on the ordeal that had resulted in the safe release of Choy and Finkelman, albeit with the balance of resolution left like a hangnail. Sitting in the back of a chauffeured Escalade on route from the congressional office building, she hardly noticed the six or seven thousand people standing in various clusters on the sidewalks in front of office buildings. When she asked one of her aides "what that was all about" and got the obvious response "Walkouts," she barely raised an eyebrow. It was as if she had casually forgotten—or never bothered to acknowledge—that the Walkout was not ethereal, real people everywhere were involved. Of course these people could not vote for her. Montana's share of the total national Walkout was about a quarter of a percentage point, and the odds that those few people could impact her electability were not worth calculating, they just did not matter.

Payne felt entitled to as much credit for the return of Choy and Finkelman as she could extract. The taking of the talk show host, Balthazer, and the continued holding of Chairman Steyer were surely troubling, but she knew with a promise of near wrap up she could spin that to her advantage. The point of the press conference would be to explain why the hijacked jet was not another government screw-up but a positive step forward, even then hardly relevant to the true issue that mattered—getting people back to work. The key to selling that story required turning the tables on Balthazer, a delicate balance of impeaching his message while maintaining sympathy for his plight. Payne had to hang him in captivity as an anti-American socialist, then position herself for acclaim when the chain of events she could not predict would return people to their jobs. The national Walkout was going to end somehow, some way, and she wanted the spotlight for staging the endgame, setting in motion the events that would make it happen. It was a reach, but Payne's political success almost always equaled her ambitions. In the past week, she had come 180 degrees from unrealistic reelection candidate to party leader, as only she had confidence she would. The key was always the same: proper stagecraft.

In her introductory remarks, Payne knew she had to be inspirational, but also remorseful, and stylishly humble. She had rejected a dozen drafts of the statement after her usual writers failed to capture the spirit of the opportunity, then farmed out the assignment to her election committee regulars, then just wrote it herself. If there was any hope of running for higher office, it would begin here, outside the structure that housed the inventiveness of the Wright Brothers. She knew this was a gateway to grander levels of esteem. As she looked past the microphones and the cameras behind them, she observed a few hundred more Walkouts, these of the federal flavor. Once again, it did not even faze her as she commenced the business for which she came: projecting the sound of her voice, enunciating clearly, nailing the perfect viral sound bite.

"I want to thank you all for joining me today here at the immortal Smithsonian Institute, an icon that celebrates American innovation," began Payne, delighted with the turnout of not less than a hundred reporters, all hand-picked and assigned to monitored rows by her campaign management. "I will share a brief statement of reflection, and then take a few questions. The events of the past few weeks have been trying for all of us. Much has been written about the abduction of the great American entrepreneurs, Calvin Choy and Stephen J. Finkelman, who due to the fine work of many unusually cooperative government agencies are safely back on the job, rebuilding their company and inspiring workers to return to their jobs. Our nation has been in discomfort too long. As we seek a return to normalcy, I think it only appropriate to recognize in particular the extraordinary and selfless work of the Federal Bureau of Investigation in addressing this situation at tremendous personal risk. We must also remember the criminals, Swerlow and Kisinski, along with their remaining hostages, are now largely under government control on a military runway surrounded by the Pacific Ocean. As witness to all the critical events in this timeline, I can assure you I am comfortable this matter continues to be properly handled. Justice is being done."

Payne took an authoritative breath to allow the polite applause that followed. A few digital camera lights flashed, but

DC bureau journalists were naturally reserved, even when they were specially invited and knew there was an expectation that their presence served as an endorsement. Payne was keenly aware the political media knew posturing when they heard it, and they knew how to separate dramatization from documentary. She had learned how to feed them the gossip that kept them employed, wrapping nutritional supplements around empty calories without compromising the interesting for the newsworthy. That was her act, and it usually warranted ovation.

"One important comment before I take your questions. The current situation of five million people voluntarily walking off the job is no small matter. I suppose given the shock the nation has been through with this extended and uncertain incident, some of this can be explained by raw emotion. But the impact on our nation's economy and particularly the stock market is devastating, and it is my sincere hope this will end soon. Restoring order to the trading exchanges is of the utmost importance, because stocks don't trade well in uncertain times, which makes it hard for investors to make money. That uncertainty can be easily ended by people choosing to go back to work — not something that has been strongly encouraged by the radio talk show host, Kimo Balthazer. While I do not wish to speak ill of Mr. Balthazer given his immediate circumstances, his message to date, of encouraging the Walkout, has not been helpful. Now that he is off the air, I encourage the five million people who have walked from their jobs to reconsider that decision. While this is a private matter between employers and employees, I can only point to the historic leadership of the gallant Ronald Reagan. President Reagan did all he could to help our nation's air traffic controllers before he had to act in the best interests of The People, and in light of their lack of cooperation, dismiss them. I would hate to see anything like that happen again when it is so clearly avoidable. Are there any questions?"

Payne felt victorious. Balthazer had been bulldozed, but not steamrolled. She made her point and maintained her dignity. Undoubtedly a follow up question would give her another

chance to spread his remains in the airstream. Hands of the assembled elevated toward the sky as if gravity itself had been
given the hour off.

The first question acknowledged by Payne came from the
grizzled bureau chief of the *Wall Street Journal*: "Representative
Payne, it's Friday afternoon and the equity markets are closed.
Normalized market movement in the past several sessions has
been sub-measurable with trading volume at an unprecedented
low. Prior crashes of the last decade were soon followed by some
counter to overreaction. We have seen no dead cat bounce, no
wild swinging volatility, no bottom feeder buying, frighteningly little float, in essence no evidence of a window on recovery.
What is to make us believe that this is not the new norm, and
that we aren't only headed for recession but something worse?"

"Excellent question and I thank you for that," answered
Payne confidently. "Let's be careful with the R word. We are
eons distant from any warrant for panic. The key critical factor
we must keep in mind is that we do not have a situation of unemployment. We have a condition that approximates a volun-
tary strike — with no union governance, no recognized collective
bargaining, no legal authority. As Chair of the House Committee on Education and the Workforce, I know a bit about labor
and its impact on economic conditions. To put it bluntly, when
more people work, the economy improves. Everyone who has
made the choice to walk from their jobs has the same choice to
unmake that decision. Call me an optimist, but my sense is that
when the reality of eliminated payroll starts to impact mortgage
and rent bills, workers will do the right thing and a correction
will begin. Hey, someone has to be an optimist, right?"

There was a nervous laugh following Payne's button up.
This was her genius, she could be on-the-money charming when
her peers succumbed to gravitas. She also knew not to overstay
her welcome or extend an appearance for vanity, which might
tempt unnecessarily clever interrogation. There was little upside
playing into overtime once she found an upbeat exit line. The
regulars in attendance knew she would not stay for much more.

She had accomplished all she had wanted, the appearance of openness and transparency, a heap of value that could only be compromised by potential contradiction.

A question from the *New York Times* reporter, whom Payne cordially next acknowledged, would be her last for the day: "Congresswoman, you seem to be flip flopping on the matter of Kimo Balthazer. You attack him, then embrace his assistance. Today you seem to feel sorry for him while still indicting him. What are we to make of this rollercoaster ride you are taking with Mr. Balthazer, and why are you paying attention to him at all?"

"Leave it to the Newspaper of Record to question a government leader about her theme park excursion with the popular media," replied Payne to the expected chuckle from the crowd. "You know, you are probably right. In the grand scope of the cosmos, Mr. Balthazer is not all that significant. To be clear, he has been a bit of a parasite, an egomaniac of the worst form, so unpolished that his rage can bring harm. My concern with Mr. Balthazer is that he is misunderstood, and thus the current flavor of the day. When people go to the ice cream shop, they usually pick something reliable like strawberry or chocolate chip, but every now and again a flavor of the day catches their fancy and they just don't know why they are devouring bubblegum swirl. The problem with Mr. Balthazer's bubblegum swirl is that it is unexpectedly influential—it is getting under people's skin like a narcotic and causing them to make poor decisions. Have I been trying to play along a little until we can get the swirl back in the spout? I confess, I have. I have been trying to do whatever it takes to get Mr. Balthazer to be helpful and cajole his audience into making better decisions about their future. I have seen fragments of light in Balthazer's dialogue, but ultimately, he has let us down. He has let me down, he has let himself down, and his has let the American people down. Thankfully, as a beacon of radiance in the storm, his show has been taken down. That's a step in the right direction. My sense is, until Mr. Balthazer seeks redemption and steps into a path of worthiness, we are not going to return to normalcy. People need to go back to work, the markets need to recover, and Kimo Balthazer needs to be forgotten, not necessarily in that order. All this must happen so prosperity can return. I thank you again for your time today, and I look forward with you to better days ahead, a spirit of optimism, which is the American way."

Payne thought she had them on that end note. She built carefully to a choral crescendo, but maybe she was trying too hard. Applause was polite but tentative, camera flashes were fewer. The good news was that if she did not like what she saw in a few hours on television and internet streams, her own people were in the audience recording the same material, which she could edit and release at whim to her followers and soon-to-be followers, all of whom would know she was on the side of right. Payne was just about to make a clean exit from the stage, when a thin woman in her mid-thirties wearing no makeup and a frayed plaid sun dress stepped in front of the podium. She had no press badge, and her hard leather shoes looked like they had floated downriver in a flood.

"Congresswoman, may I ask a question?" queried the threadbare woman.

Payne stopped in her tracks before she reached the stage stairs, uncertain and off guard. The woman speaking was not a journalist. From the looks of her, she was not likely employed. Payne's eyes were on her reluctantly. The moment was not scripted or rehearsed. Payne had not prepped today for the extemporaneous. The woman with the muddy shoes was not part of the show. She was not supposed to ruin the curtain call.

"The press conference is over, ma'am," stated Payne. "You can certainly submit any subsequent questions via email to my staff."

"I'm not a reporter, Congresswoman. My name is Haley. May I ask you a question?"

Payne looked left and right at her staff. She couldn't find a safe exit, particularly with so many video cameras hot. She did not want to engage, but her choices were few.

"If you are one of my constituents from Montana, please feel free to set up some time to meet with me in my office. I would be pleased to do that at your convenience."

"I'm not a constituent, and I'm not from Montana. I have no home state. May I ask you a question?"

"Generally we don't take questions from the public at a press conference, Haley. Can we possibly do this in a follow up at my office?"

"No, because you'll blow me off, like you're doing now," replied Haley, softly but drawing curiosity from the journalist pack, which remained solidly in place, the entertainment value of the afternoon improving. "I'm not from the press, and I'm not a voter in your district, so you have no reason to speak with me. If you don't answer my question now, there's no reason for you to consider doing it later."

Payne looked again at her staff, then into the audience. The video cameras were glowing red. She could not get off that stage without her poor manners making the evening news. She did not want to be on the record, but she was. She had no choice.

"Certainly, Haley, I would be delighted to answer your question. What is it?"

"Thank you, Congresswoman, I appreciate that," said Haley. "My question is, why do you hate people who play by the rules?"

"That's ridiculous, Haley," responded Payne in as gracious a manner as she could. "First off, I don't hate anyone, not anyone at all. My ethics and values speak for that. As for people who play by the rules, we all should play by the rules. No one should ever not play by the rules. That's why they are rules."

"Do you think fairness is a rule?" asked Haley.

"Of course I do," agreed Payne. "Fairness is only right. Fairness is the golden rule."

"Do you think reasonable pay for a job well done is a rule?" asked Haley.

"Again, that's obvious," said Payne. "We have many laws to support employee rights. If you do a good job, then you must get paid what you were promised."

"Well, I did all that," said Haley. "Now I am homeless."

"I'm very sorry to hear that," replied Payne, generously em-
pathetic, a sound bite cued from her Random Access Memory.
"We have many assistance programs for people in your situation. I'm sure someone on my staff can help point you in the
right direction."

"That's not what I'm looking to clarify," said Haley. "I
worked as an accounts payable clerk at a grocery store chain for
sixteen years out of high school. I supported my two children,
whose father lost his job when they were three and five. Then he
left us. The store I worked for was bought by another chain. I
was given sixteen weeks severance pay and told I wasn't needed
anymore."

"Well, sixteen weeks pay isn't a treasure, but it is something," commented Payne.

"That was four and a half years ago," said Haley. "I haven't
worked since. Social Services took my children. I have no home.
I have no health insurance. Where you are standing on that podium, when you take the podium down, that's where I'll sleep
tonight. Tell me, do you think all that is fair?"

Payne was under pressure, the heat lamps were on her and
the cameras were recording. More than anything, she wanted
off that stage. She was impossibly jammed, perspiration leaking
through her tapered silk collar, trapped by the proscenium of
her own making.

"I don't know if it's fair, Haley. Business is difficult. You
see how things are now. The stock market has lost a substantial
amount of value and no one is certain when it will recover."

"I don't own any stocks," said Haley. "I'm worth the same
today as I was a month ago. Are the people who lost money in
the stock market this week worth nothing?"

"I suppose some of them are," said Payne, attempting a
thimble of levity but falling flat. "But I would agree, most of
them are not worth nothing."

"And I'm sure they all played by the rules, just liked I did.

By the way, when I got laid off four and a half years ago, the stock of my company was at an all-time high. Our CEO retired. He was paid $70 million. Maybe now that is only worth $30 million. Or maybe in a few years if he plays by the rules it will be worth $130 million. I'll still be worth nothing. And I won't have a home or my children. You see why I wonder about playing by the rules? Because I always do. As a result, you're standing where I sleep."

"We're going to get you some help, Haley. I promise you that. There are five million troubled people out of work right now who don't have to be, with you that's five million and one. Besides taking that plane back from those renegades in Hawaii, getting all of you back to work is our Job Number One."

Payne knew that did not come out right. She had spoken beyond her plan and that was not good.

"No, that's okay," said Haley. "I'm not asking you for any-thing. Those people walked off their jobs on their own, to make a point before their companies are bought. I'm what happens afterward. I just wanted to ask you the question. That's all."

Haley disappeared into the crowd, without acknowledg-ment, without demand. Payne was silently fuming. She had traded a carefully orchestrated arrangement for a cacophony of uncomfortable improv that was 100% more likely to make the evening edits and be immortalized on YouTube. She had succeeded in nailing the perfect viral sound bite, but not the direction she had intended. She played back the words in her head, the slip she had just launched to infamy: "There are five million *troubled* people out of work right now who don't have to be, with you that's five million and one." If only she hadn't said "troubled."

Payne at last stepped off the stage, forcing an awkward grin for the remaining assembled. Before she could catch her breath, one of her assistants handed her a live cell phone and a laven-der Post-It note, marking it unmistakably a call she could not refuse. It was Hussaini.

"How hot is it on that runway?" asked Payne, trying to

regain her composure.

"Fahrenheit or Celsius?" replied Hussaini. "It doesn't matter, more than warm."

"Have they figured out yet they are out of negotiation leverage?" she asked. "How much patience can your boss have left?"

"Not much," said Hussaini. "But I don't think that's the way you want it to end."

"I know the gas scenario is off the table. Last thing in the world we want is a gagging, deceased talk show host."

"I'm glad you understand that," said Hussaini. "I think they know they're not going to Shanghai. It's been forty-eight hours and nothing has changed. We're stuck, but I think they're ready for a way out. Can you get them a package?"

"You want me to go to bat for them?" growled Payne, almost as insulted as she was caught off guard. "I don't make criminal justice deals. That's your thing."

"My boss won't touch it without a sponsor. Too many crimes, cross state borders, FAA, terrorism, it's a mess. He says it has to come from you."

"I'm not touching it," batted away Payne. "How do I know you can even sell it?"

"Swerlow is losing his mind. He's pacing and sweating and waving the gun like a parade baton. It really is hot in here. They're keeping us rationed but not comfortable. We don't have much time before Swerlow flips and shoots one of us or my boss calls in the plow. We don't know how many people get hurt if that happens. I'd prefer a surrender."

"What makes you think you can get one?" reiterated Payne, even more irritated.

"Kisinski knows it's over. If we can find a way for them to cave without a stampede, I think he can get his cousin onboard."

"I still don't know what makes you think that," countered Payne.

"Swerlow let Balthazer send his email. Then he told me to call you."

"You know there is no way they walk, no chance of any

kind," stated Payne.

"Yes, I understand that," said Hussaini. "I'm sure Kisinski does as well, but I don't think he wants to die. Talk to your friends at Justice. See what they can do. If we get Swerlow to toss in his hand, we can fold up the table and the whole thing stays sealed. Then all you have to solve is the Walkout. If you get us out of here, I'm guessing Balthazer will get onboard too. He's close to turning the corner."

"People will be going back to work soon, that's the natural way of things," said Payne. "The longer they stay out of work, the more they risk losing their jobs in perpetuity. All of this will soon be less memorable than last year's Academy Award for Best Picture."

"You do know Choy and Finkelman have conference calls this weekend with dozens of other CEOs to discuss Balthazer's Merger Bill of Rights, do you not, Congresswoman?"

"I do now," said Payne. "That won't go well. They're idealists. Business is not best conducted by idealists. It is best conducted by pragmatists. They're about to learn that, which is good learning. However wealthy they might be, they are young and emerging, the lesson will be worthwhile. I'll look into a deal for Swerlow and Kisinski, but I'm not hopeful."

"Get your friend Henderson to help," said Hussaini. "He knows no one on the government side of the equation needs any more embarrassment. We make it look like a unilateral surrender, then we take their plea. My boss has to know he has cover."

"I'll see what I can get," said Payne. "Try not to watch me on the evening news tonight. Balthazer already has enough to gloat about."

"You think you're having fun," said Hussaini. "Imagine my joy listening to Balthazer and Steyer go at it all day, locked in steaming close quarters."

"That's the only laugh I got today," said Payne with a half-hearted chuckle.

"I'm glad you're laughing," said Hussaini. "That makes one of us."

Payne hit the end button and handed the phone back to her assistant. The press conference crowd had mostly disbanded, the makeshift platform already being disassembled by government subcontractors. The Walkouts remained in place. Haley was nowhere to be seen. Payne's handlers were skillfully in motion, leading her from the Smithsonian to her next important commitment. Her Washington dance card was always filled, she would not have it any other way. Still unnaturally perspiring, she was escorted to the waiting Escalade.

$ $ $ $

<u>3.3</u>
Fundamentals are for Mortals

To My Loyal Listeners:

The response from so many of you to my email yesterday was overwhelming. Two things are clear: first, you want me off this plane, and second, you want me back on the air. I thank you for your support, and for your understanding. For what it's worth, I'm doing fine. The focus now is on you. It's all about you.

I thought I would share a snippet from one of the emails I received. This is from Darcy, an engineering VP for a chip designer currently on watch in a parking lot in Austin:

"Kimo, thank you for letting us know you are okay. You are standing by us, and we are standing by you. There are at least a hundred in this parking lot and maybe another thousand or so in the complexes nearby — probably two hundred thousand across the state, but who can tell. Texas is a really big footprint, not an easy place to get on the radar, especially for dissenters. We see the other Walkouts online and we are connected to them because of you. The police are coming out in heavy force. They kind of look ridiculous, the ones in riot gear. No one I know in the Walkout is danger- ous. We're office workers, not the Warriors. They're starting to form a perimeter around us. I hope they stay cool. We wouldn't know what to do if they didn't. We just want to make a quiet point.

"My situation is different. I have never been laid off. I've had steady work for almost twenty years and been through two IPOs. I have been very fortunate, but I have had to let go hundreds of employees as a boss and I can't stand it anymore. Every time my company buys another company, the bodies fall like leaves. It's not allowed to be emotional. We are told to do it to justify the purchase price and then we do it. Last year I let go a director of operations who had been with me for seven years. Five months later he lost his home. He moved into his mother-in-law's one bedroom apartment with his wife and kid. He is standing four feet from me as I write this email. He still can't find work at anywhere near his previous salary. Now he works part time in a warehouse without health benefits, and he has an MS in computer science from UT. Last quarter, after our ninth acquisition in four years, our company had another record quarter of earnings growth, and before the bubble popped last week, our stock was at an all-time historical high. I got a bonus last year for beating my cost targets. I gave it to the employees I let go, but it's not enough. Please help us make this nuttiness change. Please make someone listen. That is why we are out here. It's way past time."

Darcy is one of the good eggs in management, so remember, they are there. Record profits, record share price, record bonuses, record layoffs. Makes sense, huh? No, it does not make sense. We have to make them listen. We made this Walkout happen. They have to make it go away.

As we approach the weekend, I ask you to

keep standing tall and don't forget to help each
other. There are five million of you plus one of
me, and everywhere you look, there is someone
from the media who wants to retell your story,
just like Darcy. We are on the verge of a breakthrough. I continue to receive information that
makes me believe Choy and Finkelman are
on your side, they are doing everything they
can to carve out a Merger Bill of Rights, our
MBOR. I hope to have something ground-
breaking to report to you soon.

Stay out there, stay calm, make your voices
heard. Your jobs should belong to you as long
as you do them well. Make it religious. Make
it our fate. Make your employers see what it
means to try to crawl out of the slime without
you. Don't Cave.

This Is Rage!
Kimo

$ $

"It's a curious letter, don't you think?" proposed Professor
Yamanaka, standing before his class of MBA students, reading
aloud the words of Balthazer. It was risky to be talking about a
set of circumstances with which he was so closely associated, but
Yamanaka could not help himself. He had tenure, and as far as
he could tell, he was not violating confidentiality. The next Choy
and Finkelman might be sitting in this lecture hall, and if there
was a way to surface them, candor was his best bet. He also still
had some work ahead of him coaching the current Choy and
Finkelman. In his mind, they would always be his students. No
matter their success, he knew he could be helpful to them if they
were open to it. He respected their towering accomplishments,
even their untested world view, but if they forgot how to listen,
that would be their undoing.

"I want to talk today about Market Forces—about
fate, chance, circumstances beyond our control," continued

Yamanaka. "That is what you will face as a start-up CEO, so let's start getting used to facing it. Who can summarize the Butterfly Effect?"

Numb stares returned to him from the tiered amphitheater. The Butterfly Effect was not mentioned in the required reading, so no one had a clue. Yamanaka worried about them, all of them. They were supposed to be top management in the making, but they never deviated from syllabus assignments, high or low. They wanted grades, credentials, networking, and introductions. Were they abstract thinkers like Choy and Finkelman who unquestioningly embraced creative destruction? Was the ethos of Joseph Schumpeter running through their mostly unclogged arteries as an essential nutrient, with innovation and reinvention a brew of life fluid more than academic theory? Not enough of them. Maybe that was why the economy was out of control. Enterprise was too commonly led by stealth followers who wanted sticky gold stars on their foreheads, not courageous standouts who were not afraid to be difficult. These studied carpetbaggers cared too much about cash payouts and not enough about sustainable value. What mattered to them was what would collect in their pockets, not the annuities they could cement for the down line. The real lesson of arrival had to be recited, that the self-serving cash box was no reflection of bravery, value creation was.

"Fine, let's talk about butterflies," continued Yamanaka. "The Butterfly Effect is a subset of Chaos Theory, largely the work of mathematician Edward Lorenz. Come on, you're not that young, you remember Jeff Goldblum in *Jurassic Park*. Migrate it from movies to something that matters, your hopes of great riches. The presumption is that in nonlinear systems, a small, seemingly meaningless, change of events in any one part of the world can have a profound, unforeseen impact somewhere else. Specifically, the notion is that the presence or absence of butterflies flapping their wings on one side of the planet can result in the creation or nonexistence of a hurricane on the other side of the planet. The connection between the minor and major

events is inarguably nonlinear, but traceable through careful cor-
relation, the corollary being that understanding the unintended
consequences of any single event, however modest, could have
profound impact on intended or unintended outcomes. We see
this conceit regularly in popular fiction, particularly time travel
adventures, where a protagonist must find a way to go back in
time to do or undo something that can change the present. If
you remember the *Back to the Future* films, you have a layman's
understanding of the Butterfly Effect—Hollywood's adaptation
of special relativity."

Yamanaka's students were questionless. They had been expecting today's lecture to be on analyzing complex formulas for
designing derivatives, which they had previously been taught
was a necessary component in achieving ridiculously favorable
return on investment regardless of whether the stock market
was going up or down. They liked those kinds of lectures—
those secret formulae were why they were willing to go into debt
for a prestigious MBA, because it gave them the best possible
shot at getting back their bait plus some at the earliest possible
window. Of course they were aware that their teacher was on
the board of EnvisionInk Systems and was tied to the turmoil in
the headlines, but perhaps they believed it was taking a toll. Yamanaka was talking about Spielberg and Michael J. Fox movies
toward a purpose, yet he did not have their engagement. He
advanced the sermon, undeterred by the incoherent stares from
the amphitheater.

"You are all exceptionally bright individuals, and likely believe you will have a great deal of control over business once
you reach the corner office. I must disavow you of that hubris.
Most of your companies will fail. You will build them with every
fiber of your being, and they will crater or be sold. There is no
getting around that, the odds are stacked infinitesimally against
you. It used to be if a company lasted one hundred years it was
major league special. Today the numbers tell you a start-up is
defying gravity if it celebrates its tenth anniversary. Invention
is a cycle that consumes itself. More powerful than strategy,

more powerful than execution, more powerful than competition
and talent are the Market Forces. Understand what I am saying about the Butterfly Effect. You cannot save the butterfly in
central Brazil if someone wishes to swat it. There is absolutely
nothing you can do, nor can you know what its death means
to you. You cannot prevent it, you cannot protect against it, all
you can do is be ready and anticipate any potential outcome
it might bring. Does luck matter in business success? It does.
Does timing matter in business success? It does. Will you be
thrown curves by your competitors and observers you never anticipated? You will. World heavyweight champion Mike Tyson
famously said, 'A plan is something you have until you get hit.'
My question to all of the aspiring CEOs in this room is quite basic — in assuming your forthcoming profit and loss responsibilities, are you ready to get hit? And if you are, do you know how
hard you can get hit, and what it will be like to pick yourselves
up off the ground when no one is handing you a towel or water
bottle — they are instead standing on your fingers asking to get
paid for the privilege of watching you suffer in disgrace?"

Yamanaka was certain his students had to be thinking he
needed a leave of absence. First it was butterflies and time travel movies, now the wacky professor was invoking the advice of
felon Iron Mike. Of course the syllabus declared they should be
learning how to beat the sector indices with obnoxiously clever
math. These were not graduate students in the humanities. No
one before him was preparing to apply for a religious mission
or non-profit do-gooder austerity. This was Stanford, birthplace
of HP, and Yahoo, and Google, and EnvisionInk, the latter of
which would not have come into being without Sensei Supreme
George Yamanaka. Yamanaka had to convince them he was not
out of his mind. He motored on, a steam engine gaining inertia
under reserve power.

"The Butterfly Effect, Market Forces, that which you can't
control — each morning this week we awake, we look at our
headlines online or in print, and what do we see? Five million
people voluntarily out of work. How does that make sense?

What led the nation to go on strike? The kidnapping of Choy and Finkelman? A mouthy online talk show host who emails from captivity? What are we to make of that? I am about to tell you. Close the lids on your laptops, power down your tablets, reach for a writing implement, and write this down on a piece of paper you can keep for the next forty years, through your retirement if you happen to be so lucky and work does not kill you."

Yamanaka had their attention. He was going to give them something of value. He had not gone mad. He had a point to make. The lecture was going to pay off, even better than derivatives. Their computers were closed, their laptops were powered down. Most had a disposable Bic pen buried deep in their shoulder bags, but those who did not borrowed from a classmate. Archaic yellow lined paper was torn from pads and shared. Yamanaka would now need to deliver to maintain his credibility. He continued, following dramatic pause, without anxiety or retribution.

"Resilience," he said, looking into the eyes of his unmoving students. "You must have missed that. I said Resilience. Write that down on the piece of paper before you."

The class stared back in disbelief, as if the once brilliant Yamanaka had abandoned his own consciousness, the EnvisionInk crisis simply too much for him. He stared back, resolute, unapologetic. Reluctantly they did as they were told, forever fearing the mark down in grade point average that could result from any instructor who held them in disfavor. Everyone was aware a few basis points below 4.0 GPA could mean a 30% swing in starting salary post graduate degree. Yamanaka knew no one would risk that, no matter how skeptical their belief set. He continued, bringing it home.

"Why do I mandate that you embrace Resilience? Listen now, I am sharing with you the worst kept, but least embraced, industrial secret of all time. One of the most critical components of a successful entrepreneur or corporate leader—from the freshest newbie to the most seasoned veteran, from the fast rising star to the battle worn chief executive officer, from the biggest loser to the windfall winner—is the ability to let go of the past and look forward. It seems terribly intuitive, but it is not easy to do. Pain sticks and holds people back. Getting unstuck is a rare talent. Jack Welch would teach this at the General Electric Training Center in Crotonville—you can't do anything about the past, it already happened; look forward, look forward, look forward. Those who have failed did so for any number of reasons. Those who have succeeded—who have defied Market Forces and harvested luck and rode the wave of timing—have largely done so for one reason: they don't give up. They have vision and ability, a good idea and capital, all of that matters. Survival matters more. When I looked at Calvin Choy and Stephen J. Finkelman in our boardroom yesterday, I knew why they were alive. I knew why they were back at the table. I knew why their company was once again theirs. They are indefatigable. Their will led them to the endgame. They never, never look back. They live in the present and the future. What happened yesterday, right or wrong, good or bad, is an artifact—worthy of study, unworthy of obsession. Did they mean to be kidnapped? I think not. Did they mean for their employees to walk out in anticipation of a merger that never occurred? I think not. Did they anticipate the Walkout at EnvisionInk leading to a nation-wide Walkout of five million people and a stock market crash that now sits squarely on their shoulders to solve? They did not. Are they challenged by this? They are. Are they inspired by this challenge? They are. Are they taking time off to recover from the abduction? They are not. Choy and Finkelman understand and embrace resilience. They are intellectually and emotionally invincible. They have always possessed this too rare trait, and it has served them well, but it will never serve them better than at this very moment, back on the job, facing unprecedented crisis, this strategic inflection point. That is why I am betting not on the butterfly, but on Choy and Finkelman. You want to be successful, learn to look forward and forward only. Learn that, and your time here in business school will be well spent."

Normally students only applaud an instructor on the last

day of class, at the end of his final lecture. Today was an exception. Yamanaka stood before the room to a spontaneous mid-lec-
ture ovation. He had reached them, the lesson he had taught
in those few articulate words would be one his students would
always remember. Yamanaka wondered how his wunderkind
Choy and Finkelman were going to live up to the billing, but he
knew they would.

"The Operator drives, the Banker dances, the Investor must
win. It is not meant to be fair, it just is. The rewards to which
we aspire may be intrinsic or extrinsic, but those we receive are
not necessarily those we choose. The butterfly can decide for
us. Fate is factored, but it is not determined. Leadership is Resilience. Now, shall we resume our discussion of derivatives?"
prompted Yamanaka, turning on the ceiling projector which
blasted a wall full of Cartesian graphs. Yamanaka looked up at
the small control booth beyond the back row of stadium seat-
ing, where his staff media technician slightly lowered the lights,
ready to follow him with PowerPoint slides. As a matter of routine, the media tech was also recording Yamanaka's lecture on
video for student log-in use during study sessions, as well as
university posterity. One thing Yamanaka could count on, his
bit on the Butterfly Effect was on its way to being excerpted on
YouTube, on the same page of search returns as *Jurassic Park*.
He was counting on that, which is why every word had been so
carefully chosen.

$ $

Partner meetings for top venture firms are typically held
on Mondays, the day partners set aside not to travel, since all
partners must be present for any definitive action. The rest of
the week partners routinely spend traveling to portfolio companies, attending board meetings for their sponsored start-ups,
engaging in discussion with limited partners, or prospecting potential Investors for their next fund. SugarSpring Ventures long
ago agreed that its partners would spend time with each other
in Palo Alto every Monday, at least until lunch, regardless of
whether they looked forward to the dialogue, unless they were

on vacation beyond the reach of telecom or other extenuating circumstances. In the true spirit of trust but verify, partners did not like to miss partner meetings, nor did they look fondly on fellow partners who missed them.

Steyer joined the conference call in Palo Alto with the four other general partners who called the shots at SugarSpring Ventures from the Boeing Business Jet stuck on the tarmac at Hickam Field. Steyer interpreted the permission he had been granted as a desperate goodwill gesture by Swerlow and Kisinski, who had to know their time was running out and that it was in their best interest to be as cooperative as possible as long as they remained surrounded by armed militia. It was not a perfect setup and Steyer had no privacy in the forward office of the 737 with the door ordered open by Swerlow so he could hear all, but it was better than nothing and at least served to keep Steyer connected during the worsening national financial crisis. Steyer had asked for only one accommodation, that Balthazer be held in the aft sleeping quarters of the plane with the door shut while he was on the call, so anything he said did not leak via email. Swerlow had obliged without argument, offering to fit Balthazer with a muzzle if Steyer had the guts to secure it. Steyer was not sure if Swerlow was kidding, but politely passed.

It was critical that Steyer attend the partner meeting given all that was at stake, not only with EnvisionInk Systems, but now their entire investment portfolio, public and private, as the bottom had fallen out of the capital markets with no sign of rebound on the horizon. Steyer and his partners oversaw placement of the current SugarSpring 12, a $1.25 billion venture fund targeted at digital media, wireless, ecommerce, and clean tech, all sectors which had been good to SugarSpring, except perhaps clean tech, where positive returns remained nascent but government subsidies were enticing. EnvisionInk had been part of SugarSpring 7, a seed bet of $50 million placed over ten years ago for 20% of the company fully diluted. About half that stake had been methodically liquidated over time, providing healthy contributions year after year to take home bonuses at

SugarSpring. The approximately 10% of EnvisionInk that SugarSpring still held at the market peak just a few weeks ago had
been worth over $6 billion, today it was worth about a quarter
of that. While that kind of return would be considered hardly
a failure by anyone with the guts to play at this table, much
of it remained a paper gain, locked up in EnvisionInk equity,
due in part to SugarSpring's belief in the investment's long-term
growth prospects, and in part because selling it off in high volume could spook the market and crash the price, had the price
not already been crashed by other market forces. The partnership would never admit it had been greedy letting the bet ride,
only that their exuberance was warranted by the unique value proposition and inspired management team. Today they just
wanted out, any path to liquidity. They had other even weaker
positions that needed to be covered, given the market crash, and
the wind was no longer at Steyer's back on this one. Headwinds
on EnvisionInk were suddenly blowing hard with no forecast
for reversal, leaving the general partners with little choice but
to be responsible to their own backers, the limited partners, big
money institutions including major university endowments with
whom their reputation had never before been in question.

Etiquette for a partner meeting was always the same, any
partnership vote on allocating capital or seeking exit had to be
unanimous. Every project, deal, or company had an individual
lead advocate from the firm, but when it came time to decide
what to do with an asset or investment, that partner could become a hair-on-fire barrister, as if making his case before a high
court where he too was a judge, but majority was meaningless.
There were no ties, no dissenting opinions to an action on any
split vote. Five partners meant five yes votes were required to
move forward, anything less was a stalemate. Steyer faced that
singular challenge, uniting four partners plus himself. When
Atom Heart had approached them, they had agreed selling
their stake in EnvisionInk was the right thing to do, provided
this was amenable to the company, the only way they could get
out with a path to full liquidity. Steyer's counterpart at Tehama

Capital, the other VC that had invested alongside SugarSpring in the original EnvisionInk deal, had delivered the same consensus. When that deal fell apart, Steyer had egg on his face that was hard to wipe clean. Today he needed to leave the meeting with a new consensus. He had come to the speakerphone with a direction. He absolutely had to sell it.

The boardroom 2400 miles away was all too familiar in Steyer's mind. If he had been at the table he would be surrounded by the same lineup he saw every Monday morning, all present and ornery. Malcolm Kent, the firm's co-founder with Steyer, had thirty-two years in venture, all of them at Sugar-Spring, junior to Steyer only in charisma and visibility. Dorothy Fabre had twenty-nine years in venture, the last fourteen of them at SugarSpring after she jumped ship from a competitor on Sand Hill Road when that Menlo Park firm failed to raise a new fund after several years of losses on deals she had been corralled to support. Bernie Singh had eighteen years in venture, all at SugarSpring, prior to which he was a Founder/CEO who took a chip maker public and then sold it to Intel, two bites of the apple that paid off well for his SugarSpring backers who kindly welcomed him to their ranks. Johan Shauk was the kid in the group with nine years in venture, all at SugarSpring, although he had only been a partner the past two years after seven years training as an associate, taking the seat of Steyer's other founding partner, Gerhard Untermann, who had retired at age sixty-five, an impatient tennis enthusiast way too rich to care about sitting through any more Monday meetings.

Partner meetings were always civil, however awkward, because no matter what might be said, Monday would come again next week. Perhaps the most oblique aspect of partner life was that for the most part they were stuck with each other, if not for their full careers, at least half or more. Venture partnership was like marriage — entered with the greatest sense of romance and adventure, long-term impossible for the participants not to get on each other's nerves. As often as the idea of separation might be entertained, the cost of pursuing dissolution was onerous to the point of deterrence. Each partner would inevitably know the idiosyncratic speech patterns, the oft repeated metaphors, even the half-hearted attempts at humor of the others. They had to listen to each other even when they all knew what each was going to say, teeth often grinding away generous chunks of calcium or needlessly breaking bridgework, pencils snapped like sunbaked twigs as compelled endurance eroded. Civility ruled, order was expected, grace under pressure was the norm no matter how much capital was gained, lost, or held at stake. The bizarre circumstances of the recent five-alarm crash and Walkout may have been exceptional, the dial-in logistics of Steyer's participation unconventional, but the tone of this partner meeting had to be no different from any other, at least on the surface, if they were going to get to the right place by adjournment. Any outcome other than civil agreement and definitive action was not an option.

"Are you sure you're in a position to carry on this conversation, Daniel?" asked Kent at the outset, his voice replete with respectful trepidation. "We have a good deal of concern for your well-being. This is not an ideal situation, hardly what anyone could consider normal."

"Yes, it would be difficult to classify the past few weeks as normal," transmitted Steyer's voice through the polycom. He had become his own version of Henderson, although under more hostile circumstances. "Dennis Swerlow knows I'm on the call and is listening from the aisle. Anything we can do to help his negotiation will be appreciated, which is why he is allowing me to do this. Other than a little heat exhaustion and not enough variety in diet, I'm fine for the moment. Our hosts are looking for a good outcome, as am I."

"I appreciate your situation, as well as the flexibility you've been afforded," said Kent, obviously presuming he would be overheard by Swerlow. "The markets remain in a dire state and these five million Pollyanna numbnuts aren't budging to help make things better. Thus far we have seen no violence, but who knows how long that will last. Daniel, please tell us what you can about these CEO conference calls we've been hearing about all weekend. It seems there might be a potential outbreak of Marxism at your beloved EnvisionInk. Is there something we should know?"

"I don't keep secrets," replied Steyer. "Choy and Finkelman have a lot of youth in them to reconcile. The tannins need to soften. They mean well, but sometimes they can be a bit naïve."

"This Merger Bill of Rights, the grapevine says it was drafted by the general counsel at EnvisionInk," commented Fabre. "That does not seem like a very good use of her time. Have you seen the document, Daniel?"

"I have not," said Steyer, silently irritated by the distraction. "I'm guessing it will find its way to the Internet soon enough, and I'm sure it doesn't have much in the way of teeth. That's not Sylvia's style. She looks out for the company."

"Why do you sense that Choy and Finkelman have invested their energy in this?" asked Singh. "They can't really think anyone in the corporate world would take this seriously. I wonder, after this, if anyone will take them seriously."

"They have been through a lot," offered Steyer. "There's still a lot of emotion tied up in their contemplation. They got kidnapped when it was supposed to be me, one of them was shot and then they were held hostage in their own plane. The day they were taken, the company they founded and the world it inhabited were functioning in accordance with the laws of nature. When they returned, the company had lost more than half its value, and half the professional world was on strike, started by people they hired and thought liked their jobs. It's a lot to digest. I'm guessing they are just trying to find a way to help."

"Five million people is not half the world," corrected Kent. "It's a lot of people, but we needn't exaggerate."

"I was painting a picture," rebuffed Steyer. "Forgive me for storytelling. I've had a good dose of emotion as well."

"We need to get our money out of EnvisionInk, Daniel," stated Fabre without emotion of any kind. "Our portfolio is battered, and the asset least likely to recover at scale is EnvisionInk, given it still represents such a large part of our holdings. Raising the balance of capital we are seeking for SugarSpring 12 is going to require an upbeat report to the remaining position holders in SugarSpring 7, since we took such great risk and held as long as we did."

"We all have a keen interest in the recovery of our portfolio," continued Steyer, avoiding escalated confrontation. "You are correct, Dorothy, our capital in EnvisionInk is of special interest since it represents such a sizeable portion of our positions. Precisely what I would like to discuss today is an acceptable strategic path to exiting EnvisionInk, which has consumed considerable amounts of our time over the past several months."

"Isn't that how we got here?" asked Kent, prying but pithy. "We were stuck holding the shares of EnvisionInk because to dump them would have risked tanking the share price, so the only real way out was a clean purchase. Your buddy Sol Seidelmeyer was supposed to be our conduit there, but it didn't work out the way we intended."

"Right, we ended up with a mess on our hands, I get that," bridged Steyer. "Now comes the interesting part. Seidelmeyer is still interested in a deal, particularly at current depressed prices. He texted me."

"I may be the newest partner at this table, but I recall Seidelmeyer resigned," said Shauk. "Is there some creative construct of which I am unaware under which a former CEO can direct M&A for that organization?"

"Don't make me sorry we voted you in," said Steyer, somewhat joking but keeping Shauk in his place. "Seidelmeyer is a power magnet in media. He was a top packaging agent, an exceptionally clever dealmaker long before he was a studio CEO. He remains a major stockholder in Atom Heart Entertainment and his old job is open. Putting together the companies as a broker could be his ticket to a fast comeback. If anyone can make that happen, it's Seidelmeyer."

"I'm sorry," said Fabre, "Seidelmeyer crapped out trying to acquire EnvisionInk, humiliated himself on national television, helped bring on the market crash and the Walkout, and now you think he is going to make another run at EnvisionInk. That seems like a hell of a stretch, don't you think, Daniel?"

"I am equally confused by the proposition," commented Singh. "EnvisionInk stock is down, but so is Atom Heart. Even if Seidelmeyer wanted to do the deal, even if he had the authority, which he doesn't, I don't see how he leverages in this equation to come up with the cash to buy EnvisionInk."

"He doesn't," countered Steyer. "We do it the other way. EnvisionInk goes after Atom Heart. We put the two together, the market gets a little inspiration, we have a smaller piece of a vastly bigger pie. EnvisionInk takes on the leverage since we look stronger on recovery and our multiples are better. No question we can raise the debt if we lead. Our stake is reduced, so is the price dependency on our holding. We let it settle, wait for the spring back, then slowly start to exit the big game without jacking it. We get everything we want, just not all at once."

The phone silence Steyer experienced following those remarks spoke to the incredulous nature of his proposal. He had to keep selling. "Okay, it's not exactly what we had in mind, but it's a way forward that helps the market build confidence in itself."

"It's another head fake," said Fabre. "Too much frosting, not enough cake. Even if both EnvisionInk and Atom Heart did go for it, how do you factor the Walkouts? You start talking a merger of those two again and you know the Walkouts aren't getting behind it. It all stays frozen."

"That's the beauty of it," added Steyer. "They announce the merger and promise not a single layoff. It becomes a model for the future, and everyone is happy. No proclamations, no manifestos, they just do it. Once the EnvisionInk Walkouts come off the line, the movement loses its leadership. The trading desks heat up with a payback rally. Everything starts to go back to normal."

"They can't do a deal of this size without serious cost reductions," insisted Shauk. "Arithmetic won't work, not a chance.

We have to get a valuation on fundamentals."

"You think you can make money selling on fundamentals, get out of venture," shot back Steyer. "Fundamentals are how the mutual fund guys get paid, the retail guys who still wear ties to work. Some of them even believe they really can beat the market throwing darts outside the pub—that's not what we do. We see what others don't see, what isn't there to be seen. That's why our clients let us charge them what we do, because we embrace imagination in our math."

"He's right about that, Johan," added Kent as a quiet aside. "Listen to what he's saying, you could learn something."

"A deal without strewn bodies is the only way we get Choy and Finkelman onboard," argued Steyer. "I'm going to have a hard enough time selling them the deal in any form, layoffs can't be on the table. Right now I would have a hard time selling them that the sky is blue, but hopefully they'll listen to Yamanaka, their teacher, they trust him. If he can get them to believe they can make their point leading by example, help our company and set the stage for a comeback, that's something they might buy."

"What about that freak show, pulp head Balthazer?" asked Singh. "What happens when he gets word of the deal, when the two of you are released and he starts pooping on it over the public airwaves? You think the EnvisionInk staff is going to follow Choy and Finkelman over the great radio god?"

"Balthazer is going to stay out of hearing range, he's not going to know about this until it's publicly announced," said Steyer. "Choy and Finkelman have managed to build a bridge with him. If they're onboard, they can get him to support it, especially if there are no layoffs. Balthazer has his own set of problems. He's got that hammer heavy congresswoman from Montana eyeing his kneecaps. If Choy and Finkelman can position him for helping end the Walkout in spite of himself, he walks away clean and gets his show back, which is all he wants."

"I don't see any action items before the partnership, Daniel," summarized Fabre. "There is no motion to consider. Everything you have suggested is theoretical. What exactly are you looking for from us today?"

"I guess I wanted to float the idea over the phone, Dorothy," replied Steyer. "Hypothetically, if the opportunity came about for EnvisionInk to acquire Atom Heart Entertainment, allowing me to leave the board and Sol Seidelmeyer to assume my seat as chairman, is that an action the partnership would support? I need to know because if I'm going to have my fellow board member, Professor Yamanaka, open that door as my proxy. I want to be sure I'm representing the firm's interest as well as enacting my fiduciary duty on behalf of all shareholders."

Steyer stopped talking, having said more in a partner's meeting than ever was his norm. He waited for someone else to continue the dialogue, but no one seemed sure where to go from here. He tried to imagine the confused looks on their faces, his partners stalled without precedent. He needed eye contact to read the room, but all he had was the silent handset. This was the waiting game. Whoever spoke next lost.

"Are you looking for a sympathy vote?" asked Shauk. Steyer exhaled with his mobile on mute. Shauk had stepped into his bear trap, the only partner in the room rookie enough to snap the discomfort, willing to take the hit if he said the wrong thing.

"No, as Dorothy pointed out, a motion would be premature," rejoined Steyer, bringing his phone back to life. "There is no reason for anything today to be recorded other than we discussed EnvisionInk and approaches to our remaining investment there. What I am looking for is consensus, directional consensus. Did what I suggest sound like a potential way forward?"

"If it gets us out over a reasonable period of time, I'm for it," responded Kent, who like Steyer never wanted to say more than was required. "But I want skin in the game from Seidelmeyer. His cash becomes EnvisionInk's cash, and I want some of that cash on close as a hedge against whether the market likes the deal, which I have no clue."

"I agree," volleyed Steyer. "Seidelmeyer will understand that. Whether he is a buyer or a seller, he knows we're playing for the exit. He's playing for the ego. Everyone is happy, and maybe a few million people will find their way back to work. Others?"

This time the quiet was a positive signal to Steyer, who could practically see the heads bobbing around the table. Kent had been with Steyer a long time, and if he was in agreement, the others had to go along. It could not be otherwise, because sooner or later they were going to need Steyer and Kent to support their deals. Individual memory was always much longer than institutional memory, a favor was as easy to remember as a roadblock, in most cases easier. That was the beauty of partnerships, the stuff that made them work, the placing and playing of markers. Partnerships were relatively easy once you understood how they functioned, easier for most than husbands or wives. Steyer had what he needed for the moment. All he had to do was get Yamanaka to convince Choy and Finkelman he had not completely lost his mind.

$ $ $ $

3.4
Exit, Stage Left

To My Loyal Listeners:

You may have heard that over the weekend a
number of conference calls were scheduled to
take place, originating with Calvin Choy and
Stephen J. Finkelman at EnvisionInk Systems,
reaching out to as many Fortune 500 CEOs
around the nation as they could contact. There
has been plenty of wild speculation from the
media flooding the Internet, TV, and even old
fashioned newsprint about the nature of these
calls, with countless corporate leakers adding
their touch, but let me assure you that the calls
are real. I remain in direct contact with Choy
and Finkelman as we eagerly await the results
of their efforts.

If you're looking for a moment of hope that
your corporations might actually be ready to
care about you, this is as close as we have been.
Choy and Finkelman are proposing a simple
and benign draft of a Merger Bill of Rights
that goes like this:

Whereas most everyone in the business world
is aware that corporate growth is desirable in
a free market economy, with increased revenue and profits fundamental to the creation of
shareholder value; and

Whereas companies can improve business either through innovation in their own enterpris-
es or through combining their efforts through
mergers and acquisitions; and

Whereas corporate executives must have the freedom of action to enter into mergers and acquisitions, understanding that cost savings in combined operations are often needed to make the economics of a merger viable.

Now, therefore, be it be resolved that CEOs acknowledge that the reduction in work forces to improve the economics of mergers comes at the cost of some human impact among those who lose their jobs by no fault of their own;

Resolved further, that in acknowledging the loss of these jobs can create personal financial difficulty, the CEOs wish to offer fair and much needed assistance to those in transition;

Resolved further, that employees who lose their jobs because of a merger or acquisition, will receive reasonable support to help maintain their prosperity at a level commensurate with the benefits realized by the company that eliminated their positions solely as a means of cost savings and earnings enhancement.

That definitely has lawyer written all over it, but I don't think it's so bad. It's sure better than what we have now, which is nothing. I would love to hear from you on this. Post your thoughts on ThisIsRage.com and let's see where people stand. I know you're hanging tough on the line, still five million strong and well behaved no matter the intimidation, eagerly awaiting word from Choy and Finkelman what their fellow CEOs think of it. Don't Cave.

This Is Rage!
Kimo

$ $

It was no accident that Balthazer had the draft of Sylvia Normandy's proposed Merger Bill of Rights. Choy and Finkelman had sent it to him over the weekend and then told him to e-blast it late Monday night to put pressure on their fellow CEOs. If the media had the actual working copy subsequent to the pitch, no one could say they were overreaching, and by taking it public after the pitch, they kept the noise factor at the right level. Everything would be cleansed in the camera lights, and that would either help the manifesto build a platform of community support or scorch it to a fizzle.

Balthazer had no delusion the MBOR would have any teeth. The draft he saw and sent was as thin as the single sheet of paper required for a printout, but it was a ceremonial bridge to the future, a latter day Magna Carta. As long as enough business leaders of importance acknowledged that it existed, Balthazer could call a draw a win and in good conscience rally people back to work. He could also get on with the next chapter of his life—be it a cinder block federal cell, some half-blazed trail in the Himalayas, or a grandiose return to the airways—provided he got off that sweltering grounded jet alive. Swerlow was getting antsier as the hours passed, and the increasingly high temperature was taking its toll on his restraint. Balthazer cringed as Swerlow habitually waved the gun like a laser pointer, part prop and part hand gesture. With no deal coming from the other side of the runway, time was no longer their friend.

When he was not arguing with Steyer about the meaning of existence and its bottom line, Balthazer had spent the weekend surfing the web for news of the Walkout. Seeing no signs of a pullback in participation, he nervously waited for Choy and Finkelman to contact him with an update on their conference calls. Balthazer remained hopeful that Choy and Finkelman could sell the MBOR to at least a dozen fellow CEOs, even a half dozen would constitute a road trip victory. Just one big company announcing adoption could give it enough credibility to let Balthazer sound the victory trumpet and send the first wave of Walkouts where he knew they needed to be, paychecks again in hand, proud they had made a stand and been heard. The Walkouts were counting on Balthazer, and Balthazer was all in on Choy and Finkelman.

$ $

The stock market had barely moved during the trading sessions on Monday or Tuesday, not unlike the previous week, with volume so weak it almost was not worth the bother for the few trades that were placed to be settled. Since the crash, the market had not moved up or down more than 0.05% on any trading day or in the aggregate. Until the Walkout was resolved, no one but the most radical speculators wanted to buy, and no one but the most destitute leveraged wanted to sell. The market just sat there, hardening sludge, dead at its bottom. Any good word from Choy and Finkelman could change that, but their news had to give the Walkouts noble reason to retreat. That was only going to happen if there was some sympathy — any sympathy — for the high level concepts suggested in Normandy's draft resolution.

In the parking lot at EnvisionInk, expectations were on the rise following Balthazer's latest email containing Manifesto Lite. The release of Choy and Finkelman had been an injection of positive energy among the Walkouts, with the leadership Walkouts at EnvisionInk alternating between despair and hope. The weekend anticipation had yielded tremendous anxiety, but the Walkout was never intended to be a wake, and from it came flash mob moments of gallows humor. The latest bit of dork glam to emerge from Santa Clara was a music video on YouTube sung to the tune of the Village People's "YMCA." It had gone viral, and it had inspired on the spot dance renditions for exercise interludes in parking lots from New Hampshire to New Mexico in all its redundant refrains:

> Boss man, you're a real rich dude.
> I said, boss man, do you need to be rude?
> I said, boss man, 'cause you've got a bad 'tude.

There's no need to be so crappy.

Boss man, gotta keep me this job.
I said, boss man, do you work for the mob?
You can fire us, and I'm sure you'll save cash.
And then keep it in your stash.

It's time you give us an M-B-O-R.
We need to have us an M-B-O-R.
You have everything that a boss can joy enjoy,
You have planes and homes and toys.

It's time you give us an M-B-O-R.
We need to have us an M-B-O-R.
You can just let us work, you can have us real
cheap,
You can please just not cut so deep . . .

Boss man, are you listening to me?
I said, boss man, just how rich will you be?
I said, boss man, we have quite simple dreams.
But you got to know this one thing!

No chump likes to go on welfare.
I said, boss man, it's my job and I care.
When you merge us, and you take all our pay.
There's no place for me to live today.

It's time you give us an M-B-O-R.
We need to have us an M-B-O-R.

The MBOR flash mob anthem was an instant YouTube classic, with a total life-to-obscurity span of maybe seventy-two hours. Perhaps the only usually fun-loving person at Envision-Ink who wasn't Bollywooding in the parking lot was Monty Dadashian. The company's CIO clearly had too much on his mind. Choy and Finkelman had received an ALL CAPS TEXT from Dadashian saying they absolutely had to meet him on the front lines in the EnvisionInk parking lot with the Walkouts first thing Tuesday morning, no excuses. For one thing, they were overdue to see and be seen by the Walkouts—it was insulting that they had driven past them to their office for the past few days and not stopped to offer a Starbucks fix. The Walkouts needed to see that their co-CEOs cared, and the co-CEOs need-ed to encounter the scope of the Walkout in the flesh, there was no substitute from afar. Second, and much more importantly, Dadashian referenced a crosscheck on some test cells he had run that had not gone well. Choy and Finkelman were not yet clued into the specifics, but anytime their CIO called out batch data as damning, they knew they needed to hear what was on his mind. Dadashian never exaggerated when it came to data. Data was truth. Data was sacred. No long-serving CIO could be an alarmist when it came to data. When Dadashian's text implied he had critical data that would matter to their decision making, he had Choy and Finkelman's attention.

Choy and Finkelman had spent the entire weekend and most of Monday trying to sell the MBOR to their fellow CEOs, but agreed to meet Dadashian as he requested, on Tuesday morning in the open. When Choy and Finkelman encountered their old friend at the EnvisionInk main driveway, it was part reunion, part dread. Sight of the faux coonskin cap reminded them how much they missed Dadashian, but the drain on humor brought on by so much mayhem in such a condensed period of time was inescapable. Dadashian looked into their eyes and they could tell immediately he knew they had nothing.

"Monty, did you write that MBOR song?" asked Finkel-man, balanced on crutches, his souvenir leg cast still affixed. "It's got your rhyme scheme built into the beat."

"Not my work," said Dadashian, an uncharacteristically sto-ic response. "I've had a few problems, no time for tunes. How's the leg wound?"

"It'll be a few months, but I should make a full recovery," replied Finkelman. "At some point I'll wind surf again, at least at low tide. Wish I could say the same for the NASDAQ. All the numbers are bleak."

"I did happen to see some online video of your old teacher Yamanaka singing your praises," said Dadashian. "Have you seen the Chaos Theory clip? It's bringing YouTube to a crawl. Someone on the inside tagged it Stanford Full Frontal Steaming Hot Butterfly Tease. That got it moving across the grid."

"Yeah, the Butterfly Effect, we heard about it," replied Choy. "Not sure how that helps us. Speaking of chain of events, we read your report. You found anomalies in the algorithm."

"Tell me your worst fear," posited Dadashian, the melodrama unavoidable.

"Nuclear winter, followed by impure drinking water, global starvation, and mass untreated surgical needs, plus permanent damage to the earth's ability to heal," said Choy.

"As it pertains to business," rephrased Dadashian. "Stephen, you try."

"That if I live long enough, I become like Steyer."

"Closer," said Dadashian. "What I have to share could transform you into a habitual liar for the sake of survival."

"Sounds like Steyer to me," parried Choy. "What have you got?"

"The value of the algorithm is deteriorating. It's like it's been cracked, the source code handed over to the search engines. I think they reversed engineered us. We are less and less an effective inoculation against moron bidding. They are beating us at their game by making us play their game. Our long term usefulness is in question."

"That sounds like panic," said Finkelman. "Don't we have enough to worry about with the Walkout and getting those guys off our plane?"

"The stats are real," said Dadashian. "The numbers are in constant, steady decline. Anything that can be engineered can be reversed engineered, as long as you're subtle about it. It's kind of like what we did to them to get into business. They did it to us. Reverse creative destruction. The key word recommendation blocks we're serving up are being overridden. Search revenues and profits have been up for them. Ours were flat.

Now we're declining. Pretty soon we'll be in free fall. Stopgap vaporized free fall."

"Then we'll rewrite the algorithm again," said Choy confidently. "We've seen dents in the armor before. Our eye has been off the ball all of two weeks. We can't lose our company in two weeks."

"We are," said Dadashian. "They've developed a core resistance. Their algorithm to drive up bidding trumps our algorithm to thwart it. They leapfrogged us in the arms race."

"No algorithm is definitive," replied Finkelman. "We'll fire back."

"It's all about time and distance," countered Dadashian. "Leapfrog is too far too fast. Our code got dusted and we'll be playing defense instead of offense. You can't catch up, you have to leapfrog again. They went too far ahead."

"The advertisers won't figure that out for months, maybe a year," said Finkelman. "They love our value proposition, our vision. It's in their interest to be patient and stay with us."

"Our value proposition will soon be all theory, no practice," challenged Dadashian. "Code is code. The best code wins. It's a zero-sum game. They win, we lose. My advice, FWIW, if there's still an offer from Atom Heart, take it. Take all their money, quickly. Tell them nothing. Stick them with the stricken beast. Let the law suits catch up later. By the way, on the stand, I never said any of that. We're old friends, I'm telling you the truth. We have nothing. It was a good run, but it's gone."

"That's ridiculous," asserted Finkelman. "How did they get the source code while we were gone? Steyer wouldn't give it to them. He is that evil, but he's not that stupid. It would cost him everything."

"You know the drill, the best way to steal information is in people's heads," replied Dadashian. "The search engine guys have been poaching our engineers ever since our stock went flat a year ago. You never know who gave up the goods. It only takes one, could have been anyone. You'll never trace it, but they have it. The result is we're toast."

Dadashian handed Choy and Finkelman a set of printouts, more than a hundred pages of spreadsheets, graphs, and charts, all with hockey sticks going in the wrong direction. All around them the eyes of their employees were transfixed on their leaders, everyone looking to them for an answer, with no idea what they were reviewing. Choy and Finkelman had thought sales were flat because of saturated market share, because they had won their war. The documents that Dadashian had compiled told a different story. They had slowly, invisibly been under attack for months, probably for over a year. Choy and Finkelman had been caught up in other things, distracted by operational interruptions, not paying attention to the code. They had tripped over nimbleness, misplaced focus, gone inadvertently soft in success. All that they had engineered to help advertisers beat the search engines had been reverse engineered, a little at a time. Then when they disappeared ever so briefly from the landscape, the competition struck hard to see if the counterattack would scale. It did.

Calculations raced through their minds, the outcome pointing to a single variable. The core intellectual property holding up the pillars at EnvisionInk could soon be worthless. Not worth LESS, worth ZILCH. A strategic inflection point had hit them that hard. They had fallen victim to classic tech subterfuge, mostly of their own making. The Walkout may have been caused by the Butterfly Effect, but the algorithm corruption was strictly human failure. Arrogance. Laziness. Leadership failure. Their failure.

"We'll sue," said Choy. "Reverse engineering is completely illegal."

"It will take years to prove anyone did that, who knows how many millions of dollars in legal fees," said Dadashian. "No judge will give us a restraining order to counter the real time damage. Business goes on while disputes are sorted out, that's the way it goes. The company will become an abandoned shell with almost no revenue, suing giants with monster cash reserves. Our stock price will go to zero before a jury is interviewed. Even if we win, we lose."

"I'm not so sure," argued Finkelman. "We'll see where we are after we get through our current crisis. We have plenty of problems already, one day at a time, okay?"

"Right, well, I'm hoping the MBOR phone calls went well this weekend, but I'm not getting that from you either," continued Dadashian. "Anyone bite?"

Choy and Finkelman looked at each other. They could not hide anything from Dadashian, not after all these years. They had to tell him the nasty truth.

"Not a one," confessed Finkelman, utterly matter of fact. "On a scale of ten, where ten gets the bill into law and one uses it as kindling, we're a negative integer. Fair description, Calvin?"

"I might give it a 1.25, but only because no one we talked with in the last three days threatened to kidnap us again, although I'm guessing they might have been thinking it."

"It's words on a page," said Dadashian. "It's practically a press release. It says almost nothing. The theme song is more volatile. What did they hate so much?"

"Starting with the first capital letter and ending with the final period, every keystroke of it," said Finkelman. "The chances of the MBOR getting any corporate support are as good as Swerlow and Kisinski getting off with a warning and finding a new source of capital for their Shanghai company—although in this town, if they could prove a path to liquidity, that could happen. This won't."

"Just like that, dead on arrival?" asked Dadashian.

"D-O-A," echoed Choy. "We pitched to Apple, Intel, HP, eBay, Cisco, Microsoft, they all thought we were completely out of our minds. Google laughed out loud, they thought we were playing a practical joke, unworthy of being indexed. Facebook threatened to unfriend us. Everyone wants their employees back, but not if they have to promise to keep them."

"We even took a run at the start-ups," added Finkelman. "You'd think there might be slightly more sympathy there, given that most of them were started by people who got canned or were likely to get canned on combination. They were even more adamant—no way, no how, that's not how business works. When you're gone you're gone, that's the way it has to be. Zero acceptance, zero receptiveness, universal disdain. When the entire world says an idea is bad, it's either the best idea no one has ever thought of, or it truly rots. I'm not sensing we've stumbled onto a breakthrough in enterprise thinking. This idea will never get momentum."

"We heard this consistently from the other CEOs," said Choy. "They have enough problems with the Walkout and the market crash. No one is ready to sign up for an endless set of costs, and when you think about it in terms of economics, that's all the MBOR really is. Cost without revenue. When you look at it that way, it's hard to rally behind it."

"What do we do now?" asked Dadashian. "We have to give everyone a reason to go back to work. We have a company to fix, or sell."

"When the wipeout goes wide on the web, which should take another few hours, the next thing that happens is that Congresswoman Payne starts to draw a line in the sand to blanket protect the companies," said Finkelman. "Walkouts are going to start getting fired. That's not exactly the outcome we wanted."

"It won't just be a nightmare for the Walkouts," said Choy. "It means the market doesn't recover, the economy sucks, maybe it's a recession. Everyone loses."

"Except the Honorable Sally Payne," reflected Finkelman, thumbing through more pages of the report. "She follows this smoke straight into the Senate. Maybe she gets offered VP on the next ticket. She lets everything crash and positions herself as the solution. No one has reason to think she's wrong since she called the implosion from the outset and warned the Walkouts to back down. She becomes the voice of strength, calm, and reason."

"Yeah, Madam Clairvoyant, she saw it all coming," announced Choy, hardly believing his own words. "More like she let it all happen. Where do we go from here? The MBOR is dead and our company may have no core value. What's our next move?"

"Balthazer is not going to be helpful with the Walkout when he finds out the MBOR is history," said Finkelman. "We need to get a new story out to the employees before he goes off the reservation."

"Here you are among them," said Dadashian. "What do you want to tell them?"

"I wish I knew," said Finkelman. "Professor Yamanaka asked to meet with us. He said it was urgent, same as you. Maybe he'll have a point of view."

"He always has a point of view," commented Choy. "That doesn't mean he can help us."

"All I can tell you is that all these people here, all the people we hired, they need to hear something from you, and they need to hear it soon," said Dadashian. "See how they are looking at you? They're confused. They've never looked at you like that before. You need to give them something or the decision is going to make itself."

"You think they want to listen to us?" said Choy. "We're the enemy, remember. Management is exactly who they don't trust."

"Then stop being management," suggested Dadashian. "See the world again through their eyes. Then maybe they might care about what you have to say."

"I'm not getting where you're going," said Finkelman. "You want us to walk off the job and join them in the Walkout?"

"How many CEOs do you know who willingly throw themselves under the bus for a principle, without a golden parachute?" said Dadashian. "Want to make a statement? That's a statement."

"But we just got back on the job," said Finkelman. "We haven't even been in the office a week. How does our joining the Walkout position everyone to go back to work?"

"You stay out here on the front lines and tell the gang you're not going back to work until they do," said Dadashian. "You tell them you tried for the MBOR, but you couldn't sell it, so you're joining their ranks. If they want to go back, you'll go back, but they have to know you believe they come first. The rest of the five million will follow."

Again Choy and Finkelman looked at each other. Dadashian had an interesting enough point of view, but they needed to huddle. He was a friend, a C-level executive, but he was also an employee. The next calls would be the toughest ones, they had to be made with privilege.

"Monty, we're going to step aside for a moment, if that's okay," said Choy.

"I have work to do anyway," said Dadashian, probably not surprised that his time with them was up. "I can hold up the data for a few months before the search engines obliterate us, but you need to have some story ready before we implode or we'll never come back. You can try out your story on me before you tell anyone if you want. It will need a dry run. And yeah, I did write the MBOR song. But I didn't choreograph the video. Too depressed."

Dadashian departed, his coonskin cap askew following their heated conversation, always the hood ornament on his lanky frame. Choy and Finkelman watched lifelessly as he departed into the crowd with his endless pages of doomsday reports, leaving them an executive summary. They felt awkward, surrounded by their followers, no answers of any kind to announce.

"What are you thinking?" asked Choy after another discomforting interlude.

"I hate to say it, but I think we're going to need Steyer," answered Finkelman. "We have to get him and Balthazer off that plane."

"Then what?"

"I was thinking exit strategy," said Finkelman.

"We think alike," said Choy. "Maybe Yamanaka can help get us there. At least he thinks we're resilient."

"Resilience isn't staying onstage past the curtain call," said Finkelman. "Sometimes it's coming to terms with what needs to happen, having the courage to move onto the next new thing. We've had a good run," said Finkelman.

"We've had an excellent run," reinforced Choy. "Let's start

working on the story."

They folded up the summaries that Dadashian had given them and stashed them in their backpacks. It was time to greet the troops around them, put on the face of confidence, stand tall however alone, leaders of the pack. None of their employees had to know a new normal had not been delineated, not now anyway. Choy and Finkelman slapped on a pair of smiles and disappeared into the maze of Walkouts dotting their parking lot.

$ $

Dennis Swerlow was not as stupid as everyone but his cousin had come to believe. For an untrained criminal, he had done remarkably well. He had gotten halfway to his getaway on a private 737 owned by a pair of tech luminaries, been taken overly seriously by the FBI, and was holding his own in a standoff on a US Air Force Base. If he was stupid, the other side was not doing much better. Emotion and exhaustion were wearing him down, yet he was smart enough to know that. He also knew he was nearing the end of his timeslot. His career in corporate crime was going to conclude on this government runway, that milestone was inevitable. He was like the CEO of a company that was already bankrupt, the zombie start-up that hadn't yet filed for Chapter 7. He knew the jig was up. The only thing left to negotiate were the terms and conditions of surrender. It was time to craft his exit strategy.

What that meant to Swerlow was that he was going to have to figure out what was desirable and achievable. Like any well-formed business goal, the conditions of desirability and achievability both had to be met for a win-win outcome. Swerlow knew his options for the achievable were not going to be numerous, given the public hazard he had created, so he needed to figure out what he considered desirable. If he was going to throw in the towel, what did he most want, and was it possible he could get it? Between Steyer and Balthazer, he had in his presence two of the foremost subject matter experts on give and take. The irony had not escaped him. The question was whether he could humble himself enough to seek their help. He could.

Steyer and Balthazer were in the main cabin of the aircraft, doing what they had been doing since Balthazer boarded when not wiping perspiration from the back of their stained
necklines — arguing about what made the planet spin. At first
Swerlow and Kisinski — and even Hussaini — found this mildly
entertaining, but after almost a week in close quarters the irritation factor had escalated to migraine inducement. Luxurious
as it was under full power in flight, the unventilated business jet
had become claustrophobic, tense, each day with less bearable
odors. Supplies had been purposely limited by intervention to
essentials — water and dry packaged foods. The pilots had been
excused as a concession to the standoff, thus the plane remained
in power down mode without air-conditioning and most other
hygiene sustaining amenities. The plane was on back-up electri-
cal, powered by a low amp generator to allow recharging of mobile phones, laptops, tablets and the like so that communications
with the outside world could continue, but beyond that, the
fuselage had become a suffocation tunnel. Swerlow, more than
anyone, knew an assault from the outside could be unleashed at
any time.

Swerlow could see that Steyer did not like Balthazer from
the outset, the Great Mouth Prince was not his idea of *Entertainment Tonight*. Balthazer likewise never concealed his disdain for Steyer and his repugnant life plan. Stuck sweating
beside them, Swerlow hated Balthazer for humiliating him
on the air and Steyer for complicating their plans. Swerlow
knew that cousin Sam desperately wanted closure, worried
for good reason that Swerlow's patience could pop at any
point.

Special Agent Hussaini remained the wild card for Swerlow.
In Hussaini he saw a tired technocrat who could not believe this
crime scene had not been closed down, a family man facing the
absurdity that his life was held in the balance for reasons surreal. Hussaini had remained point on the outside negotiation —
all it would have taken was a word from him and the jet way
door would be blown down with an onslaught of machinegun

fire—but he had managed to rebuild credibility with Swerlow and was clearly the key to breaking through the impasse. Just out of participation range of the main cabin debate pit, Hussaini waited in the forward private office for word to come back from Payne that some deal could be presented to Swerlow. Short of that, the chances all five of them were going to deplane alive were almost nonexistent.

The more Swerlow heard Balthazer rant, the harder it was for him to believe that anyone with more than a fifth-grade education would listen to him for more than ten minutes, let alone every afternoon for three hours in drive time. Swerlow found Balthazer's arguments thin, unformed, a setup for jerky punch lines and caller bashing more than well-considered opinions of business, government, and how the world functioned. Swerlow found Balthazer's vocabulary to contain endless clichés and almost no insights—little guys were pawns, big guys were mutants, elected officials were delinquents; the rich viewed the poor as low margin customers. Ho-hum. Balthazer's spiel was a set of bumper stickers for old VW vans, not an assessment of how companies were built and people got fed. This wasn't entertainment. It was spew.

With animus on par, Swerlow found every concept that Steyer articulated grating and despicable. He tried to listen for the first few days, then gave up. If he heard the words "value creation" one more time he thought he might shoot Steyer dead solely to make it stop, the repercussions of less bother. Swerlow found Steyer's lack of empathy so complete, he wondered how the job of venture Investor could be legal. The more they all sat together and sweated, the more precarious each hour became. Steyer and Balthazer could not shut up, driving tension levels in the cabin increasingly closer toward Swerlow's unwind point.

"You don't at all understand why those employees walked out," railed Balthazer in another muggy, mid-afternoon skirmish. "You take their dignity when you fire them. You see it as cost savings. They see it as loss of their identity. Why is that hard to understand?"

"Should we keep everyone employed forever?" asked Steyer in his standard detached tone. "Classic European socialism — worked out well for the Euro, hasn't it?"

"That's campaign rhetoric, not a point of view," argued Balthazer. "Leave the labels to the politicians, ignorance is in their job description. Do you really see American quality of life better for the average guy? The four hundred richest guys like you have more wealth than the bottom fifty percent of everyone else. Is that the way the equation for middle class life is supposed to work? If people are so damn happy, why do they call me? Why do I have a career?"

"Exceptionally meaningful question," answered Steyer. "Why do you have a career? Because you feed people watered down Xanax. You let them wallow in public sorrow, with just enough sympathy to get them to tune in tomorrow, but no real world advice that helps them advance. You pay the tiniest bit of attention to them when they get rejection from everyone else, unless you don't like what they say, then you hang up on them as a gag. And don't forget the real irony — you get paid decent money by ghastly exploiters like me. All your life, you've worked for guys just like me. You complain about what we do, but you cash our paychecks. You think I'm a mess of ethics? You're a walking conflict of interest, with a cheap haircut."

"I may work the system, but I'm not a corporate criminal," replied Balthazer. "I didn't create the savings and loan crisis. I didn't make money on Long Term Capital Management. I didn't jam home mortgages that could never be paid back for the commissions. I didn't merge all the banks for deal fees, say oops when they collapsed, and take bail-out dough to pay bonuses while writing up the layoff lists. You and your buddies did that. That's why five million people walked off their jobs. We could still be having a good run in this country, but you and your pals decided your share wasn't enough. You were so much more clever than the rest of us. You took it all."

"You don't get technology, the profound impact of innovation on our lives," pontificated Steyer. "I know your education has been underserved, and I know you are by nature an endless talker and a poor listener, but please, let me explain why our economy is the way it is. If I have screwed up the world by investing in technologies that have changed it, then yes, I am guilty."

"Yes, you are guilty, on that we agree," declared Balthazer. "Don't lecture past the punch line. It's bad radio."

The banter was going on too long. Swerlow needed it to stop. He was not amused. He was in hell. Thick sweat dripped down his nose, but they were not looking at him. They seemed to have forgotten he was even there, the captor in charge. They could not restrain themselves.

"Try tuning into reality," persisted Steyer. "Three fundamental changes are behind all the supposed evils you get paid to babble about. First, technology means we're all living longer than anyone planned. Medical science is a good thing if you're the one on the table, but our longer life spans were not projected in the original math for Social Security and Medicare. If the math doesn't work, we have to change the math. Leave pensions in the formula and no one can balance the equation. Second, technology has automated most of the factory jobs and back office work that a lot of people hoped would last forever. We have computer programs and robotics to do those jobs, they aren't coming back. Third, technology accelerated globalization. Today we compete with the rest of the world for commodities, and the rest of the world competes with us for employment. You want to blame an employer because he can find someone who wants to join the middle class in India or China to make his margins work, blame him for being a smart business person. Those three things, that's why people lose their jobs."

"And greedy corporate assholes like you who take all the profits and turn them into a shell game called the stock market, only you leave the table a winner while the fools you've duped think they have a chance against the house. You train them to become addicted to bad gambles."

"This is ridiculous, you keep saying the same things over

and over without any facts," proclaimed Steyer. "That's show-biz, right? Say whatever you want for the impact. Technology creates problems, but it creates opportunities. Without guys like me willing to take that risk on innovative products and services, there is no way out—the Walkout may as well be permanent. People like me willing to take on risk are not the problem, we're the solution. Only risk can make the market come back."

"Can I smack him?" proposed Balthazer, turning to Swer-low, like a second grader taunting his teacher. "Come on, one good smack. Or maybe you could shoot him. Or shoot me so I don't have to listen to him anymore."

"You're not on the air, Balthazer," hammered Steyer. "Enough with the theatricality."

Swerlow could see that Steyer had pushed Balthazer be-yond his sanity quotient, and Swerlow wasn't far behind. Swer-low had heard too much of both their voices. He had absorbed an overdose of the incessant heat. He had breathed in enough foul smells of airless confinement. Then without further warn-ing, Balthazer charged full press at Steyer, Bat Out of Hell, div-ing onto the sofa at his bruised torso. Swerlow drew down on them both and cocked the trigger.

"Enough, you're insane!" roared Swerlow, the raised gun once again a tie-breaker. "Park the dueling sermons and tell me what it's going to take to walk off this jet."

Balthazer stood down on impact with Steyer's wired jaw, lowering his crimped hands before they reached Steyer, still fragile from surgery. That was the first time Swerlow had let out a hint of compromise. It had weighed on his mind for days, but this was the first he let anyone hear him say it. That was no accident.

"Don't ask me," said Balthazer through a wheezing breath. "All I do is repeat myself without any facts."

"You want off the plane?" asked Steyer. "Open the door. We walk off together. No one gets hurt if we walk off together."

"I'm not spending the rest of my life in a federal prison," de-manded Swerlow. "That isn't going to happen. Not an option."

"Take him seriously," added Kisinski, until this moment silent on the sidelines, but fully with his cousin's back. "That hasn't changed since we started."

Swerlow did not know what to say next. It was hard to imagine a scenario where, if he and Sam were not gunned down in an assault, they did not get a life sentence. Balthazer and Steyer remained quiet, for the moment they had no more to say. Swerlow secretly wished they did, some ingenious suggestion, but they had none. With the argument interrupted, Hussaini entered the main cabin lounge from the private office. All eyes were on him.

"Okay, I have word back from Payne," began Hussaini. "You won't like this, but here's the deal. We all walk out together, they'll consider recommending leniency."

"That's not a deal," blurted Swerlow. "That's not even close to a deal."

"The deal is you throw in the towel and they'll consider a deal," continued Hussaini. "You have to surrender first, unconditionally. That's all you're going to get. This doesn't go into the weekend. Next week it can't be a story."

Hussaini had positioned himself as the messenger, but Swerlow was not sure if he had helped or ended it. Hussaini's tone made it clear this was not another bluff. If they did not accept this final offer for a safe walk-off, whoever was calling the shots was willing to live with the consequences. Swerlow knew it ended here—the last, best, and final offer was on the table. A recommendation for leniency meant he and Sam would not be gunned down with any collateral damage that might follow, nothing more. It was a simple deal, impossible to misinterpret the terms and conditions.

$ $ $ $

3.5
Buy Low, Raise Cash, Sell a Story

To My Loyal Listeners:

There's no joy in Walkoutville. At least I don't have to be the one to break the news. The Internet has been very efficient and you all know what No sounds like. The Merger Bill of Rights is officially dead even before it had a chance to be born. Not going to happen. Not coming to an HR office near you. Not going to give you a reason to go back to work.

The answer to all your thousands of ideas on ThisIsRage.com is No.

The answer to considering the boneheaded lawyer draft I sent you yesterday is No.

The answer to whether you deserve any protection or security of any kind is No.

Our friends Choy and Finkelman went to the high rollers table with our backing and tossed snake eyes. They went looking for anything we could call a win and were shut out. They got nothing, so we've got nothing. I want you to understand what nothing means. It means there's no counter, no discussion. No one in a position of authority at any company they contacted gives a half-ounce of squashed mosquito gunk what's bugging you. They desperately want the stock market to come back, but they don't care if you come back. Maybe they think they can have one without the other. I don't think that's true, but the only way we can find out is if you stay out there on the line and maybe each yank in one of your friends who hasn't yet walked out to share your outrage. That would double our numbers, from five million to ten million. Don't retreat — recruit! We still won't get an MBOR, but they won't get back any of their Monopoly money, which is real money, or at least it used to be. They don't show any respect for you. Show how little you respect them. The longer the stock market is dead, the more money they'll never recover. Seems like a fair lose-lose to me.

I'd like to tell you my own situation was better but that would be stretching it. We are on a wind down clock. The stalemate on this runway is coming to an end. We are facing a hard deadline that, unlike your situation, is a lot less governed by free will. I will make you this promise: If I am able to do it, I will be back on the air next Monday no matter what you are doing or how the rest of the nation's idiocy is being expressed. If I am not on the air Monday, you know why.

I wish I could tell you this was going somewhere, but when arrogance and greed go to war with integrity and reason, there are no longer two sides to argue. It isn't civility to play along with intolerance. That's apathy, and that ain't me. At least we now know the rules. We know they don't care, and they don't want to care. The only right thing to do is keep hitting 'em where they feel it, banging on their net worth. Don't Cave.

This Is Rage!
Kimo

$ $

"Smart move, spending the night out here with your employees in the parking lot," said George Yamanaka, abruptly waking Choy and Finkelman from an uneasy sleep on a pair of REI air mattresses. Sunrise had broken through the bay fog and the morning peninsula air held its usual chill. Yamanaka had just read Balthazer's latest missive on his smart phone, worried about the impact, hopeful the crowds would remain peaceful. Choy and Finkelman were among at least a thousand Envision-Ink Walkouts, maybe more, the lucky ones finding open patches on the perfect lawn, the rest settling for available asphalt. They had already read the dispatched email from Balthazer, setting their mobiles to ping on its incoming status, then going back to sleep.

"You're still an early riser," said Choy, half opening his eyes. "We don't get up this early when we sleep out at Burning Man."

"You don't wake up until nightfall when you sleep out at Burning Man," sniped Finkelman. "But we always let you come back."

"Can I buy you both a cup of coffee?" asked Yamanaka.

"It's free in the cafeteria, breakfast served all night," replied Finkelman. "Perks have yet to be revoked, pending restated earnings."

"Excellent, my stock options are currently underwater, so the price is right," quipped Yamanaka.

Choy and Finkelman fumbled a bit, then rolled up their sleeping bags and followed Yamanaka though the mostly sleeping crowd to the main commissary. Yamanaka looked the perpetual role of northern California business professor, summer suit without tie, last steam pressed the prior semester. It would have been without precedent for him to look otherwise. Choy and Finkelman looked their old selves, the all-nighter student variety, as unpolished and close to their earthy roots as co-CEOs could be. They seemed a lot happier in their unwashed sweats, more like engineers, less like executives. Somewhere between captivity on the 737 and returning to work crisis, they had taken a small step back toward verisimilitude.

"Thanks for seeing me," said Yamanaka, with his dark roast and fruit cup. "I talked with Daniel late last night and he was doing reasonably well, but the tension level on your plane reflects the high heat there. The officials in charge have extended a mandate, and I don't sense the standoff is going to last much longer. It could end badly if Swerlow and Kisinski don't opt otherwise."

"Don't you think it's strange the FBI was willing to be patient when Calvin and I were on the plane, but with Balthazer and Steyer, they couldn't seem to care less?" asked Finkelman, downing his first Diet Coke.

"I think it's more about time than personnel," replied Yamanaka. "This has gone on too long. The situation was a lot more visible when it was you in your backyard. Everyone's attention has since shifted to the Walkout, so if something awful happens on that runway, it will fight for headlines rather than lead the news. That's the nature of the twenty-four hour news cycle you and your peers created."

"You can thank Congresswoman Payne for the shift in focus more than Stephen and me," said Choy behind a cup of hot green tea and a honey crème donut. "The whole thing is a mosh pit, and we need to find a way to crawl out of it."

"As usual, your attention is well placed," said Yamanaka. "Have you given any thought to how that happens?"

Choy looked at his partner for guidance. Stephen's caffeine-stoked eyes told him not yet. They had tremendous admiration for Yamanaka, their deep history with him could not be dismissed, yet they knew he was owned by Steyer and they had to be careful. The stakes had moved up considerably since their release and trust remained a limited currency. They needed to draw out Yamanaka, see what he knew before they coughed up Monty's slaughterhouse discovery. Yamanaka could help them, but only if it was in his own interest, and only if Steyer supported his point of view. They weren't there yet.

"We were thinking it would be helpful to have Steyer at the table, and Balthazer on the air to sell a new story," said Choy.

"The MBOR is a buried carcass, that's today's buzz. We need something to replace it for tomorrow or the crowd may lose its cool."

"Five million pissed off people in fifty states can do a lot of damage with a reason," said Finkelman. "We can't take the peaceful nature of the Walkout for granted, especially not with Payne trying to spin this. What are you and Steyer thinking?"

"I'm glad you haven't shut down completely on Daniel," said Yamanaka. "I was afraid you might have entirely turned against him. He is a unique individual."

"He tried to sell our company out from underneath us while we were held hostage," noted Choy. "That was unique."

"The board rejected that unanimously," countered Yamanaka. "Be clear on the facts. The facts are what matter in your decision making. You know that."

"The facts are what they are," stated Finkelman. "So how do we solve the problems of the world?"

"Just as you have remained somewhat open-minded about Daniel, is there any room in your thinking for further discussion around Atom Heart Entertainment?" asked Yamanaka, as delicately as he could form the words.

Again, Choy and Finkelman were not ready to show their cards. Yamanaka did not have to know that EnvisionInk was a dead company walking. If he was going to re-propose selling to Atom Heart without them having to bring it up, maybe they could skirt the whole notion of the morbid algorithm. It would have to come up sooner or later, but later was irrefutably a better idea. Transparency would be ethically required, but timing was always a variable. The more awful the disclosure, the later you wanted it introduced as data, hopefully past any affordable ability to unwind an announced deal. Their capacity to know each other's thoughts on this sort of thing without exchanging a word was what made their shared CEO status work.

"I don't see how an Atom Heart deal gets people back to work and the markets to recover," responded Finkelman. "That's an awfully big reach, don't you think?"

"There is some conjecture, but these are extraordinary times," replied Yamanaka. "A lot has to happen to restore confidence in the system. That will likely begin with a single event."

"The Butterfly Effect?" asked Choy.

"Not exactly, something derivative," answered Yamanaka. "The Butterfly Effect most often begins randomly. It starts an unrelated chain of events with an event that cannot necessarily be traced. It is causal, but not proactive. What we need is a catalyst, a deliberate action that directs a specific chain of events to occur in sequence. Daniel and I were thinking since Atom Heart was the catalyst for the decline, perhaps it could be the catalyst for the recovery. The icon offers resonance as well as symmetry."

"Truly spiritual, Professor, but Sol Seidelmeyer resigned," asserted Finkelman. "How do you see Atom Heart moving forward to buy us when their CEO crashed and burned trying to make it happen? I'm not saying it's not worth discussing, to your point on having an open mind, but the physics factor there is wildly theoretical."

"I do appreciate your open-mindedness," said Yamanaka. "Even more so when I tell you what we really have in mind. Before the market crash there may have been a persuasive argument for Atom Heart to buy EnvisionInk, the combination of assets revealed potential merit and synergies. In terms of capital structure, that transaction could only have gone in one direction, but things are different now. Atom Heart has been knocked down harder than EnvisionInk on all multiples. EnvisionInk has leadership, the two of you are back at the helm. Atom Heart does not offer the same stability."

"You make it sound worse," responded Finkelman. "I don't see how any deal gets done that the shareholders would rally behind. What am I missing?"

"You are only seeing a linear equation, which is unlike you," replied Yamanaka. "Try reversing the variables. What if EnvisionInk bought Atom Heart?"

"A massive leveraged buy-out?" said Choy, only now

comprehending where the Socratic process had led them. Ya-manaka was proposing that Nemo swallow Jaws. Luckily they had not yet spilled the beans that their company would soon be worthless. "It's interesting," continued Choy.

"It's wacky," said Finkelman. "But it is interesting. The economics are crazy unbalanced. Do you think we could pull it off?"

"We do, or we wouldn't have floated it by you," said Ya-manaka, apparently not surprised by their receptiveness. "Og-den Feretti thinks his investment bank can put the financing together if we can reach agreement in principle on valuation with Atom Heart. He has a contract to represent them, which is binding beyond Seidelmeyer's tenure, so he is motivated. As you are too well aware, Bankers only get paid if there's a deal."

"Who makes the decision for Atom Heart?" asked Finkelman.

"Seidelmeyer is still much respected there," said Yamana-ka. "He is also a major shareholder. His entire life is tied up in that company. If, as a consultant, he takes it to their board — the board he created, person by person, all of whom have done well by their stock options — he can get it done. You sweeten the pot by allowing him to become non-executive chairman after the close. It would be a nice gesture that would cost you nothing, but it would mean the world to him."

"That would be one way to get rid of Steyer, if he comes back," said Choy. "The whole scenario sounds like Alice in Soft-wareland, but suppose it all fell into place. Suppose we made a deal to acquire Atom Heart, agreed on valuation, landed the debt instrument, and got Atom Heart and our shareholders to approve it. How is that a catalyst for a market recovery and handing a win to the Walkouts?"

"What's the one thing you hate most about mergers?" asked Yamanaka. "The one thing the Walkouts hate most as well?"

"Do it without layoffs?" posed Finkelman. "Is that even possible?"

"You're the co-CEOs, you call the shots," said Yamanaka.

"All you need is a compelling synergy story."

"If we attach the algorithm to their content, their traffic acquisition costs will drop across the board, so there's a lot of savings there," said Finkelman. Choy looked at him, reminding him that was temporary at best, if at all. "What's even more interesting is that if Atom Heart cuts a broader deal for sponsored search with improved revenue sharing, we don't necessarily need to apply the algorithm to every advertiser who wants to be associated with their content. Today we are not a content company, so the algorithm is to our advantage, but the day we become a content company, every ad dollar matters to us. We actually could benefit from the inefficiency we currently eliminate today for others."

"That's a little cynical, Stephen, don't you think?" asked Choy.

"Creative destruction, you know," replied Finkelman. "You roll with the punches. What mattered before may not matter in the future. The important thing is that we quickly reinvest the profits in innovation and come up with the next big thing before we lose our runway. We've been riding the elimination algorithm for a long time. We can up it, improve it, replace it. If we don't have to lay off anyone, we bulk up on pure R&D, become our own incubator, only with real deadlines. Monty would love the challenge."

"Your logic has never been sharper," proclaimed Yamanaka. "The announcement of the start-up EnvisionInk Systems acquiring the giant Atom Heart Entertainment without a reduction in workforce is precisely the kind of catalyst the market needs to spark it. If you issue the statement and your own people go back to work, the Walkouts will have reason to call it done. They may not have a bill of rights, but they'll have a success model for reference. At this point I don't think they are going to get much else."

"It feels slimy," said Finkelman. "Unfortunately, I don't think we have a choice."

"We don't have a choice," added Choy. "We really don't

have a choice."

"I can arrange for you to meet with Feretti and Seidelmeyer tomorrow," offered Yamanaka. "It has to be something you want to do. If you don't believe in it, you won't get it done, no matter how low the price."

"We don't have our plane, so they'll have to come to us," said Choy. "We need to be careful so the press doesn't see us together. Can we meet in your office at Stanford?"

"It shouldn't be a problem," said Yamanaka. "I'm guessing I can count on you to shower between now and then."

"We won't be able to sleep out tonight," said Finkelman. "We'll be crunching data ahead of the meeting. Yes, we'll remember to wear clean clothes. We appreciate the guidance, Professor."

"It's my pleasure, and my fiduciary duty," commented Yamanaka. "Thank you for the breakfast and the inspirational discussion. I hope the government authorities find themselves equally innovative in rescuing Daniel and Mr. Balthazer."

Yamanaka collected his utensils on the serving tray before him and pushed back his chair from the table. Choy and Finkelman did the same, but held themselves a moment in position.

"One more question, Professor," said Choy. "Why did you leak the Butterfly Effect video on YouTube?"

"I thought it would be a morale booster," said Yamanaka. "You were down, you needed to be up. I wanted you to know my assessment of your talent is unwavering."

"I don't think I buy that," said Choy, resuming an accusatory tone.

"Me either," said Finkelman. "You tagged it for the salacious. I think you did it to position us with the public as stronger than we seemed. Now it makes sense. You were accelerating the groundwork for us to go after this deal, even before you pitched us."

"You could only go after something like this if your confidence was at a peak," said Yamanaka, not getting any visual buy-in. "Perhaps a byproduct would be to seed its acceptance with any number of stakeholders. To me it's all the same. I said what I believed, and as a teacher, it felt right to share it. May I ask you a question in return?"

"Fire away," said Finkelman.

"Why didn't you tell me the algorithm was dead and you were ready to sell?"

Choy and Finkelman knew in that instant that Monty had come to him first. How else could he have known? How else could Monty have been able to position it with them? How else could he have spun a sell into a buy? They were even less convinced there was anyone they could trust, but then, they had put themselves in the same bucket—first shielding Yamanaka, then preparing to gloss over a few important details for Seidelmeyer. Feretti would trust them even less, but he was a Banker, which meant he didn't care. The only thing left to do was get the deal done without having to fire a single employee. They could not lie, but they had to make their way to a lightning fast close.

$ $

The temperature inside the parked 737 never got below eighty degrees at night, and by each afternoon it would climb to the mid-nineties. The only openings for ventilation were the front jet way door and the aft emergency door, both of which let tiny streams of air into the cabin, and neither of which, when open, anyone dared stand near for fear of trained sniper fire. Whoever decided to let the Swerlow party literally sweat it out had made either a very good or bad decision, depending on how it all ended. Swerlow and Kisinski wanted off the plane every bit as much as the others, but as they huddled in the forward office trying to figure out a plan, the incessant heat was having an undeniable impact on their thought process. There was no way it couldn't.

In the main cabin, Hussaini sat with Steyer and Balthazer, their shirt sleeves rolled up, their shoes off. Boredom had been introduced to the equation as a tactic, but it was everyone's boredom, it was a dangerous boredom where any breaking news could alter the mood in a millisecond. Hussaini assumed the role of chaperone, taking on ad hoc responsibility for keeping Balth-azer and Steyer from dismembering each other. The last thing Hussaini wanted to be was body guard to the detained, but with the risk of another clash ever looming, he had no choice but to position himself between them as a no man's land of the mo-notony. Once Balthazer sent his morning email each day, there was not much for him to do but check the latest postings on ThisIsRage.com, all of which had shifted to a decidedly sour tone since the swift massacre of the MBOR. Steyer checked the financial headlines from time to time, but he had even less to do to pass the hours other than watch the stock market sit at bot-tom, with virtually no movement and impossibly light trading volume. Hussaini remained, by edict, in a holding pattern—his job was to deflect, to keep everyone non-reactionary until ei-ther Swerlow and Kisinski came to their senses or a platoon of storm troopers hammered through the humidity and shredded the leather upholstery.

"You know the worst part of the market crash?" mumbled Steyer, gazing at his phone screen.

"You can't buy the Empire State Building and turn it into a personal condo with tax advantages?" snarled Balthazer. Hus-saini forced his brow to wrinkle, staring into his laptop, silently praying his wards could be of equal silence.

"It has nothing to do with me," replied Steyer. "I'm insti-tutional. I play with other people's money, and I can afford to hold. When the market comes back, we ride it up. The poor guys in retail are the ones who get killed, every time."

"You mean *if* the market comes back," said Balthazer.

"It always comes back," said Steyer with certainty. "Even af-ter the Depression it came back. Bear markets are when wealth is transferred to the rich in abundance. No one seems to get that. The guy who thinks he's going to retire on his 401k—the same guy who went to cash last week in the panic—he misses the re-bound. He never gets his savings back. No one taught him the game, so he loses every time."

"It's a lovely world you created," said Balthazer. "Democracy and free enterprise, precisely why General Washington let his men shed buckets of blood fighting the king's army."

Steyer rolled his eyes disparagingly and looked over to Hussaini for a sanity check. With no interest in taking sides, Hussaini remained purposefully focused on his computer screen and noticed a sudden refresh to his RSS feeds.

"Payne just released a statement," said Hussaini, reading from the angled LCD. "Tomorrow she's introducing legislation on the House floor that would allow every corporation in America to fire the Walkouts without obligation. No severance, no liability, blanket indemnification. That's bold, even for her."

"I guess in addition to forgetting about separation of church and state, she forgot about separation of powers," responded Balthazer. "She thinks she's Reagan reincarnated, or a substitute for the Supreme Court."

"If she gets a sweeping vote on her bill, she might be the next President Reagan," suggested Steyer.

"Right, like that bill is going to pass with tickertape bipartisan cheers on the first draft," said Balthazer. "She probably wrote it in longhand on a roll of paper towel. It will take a month just to fix the typos. With our dysfunctional Congress, they won't even get to a vote on it until everyone is back to work and the stock market hits a new historic high."

"She knows that," said Steyer. "Don't confuse her lack of textbook knowledge with a lack of street smarts. She knows what she's doing. It's storytelling, pure and simple."

"Steyer is right on that," added Hussaini. "She doesn't have to pass the bill to own it. She just has to have her name on it. If it works as a scare tactic and people go back to work, she wins, even if not a single one of her colleagues reads it. If her adversaries oppose it and issue their own statement, she looks like the leader since they are challenging her and at least she's put forth an idea. If there were a vote and it were defeated, she'd be set up as a sympathetic figure who tried to win in a losing environment. She wins on every outcome."

"And if she were to pass it, this year, next year, or any year, she probably could run for any office she wanted on national name recognition alone, which this will give her," commented Steyer. "She understands her job. She puts on a darn good show."

"Maybe I should consider Shanghai," said Balthazer. "A change of scenery might be good for me."

"As soon as we get off this plane, I will gladly back you in that move," offered Steyer. "You don't even need to pay me back. My firm will furnish you with an overseas studio, as long as you agree not to send the signal back across the Pacific."

"I'll discuss it with Producer Lee Creighton," said Balthazer. "We'll see how fast he can learn to build a website in Mandarin."

"Shanghainese," corrected Steyer. "We learned that before you joined the band."

"We need to figure out a way to help Swerlow make the right decision," said Hussaini, forever composed. "For the first time, I think our side is playing it right, waiting them out. He knows what has to happen. We have to make it easy for him."

"I don't see how that happens," said Steyer. "Swerlow is right, the deal your folks came back with isn't much of a deal. All it means is we don't get gunned down. What do they care?"

"Kisinski doesn't want anyone else to get hurt," said Hussaini. "I'm sure they're in there talking about it. The fact that they got any response at all is a good sign. We have to hope the waiting and Kisinski wear him down."

"For once I agree with Steyer," said Balthazer. "I don't see what's in it for Swerlow. Leniency? Maybe leniency? What happens when they're on the other side of that door? Do you really think Payne won't ride that pony until it drops flat on the trail?"

"There's no promise binding her," added Steyer. "Once they're in custody, it's over. They know that. So the three of us get to go back to normal — Swerlow gets to think about that in a solo cell every day for the rest of his life. He's not going there."

"We can't take that point of view or it's self-fulfilling," argued Hussaini. "We have to find a way to coax Swerlow to make the right decision. Balthazer, you know how to empathize with confused people who are down on their luck. Steyer, you craft impossible deals out of nothing, the higher the stress the better. Between the two of you this should be a milk run."

"Swerlow won't listen to me," said Balthazer. "He only yanked me on this plane to get me off the air. I did what you told me and tried to help him but it backfired. If I got gunned down that would probably be his favorite outcome."

"We share that as well," said Steyer. "Strange how much we have in common at the moment, given our differences in viewpoints."

"If you give up now, then you write your death certificates," continued Hussaini. "We have to try. We have to walk them down the aisle and to the door or no one gets a ticket home."

As if timed to Hussaini's guiding remark, the door to the front office opened. Swerlow and Kisinski emerged, looking even more haggard than they were before given zero air flow in the closed chamber. The jet way door was propped open just enough to let some new oxygen flow into the cabin, but not enough to see in or out. Given the clear shot daylight, they crawled past it, rightly expecting a zealous sharpshooter might be waiting.

"You're wrong about the ticket home, Special Agent Hussaini," announced Swerlow. "Sam and I have decided to let you go."

"Why is that?" asked Hussaini, completely caught off guard.

"We don't have to tell you why," ripped Swerlow. "Call your friends, tell them you're opening the door and walk out now, before we change our minds."

"Maybe you should change your minds," said Hussaini, squirming under the implications. "I think you need me here to bring this situation to its best resolution."

"I think we don't," countered Swerlow. "I think you're as much a part of the problem as anyone else. We trusted you. We let you have free access to negotiate and now we have nothing. We'll take our chances from here."

"If you have anything you want to take with you, get it

now," offered Kisinski. "This is a gesture of goodwill, like the pilots, but it's not optional. The four of us will take this to the finish line. We don't need you."

"We don't want you," emphasized Swerlow. "Call your pals and get off the plane, or I'll toss your body off the plane."

"You won't do that," said Hussaini with resolve. "You kill a federal agent, the lights go out before you reach for the switch."

"That's why you have to go," pressed Swerlow. "No one cares about them. Someone cares about you, for whatever reason. Please go."

Swerlow then glared without words at Balthazer and Steyer. Hussaini knew this did not bode well for them and surmised they did as well. If Swerlow wanted to free himself of the liability for killing an FBI agent, he could not be planning an ending in their best interest. Hussaini understood his exit was not up for further discussion, whether or not they were bluffing about shooting him, which it had become clear to him they were. It was not like Hussaini to leave a crisis in this state, but he had no choice. He made the phone call to the outside, made it clear that the door was opening and he was coming out safely. That could be considered progress, so he advised no further action, hoping they would listen as he headed down the aisle. There was nothing on the plane he wanted, no personal effects he needed beyond retrieving his worn shoes to exit. The closure he intended was beyond his will.

"Consider what I suggested," reiterated Hussaini, a gentleman's goodbye to Steyer and Balthazer. "You're smart guys. Talk to them. Help them make a good decision."

"We'll all have a nice chat after you're gone," concluded Swerlow. "Aloha."

Hussaini looked back at Balthazer and Steyer and quietly said, "I'm sorry." The words were barely audible, but they were heard, everyone knew what he meant. He had failed to disarm Swerlow when he had the chance, and he had failed to negotiate their surrender on the runway. He was a career desk jockey, no matter what he had been prior. Leaving them alone with

Swerlow was nothing positive, it simply cleared the deck for Swerlow to do whatever he next had in mind, however unstable.

Hussaini advanced to the jet way door, slowly pushed it open and showed that his hands were empty. He stepped onto the air stairs with summoned care, one stride at a time. At the top of the air stairs were a pair of model military police with weapons drawn. Below him were at least fifty more, all in the same ready state. They could see Hussaini's report was consistent. He was alone, he was safe, and he was the only one coming out. He closed the door behind him and descended to the tarmac. As his weary feet hit the runway, it hit him that he had achieved the impossible. He had escaped, free, alive. His knees began to buckle, but a hefty guard nearby grabbed him before he collapsed to the concrete. Hussaini knew that his work was excusably unfinished. He would soon be going home to his family, which was all he had wanted since his first day on this miserable, warped, outrageous assignment. Now he wanted something else.

$ $ $ $

3.6
There's a Reason for Out of Town Tryouts

There was no email Thursday morning from Balthazer to his readership. There was also no statement to the press that Special Agent in Charge Hussaini had been released from the plane, mostly because there had never been any public statement that he was on the plane. Swerlow and Kisinski seemed to have decided that Balthazer's outside communication was no longer useful to them. Quite the contrary, Balthazer and Steyer had both been completely cut off from the Internet synchronous with the release of Hussaini. At the same time, government control of the runway standoff had adopted an equivalent posture of silence, with no journalists allowed beyond the base gate. The crime scene in Hawaii bad been blanketed in obscurity precisely as it reached its final chapter. Global digital communication had to be fed or the rumor mill took over, and the feeding tube had been pulled from Hickam.

Balthazer had made a promise to be back on the air Monday morning if he could. He had also warned his listeners that if his communication were suddenly shut down, they should think the worst. This fueled an ominous flow of gossip among the five million Walkouts, not to mention everyone else who was checking ThisIsRage.com for official updates, of which there were none other than Producer Lee Creighton continuously advising site visitors to stay patient and not think the worst. Producer Lee Creighton was ill-quipped to be on his own, but that's where he was. Emails, texts, posts, and phone calls flowed to him endlessly—speculation and hyperbole badgering him for response—but he was aware that one wrong retort could turn the peaceful protest into something much worse, so he restrained himself and sat out the dance, awaiting further word from the tarmac.

Lack of communiqué from Balthazer gave pause to Choy
and Finkelman, who for the past seven hours since mid-morn-
ing had been locked behind closed doors in the Stanford office
of Professor Yamanaka, who was voluntarily not in attendance.
Backing up Choy and Finkelman were Counselor Normandy
and CFO Basru, sitting across from former Atom Heart Entertainment CEO Sol Seidelmeyer and his investment Banker,
Ogden Feretti. In an attempt to show strength, the EnvisionInk
team had elected not to bring along a Banker, thinking instead
if they could construct a high-level deal that would largely be
acceptable to Atom Heart, the details could be worked out over
the weekend in a marathon negotiating session that would yield
a preliminary public announcement first thing Monday morning. It was not lost on Choy and Finkelman that Feretti was
the Senior Managing Partner at Dardley Scott Silverman, who
had lost employee Charles McFrank the day of their original
capture at Steyer's home. Everyone present had been advised
via a call from Hussaini that he had been kicked off the plane,
but he offered no speculation as to what Swerlow and Kisinski
next had in mind. Hussaini agreed that a cordial deal between
EnvisionInk and Atom Heart to merge without staff reductions
might provide a path to ending the Walkout, but it did nothing
to help solve the problem of how to get Steyer and Balthazer off
the plane and Swerlow and Kisinski to take the surrender deal.
It was also no secret the stalemate in Honolulu was likely to be
resolved one way or another before any announcement would
materialize from the calculating minds currently gathered at the
illustrious Stanford Graduate School of Business.

This was not only the first time Choy and Finkelman had
met Seidelmeyer, it was the first time they had met anybody
like Seidelmeyer. Their world was filled with passive-aggressive
sharpshooters like Ogden Feretti, and they knew not to listen to
a single word that came out of his mouth, he was simply there
so that Seidelmeyer looked less alone. Steely cold Investor types
like Daniel Steyer were as common in their Silicon Valley circle
as non-conversant engineers auctioning off their own mercenary

services without saying more than a few sentences in the entire course of a salary hijacking. Choy and Finkelman were equally cognizant that, other than an occasional summer job lifeguarding at a community pool or tutoring rich kids after school to bump up their SAT scores, neither of them ever had a real job. Not having a real job meant never having a real boss, and if they would have had a boss, it would have been someone like one of them, or even someone like Steyer. They understood Normandy and Basru, their style was understated and peninsula cynical, but it was seldom dramatic and words were kept sparse.

What was curious about Seidelmeyer was that even in a room of four on two, even though he had no official title, even though he had resigned in disgrace, he was certain he was in control—and by the very virtue of thinking he was in control, he was de facto in control. He said three words for everyone else's one. If an anecdote were to be told, Seidelmeyer would tell it. When awkward silence would ensue, Seidelmeyer could be counted on to break it. When food and drink menus were slipped under the door—which had happened twice for early lunch and dinner—Seidelmeyer took it upon himself to order for everyone. The remains of those feasts were now decaying around them in the form of half empty bottles and soggy cardboard containers, since Yamanaka's office door had not been open for more than a minute to let provisions arrive without allocated attention to let the dregs escape.

"You really need to explain to me more convincingly why I should let you steal my company," proclaimed Seidelmeyer, predictable in that he had said this at least a dozen times and each time their ability to respond was less imaginative. "I know you engineer types are excellent with mathematics, much better than I ever will be, but I do know the difference between a tiny pail of coins and big bucket of dollars. How can I take the pail when I am worth the bucket?"

"I think what Sol is saying is that he just wants you to be fair," interjected Feretti, discarding the last few bites of an egg and cheese burrito that stopped being desirable an hour ago.

"We are not looking to gouge. We understand the circumstances, but face value is not something we can sell when we take this back to his board."

"You keep referring to Atom Heart Entertainment as *your* company," stated Finkelman, looking Seidelmeyer in the eye. "I am having a hard time with that. You don't really work there anymore. The company is owned by its shareholders."

"You put in as many backbreaking hours as I have, you get a movie nominated for the Best Picture Oscar fifteen out of the last seventeen years, you program a television network seven days a week, and then bundle the sale with a basic cable lineup you built to ninety million households from zilch, zippo, nada — that's *your* company. You don't need an office. You don't need a title. It's *your* blood in the chemicals they use to develop the film, even when we stopped using film, it's still in there. We were going to buy you, remember? And the price I offered was fair."

"But it was rejected," said Choy. "Stephen and I weren't here to receive the offer, so no, we don't remember. Fair is a moving target. Now we are here, now we can discuss fair."

Seidelmeyer poured the melted ice in his cup into another empty cup, then poured it back into the first cup. Basru shrugged. Normandy did not look up from her laptop. Everyone in the room knew a deal needed to happen, and everyone in the room wanted a deal to happen, but all of them had been to this meeting before in various guises. All negotiations ultimately came down to valuation, or in layman's terms, price. The public markets currently valued EnvisionInk at $17.5 billion, down an astonishing 71% from its recent run up to a new historical high, but more distressingly, off more than 50% from its pre-abduction yearlong stable run rate. That meant ENVN was trading at just less than three times annual sales volume, and about eleven times earnings — not a bad picture for a dividend bearing value play from the Old World, but that was not the way any Investor wanted to think about EnvisionInk. Atom Heart had lost 55% of its pre-crisis value, descending to a market cap of $27 billion, much less than one time annual sales and under seven times earnings, making it a virtual steal if it could be acquired outright for anywhere near that price, which was certainly not what Sol Seidelmeyer had in mind.

There was just one problem in the divide between what Seidelmeyer wanted and what Choy and Finkelman could pay—it was going to be a stretch for EnvisionInk to acquire a company worth one and a half times its own current value even without a premium, as any debt issuer would ultimately cap EnvisionInk's debt load at some reasonable level to assure interest payments and secure the asset. Even if they issued a substantial amount of dilutive stock and only took on debt for about half the price, interest on a $13 billion note would easily cost the new entity well over $1 billion per year in payments, wiping out most of EnvisionInk's current annual profit before consolidating Atom Heart. EnvisionInk had amassed over $6 billion in cash, a helpful chunk of change shimmering on its balance sheet that made a deal at par creatively doable, but not much more. That had been the subject of a circular argument for most of the day.

"We seem to be stuck on price," acknowledged Feretti. "Why don't we try a different topic for a while and then come back to price."

"What other topic is there?" posed Basru.

"He's right," said Normandy. "Once we agree on price, the lawyers and IBs can take it the rest of the way. We've already agreed on management. Choy and Finkelman stay as co-CEOs. Mr. Steyer exits. Mr. Seidelmeyer becomes chairman of the board."

"Terribly gracious of you," chided Seidelmeyer. "The depth of our management bench will reassure our joined shareholders that the company is in superb hands for the foreseeable future."

"You can keep Sanjay and me or not, that's a nit," returned Normandy. "We both have contracts with concise change of control provisions. We can be liquidated without controversy if that is desired."

"You'll find that I accept liquidity graciously, but first we need to agree that the only price we can pay is your current market value," said Basru. "There is still a lot of risk that we can take on that much debt."

"There's very little risk," countered Feretti. "The book value of Atom Heart is greater than its market value. If an enterprise lender had to foreclose, the sell-off value of the individual components of Atom Heart would easily retire the principal. The same can't be said for EnvisionInk. Your primary assets are millions of lines of program code that could be antiquated at any time. Your break-up value is almost impossible to quantify. The risk our shareholders are taking is substantially greater than the risk yours are taking. We are taking your virtual assets and exchanging them for physical inventories of proven substance. Don't blame the lending platform. You're being unreasonable."

"Then why are you here?" asked Choy directly.

"Out of respect for my friend Daniel Steyer, who suggested we meet," said Seidelmeyer, heating up. "His life is on the line. He asked me to meet. I'm here."

"He asked you to take this meeting?" queried Finkelman.

"It doesn't matter who asked who, who mailed the invitation and who broke the sealing wax," argued Seidelmeyer. "We're here. We might as well get a deal done."

"Again, I suggest we try another thread instead of price, to cool off for a bit," reiterated Feretti.

"What else would you like to talk about?" asked Choy.

"How about this mishegas about no layoffs?" asked Seidelmeyer. "That's what's holding back our discussion. You can't pay the increased interest on more debt because you won't let go of staff. That's holding back my price and that's plainly wrong."

"That's the very reason for our discussion," countered Choy. "You say you're here out of respect for Steyer. We appreciate that—we applaud that—but we really don't have to do this deal. We don't have to do this deal, you don't have to do this deal. This deal is 100% fully optional. If you don't like the price, and you want us to pay a bigger price and fund it through layoffs, let's call it a day and go back to what we were doing."

"Nothing gets fixed in the status quo," said Seidelmeyer.

"We're here for the national good, to give people hope that business will resume as normal and give the stock market a little defibrillator zap."

"Exactly, which is why we can't have layoffs," said Finkelman. "That's the story the Walkouts need to hear—deals can be done without killing jobs."

"But they can't," challenged Feretti. "You may be idealistic, but you don't believe that. When you're co-CEOs of the sprawling NewCo, if you miss earnings, what are you going to do—say how nice it is that everyone still can eat for free in the cafeteria? Any way you look at it, you lose control in this merger. You're going to have a whole bunch of new shareholders, and our shareholders aren't as Zen as yours. They don't forgive. You miss, you're compost."

"Reason again for them not to do the deal," commented Normandy. "Are you Hollywood gents trying to get to yes or no?"

"We're trying to help the nation," asserted Seidelmeyer. "We're trying to inspire confidence and jumpstart securities trading."

"You're trying to create a new role for yourself," snapped Basru, the words leaping from his mouth unchecked.

"Another putz," stung Seidelmeyer. "What is with this Silicon Valley crowd? You don't laugh and you don't help. You just want to be right."

"I apologize," said Basru. "That was out of line. I do that sometimes."

"No, you said what was on your mind, and it was largely correct," asserted Seidelmeyer. "It just wasn't very funny. Or helpful. Let's go back to something we all understand: valuation."

"Don't look at us," said Choy to Feretti. "He's the one who brought up price."

"I know, I understand," said Feretti. "What you have to appreciate is that our shareholders are entitled to a premium, some offset for staying with us. Risk premium is what drives Investors, at least smart Investors. Most of these civilians who jumped out of the market are going to get killed when the market recovers, but for the ones who stayed with us, they have to get something, just like the ones who stayed with you. If there's no risk premium, why assume risk? Risk is the basis of all investment, however misunderstood by the public. Think of all the money that's incinerated in the market. It's not gone, it just shifts owners. Then those who have balls and cash scoop up the wreckage and watch it blossom. For the institutions who hang on, the winners have to pay for the losers. In this crash there's been a lot of losers. Together we can be the first recovering winner, but you have to give us something. You have to work with us."

"You're giving us a lecture on economics—to get us to pay more to make a point?" asked Normandy. "I've heard a lot of sob story Banker pitches before, but pay more to prove the textbook case that risk is warranted by exemplified return, that line is Hail Mary Hall of Fame."

"And not going to work, however true it may be," said Finkelman. "Well played though."

"Yes, excellent volley," said Choy. "We'll have that framed for Yamanaka's office as a memento, Risk Commands Reward, Thus Spake Feretti. We'll make bumper stickers."

The dialogue continued for another two hours without progress. Then another three, which included a third catered meal, takeout line caught sushi and no-cheese organic shiitake mushroom pizza, again selected by Seidelmeyer. Yamanaka dropped by around 9:00 p.m. to see if they were nearing agreement. EnvisionInk was still proposing to acquire Atom Heart at par. Seidelmeyer was sticking to his script, demanding a sweetener. They had reached resolution on no layoffs, which Seidelmeyer knew was a deal-breaker for Choy and Finkelman. Seidelmeyer also knew Choy and Finkelman understood with a merger of this scale, their personal stakes would be diminished to minority positions. If they missed future earnings they could be fired, but the initial deal announcement had to be without layoffs or they would never get their own employees back to work. If Choy and Finkelman could simply get their employees back on the job, there was a decent chance the nation would follow. Seidelmeyer was clear if Choy and Finkelman failed to find revenue synergies after the merger and their new amalgamation of shareholders revolted, they would take the hook when it came and let new management implement staff reductions, but that was not going to happen on their watch or in their world view. Even so, Seidelmeyer sensed something unbalanced. The notion of increased leverage was unnaturally troubling to Choy and Finkelman, who by now should have been able to come forward with some movement above par. They were too focused on keeping profits whole, too pedestrian in their vantage point, too firm in deflecting risk. Steadfast was one thing, timid was another. They talked a good game around transparency, but Seidelmeyer saw anything but all their cards on the table. The less they spoke, the more he suspected something was wrong.

$ $

As most of the Stanford campus retreated for the night, Yamanaka suggested before departing that Choy and Finkelman continue their short break to touch base with Monty Dadashian, who had been pacing for hours in the well-tended courtyard of the business school. Choy and Finkelman had once again been so distracted that they had missed a full day's worth of their CIO's calls, emails, and texts. They asked to be excused briefly and met Monty outside under a clear starlit sky.

"If I'm going to stay with you, we need some kind of system so when I want to be in touch with you, you pay attention," griped Dadashian. "I won't abuse the privilege."

"We're sorry," said Choy, almost convincingly. "What have you got?"

"What have I got?" echoed Dadashian. "What have you got?"

"I can tell you what we don't got," answered Finkelman. "We don't got a yes."

"Valuation?" asked Dadashian.

"What else?" said Choy.

"Maybe I can help," offered Dadashian. "What kind of forecast are you giving them?"

"Conservative," said Choy. "We're saying five to seven percent annual sales growth with no meaningful impact to margin."

"Steyer has taught you to lie like pros," remarked Dadashian. "You've ascended to Olympus, thatched thrones and scepters."

"Don't call us out," jabbed Finkelman. "What you showed us is early, unsubstantiated, and immaterial to disclosure. We don't have to introduce it to discussion because it's still mostly conjecture and hasn't been reviewed by the board."

"Counselor Normandy script that bit for you?" asked Dadashian.

"What if she did?" asked Finkelman. "We're a management team. We rely on each other's expertise."

"What if this member of the management team told you that you could increase your revenue and profits before they declined?" proposed Dadashian.

"It would mean we could tell Seidelmeyer there was more reason to take our offer at par," noted Choy. "The NewCo would be even more profitable than we anticipated, so when the market recovered, his shares would be tied to ours and yanked north. It would be a deal he could sell to his board."

"What's the magic?" asked Finkelman. "Did you fix the algorithm?"

"Sort of, but better," said Dadashian. "But I want three things first."

"You're negotiating in the middle of battle?" asked Finkelman. "With us?"

"Someone has to teach you," said Dadashian.

"Spill," said Choy.

"First, whenever I send you a note with a red exclamation point on it, you promise to respond promptly. Second, you agree to spend at least two out of five days each week out of your offices, one with the engineering team, one with the sales and marketing team, so you always know what's going on in our company. Third, I want CTO."

"Wow, going for the title jugular, are you, Monty?" said Finkelman. "Didn't think that was your style."

"It's not, but I need to give the CIO title to someone else, to get him to bail from the search engine team that has our code," said Dadashian. "He hates it there much more than he hated it here. He wants to come back if the place is more like it used to be."

"You found the renegades that flipped on us?" said Choy.

"Yeah, I ran a bunch of queries on the Merger Bill of Rights section of ThisIsRage.com. Figured out the common themes, the IPs of their origin, sent a blind inquiry and our own former guys ponied up that no grass is green, it's all brown, but at least our brown grass wasn't sprayed with toxic piss. They said if we wanted them back, no questions asked or prosecution, they were up for it. Now the good part?"

"You just saved the company, there's more good part?" asked Finkelman.

"Yeah, while we were figuring out the damage, we discovered that with what we know about the keywords you don't want to buy, we can launch our own competitive search engine with the keywords you do want to buy, at a discount. It's the same relevancy database. We didn't even know we built it, a mountain range of historical data — Big Big Big Data — only our auction doesn't have to be blind. We can let people see the prices of the competitive bids in real time because it's a secondary business to our core. Dual revenue streams, total transparency."

"They'll sue us," said Finkelman. "It will be a steel cage death match if we bring back that team and launch our own keyword ad platform. San Jose will have to build a new courthouse to house all the lawyers."

"Right, like we can't sue them back for doing the same thing?" parried Dadashian. "Come on, you're CEOs, get tough. You point grenade launchers at each other's head, no one pulls the pin."

"Plus we'd enter the search market with less than 1% market share, hardly a threat to Entrenched dominance," said Choy. "We'd be favored by a jury, an underdog gasping for breath. Hell of a bonfire story for Burning Man."

"We'll also be the company that ended the Walkout and got

the trading floors lit up again," added Finkelman. "Hard to believe if we did go to war, the Justice Department would let us go under. We'd be the remedy to future antitrust."

"Think about the upside on the Atom Heart deal," said Dadashian. "If we put our own branded search box on every one of their zillions of pages of bozo content and sell the keywords at half the market rate, all that inventory is ours at no acquisition cost. It's monster, might pay for the deal in a few years just on CPC."

"You want to start a price war in search?" asked Choy.

"No, I want to start a transparency war in search, where our search engine reveals the auction and our efficiency algorithm continues to protect clients in the blind auction," said Dadashian. "I'd call it leveling the playing field with real competition. Toss in Seidelmeyer's content library, we might be the next you know who."

"Monty, I have not yet fully conferred with my partner, but I'm guessing if all this goes as described your three conditions can be met," said Finkelman. "We need to get back to our negotiation and show them some new numbers."

"I'd say we have our first CTO," said Choy. "Go get that team back, before some rich retiree backs them in their own start-up."

Choy and Finkelman high fived Dadashian and headed back up the stairs to the awaiting Seidelmeyer and Feretti. Their ace in the hole now was that they truly did not need to do the deal, their company was protected. The merger would be a matter of the public good, a deal with unlimited upside for all who came onboard on their terms. If that did not work for Seidelmeyer, he could go back to what he was doing, which was nothing. If he wanted to join the future and help lead the team through reinvention, he would be welcomed to the team — he would just need to tell a few less stories when he was outside Los Angeles. Almost impossibly, technically miraculously, they had discovered an honest way to get to yes.

$ $

The Honorable Sally Payne knew it was time to go national or draw the curtain. There was no longer a middle ground. She was either going to ride the Walkout resolution to eminence or go down in flames as a martyr for capitalism. She knew where that was likely to come out—there was only upside in getting the Payne Economic Safety Act to the House floor with the biggest splash imaginable. It did not matter that it was unlikely to survive committee review in anything close to its initial fourteen pages of slop. What mattered to her was that it was widely known that it existed because she caused it to exist—that she had acted with urgency in response to the crisis at hand, and that she got legislative credit for offering a farsighted resolution. Attempted definitive action of any kind could always be touted as leadership.

There was one key point Payne wanted emblazoned in the national consciousness: any corporation was free to fire a Walkout immediately without Recourse, Retribution, or Remedy. Those were her carefully constructed keywords: Employees at Will can be Fired at Will. Companies should feel free to Fire at Will, without Recourse, without Retribution, and without Remedy. Whatever final form the bill would take in a vote, those words needed to survive, if not in law, then in people's minds. Win or lose, Fire at Will would make Payne a household name.

Payne pondered the best way to get out the word. It was a nonconventional statement that required non-conventional visibility. A press release would get lost in the noise with all the other congressional press releases, no one read them other than Think Tank Watchdogs and no one in the public much cared. She had just given a press conference, so giving another so soon on such a similar topic might seem gratuitous, plus that last one had not gone so well. With five million Walkouts freely roaming the grand electorate, she could no longer predict who might show up in a crowd attempting to steal her Soap Box. She could count on C-SPAN video coverage and reposting the announcement online from the House Floor, but that would draw fewer plays than the average squirrel missing a tree-to-tree branch leap. National broadcast news was only a small step up from C-SPAN and probably would not touch the story until the full bill came out of committee, and cable news was too divisive and partisan for as polarizing a figure as she had become. She was looking to broaden her public appeal, not fix her visage in caricature.

The more Payne mulled it over, the more she knew she needed a big idea, and the more she needed a big idea, the more all other ideas seemed trite. Then she came upon it—out of the box, unconventional, not what anyone would be expecting, the perfect tactic to make it known that she was at the forefront of civil resolution to the unnatural matter of people voluntarily leaving corporations in the lurch. If only she could remember the name of that fellow who worked with Balthazer, the unkempt producer guy who was always there. No matter how she tried, she could not recall his name, so she asked someone on her staff to track him down and get him on the phone, which was easy enough given that ThisIsRage.com was currently the number one vertical internet property in the nation.

"Please hold for Congresswoman Sally Payne," said the flat female voice of one of Payne's amorphous assistants into the VOIP line linked to Producer Lee Creighton. The congresswoman's research team had traced Creighton to a makeshift office he had been loaned by a satellite retransmission outpost in Los Angeles. Payne listened in the background, her bear trap being plied into readiness.

"I can hardly contain my patriotism," answered Producer Lee Creighton on the other end of the call. Payne reveled hearing his muffled sardonic voice, likely obstructed by a cheap computer microphone. His arrogance would be his undoing in too few milliseconds.

"You're the fellow who helps with the Kimo Balthazer show, correct?" followed the voice of Representative Payne.

"I am, this is Lee Creighton. We have met. I produce *This Is Rage*, which is currently not on the air due to an illegal abduction you helped facilitate."

"I don't remember it that way, but I'm glad we found you," replied Payne. "I have a proposition for you."

"You're not my type," said Creighton. Damn, he was the unwashed.

"You are so clever," said Payne. "It is a business proposition. It goes like this. I have recorded a brief video announcement of a piece of legislation I plan to introduce on the House Floor tomorrow. It's called the Payne Economic Safety Act. I would like to upload that video immediately after midnight and provide a single link to it from ThisIsRage.com. Does that sound like something your audience would find compelling?"

"Is this the one where you tell all the corporations they can fire the Walkouts and not owe them a dime?" asked Creighton.

"It is precisely," replied Payne. "I would like to offer you an exclusive."

"Why would I want that, and why would you want it on our site?" asked Creighton, mockingly dismissive, but as she anticipated, not hanging up on her.

"Where better?" asked Payne. "The visitors to your site are the target audience. I want word of this out before I appear on the House Floor. I'm comfortable with controversy. I can't imagine a better way to share my message."

"I don't know, Congresswoman, it feels awkward to me," said Creighton. Payne knew she had him, that this clever geek thought he could get the better of her, but he would play her to get something in return.

"You can't possibly be that gutless," continued Payne. "You're in the entertainment business. I'm in the information business. They are two sides of a coin. We both have the same interest, drawing attention. Balthazer would want you to post it."

"I think I have the tiniest bit more insight into what Kimo might want," responded Creighton. "Insulting me is not an optimal strategy to help you get your way."

"Yes, got it, you don't want to be told you're a coward," said Payne. "How about this for an incentive—you upload the video,

I'll give you my commitment that no one will seek legal action against Balthazer for any past crimes if he lives, carte blanche."

"You've got that pull at the FCC?" asked Creighton.

"I do, and I will give it to you in an email, so if I break my word, you can forward the email to the *New York Times* and let them use it to roast my goose."

"Give me the email and the video and you have a deal," confirmed Creighton, almost too matter of fact. Payne wondered for an apprehensive moment why he was so easily compliant, then shrugged it off. She had what she had called for and her plan was what mattered.

"Be prompt, 12:01 a.m., the video contains the words 'Today I will introduce a critical bill . . .' and it needs to be one hundred percent truthful," said Payne. "Look for the email and the video coming your way shortly from my office. Good doing business with you, Mr. . . . ?"

"It doesn't matter, you won't remember," said Creighton, killing the VOIP line without another word.

Payne never liked to be the one who did not end the call, but this time she could live with it. She was satisfied. All that she had envisioned was tracking to her advantage.

$ $

Ten minutes later, Producer Lee Creighton received the promised email with video attachment, not from one of Payne's nameless entourage but from the congresswoman herself. She was serious about making the point that if he posted the video as directed, Kimo would be off the hook for any and all crimes he did or did not commit. There was no confusion in the email, no mincing of words, no game playing. Hers was a promise that Balthazer was irrefutably returned to free speech status if he found his way off that plane. If for any reason he did face charges, a release of her email would inarguably indict the congresswoman for asserting a level of authority she never had. Producer Lee Creighton felt very good about the deal, tremendously good about the email, and ecstatic about the video clip which he reviewed immediately. When he launched the video

player, there she was behind her enormous oak desk, family por-
traits on the credenza, American flags capped with gold eagle
clusters and yellow fringe in the background. If she were audi-
tioning to play the role of President in the Oval Office on the
cold open of *Saturday Night Live*, she could not have built a more
perfect set. Her delivery was straight off the teleprompter, eyes
to the camera, as commanding an image as she could portray.
She delivered the micro address with metronome rhythm:

"Friends, many of you outside the State of Montana may
not know me. My Name is Sally Payne. I am a seven-term member of the United States House of Representatives, and current
Chair of the House Committee on Education and the Workforce. Today I will introduce a critical bill on the House Floor
which you will be hearing much about. It is called the Economic
Safety Act. There are two key drivers behind this bill, which
I am hopeful will soon become law. First, the Economic Safety Act provides vital and necessary protection for corporations
across the nation, regardless of their business enterprise, in a
much needed time of public market turmoil. These corporations
need our help, our trust, and our support. If our corporations
cannot function, our economy cannot function, which means
our families cannot function. That would be in no one's interest,
and it would be ethically, as well as morally, wrong. Second,
the millions of misguided employees who have voluntarily left
their jobs in the so called Walkout Movement need an incentive
to return to work immediately, and the Economic Safety Act
provides such motivation. In briefest description, the Economic
Safety Act is not a new law, it is reinforcement of existing law. It
reiterates the fundamental notion of Employment at Will. Unless an employee has a formal contract with explicit stipulations
to the contrary, or is represented by a legally recognized collective bargaining agreement, employment in our great nation
is in most cases known as Employment at Will. That means an
employee may freely depart a job without explanation any time
he or she chooses, and an employer has the same freedom to
sever that employment without any obligations other than those

which an employee has accrued at the time of separation. The Economic Safety Act makes it absolutely clear that any employee who has joined the Walkout of his or her free will may immediately and without further benefit or reward be terminated by his or her employer, as I believe is already the case under the law. An employer must be able to Fire at Will, without Recourse, without Retribution, and without Remedy. This lets our corporations conduct business as usual, replace someone who does not want to work with someone who does, and return their businesses to prosperity so that our equity markets can return to prosperity. The Walkouts have been warned repeatedly, and even as some of them may have opportunity to view this brief video statement by virtue of its thoughtful online distribution, they may return to work immediately and face no retribution. My hope is that even before this bill becomes a law, the Walkout will have ended by exercise of goodwill and common sense. In the event that it does not, I want to be on record having given my promise to the great corporations upon which our democracy and freedom depend that if they need to move forward, they can, and they will be safe from frivolous legal action or costly penalty. As I said, you will be hearing a good deal more about the specific provisions of the Payne Economic Safety Act soon enough, but I wanted you to hear it from me first, and to know that I am putting my record and reputation on the line for this bill as necessary to restore the wellness of our great nation. An employer simply must maintain the Constitutional Right to Fire at Will, without Recourse, without Retribution, and without Remedy. Thank you, God Bless You, God Bless our way of life and all the bloodshed for which individuals have suffered in the name of free capitalism, and may God Bless the United States of America."

Producer Lee Creighton wondered how many times she had rehearsed it, how many takes she recorded to get it done without a single stammer. He could not have been happier with her performance. He teed up the video to execute on ThisIsRage.

com exactly at 12:01 a.m. per their agreement. That clip had the power to blow the roof off the site and launch the URL into legend. There was no way he was not going to deliver his end of the bargain.

$ $ $ $

3.7
Milestones Make the Wicked Cry

If there were a political award for fastest ever moving on-line stump video, the Honorable Sally Payne would have just claimed it with a self-purchased bouquet of roses. Between midnight and breakfast on the East Coast, her video on ThisIsRage.com had been viewed 2.7 million times, which in total volume would have exceeded the entire *This Is Rage* email list, over half the national Walkouts, or some combination of individual contacts plus forwarding. By California breakfast time, the video had seen more than 6 million global plays. A viral tsunami had been her goal, and with this breaking wave she could put a check mark in that box. The extreme of heightened fury it created among the disenchanted—to a lesser degree incorporated in her expectation—only mildly surprised her, accompanied, as she intended, by the polarizing support that chimed in. She had skillfully vexed her opponents, while fully rallying her base. There was no more dialogue, no discussion, no conversation to be had, just entrenching venom.

The last thing Payne wanted to do now—if keeping all her limbs was of importance—was make an appearance in any parking lot. Walkouts to date across the nation had embraced no-violence-allowable almost as religion, but with her fighting words, restraint teetered on combustion. Obscenities shouted across the line became the day's norm. Increased police coverage shifted to high alert. She had purposefully made the simmering teapot unstable. The lid might blow without warning, triggering riot response, possibly even National Guard.

This she deemed success.

$ $

Balthazer and Steyer had no idea the Payne video existed, let alone that it had been posted on ThisIsRage.com. They had been cut off from the outside world ever since Hussaini was excused from the sunbaked aircraft. The two remaining captives were sitting alone in the sweltering main living area shortly after mid-Pacific sunrise, half a liter of pineapple juice in a cardboard container left to share, with Swerlow and Kisinski sequestered again in the forward office. Balthazer suspected they would not be left alone long. Steyer was equally apprehensive. There was little to say, yet so much they needed to exchange to plot an exit. They needed a bridge between them, a path to trust, fast agreement that would go unnoticed. Neither wanted to talk, but continued separation was a worse choice, foolish to the point of life-threatening.

"How did you get the name Kimo?" asked Steyer with authentic curiosity, seemingly out of nowhere.

"What makes you ask?" replied Balthazer, unsure of Steyer's purpose, but glad to be communicating.

"I don't know, too much time sitting around, I was just thinking about it," said Steyer. "We're in Hawaii. If memory serves, it's a Hawaiian name. I didn't get the sense that you're Hawaiian."

"I'm from Ohio," said Balthazer, more open than usual. "My given name is James, same as my father's. When I was a kid we used to watch the original *Five-0* together, black and white when it started. In one of the episodes we found out that Kimo is the Hawaiian version of our name, so he just started calling me that. It stuck, kept it cleaner for people to call him Jim and me Kimo. When he was gone, I hung onto it. Neither one of us ever made it to Hawaii, until now, if you call it that."

"I'm sorry about your father," said Steyer. "When did you lose him?"

"It doesn't matter," answered Balthazer. "Too long ago."

"Me, too," said Steyer. "We have that in common. Hard to keep going without him."

"Looks like you did okay," responded Balthazer. "I got by.

Mostly I got lucky."

"Both of us," said Steyer. "My father worked much harder than I did. I worked hard, but a lot broke right for me. I didn't realize most of that at the time, probably took more credit than was coming to me."

"Sure," said Balthazer, lowering his voice to a near whisper. "So how do we get a little luck to break our way now? We don't have a lot of time left."

"Luck won't do it," noted Steyer, also taking down the volume in grim hope that Swerlow and Kisinski would not hear them. "We're going to have to take him down, catch him off guard. No choice, we have to get the gun."

"I'm game," said Balthazer. "He won't be expecting it after so much obedience. What do we have to lose?"

"Absolutely nothing," said Steyer. "You want to make the move or should I?"

"I'm younger and don't have a broken jaw," said Balthazer. "I'm guessing it should be me."

"I won't be far behind you," said Steyer. "Go for his gun hand, I'll try to pin it with you against the wall. Best thing that can happen, if the gun goes off, the guys on the runway will be through the door in seconds."

"As long as a bullet doesn't bounce off the frame into one of our heads," said Balthazer.

"That's where luck will be helpful," replied Steyer with a small smile. "If it looks like we're losing the gun, I'll go for Kisinski and put him between us and Swerlow, to slow things down. Let's hope it doesn't play out that way. No way to predict Swerlow at that point."

They were quiet after that, staring out the window portals at the armed militia on standby all around the plane. The cabin stunk, the air was foul and none of their clothes had escaped the drench of sweat. Humidity had been unkind, draining them of will, but not entirely. They had eaten bits of this or that, but they were hungry. They had been provided plenty of water, but they did not have the energy to drink enough so they were dehydrated. It was Friday. No one expected the standoff to go into another weekend. With Hussaini off the plane, the base police had to be planning to board. What Swerlow and Kisinski were planning was still a mystery, perhaps even to them. As they emerged from the office, Swerlow with the gun glued to his hand, Balthazer's eyes were fixed on the handle of the pistol. He did not want to know what Swerlow had in mind. He just wanted to get his hands on that weapon and tear it away from the dunderhead. He wanted to snap the punk's wrist, pull his elbow from the joint, do whatever he needed to disarm their assailant and get on with his life, his show, his rebound. He would get a chance, but no practice run.

"Last milestone, we're late on final deliverables," declared Swerlow. "Here's the drill: We're going to form a bundle and walk out together. I'm going to put a rope around us. We become a single object, or target, however you look at it."

"You think you're just going to walk off a US Air Force Base?" asked Steyer, astounded again by Swerlow's delirium. "You're not thinking straight."

"They'll put you down like a rabid dog," added Balthazer. "They don't care about us anymore, just you."

"I don't think so," argued Swerlow. "They can't take a shot if you're in the pack. They won't do it."

"You think we're going to follow you off the base?" asked Balthazer, eyes widening under the sweat.

"I do," declared Swerlow. "You'll do what I tell you to do, like you have since the beginning."

"You overstate your authority," advised Balthazer, reaching for the remaining pineapple juice in the half empty carton, entirely nonchalant. "I'm done. Pull the trigger."

"Please don't push Dennis to be combative," enjoined Kisinski. "Just because he hasn't doesn't mean he won't."

"He can or he can't," said Balthazer, pouring himself a paper cup of juice and taking a sip, further to his posture of indifference. "I don't care. I'm not walking off this plane onto a runway surrounded by semiautomatic rifles and machine guns. You have nowhere to go, so we end it here. Daniel?"

"Agreed, you have one gun, they have a lot more, chances are better in here," said Steyer. "Balthazer's right, you've overstayed your welcome. All they need to do is hear a shot and the sides of this can peel open."

"You walk with us off this plane or we're all dead," demanded Swerlow

"Fine, get it over with," goaded Balthazer. "If we're not going to make it to the beach, put us in a box."

"You're reading the end game wrong," threatened Swerlow. "This is not a joke."

"You're right," countered Balthazer, blissfully deadpan. "I do the jokes."

Without further telegraphing, Balthazer hurled the remaining juice in his cup and the container into Swerlow's eyes. Swerlow had not been expecting it and was instantly distracted by the acid hit, enough impact for Balthazer to a land a hand on his wrist, immediately below the gun handle. Balthazer bent back Swerlow's wrist, and thrusting his arm forward was able to pin the barrel against the fuselage wall. Swerlow recovered quickly and tightly maintained his grip on the handle, steadying his feet and holding his weight against Balthazer's advance.

"You want us all to be dead, asshole?" bellowed Swerlow.

Steyer followed Balthazer's lead and dove against Swerlow on the wall, but Kisinski plunged onto Steyer's shoulders and held him partially back. Balthazer pried back Swerlow's wrist, but Swerlow shifted his arm to relieve the pressure and maneuvered the gun only inches from Balthazer's chin. Steyer briefly shook off Kisinski and crawled forward with him in tow, Kisinski now latching his arms around Swerlow's knees, keeping him from nearing Swerlow's wrist to help unhinge his grip. Kisinski grabbed a laptop from the coffee table and used it to pound on Steyer's shins, separating Steyer from the struggle with Swerlow. Having broken the screen from the laptop in a second blow to Steyer's torso, Kisinski sloppily wrestled Steyer to the floor.

"You want it to end, we can end it," hollered Swerlow,

straining to shake Balthazer's fingers from the stuffed trigger mechanism, where Balthazer had worked his own fingers to keep Swerlow from taking a shot.

"Let go of the gun," fumed Balthazer, pushing upward on Swerlow's wrist above a closed window portal, cutting open Swerlow's forearm against the window shade handle. Balthazer saw Swerlow's blood in his palm, struggling to release the pressure of his own fingers being crushed in the trigger.

"You will not walk off the plane without us," yelled Swerlow, using his alternate hand to pull Balthazer's cramped index finger from the trigger mechanism—even more painful for Balthazer, with no way to stop it but to let go, which he would not.

Steyer grabbed the broken laptop console from Kisinski and threw it to the rear of the plane, out of reach, then pulled himself to his feet and moved toward Swerlow again. Kisinski grabbed Steyer again by his feet and brought his broken jaw to the floor, a perfect infliction of pain that slowed Steyer but did not stop him.

"Keep Steyer away from me, Sam," roared Swerlow, attempting in the reverse direction to twist himself free of Balthazer. "I'm going to shoot this fat ass loudmouth and then I'll take out Steyer."

"You've got nothing, you can't pull the trigger," barked Balthazer. "I'll break your fingers off one at a time if I have to."

"This is over," yelled Swerlow, unable to get any leverage on the trigger, fighting to keep his wrist from breaking. "One way or another, this is over."

Steyer fought the pain numbing his face, rolled over and kicked Kisinski in the chest, jolting himself free to join Balthazer. Kisinski fell back into the main cabin area, hitting his head on the edge of the coffee table as Steyer's hands finally joined Balthazer's on Swerlow's wrist. Kisinski regained his balance and sprung back at Steyer, easing Steyer's weight from Swerlow's grip. Swerlow's arm rebounded on reflex and the pistol handle hit Balthazer in the nose, knocking the wind out of him and forcing him backward. Steyer saw that Balthazer had lost his hold on Swerlow, whose arm and trigger finger were free. Summoning all his final strength, Steyer yanked Balthazer behind Kisinski, the two them deftly holding Kisinski in front of them in the direct line of Swerlow's fire. Swerlow regained his balance, but he had no clear shot at Balthazer or Steyer with his cousin sandwiched between them.

"Let go of Sam!" ordered Swerlow. "I'm not giving you an option."

Balthazer and Steyer stood frozen, Kisinski wedged in an arm lock in front of them. They were not taking orders. They were not going to move.

"It's your option," said Balthazer. "Maybe you hit us, maybe not. You want to shoot your cousin, do what you need to do."

Swerlow was stuck, seething, drained. He had no more options. He could fire a shot and take his chances, but he knew he was no marksman. If the weapon kicked even slightly and altered the trajectory, it was more likely Sam would fall than they would.

"Dennis, listen to me, this is not just about what happens to you, it is about what happens to your cousin," pleaded Steyer.

"You have nothing to say, Steyer," heaved Swerlow. "Sam is in this with me."

"If you pull that trigger, even if you drop me and Balthazer, this plane is going to be flooded by the guys outside," replied Steyer. "Don't take your cousin's life. Whether you shoot him or not, if you pull that trigger he's dead. Both of you will be dead. You don't have to be."

"What happens to me happens to Sam," rejoined Swerlow, his voice rising with his temper. "Balthazer and you mean nothing to us. You're both useless, no-value parasites. Corporate criminals."

"Don't blow this, you came a long way to get here," coaxed Balthazer. "You had a following. You got credit for the Walkout. Don't end it like this."

"Let go of my cousin or I'll kill all of you," shouted Swerlow, no logic remaining in his access. "I'm not negotiating."

"We're not negotiating either," replied Steyer. "Put down the gun and we all walk out together."

"I'm not going to rot in a federal prison," declared Swerlow. "That's not going to happen."

"The only way we walk off this plane is together, no ropes, no bundles, just single file down the ramp," said Steyer, who then unexpectedly turned to Balthazer. "Kimo, can you please take Sam and step toward the door while I wrap this up with Dennis."

"Are you nuts?" asked Balthazer. "That's not the best idea I've heard today."

"I want us to show Dennis we don't want his cousin hurt," expressed Steyer. "Take him aside, away from the gun."

"Really?" asked Balthazer, entirely baffled, the script missing pages in his mind. "We never talked about this part."

Steyer nodded confidently. Balthazer looked at Steyer again to be sure this was what he wanted, then took Kisinski by the arm and led him out of the line of fire, toward the front exit, door to the stairs outside. Swerlow was left with a clean shot at Steyer if he wanted it. All he had to do was pull the trigger.

"Don't go anywhere, do not leave this aircraft!" commanded Swerlow, his extended arms showing signs of convulsion, his rage so overwhelming he could barely steady the gun.

"Gentlemen?" nodded Steyer, motioning for them to continue down the aisle toward the jet way exit, further isolating himself in juxtaposition to Swerlow.

Swerlow was sweating heavily again, through his armpits and down the back of his shirt. He did not know what to believe. He was working it forward and backward in his head. What was his best outcome? What was the best outcome for his cousin? How in a few blinks had he lost control after so many moves in his favor? Balthazer held Kisinski in front of him, no shot there. Swerlow looked away from Steyer and made direct eye contact with his cousin, the gun line moving from Steyer to the obstructed Balthazer, then back to the unprotected Steyer.

"Dennis, is this how you want to be remembered?" asked

Steyer, his usual stoicism tempered by true humility.

Swerlow looked hard into Steyer's eyes, considered the question in its fullest, then responded with surreal hallow: "Yes, this is how I want to be remembered, the guy who put down Voldemort, the programmer who killed Daniel Steyer."

Swerlow pulled the trigger. Steyer braced. Balthazer dropped to the floor with Kisinski short of the cabin exit.

Click. No bang.

Swerlow squinted, direly confused. He pulled the trigger again.

Another click. No bullets.

In a debilitating moment of clarity, Swerlow knew what had happened. So did Steyer and Balthazer. Cousin Sam had emptied the chamber, who knows how long ago.

Swerlow dropped the useless weapon to the floor, fell to his knees and began to weep. Kisinski did not move, barely breathed. Steyer moved toward Swerlow, followed without prompting by Balthazer, who reached for the gun and checked the chamber. Sure enough, it was empty.

"How did you know?" asked Balthazer, hardly believing they were all still alive.

"I didn't," replied Steyer. "I thought he'd come to his senses. I bet it wrong. Kisinski bet it right."

"Sam, you didn't trust me?" cried Swerlow, almost pitiable, turning to Steyer and Balthazer. "You owe him. He saved your lives. I would have killed you both. I still would."

Steyer and Balthazer sensed closure, a moment they had earned but that could not be properly explained. After weeks of failed mouse traps and misplayed calculations, interference and interruptions and doubt, they had forced the hand of their adversary to let emotion create a mistake. It had not played out the way they predicted, but they had made it to the finish line. For Steyer and Balthazer it would finally be over. For Swerlow and Kisinski, not so much. Steyer retrieved his smart phone from the forward office and texted Hussaini, who was inside the adjacent terminal. Everyone was safe, alive, and about to deplane—an unconditional, non-controversial surrender. The FBI would be happy, the base commander would be happy, the EnvisionInk board would be happy, even Congresswoman Payne would be happy. Steyer let Hussaini know it would be extremely helpful if everyone readily armed outside could be advised to hold their fire when the jet way door opened. Hussaini agreed that made very good sense.

$ $

The Four Seasons Silicon Valley—erected in unapologetic postmodern massing—was without peer in Palo Alto. Conveniently located overlooking torturously jammed Highway 101, its grandiose glass edifice was about the most conspicuous place a high tech company could select on the West Coast to hold an important meeting. To the contrary, if you wanted to feed the rumor mill, nothing beat a cross-company mixer in the lobby bar.

As the commission-hungry Bankers and staggeringly high-priced attorneys for both EnvisionInk Systems and Atom Heart Entertainment poured past the hotel's registration desk, the MoneyPalooza festivities were already leaking real-time to the parking lots of the peninsula, fueling especially feverish buzz a half hour south on El Camino Real in the heart of Santa Clara. EnvisionInk Walkouts and on the job non-Walkouts found themselves with little else to talk about when a digital photo of Choy and Finkelman sitting at a patio lunch table with Sol Seidelmeyer hit the web. It was perfectly staged. No one had to explain a thing.

Arrival time of the executive parade had been carefully coordinated with hotel check-in not to be allowed before 1:00 p.m. Pacific Time, when domestic trading desks closed on the East Coast for the weekend. Although the market remained at bottom without any significant volume, a gathering like this with the market open easily could have ignited frenzy, and that was not meant by anyone on the inside to occur until market open Monday morning. This would be a traditional weekend marathon session, also known as a Death March, intended to produce a signed letter of intent that looked a lot like a contract and an *Associated Press* release before the 11:00 p.m. news in New York on Sunday night. Since everyone involved knew—wink wink—secrecy was off the table, the notion that a deal might not get done had been tossed to the wind. A deal was getting done, the people who mattered had already shaken hands, making the weekend meeting an exercise in drafting and show. Interviews would not be entertained, exclusive or otherwise, embargoed or not, until the press release was posted. Regal high drama was joyously desired.

Sol Seidelmeyer had experienced a lightning bolt to the head when Choy and Finkelman walked him through the math of what a single percentage point of market share could be worth launching their own proprietary keyword advertising system and competitive search engine. Choy and Finkelman had no delusions they could emerge out of the box as a significant player in search, but since they would get the system largely for free as a byproduct of their advertising efficiency algorithm and have zero costs of distribution across all of Atom Heart's content pages on every emerging digital platform available, every dollar of this would be unexpected upside to the equation—hundreds of millions of dollars of profits just by joining forces, without cost cutting, without optimizing or syndicating the system to other content properties in search of an alternative to the status quo. Seidelmeyer may not have understood technology, but he surely understood advertising, the need for viable alternatives to customers in any ecosystem, and the scaling power of very small numbers multiplied by extremely large audiences. All of this would be incalculable exponential growth for the combined entity, and there was nothing standing in their way except excellence in execution. It was the kind of innovation that would restart the mind turbines at EnvisionInk, a competitive rallying cry for the industry, a healthy battle that needed to be fought and would be welcomed by employees who would be proudly redeployed rather than redirected to log-on at Employment Development. With that much opportunity in the headlights, Seidelmeyer came to see "par" not only as a fair price for his former company, he would have sold it for less to get this deal done were that all he had been offered. Choy and Finkelman knew enough to be fair, they wanted the deal to sail through shareholder approval. The minute the deal was announced their stocks would adjust and trade in lockstep, richly rewarding all shareholders for their reasonable approach. No stranger to embracing luck, the gambler Seidelmeyer was most of all delighted he could return to his beloved office with a new role, helping create the future, a forward-looking icon of the old guard reborn for new wars. Not surprisingly, his framed poster collection had remained firmly fixed on the walls.

Even EnvisionInk's Eeyore poster boy, Sanjay Basru, bought into the plan. The newly incentivized CFO was stationed in a well-appointed marble suite with extra power supplies and a salivating team of Wharton MBAs banging out a monster forecast they could drop on the Street Monday morning, without one sharp pencil hitting the line item called Staff Expenses. Sylvia Normandy was certain a shock and awe lawsuit would follow the returning engineering team to EnvisionInk, and she welcomed it as a liberating mission. Outside counsel told her the cost to defend would be immense, but the attendant public relations would only draw attention to the EnvisionInk brand and help the new venture grow swiftly. Ironically, the bigger the law suit, the bigger the noise factor, and all of that would populate every search engine database and index on the planet, with endless links pointing customers back to the EnvisionInk brand. She knew they would ultimately prevail in court—any well-versed plaintiff was likely to know that as well, no matter how pressured they would feel to file offense as defense action— and the lawsuit would pay for itself in traffic gains and market share shifts driven alone by visibility.

As Seidelmeyer sat with Choy and Finkelman, lunching on the veranda and watching their troops assemble for the treaty conference, there was only one thing left for them to do to ensure the proper care and feeding of the rumor mill. The deal would get done, but the employees had to know they were safe before it was announced or the Walkout would remain an obstacle. With Payne's thundering missive, Walkout tension urgently needed to be diffused. Seidelmeyer was on his mobile, finishing up a call that would make for an even more satisfying weekend.

"We can still make deadline for the weekend edition of the *Journal*," said Seidelmeyer. "I bought a full page ad, which will run in the morning print edition, and as a value-add they threw in online banner links to a destination page on their site beginning this afternoon as soon as we get them the copy. The Atom Heart creative department has the layout ready, single sheet of letterhead, no logos, a facsimile memo waiting for text. We upload it, it will be everywhere in an hour."

"You're so wired, Sol," acknowledged Choy. "You're a class act for the digerati."

"We learn from each other," said Seidelmeyer. "Maybe I can take you clothes shopping. My guy in Beverly Hills does magic with gabardine at seriously fair prices. You software people dress worse than screenwriters. That takes trying."

"Let me read you back the latest draft," chuckled Finkelman, editing a word processing document on his laptop between nibbles of artisan focaccia bread:

> We have seen the video statement released early today by the Honorable Sally Payne. We find it objectionable, naïve, built upon a poorly constructed argument, detrimental to a positive outcome for our economy, disrespectful of individuals, not helpful to corporations, and in exceptionally poor taste. The congresswoman from Montana would seem to be suggesting that certain employee rights gained admirably over time were unjustly granted, and that is not at all true.
>
> We are not experts in jurisprudence, nor would we wish to test the legal and potentially Constitutional challenges she invokes, but suffice it to say that a mass dismissal of employees in

the current environment would not only be impractical in achieving the success of a shared agenda, it would in no way provide the type of relief suggested by her offering. In short, were companies to take her seriously, in our opinion things would get worse, not better. Much worse.

We wish that Representative Payne had sought counsel from leaders like ourselves before inserting herself in the matter of resolving a complex matter of employee relations. We are particularly troubled by the notion that the pernicious and severe resolution she suggests could transpire without Recourse, Retribution, or Remedy. This is senseless. We do not see our employees as adversaries. We see them as individuals with families, and dreams, and a voice — a voice we need to hear, the expression of which is the backbone of our nation. Those who have voluntarily suspended their employment have clearly done so for a reason, and we would do well to incorporate their frustration and honesty into our future planning. We certainly cannot speak for others, but we want everyone to know that we are listening and considering our future actions carefully. We want an end to the Walkout that works for everyone, and we believe that can be possible. Shared interests and shared prosperity are both desirable and achievable if approached with the same kind of innovation and creativity that have led our industries forward, not in spite of employees, but because of them.

We write and pay for the publication of this letter not as executives, not as company officials, but as individuals. We understand matters of enterprise, and we care deeply about employees. The two points of view should not be mutually exclusive. We hope others in the business community will share our point of view and refute the notions suggested by Congresswoman Payne. Her point of view is wrong for free enterprise, and wrong for America.

Trust your employees. They will surprise you.

Yours respectfully,
Calvin Choy
Stephen J. Finkelman
Solomon Edward Seidelmeyer

P.S. If you share the point of view expressed here, please visit ThisIsRage.com and add your name to the petition we have begun under the tab labeled: "Representative Payne — Please Resign."

Finkelman looked up from the screen, not seeking credit since the words were their collaboration, but in search of consensus. He took a breath, as did the others.

"I wouldn't change a word," said Seidelmeyer.

"Me either," said Choy. "That tells everyone who needs to know where we stand."

"I'm sure she won't like it," said Finkelman, saving the draft with a pull down menu.

"Last chance?"

None of them said a word, they all just grinned. Finkelman shrugged and hit the send button. As he did, he and Choy simultaneously heard the ding of an arriving text message on their smart phones. Steyer was back online.

$ $ $ $

3.8
Penance, Pity, or Pizzazz: Pick a Path

Special Agent Hussaini was waiting at the foot of the air stairs on the Hickam tarmac, surrounded by a steady supporting cast of military police, all weapons off safety in the ready position. He had wanted to board the plane and supervise stabilization of the crime scene as soon as he received word from Steyer that Swerlow had been disarmed, but Steyer had convinced him that would be counterproductive to a gentle surrender. He and Balthazer would escort Swerlow and Kisinski through the aircraft door, down the ramp, and into custody. No more poking was necessary. The time for composure had come.

As Hussaini stood near the locked-down business jet in the refracting afternoon sun, he kept playing back in his head everything that had gone wrong over the past few weeks, all the things he had done wrong. He was glad this mishandled incident was over, but not at all pleased with himself. It was painful to admit, but he just did not have the physical acumen or raw confidence any longer for field work. He had become a mouse pad and lumbar support guy, he knew that. He had tried to push himself past that when he was on the plane, when he tried to catch Swerlow off guard and take the pistol from him. He had tried to summon conviction within himself, but despite his best intentions, his attack had embarrassingly failed. He had hoped for another window of opportunity to prove himself, but when Swerlow dismissed him from the aircraft, he became a footnote in the case resolution file. He had expected more from himself than anyone else had, but in failing to bring the crisis to a close, he had been unable to shake off the inward critique. What he had been in the past was no longer what he was. His career was by no means over, but his self-worth had deteriorated to the incomplete. No one had called his competence or bravery into question, but his own vote on that count would haunt him for all his days going forward, planted until retirement in front of a computer screen. He would have to come to terms with that before he returned home, which would be soon.

The jet way portal door opened slowly from within, sadly anticlimactic, neither a rock star arrival nor salute to a head of state. It was quiet, so quiet, a strict measure of law, and order, and structure. Heat radiated from the sprawling concrete runway, the background frame just enough of a postcard to remind those in attendance this was Oahu, Honolulu, Hawaii, flavored by the grey material of martial decor. The first to emerge was Balthazer. He stepped out on the landing, looked down the stairs, saw Hussaini below him and waved feebly. Balthazer took in the blazing sun, looked around him, then back into the aircraft where Swerlow was standing directly behind him. He was nervous, not so much about exiting, but trying to imagine what awaited him in a world of normalcy, whatever that might mean for a last-gen talk show host with this too-strange tale to tell. Balthazer wished he did not have to say a word, that he could return to *This Is Rage* and never talk about any of this again, but that was a fantasy his listeners would never allow. He was going to be bigger than ever, yet at the same time, he felt insignificant, lucky to be alive but unlucky to have so many damaging ideas flooding his thinking. It was weird to be free, weird to be back, just weird—and it would be that weird, or worse, as far into the future as he could imagine.

"All good?" called out Hussaini, a perfunctory remark, but he had to say something to reassure those around him, managing through the intangible tension.

"Another berry-ripe day in paradise," spoke Balthazer, giving Hussaini the sign of thumbs sideways, then molding it into the local sign of cool, adding his pinky for a shaka.

"We're ready, bring them down," instructed Hussaini, intense but guarded, focused on the outcome, relieved that no media was present. The last thing Hussaini wanted to do at this moment was confront a journalist. He had nothing to say.

Balthazer took a step down the ramp, followed by Swer-low, with Kisinski behind him, and Steyer at the rear. It was a slow procession, as Swerlow and Kisinski looked around and internalized how much attention they had drawn. With a single firearm and no prior criminal experience, they had held Choy and Finkelman, then taken their private jet, then added Steyer, then journeyed halfway across the Pacific Ocean and swapped the co-CEOs for Balthazer. Now they were surrounded by more firepower than existed in all the gang war B-movies they had ever seen. In a strange way, they believed they had almost pulled it off, almost made it to Shanghai, almost had their own high-tech company financed by two fanboy idols of the NASDAQ. Yet as they looked around them, they knew that was delusional. They had never been in control. They were never going to pull this off. Every cakewalk opportunity to contain them along the way may have been muffed, but since the spectacle began back at Steyer's home when they put a wayward round into Finkel-man's leg and accidentally killed the Banker McFrank, not one additional individual had been seriously harmed. Sure they had done some minor damage to Hussaini, the guy at the foot of the stairs who had betrayed them, but betraying them was Hus-saini's job. They had lost. Hussaini was there to arrest them, just as they often imagined he would be.

Halfway down the stairs, Swerlow paused behind Balthaz-er, his footing on the steel mesh slightly off balance, the sweat still flowing from his pores, made wetter by the ceaseless sun. He had not slipped. He was simply out of step with the others, his eyes still watering, no swagger left to display. He turned to his cousin behind him, who almost bumped into him, not ex-pecting the hesitation.

"I'm not angry with you," said Swerlow.

"I know that," replied Kisinski.

"You really didn't have to do that, except you did," contin-ued Swerlow, a word at a time. "That's just you. Your mom got that right."

"Guys, keep moving," nudged Steyer from behind. Baltha-zer had not noticed they stopped, but paused and turned a few stairs below them when he heard Steyer's voice.

"Let's go," reinforced Balthazer, only a few steps from Hus-saini on the tarmac.

"We had a good run," said Swerlow hazily to his cousin. "Not quite an exit, but a damn good run."

"So go the odds," replied Kisinski. "Most things fail. All you can do is your best—learn what you can as you go, try to do better."

"You learned something," echoed Swerlow. "We both did."

Balthazer motioned with his hands in a scoop for Swerlow to keep moving. Swerlow reached for Balthazer's hands, as if to reassure him he was complying, then without warning grabbed Balthazer's fingers, pulled the radio jock toward him and thrust his head into Balthazer's chest. Balthazer was knocked off balance and the two of them collapsed on the ramp, Swerlow atop his enemy. The pair rolled down the incline to the tarmac, bumping along the remaining stairs, wrestling and clawing in the worst amateur fashion, violently intertwined in a body bun-dle. Kisinski attempted to follow them down the stairs, but Steyer grabbed him instantly with both hands and held him back.

"You're worse than Steyer," murmured Swerlow, his loath-ing uncontainable, his tackle on Balthazer ruthlessly effective. "I wasn't sure, but now I am."

"You're a freak con man," yelled Balthazer, pinned on the ground under Swerlow.

A shot rang out from the nearest rifleman without any or-der given, the conditional approval prewired by decision tree, the brief sound of gunfire echoing off the aircraft's steel frame. Swerlow was hit, not seriously, a flesh wound to his left arm. Unfazed, Swerlow locked himself around Balthazer's portly middle and continued to pound on him, using his other arm to beat him with the remaining bits of energy he had left.

"They have you at close range," blasted Balthazer, strug-gling futilely to free himself. "Let go of me before they dust you."

"I'm not going to prison," howled Swerlow. "I've been clear about that."

A second fired shot followed, an awful burst piercing their pointless argument. Unclear as to whether it was milliseconds before or after the blast, Hussaini instinctively dove onto Balthazer, wrenching him away from Swerlow's clumsy grip, rolling with him to the side and out of the range of fire. The bullet missed Balthazer's neck by inches and landed on Swerlow's upper chest, peculiarly not enough to take him down, but enough to splatter blood onto the faces of Balthazer and Hussaini. Swerlow did not waver and lunged again at Balthazer and Hussaini beside him. The third shot fired connected again with Swerlow, this time straight into his throat, ripping open his neckline. That one ended it, a fatal overlay. Swerlow had accomplished his final goal.

Steyer walked Kisinski down the remaining few stairs to the soiled tarmac, where the body of his cousin was shredded and inert. Kisinski bent on one knee, to look at Swerlow again, to accept the closure he had known would come.

"He told you what was going to happen," said Kisinski, letting go a tear. "He was honest about that."

Hussaini checked to see that Balthazer was okay, noting the thick blood on his own hands. This was not Swerlow's blood, not from the splatter. It was his own. He looked down and saw that he had been hit. The second bullet—the one that had been fired so close to Balthazer—had been deflected before striking Swerlow, tearing a clean tunnel through Hussaini's midsection. Hussaini felt the blow now, there was no slug in him, just a powerful in and out puncture. Hussaini reached for his side, acknowledged the dull pain, then looked closely at Balthazer with concern.

"Damn you, Hussaini, what's in your head . . .?" began Balthazer.

Hussaini paused, looked at his wound, took a breath. "Did you hear about EnvisionInk and Atom Heart?" asked Hussaini, paying no mind to his injury.

"What are you talking about?" asked Balthazer, noting where the bullet had struck Hussaini, that it would have been a direct angle on his lungs if Hussaini had not intercepted it. "For god's sake, are you okay?"

"Berry-ripe perfect," proclaimed Hussaini. "And there's a pretty decent rumor going around that EnvisionInk and Atom Heart are going to merge, one hundred percent friendly."

"I'm sure there's someone on the planet who cares," said Balthazer, tipping his head toward Steyer who still had control of Kisinski. "I don't own stocks."

Hussaini rose to his feet without complaint and proceeded immediately to Kisinski, binding him in handcuffs. Balthazer was winded, even more exhausted than he had been ten minutes ago, but he was unharmed. He looked at Steyer standing above him, creating a shadow over the corpse of Swerlow. Balthazer did not have to say a word. Hussaini had been there when he needed him. Steyer knew that too. Hussaini had not flinched. His head was never out of the game.

"Let's get this cleaned up," said Hussaini to the nearby MPs. He barely acknowledged the medical attendants rushing to his aid, wrapping his torso in gauze to stop the bleeding as he advanced with his perp, fully focused on completing the arrest. "I'll take care of Kisinski, mostly paperwork at this point. I'm known to be good at that."

Steyer reached down to give Balthazer a hand, pulling Balthazer to his feet as the armed militia dissipated and a retrieval team appeared from the terminal, attending to Swerlow's body. Steyer and Balthazer looked back at the aircraft, again at the body of Swerlow, then watched as Hussaini walked the shackled Kisinski into the terminal.

"What do you think happens to him?" asked Steyer.

"He goes back to his desk, only he feels a little better about it," answered Balthazer, checking his arms for bruises. "He'll sew up nicely, only feel the damage on really cold days."

"I meant the kid, Kisinski. He's why we're alive."

"Maybe," said Balthazer. "We had something to do with it.

Maybe he'll teach computers in prison, someday get another chance."

"I could make a call or two on his behalf," said Steyer. "The leniency game isn't obvious, but it can be nudged from the inside if you have long term friends. My board is good that way, plus I always keep a favor in reserve."

"Choy sort of backed up their story on McFrank, no one's completely sure who pulled that trigger," added Balthazer. "I'm sure you know the right people to help open their hearts."

"I also think he might have something to trade for a deal," said Steyer. "I heard them talking one night about some guy named Howzer who originally put them up to it, to coming after me. You were in the back, we were being separated. Maybe if he helps the FBI find Howzer we can soften the blow."

"Howzer?" remarked Balthazer. "You're kidding, right?"

"You know Howzer?"

"Of course I don't know him, but way back a guy named Howzer called the show," coughed up Balthazer. "We screened it. He claimed Ben and Jerry were numbskulls he goofed on Craig's List. Said he was an unemployed coder, lived in his parent's basement and occasionally posted anonymous kidnapping offers to amuse himself, to see if anyone was stupid enough to go for it. Ben and Jerry exceeded his expectations."

"Why the hell didn't you run it?" asked Steyer, again taken aback by Balthazer's mind.

"No credibility," answered Balthazer. "Plus we were on a roll, didn't want the audience to think our bad guys were worse losers than they already seemed. Take away the threat, take away the story. Sin Number One: bad radio."

"I'll see what I can do to get Kisinski another chance," concluded Steyer.

"Another chance would be good," echoed Balthazer.

Steyer knew he was making the right decision. No one had really called for his capture, it had all spun out of a bad, thin idea. He had seen that before, the unwinding of cross purpose and too clever response never quite like this, but not entirely different. Fools who wanted something responding to fools who claimed it was not theirs to have, rinse and repeat. He looked toward the ocean, then far down the tarmac. The cycle was ever familiar, the draw of winning a haze, the sine curve of the hero's journey perpetual.

"You know, I used to like Hawaii," mused Steyer. "Private jets, too."

"First time for me, for both," said Balthazer. "I can live without them."

"Make a good episode for *Five-0*, don't you think, Kimo?"

"What do you think about your Atom Heart deal?" asked Balthazer.

"No more deals," said Steyer. "Can't go there right now."

"They did it without you," said Balthazer. "You taught them something."

"It's a hell of a rumor," said Steyer, trying to regain his poker face. "I better text Choy and Finkelman."

Balthazer smiled, a real smile. Steyer sent his text. They followed Hussaini into the terminal, no final look back at the blistering aircraft behind them. Inside a staff medic approached Balthazer and Steyer with genuine concern, asked if they were okay, if they needed anything. They didn't need anything, just a ride home, the next flight out. Coach would be fine.

$ $

The feisty line of reporters outside Representative Payne's decorative chambers in the Longworth Congressional Office Building spilled into the main hallway, down the corridor, and past the elevators. Security tried to corral them, but it was futile. The noise was incessant and disruptive to everyone on her floor, but such was freedom of the press, blood sport in the nation's capital. Rumor had it when security was fond of an office's inhabitant, they were much better at steering and directing. When they were less enamored, they only pretended to be helpful. The journalist mob coming for Payne experienced minimal resistance. She was under media assault.

"Congresswoman Payne, have you seen the online ads

purchased by Choy, Finkelman, and Seidelmeyer?" bellowed one reporter, shouting through the door, on the other side of which was Payne, unable to restrain herself from responding.

"They're *Wall Street Journal* ads, are they not?" responded Payne with unbridled irritation.

"They are," asserted the reporter without qualification, pounding on the suite door. "And your comment is?"

"You work for the *Journal*, do you not?" barked Payne. "It's a conflict of interest for you to even be here. No comment. No comment at all."

Several of Payne's aides squeezed their way through the cracked-open doorway into the corridor and tried to push the assemblage away from the office suite, but their visitors were pushing back hard. Another set of aides guided Payne to her inner office, separating her from the temptation to shout further vapid response from their lobby, trying to get everyone to stop yelling through the door. Payne's switchboard was lit up like a candelabrum, even the dusty fax machine was churning print-outs overtime. Everyone wanted a statement from Payne. Had she overplayed her hand? Did she wish she could recall the video, which had already surpassed thirty million global streams? Was her reputation for overreaching beyond repair? Had she heard from the head of her party or any other CEOs? How did she feel about the next election?

Payne slammed the interior door of her private sanctum, grabbed her land line and speed dialed Sol Seidelmeyer on his mobile. When Caller ID told him who it was, Seidelmeyer stepped out of the common area of his suite where he had been huddled with his negotiating team, taking the call in his exquisitely appointed Four Seasons signature bathroom. When he spoke from the tiled enclosure, he tried hard not to create an echo that she should hear, but she could.

"Do you want your campaign contribution back?" thrust Payne, grasping for a way to open the conversation.

"Did I make a contribution to your campaign?" asked Seidelmeyer in his best George Carlin invocation. "My wife usually handles that sort of thing."

"What in Satan's calling did I do to incur your wrath?" fumed Payne. "I was on your side. We were teammates. What kind of backstabbing reality show is this?"

"No wrath, I'm not even angry with you, not personally. You simply crossed the line, Congresswoman. Someone had to call you on it."

"Someone, sure, that was the whole point of posting it on Balthazer's Socialist website," blasted Payne. "But not you, Sol. It was not meant for CEOs to turn on me. It was meant to make a point to those who don't matter, not people like you who do — or used to."

"I think you need to start there," replied Seidelmeyer. "You have some gnarly nineteenth century issues to resolve."

"I was with you every step of the way. I was hand walking you through regulatory approval. Who's going to do that now, Sol?"

"Not exactly sure what you're talking about," replied Seidelmeyer. "Do you know something that hasn't been announced to the rest of the world?"

"Right, like you and those two geek kids aren't making a deal right now. They're probably in the room with you laughing at me."

"I can assure you they are not in this room," asserted Seidelmeyer, examining the high-finish water fixtures. "Should there be a deal to be made, you will hear of it in good time, and it will go through normal channels of government approval. Were the commencement of that process to be announced under the proper circumstances, many insiders believe a fair sampling of the Walkouts might even begin returning to work."

"This is a crap fest, Sol. Your banner ads haven't been up two hours and already there are a million signatures asking me to resign. There aren't even a million voters in Montana. The people signing that petition don't even know what Interstate connects Montana."

"The *Journal*'s weekend edition has a nice layout coming

Saturday morning, as well. You may want to have someone on your staff reserve a copy, they could sell out. Decent price for the full pager, considering the online value-add. Or maybe the print was value-add with the online buy, I get confused these days. Anyway, the petition will definitely benefit."

"Did you really have to humiliate me just to make this deal fly?" whined Payne.

"Madam Congresswoman, you wrote, produced, directed, and starred in your own video epic. I was one of many social media reviewers. I hardly think I ruined you, but you flatter me suggesting my opinion could carry such authority. I don't think you'll have to resign, but I would think hard about running for future office. Like the old moguls used to say, I don't think you'll work in that town again. My sense is you could do quite well in the private sector, make some real money instead of hosting all those fundraisers. If you need a reference, let me know. I know a lot of people."

Seidelmeyer clicked off the phone. He looked into the giant gold-framed bathroom mirror, saw the thick lines under his dark eyes, pushed back his thin hair and washed his hands. More than two thousand miles away, on the opposite coast, the Honorable Sally Payne slammed down the receiver. She could feel the crowd pouring into the waiting area outside with only a few inches of molded door between them, question after question, request after request. She remembered that her communications director had booked her an interview on *Late Night* and a morning visit to *The Today Show*, both with a set of peppered questions pontificating that the vice presidency was not nearly as unimportant as most people imagined. She would be a no-show for both appearances. The Sally Payne who had so loved television would stay stranded in the dressing room, this dressing room, as far from the studio lights as she could keep herself for as long as she could be invisible. Somehow she would find a way to regroup, maybe, but for the first time since she could remember in her entire political career, she had nothing to say.

$ $

Monty Dadashian was in a brushed leather vest and full coonskin attire when Choy and Finkelman arrived back at the EnvisionInk parking lot. They had two all-nighters ahead of them at the Four Seasons, but they knew they needed to make an appearance on the home front before they sealed their transformational deal. This much they had learned from their new CTO.

"Monty, you're a prince," declared Finkelman. "Everything is clicking into place. Couldn't be better."

"Yeah, except someone out there doesn't like us," replied Dadashian. "We have been under massive DNS attack since our returning heroes turned in their resignations. This is going be a hell of a ground war."

"Good thing we have the best talent primed for the fight," said Choy. "Our sites are up, aren't they? Please tell me with half a hotel full of merger wonks that our sites are still up."

"You have to ask?" replied Dadashian. "Who do you think you have on the job, children running a community theater?"

"Sometimes the fake furry pony tail throws us," said Choy. "Yes, we are assuredly in good hands with you and your team."

"Our team," corrected Dadashian. "All these people are one team. You just have to motivate them to go back inside the building."

"What do you suggest, an impromptu all hands on the lawn?" asked Finkelman. "We could order a few hundred pizzas for fast delivery."

"How about walking around, saying hi, and answering their questions," said Dadashian. "Give Dilbert the rest of the weekend off, or at least leave him at the hotel. Just be yourselves."

That sounded good to Choy and Finkelman. It was almost too easy. Good leadership usually was. That's why so few people were good at it. This they understood, if you never had a decent boss the odds of being one were pathetic, and all the how-to books in the world could not teach a manager to be human. Learning to manage up was survival. Learning to manage down was elective. With no boss to teach you, you had to learn to listen harder, to the sounds of those most often receiving commands. Those in your charge would guide you if you let them. The electives fine-tuned instincts, the pitch of inspiration.

"We heard from Steyer right before we headed over here," noted Finkelman. "He and Balthazer made it off the plane. They're in decent enough shape. The FBI agent who was working with us took a bullet, but he'll be okay. It was pretty messy."

"Yeah, I saw a post on ThisIsRage.com when I was checking the count of the Payne petition," said Dadashian. "One of the two guys who was holding you went down, all the way down. The other walked away. Sort of seems like they wanted it that way."

"There's a news embargo on the story until the feds put out a statement, how did it make it to ThisIsRage.com?" asked Choy.

"Maybe we shouldn't have told Seidelmeyer," said Finkelman. "I'm telling you, that old movie dude gets more wired every hour."

"Balthazer and Steyer are on their way back, as soon as they get our plane cleaned up," said Choy. "We agreed to do Balthazer's show on Monday, right after the deal is formally announced."

"You should have good ratings," said Dadashian. "The Payne petition may crash his site yet. You still think about those guys who took you hostage?"

"You don't forget something like that," said Choy. "It's a shame about Swerlow. He isn't that far off from a lot of people we know. He was ambitious. He wanted to do something, make something happen. The idea got away from him. I'm surprised we haven't seen something like this happen before."

"I'm surprised we don't see it all the time," added Finkelman. "The crossover to insanity for someone who wants to win, you have to wonder, where is it? If it weren't for people like Kisinski pulling back from the line, more people would cross it. Sam kept Steyer and Balthazer alive. He kept us alive. For that he'll probably spend the rest of his life locked up with real criminals, but I don't think that's what he is. We owe him."

As Choy and Finkelman wandered the EnvisionInk parking lot, employees all around them were at first surprised to see them, as if it were a celebrity sighting, unsure if they were the real deal, but all smiles when they were identified for certain. The smiles they saw everywhere told them their leak was working, they simply had to confirm the rumors with a few well-placed, forced casual remarks. Wherever they walked around campus, the comments they received were encouraging.

"Great set of ads, great online campaign," shouted out one employee in passing. "Fantastic petition copy!"

"We picked our words carefully," replied Finkelman.

"Does this mean we get free movie tickets?" called out another.

"We already have free movies in the company theater and streamed to your desktop," said Finkelman. "But I'm guessing you can expect more. Maybe we'll buy Netflix. Kidding, just kidding. Really, enough rumors going around."

"Are we going to launch our own search engine?" yelled someone beyond their sightline.

"Wouldn't rule it out," said Choy. "That's a rumor worthy of consideration. I'm guessing we're going to have a lot of content impressions soon, so we should make those work very hard for our partners, the same way we make their current search ad dollars work hard."

"We need to innovate every way we can," added Finkelman. "Nothing is off the table, except cutting staff. Stay tuned for more news post- weekend."

Just a few well-placed, forced casual comments from the co-CEOs was all it took to power telegraph through the Walk-out crowd. There was another old adage—when the boss whispers it's a shout, when the boss shouts it's pure thunder. Choy and Finkelman were quiet thunder. Their words carried weight because they always had chosen them carefully, sparingly, and they were always true. If they implied a big merger was going to happen and no one was going to get cut, their employees had no reason to think otherwise. Choy and Finkelman had become remote, detached, but they had never been dishonest. They held onto that honor all their days, and today it had been its most useful.

Word leaked quickly to the Internet that there would be no layoffs at EnvisionInk, the same at Atom Heart, regardless of the wildfire rumors of the giant merger being negotiated a short drive away at the Four Seasons. The Atom Heart deal had not been substantiated, not that it needed to be given the magnifying number of digital photos of so many suits from both sides of the equation mingling at the hotel. What was substantiated was that the no-layoff promise had come from the mouths of their co-CEOs, live in the flesh, who would stay on the job and reign humbly over the expanded empire. Those words carried weight not only among the EnvisionInk Walkouts, but across Silicon Valley, migrating at an exponential pace eastward to parking lots across the nation. The renewal message was cascading outbound, one concentric circle linking another, device by device, town by town, state by state, information impacting action at a speed unimaginable even half a decade ago. There was optimism wiring across the grid, viral hope, and it was palpable.

In the few hours Choy and Finkelman spent on campus late that Friday, they could already see the crowd thinning. Tents were coming down, sleeping bags were being rolled up, kerosene cooking stoves were being dismantled, the cleanest ones on their way back for refund to REI. In the early minutes of sunset, lights started to go on inside the office complex. The darker it got outside, the more lights went on. People were not going home. They were going back to their desks. Gradually but with building momentum, employees were going back to work.

With the spreading populist posts of the Choy and Finkelman sighting, it would not be long before the mainstream media would arrive at EnvisionInk in search of verifying comment. Choy and Finkelman knew that was coming and had no intention of going on the record ahead of the Monday announcement. They thanked Monty again for his guidance, for kicking them in the ass when they needed it, for standing vigil on the endless jousts that were coming against their business from enterprise hacking predators. Then the co-CEOs gracefully exited the compound for the sequestered weekend ahead. By the time of journalist onslaught at the Santa Clara campus, Choy and Finkelman were nowhere to be found. Neither were most of the Walkouts. The parking lot looked like a County Fair that had picked up and vacated on exceptionally short notice, perhaps a germ war scare, with a few stragglers meandering about for the remaining poster boards that could be salvaged as souvenirs. It was a festival of remains the day after, only it had cleared like a crowd leaving a rock concert as soon as the band played its encore and exited the stage for seclusion. The telling bits of rubbish were evidence that something had happened, but not more than that. Resilience looked forward. Useless trash had to be discarded.

Fast, so fast. Change in Silicon Valley was never slow paced. Velocity was worshipped and rewarded, praised and celebrated. You were there, and then you were not. Timelines kept tunnel vision dead ahead. Rear view mirrors were for poseurs and deadbeats. When decisions were made, when consensus had been reached, everyone moved in lockstep. With buy-in achieved, the only thing left to do was work. Innovation was the mantra around which everyone could rally, the true force of creative destruction that inspired all who could share in its success. Without innovation, there was no value creation. The work itself was what mattered, most of all teamwork. It was not about money. It could never be about money. It was about purpose. It was about changing the world. It was all about the privilege to be able to make something, the gift to create.

By 9:00 p.m. Friday—midnight on the East Coast—the EnvisionInk parking lot was empty of people, but filled with cars and ready to be power-washed, its memory cleaned over the weekend. Inside the rebooted offices of EnvisionInk Systems, the lights burned as brightly as ever.

$ $ $ $

3.9

Tell Me Again How To Get To Sand Hill Road

FOR IMMEDIATE RELEASE
SANTA CLARA & LOS ANGELES, CA
ENVISIONINK AND ATOM HEART EN-
TERTAINMENT ANNOUNCE MERGER

(6:30 a.m. EST) EnvisionInk Systems (NAS-
DAQ: ENVN), a global leader in digital advertising platforms, and Atom Heart Entertainment (NYSE: AHE), the historically acclaimed
motion picture and broadcasting pioneer, today
announced plans to merge their companies.
ENVN co-chief executive officers, Calvin
Choy and Stephen J. Finkelman, will become
co-CEOs of the joined company. Former AHE
chief executive officer, Solomon Edward Seidelmeyer, will become non-executive chairman
of the board. The company will be known as
Envision Atom Innovations (EAI).

"This is a great deal for both our companies,
with no overlap in core competencies and no
layoffs planned for either side joining," said
Choy and Finkelman. "The combination of
EnvisionInk's unique technology to save digital
advertisers even more money in their efforts,
with Atom Heart's vast content library and
unmatched reach in traditional distribution,
will help chart the next generation of innovation. It is all we can do to contain our enthusiasm for certain new initiatives encompassing
our shared strengths, which will be unveiled as
soon as we complete final due diligence and secure the appropriate approvals to set a closing
date."

"This is a marriage made in heaven," added Seidelmeyer. "Investors on all sides of this transaction should applaud this deal as if it were
both the number one box office ticket of all
time and the Academy Award Winner for Best
Picture. Technology and media are two sides
of a coin — a lot of coin — and all we see ahead
is unlimited creativity that will without exception serve our shareholders, customers, and
employees alike. This is a good combination, a
great deal, and a magnificent new beginning."

Given projected plans for enhanced activity,
no offices for either company are expected to
close, with a new "modern green" corporate
headquarters for EAI to be constructed in an
as yet undetermined location. Financial and operational details of the transaction are available
under the Investor Relations tabs on the corporate websites of both EnvisionInk Systems and
Atom Heart Entertainment.

Final approval of this transaction remains subject to customary closing conditions including,
without limitation, antitrust review and other
federal regulatory approvals. Commentary
in this notice may contain forward-looking
statements within the meaning of Section 27A
of the Securities Act of 1933, as amended, and
Section 21E of the Securities Exchange Act of
1934, as amended . . .

$$\$ \$$

Kimo Balthazer was sitting in the EnvisionInk boardroom
in Santa Clara, a choice selection of sound modulation equipment spread across the conference table in front of him. Producer Lee Creighton sat nearby amid the top-shelf electronics,
manning a much improved makeshift control board, at the heart
of which was still his well-worn laptop. It was Monday, and as

Balthazer had promised, he had been on the air since the stock market had opened for trading, beginning his show at dawn by reading the press release into his headset microphone. Balthazer's "in-studio" guests for the day, also as promised, were Choy and Finkelman, who had wanted Sol Seidelmeyer on the air, but neither Balthazer nor Seidelmeyer were ready to go there yet. Perhaps that reconciliation would come in time, since one of the merger's deal points included an unprecedented offer to Balthazer, the biggest reach and dollar contract of his career, owned by Envision Atom Innovations, the first major voice of internet radio among other to-be-announced ventures. When the company's new headquarters opened, Balthazer thought this conference room might make a fine base of operations. All it needed was a little soundproof wall padding and a few console racks, plus the comfy chair of his choice and a high-def monitor for Producer Lee Creighton.

Balthazer wanted to be on the air throughout the day's trading session, which everyone presumed was going to be a beast, but no one could have predicted the scope of what unfolded. The single-day tally was drawing to a close, booking all time record trading volume for the major indices and a historic close up 13% for the DJIA, the largest percentage increase since 1933 and its third biggest ever. The market rebound reflected not only the breathtaking deal of the decade, but news from across the nation that employees were following Friday's lead of EnvisionInk's employees and returning to work. The few parking lot arrests that had occurred were on verbal abuse, at least half of them questionable, but no head bashings had been recorded and riot gear was methodically being returned to the storage rooms of city armories. As Choy and Finkelman had anticipated, the good-faith gesture of promising no layoffs said what it needed to say, and while it could never promise replication, the exemplary act proved to be enough to move people to action as a symbol of hope.

Inside the EnvisionInk boardroom, spirits were expectedly high as Balthazer's show drew to a close—timed with the

NYSE bell. Balthazer easily could have kept going for another six hours, maybe twelve. All he wanted to do was talk.

KIMO: Calvin, Stephen, it's been over six hours since you announced the merger with Atom Heart and your net worth is up commensurate with the market many more billion dollars than I can count. No one could have predicted the records that are being broken. The gains are across the board. How does it feel where you sit?

CHOY: To be honest, Kimo, we don't watch the stock ticker. It's distracting.

FINKELMAN: That's right. You can drive yourself nuts watching your price move around. We like thinking about new products and how people use them. That's more interesting and a lot more fun.

KIMO: Sure, I get all that, the Silicon Valley company line. But on a day like today, with volume exploding and double digit percentage increases, don't you make an exception?

FINKELMAN: We may have looked at it once or twice, but only because we knew you were going to ask.

CHOY: If it gets people back to work, it feels good. Does that get you to move on?

KIMO: I'm just the talk show host, only asking what people want to know. Based on the calls we've been getting from all over the nation, I think people are relieved. After watching their 401k's get pummeled, a little bounce back is good for morale.

CHOY: The important financials are the ones on our pro-forma, which can be found in the merger documents we posted on both the EnvisionInk and Atom Heart sites. We're being as transparent as we know how. What people will be most interested in seeing is that there's no sleight of hand. We're keeping all our people and we're increasing profits. It can be done if you look under all the right rocks.

KIMO: And hire the world's most mesmerizing talk show host, no longer a free agent.

FINKELMAN: That, too. Pricey, though.

KIMO: Listeners can also find those financials for the merger available on ThisIsRage.com, next to the tab for Congresswoman's Payne Petition, which over the weekend vaulted past an astonishing twenty million signatures from forty-three different countries and every continent, including Antarctica. If you haven't yet put your name on the list, it isn't too late. We want the Honorable Ms. Payne to know how many of you she has inspired with her incomparable vision.

FINKELMAN: At least she can sleep well knowing her real concern has been addressed. With the calls we've heard today and what we're seeing in the parking lots around here, I think it's safe to say we've come to the end of the Walkout. She can't complain about that.

KIMO: I certainly agree, and while we didn't get a Merger Bill of Rights, as least we had a good open discussion and received lots of helpful details from our listeners about all the ways they get worked over when they get canned, which should be honey to the lawyer bees the next time they negotiate a separation package. We haven't erased any of your suggestions. We will keep those archived in perpetuity on ThisIsRage.com. Producer Lee Creighton hasn't missed a day updating the website, even in my darkest hour. Producer Lee Creighton, our site holding up okay under the load?

CREIGHTON: Berry-ripe perfect, Kimo. Awesome to have you back on the air. Can I tell people again how many stations are in line to carry our signal under your monster contract?

KIMO: That would be tasteless.

CREIGHTON: Agreed, boundlessly tasteless. Let's just say wherever anyone can hear the nauseating grind of Limbaugh or Hannity, one click away will be the Smooth Sound of Sanity. And most of the dough they're paying you that's not going to your ex-wives will help to fund retraining for our listeners who want to make a career change, but need a little cushion.

KIMO: You embarrass me, Producer Lee Creighton. The Smooth Sound of Sanity—yeah, sure. Why don't you close your mic and clear the last few calls in the queue.

CREIGHTON: You got it, Kimo. Here's one for you, say hello to Gates SQL, from Salt Lake City, Utah.

KIMO: Gates SQL from the land without easy drink, Welcome—*This Is Rage*.

CALLER GATES SQL: Kimo, thanks for taking my call, but I don't want to talk to you. It's Choy and Finkelman, they're the ones I want. They're the ones I need to get to. And you've got them.

KIMO: Well, boys, aren't you lucky, another fan.

FINKELMAN: Tell me we're not being stalked. I've become very sensitive to the notion of being stalked.

CALLER GATES SQL: No stalking, Stephen, but I do have a pitch. You're open for business, I'm ready to go. You and Calvin need me.

CHOY: There's an employment application on our website, Gates. It's easy to find and I promise we'll personally review it.

CALLER GATES SQL: No thanks, I don't want a job. I want an opportunity. I'm an entrepreneur like you. I have a deck you need to see. All I need is some reasonably priced backing and I'm the next IPO.

FINKELMAN: We are being stalked. I told you we were being stalked.

CHOY: Not a wise idea to pitch us on the air, Gates. We'll need to sign an NDA, then we'll take a look.

CALLER GATES SQL: How about at Burning Man, Calvin? I'll set up camp wherever it's convenient for you. I've got a cloud-based mobile social commerce platform post-alpha pre-beta that can scale globally and accelerate without hardware via the existing grid. You've never seen upside the way I've modeled it. The per-transaction fees are customer friendly, impenetrably secure, and ARPU is off the charts. Give me the word and I'm on the next flight to San Jose, my dime, your lottery ticket. Can we confirm a meeting?

CHOY: Definite stalker.

CALLER GATES SQL: I'm telling you, this is bigger than Envision-Ink, bigger than Atom Heart Entertainment, bigger than Micro-soft and Apple combined. All I need to raise is a few million dol-lars and whoever gives me the money will make history.

CHOY: We haven't made enough history for a single day?

CALLER GATES SQL: You show me venture, I'll show you the fu-ture. All I need is the tiniest lucky break, just like you got out of Stanford. I'll even talk to Steyer. All the rumors of indictments for securities manipulation don't bother me. He will always be a legend. Kimo, you know Steyer, can you open that door?

KIMO: You know what, Gates SQL, I can and I will. You have my promise on that. Dan Steyer definitely has some demons ahead of him, but like you say, he is a legend. Hitch your wagon to his tractor and you're on your way to harvest. Leave your contact info with Producer Lee Creighton and we'll get back to you.

CALLER GATES SQL: Really, you're not just saying that to blow me off? Because I'm offering a finder's fee, cash off the top or equity. I will pay my way.

KIMO: You already have, my friend, more than the cost of admission. Let us know when you're in town. I will point you in the right direction.

Balthazer ended the call. He had let this one go on longer than normal, but he was trying a new approach, more patience and less vitriol, at least for his first day back on the job. How long that would last was anyone's guess — Producer Lee Creighton put the over-under at Friday, but somehow it did not seem right to tank an entrepreneur in waiting on rebound day.

CHOY: You're a good guy, Kimo. A real angel at heart.

KIMO: Don't tell anyone, I have enough problems right now with ties to the system.

FINKELMAN: I don't know, Kimo, an executive MBA could suit you well. You work days, you go to school nights, pretty soon you're a CEO.

KIMO: Yeah, me a CEO, as soon as I learn how to open a spreadsheet. Producer Lee Creighton, do you have another call for us, something a tad less prolonged? We're fighting the clock. The bell soon tolls.

CREIGHTON: You bet, Kimo, here's a softball for the wind down. Say hello to Septic Fallout.

KIMO: You make my job too easy, Creighton. Next time you sit on a fry pan runway for a week. Septic Fallout, Welcome—*This Is Rage*.

CALLER SEPTIC FALLOUT: Kimo, what the hell is wrong with you? Have you been lobotomized?

KIMO: Something making you unhappy today, my Septic friend?

CALLER SEPTIC FALLOUT: You go away for a week to the tropics, you come back grinning in the bowels of a corporate sausage grinder? How is that rancid meat you're swallowing supposed to feed the rest of us listening to you?

KIMO: You are a graphic wordsmith, Septic. Would you believe me if I told you I'm not in anyone's bowels?

CALLER SEPTIC FALLOUT: Garbage, Kimo. We're still getting chewed into cud. You're sitting there all cozy buds with your new bosses. They gave you the new contract, they own you. That's why you're telling us how great things are going to be—because they are for you.

KIMO: I can see how you might feel that way, but maybe we should let my bosses tell you how bought I am. Fellows?

CHOY: Gotta disagree, Septic. You can't even tell this guy what he's having for lunch. He says whatever he wants, that was contract Item One. Unless he violates FCC protocol, which he promised he won't do anymore, if we drop kick him for any reason, he gets paid for ten years, iron clad.

CALLER SEPTIC FALLOUT: That proves he isn't bought how?

FINKELMAN: I think we need to lay out a few basics here, okay? Are you basically good with the notion of how our economy works?

CALLER SEPTIC FALLOUT: I think you guys play murky games and the rest of us never understand the rules. You may have a lot of stupid people fooled with your no-layoff merger and save the stock market celebration, but most of us, we're just going back to work until the next time they tell us to go home. We'll lose our houses and you'll still be tallying your billions. You may have yourselves talked into it, but it's business as usual for the rest of us. You waited it out, the claw back is nothing but net. It's Groundhog Day. People like me pay your bills. Thanks for the precision timing, but maybe we got the wrong ending when Swerlow was put down.

Septic Fallout cut the line, leaving a stale vacuum in the boardroom, approaching dead air. Balthazer had been trying to build to a fairy tale finish, but he knew his show was about the callers. This one had a distinct voice that instantly altered the party mood, thinning the afternoon's gloss. Balthazer was on his new game, he had known better than to slam the door shut for effect, to ice Septic Fallout with a finishing move. This was a test. He needed to inhale the attack and reshape it—not his instinct, but a crossroads.

KIMO: Well, our last caller certainly has a point of view. I guess I have to agree, this cannot be a happily-ever-after moment for everyone. But let's think for a moment about what our choices were. EnvisionInk didn't have to merge with Atom Heart. We could have left things the way they were. No one had to go back to work. No one had to buy a single share of stock today. What would have been the good in all that? A lot of people who left their jobs to make a point still wouldn't have made their point, and if certain members of Congress had their way, they might not have ever worked again. Would they be better off or worse if we couldn't get things moving again? Not an easy question to answer. Not obvious at all.

CHOY: You're right, Kimo, it's complicated. Stephen and I knew that when we reached out to Sol Seidelmeyer. We knew this wasn't a perfect solution. But we knew we had to take a step, just a step, or you're right, we would have been stuck in the status quo. If we've learned anything, it's that the status quo is never a good answer.

FINKELMAN: I agree, we aren't pretending this is some wizard fix or magic carpet ride where we all sing in harmony. Calvin and I got a bunch of things wrong, but we got a few things right. If people want to work, those of us who've had a few lucky breaks should try harder to let them do good work and feel good about it. That may be a little heady, maybe even goofy sounding, but doing the opposite is a proven rotten idea, so I think we're making more of a good move than your average Dilbert.

KIMO: If you want to send a message, call Western Union, right? You have a company to run, people want to work. That's a picture where the dots connect. Try to get everyone to do the happy dance—that's a fool's errand. I get that, because I like my job. I like it a lot. So I'm going to keep doing my job. Should we take another call?

CHOY: Do we dare?

KIMO: Who do you have in the on-deck circle, Producer Lee Creighton? A bit of cosmic balance, perchance?

CREIGHTON: Got good karma on my screen. Local Lawyer, she's calling from inside the area code.

KIMO: An attorney? I ask you for balance and you give me the debate club?

CREIGHTON: Take the call, Kimo. It's a fair fight.

KIMO: I'll bet she sends me a bill. Local Lawyer, you're on global digital radio, soon the province of Envision Atom Innovations, E-A-I. Welcome—*This Is Rage.*

CALLER LOCAL LAWYER: Kimo Balthazer?

KIMO: Is that hopeful or fearful?

CALLER LOCAL LAWYER: Do you recognize my voice?

KIMO: It is familiar, but I cannot place you.

CALLER LOCAL LAWYER: An officer of the court, but not one hunting you.

KIMO: So very few of those. What do you have to share with us, Local Lawyer, or am I supposed to guess who you are first?

Choy knew the voice in a syllable, quickly scribbled a few words on a scrap of paper and slid it across the table to Balthazer. The note told him it was their general counsel, Sylvia Normandy. Finkelman shrugged, what the killjoy could this be about? Kimo nodded, tried to figure out how to play it, not knowing what it was she was playing.

CALLER LOCAL LAWYER: No giving up names on the air, please. That's not your normal rules. I'm a champion of equal opportunity.

KIMO: Fair enough, familiar voice. Any insight for us as the trading day draws to a close? What counsel do you offer?

CALLER LOCAL LAWYER: No counsel, just a shout-out to the two guys sitting with you. They did a hell of a job—and that's before we knock down the mounting pile of frivolous lawsuits freshly delivered to my desk, the hypocrite waltz in Dolby Surround Sound.

KIMO: I'd bet on these guys, no question about that. I did bet on these guys, all in. They got the dead engine started. Now we need to see if they can hold the wheel steady at Warp Factor Freaky.

CALLER LOCAL LAWYER: Trust me, they can. I've seen them do a lot. By every estimate of the analyst core, they should be toast, but they're not. We dodged one nasty melt down.

KIMO: You are expressive, Counselor, and you won't get any argument here. If you need someone to celebrate with, you know where to find me. Just give me a call.

CALLER LOCAL LAWYER: You know, Kimo, I might do that.

KIMO: You do know I'm a three-time loser.

CALLER LOCAL LAWYER: Yeah, but you're only half the schmuck you used to be. Don't hog the mic. Good show today, guys. See you around campus.

Local Lawyer hung up on her own cue. Balthazer wasn't even vaguely sure what to make of her. Neither were Choy and Finkelman, but they were locker room amused — and surprised, very surprised. Producer Lee Creighton had not seen it coming, but he was not surprised. Running the board for Kimo Balthazer, he could never be surprised.

It was time to wrap, and Balthazer was not sure how to go out. The script was a blur, and he wondered if he should be worried. How many Septic Fallouts had been left grinding their teeth in the alleys, extracted from every Main Street, maybe waiting for him? How many Gates SQLs were out there in the non-cyber world, physically real and distraught, gnawing away at conjecture with their unbaked business plans, primed to become the next Dennis Swerlow if a taut desperation switch happened to snag a mouse click? The demographic of Balthazer's audience had transformed over the years. Callers used to ask how to survive the tightrope called career on a steady ramp. Now they wanted lessons in jackpot looting or defying the creep of homelessness. The pillars of so much fear had brought strident polarity, which left him in a tough place, not knowing what to say. He was supposed to be an entertainer, but he knew he had always been something other than that — maybe not more than that, but different. He was no overnight success. There was hardly an example he could point to of overnight success, but the treasures of cobbled tech IPOs and low-talent movie stars muddled the story for his listeners. Too many people thought they could lunar leap to the stars, laugh at gravity and bypass the zig zag of plastic orange cones. They were wrong. Mind levitation was no better a get rich strategy than bumping credit cards to play the slots, but what could he tell them? So many of them were content blowing good grocery money on the gamble. He knew that, but his message was too concentrated, too tangible. He was a solo silly voice, ethereal as the cloud, elevator music in a car, and he could never be more.

Once again Balthazer blabbed as Investors went back to Investing, Bankers went back to Banking, Operators went back to Operating—nothing majestic had changed, the triad was as always, harmony accruing to the few while so many others were hypnotized by the tone. Money knew how to behave, because it had been trained well by its owners, and so equilibrium would be reassured. It was as if nothing whatsoever had been learned, no lesson, no teachable moment. Liquid found its former level and no one who mattered was listening to the terms of the truce. Balthazer could not be the only one who knew it was a temporal peace, a cease fire that could not be sustained. History was taught to everyone in high school, the dialectic was common knowledge without a label—but no one kept their notebooks, who could remember trivia? Empires fell, every single one had collapsed, corrupted in slow motion by loss of focus, charred by demented ideals and twisted values, legislated cruelty rejected and replaced by rehashed sequels. There was no reason to believe the present calendar was an anomaly. Greece yielded to Rome. Rome gave way to medieval chaos. The dynasties of China and Russia eventually puttered out. Spain, France, Germany, and Japan all expanded with voracious appetites and ambitions, all were forced to pull back. Britain sailed, then retreated, and rebranded as Commonwealth. How could current times not follow suit, what was so different?

Greed, entitlement, arrogance, whining—the dodge was all around him. It allowed him to have a show. Everyone worked so hard to stay afloat, so many laboring hours, but their thoughts had been left lazy, soft matter numbed by distraction, too many commercials, too many invented needs. The underpinnings of imminent distress could be heard in the voices of his callers, the separation of humans into structures, weakness in education driving fascination with celebrity culture. Closets were filled with logo wear. Mortgages had to go unpaid. Every day listeners were bombarded with lies, spectacularly unnecessary huckster noise with no one on the switchboard at customer service. Clever leaders with lifetime pensions picked their pockets and called it campaign donations. Public school teachers took a vow of poverty even when districts had jobs. Top dog university professors cashed their grants and refused to teach, pushing tuition beyond fair reach. Newspapers folded, free form bloggers typed at will where fact-checked journalists once risked their lives. The dichotomy of control and emergence was practically chiseled in the landscape, with opposing forces simultaneously lining up to fight while closing in on themselves. The thesis of freedom collided with the antithesis of power and produced the synthesis of struggle without TV episode resolution. Every single day, they would call him on the phone and talk publicly of their pain. There should have been no surprise of any kind coming—but always, no one saw it coming. Who to teach, whom to teach? The refrains of each call were ephemeral, but the chorus was cumulative.

Despite the rampant war in his head, Balthazer felt something in the glow around him he had a hard time identifying, a tinge of happiness. He had spent thirty-some years agonizing over what was wrong with the nation, the mass of troubles and unfairness tilled in the real estate. All this he felt, and pondered, and worried over, a reflection of his threatened spirit. His distaste with the subject matter was a full-length mirror, sad, and scary, and framed in gold plating. Now he was part of the problem, and strangely it did not all look so bad. There was time, healing, a way forward. Change was inevitable, the coin-toss mutation worth hanging around to see. The nation may not have been granted another full chance, but it was a partial chance, a stay of execution, and he was on the side of the affirmative. He had ownership in this recovery, and with gathering conviction came trust. There was good somewhere in our system, no matter the forged steel shovels needed to dig it out, and there was good in himself. His audience knew that. They stayed with him no matter how many times he turned against them—surely not all of them, you could not have his gig in earnest without pissing off a lot of folks. He could still attract plenty of listeners, so his new contract was not a gift, but a business proposition, a two-way ticket he would earn and bank. That was the free enterprise he loved, the bully pulpit of public record, and that was the kind of business that made sense. It did not come with friends, but it did come with a soap box for snide comebacks. All he had to do was pay attention.

As the closing bell of the NYSE rang in the background on CNBC, Balthazer knew he was on a roll. He signed off for the day, more hope tomorrow. The market was coming back, employees were coming back, the show was back, his audience was back, and this time he would make it work. He had a hunch his new show could help, at least for a while. His voice would keep them the tiniest bit more honest than nature allowed, and guide them to clear the wilderness ahead, one mile of trail at a time. The echo in his head would keep the rhythm. He was bringing it like never before. A lot of them were not going to like what they heard, but Kimo would make them listen.

Like a Bat Out of Hell

$ $ $ $

Letter to Shareholders

From The Desk of Daniel Steyer

To the Shareholders of EnvisionInk Systems:

It is with the greatest of mixed emotions and humility that I today announce my resignation as chairman of the board of EnvisionInk Systems. With the announced merger of our company with Atom Heart Entertainment, the timing seems appropriate and easily administered.

Simultaneous with this decision, my wife and I have elected to put the entirety of our holdings in this landmark company into a permanently restricted trust for the benefit of charities to be determined by the company's continuing board of directors.

While some may read more into this than truth will bear, the notion of EnvisionInk and Atom Heart proceeding through regulatory approval and final due diligence with undue public attention focused on my role did not seem to me advisable given the potential disruptive nature of dramatization and emotional speculation. As a fiduciary, my decisions must be, and are always, guided by duty to our shareholders, our employees, our partners, and our customers. The events of the past several weeks have been instructive and enlightening on any number of fronts, but the forward-looking nature of value creation will always be the driving force

of innovation. While leaving the most important company I ever helped create to enjoy
retirement would normally be the last thing on
my mind, these most certainly are not normal
times.

It is important to know that this choice is mine
alone, and in no way reflects on my sense of
the future financial prospects of the merged
enterprise. To the contrary, with the instantly
renewed engagement of our employees and
the demonstrated optimism disseminating
throughout the capital markets, the company's
prospects have, in my mind, never been more
encouraging.

I am also honored to have been contacted of
late by senior government officials to consider
a career change and submit my credentials for
nomination as US Treasury Secretary. While I
had never previously thought much about an
opportunity to have a critical impact on broad
economic policy, the opportunity to serve our
nation in this time of recovery is one I feel I
must pursue. I am humbled to be considered
for such high office in the public sector. When
asked to be a part of the solution, the only
appropriate answer is to sign up. It thus makes
further sense for me to eliminate all potential
conflicts of interests, further to my decisions
noted here, as my confirmation hearings will
soon be announced and scheduled.

I wish Calvin and Stephen the best in their
ongoing leadership efforts of the combined
companies. I believe they will benefit tremendously from the ageless wisdom of their new
mentor, Sol Seidelmeyer. The joined team
members overseeing our company are as talented as they are tireless, and with this recent

ordeal behind them, they exhibit an inspired
reflection of creativity that cannot be equaled
in experience. I remain confident that all of our
stakeholders will see benefit from our unified
efforts to ignite a period of global economic
growth and prosperity. If I can be of help, so
much the better.

Very truly yours,
Dan Steyer, Chairman ex-Officio
$ $ $ $

FINIS

About the Author

Ken Goldstein advises start-ups and established corporations in technology, entertainment, media, and e-commerce. He served as chief executive officer and chairman of the board of SHOP.COM, a market leader in online consumer commerce acquired by Market America. He previously served as executive vice president and managing director of Disney Online, and as vice president of entertainment at Broderbund Software. Earlier in his career he developed computer games for Philips Interactive Media and Cinemaware Corporation, and also worked as a television executive. He is active in children's welfare issues and has served on the boards of the Make-A-Wish Foundation of Greater Los Angeles, Hathaway-Sycamores Child and Family Services, and Full Circle Programs, and is involved in local government. He speaks and teaches frequently on topics of leadership, executive management, and innovation. He and his wife Shelley, who teaches English as a Second Language, make their home in Southern California. He received his BA in Theater Studies and Philosophy from Yale.